THE ELIZA STORIES

THE ELIZA STORIES

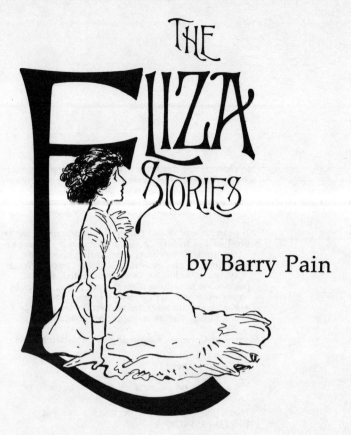

by Barry Pain

with an introduction by Terry Jones

BEAUFORT BOOKS
PUBLISHERS
NEW YORK

Introduction © 1984 by Terry Jones

Library of Congress Cataloging in Publication Data

Pain, Barry, 1864–1928.
  The Eliza stories.
  Contents: Eliza — Eliza's husband —
  Eliza getting on — [etc.]
  I. Title.

PR6031.A25A6   1985   823'.912   84–24472
ISBN 0–8253–0288–9

Published in the United States by
Beaufort Books, Publishers, New York.

Designer: Lawrence Edwards
Printed in Great Britain
First American Edition

10 9 8 7 6 5 4 3 2 1

Contents

Introduction

Congratulations! You have just picked up some of the funniest books in the English language, for this volume contains all the five books about Eliza and her dreadful husband that appeared between 1900 and 1913.

In their day, these books were phenomenally successful. 'They opened up a new vein of humour and parody' according to one contemporary, and they established their author, Barry Pain, as a popular humourist. Today they are as fresh and as funny as if they had only been written this morning. In view of all which you may rightly wonder why you have never heard of them or him before.

I wish I knew.

Perhaps the Eliza books were *too* successful and popular. You see, eighty years ago it wasn't really respectable to be funny. Heavens knows even now there are people who think that comedy isn't serious. And there was Barry Pain, a Cambridge graduate, making his living being funny. Even early on in his career the eminent poet and critic, W.E. Henley, had advised him to devote himself to serious work. And a mere year before Barry Pain died Sir Alfred Noyes wrote of him:

'It is a real obscuration of the genius of a great artist that the general public should so often derive its knowledge of him [Barry Pain] from the mere by-products of his pen that are to be found on railway bookstalls ... Mr Barry Pain ought not to be allowed to go scattering his masterpieces about so carelessly, while the bookstalls call attention only to his more ephemeral work. Even this has more genius in it than ninety per cent of the solemn "Art" of our day.' (*The Bookman*, December, 1927)

Perhaps the distaste which men of letters felt for the railway bookstall damaged Barry Pain's credibility in the eyes of lesser intellectuals than Sir Alfred. And perhaps when the railway bookstalls no longer carried his popular works (like the Eliza books) there was thus nothing left to sustain his memory. Anyway, I hope this volume will do something towards restoring the reputation that Barry Pain enjoyed when he lived.

Barry Pain was born in 1864. He died in 1928. From the *Dictionary of National Biography* I learn that he went to Sedbergh School and Corpus Christi College, Cambridge; that he became an army coach in Guildford for four years, and then sought his fortune as a journalist in London. In 1892 he married Amelia Lehmann (daughter of the portrait painter, Rudolph Lehmann, and sister of the composer Liza Lehmann). In 1897 he succeeded Jerome K. Jerome as editor of *Today*. He lived in Pinner, Bushey and, finally, St. John's Wood, and generally became well-known as a novelist, short-story writer and one of the foremost humourists of his day. Otherwise, apart from an article called 'Mr Barry Pain at Home' in *Sylvia's Journal* (February, 1894), there seems to be little written about him. As Sir Alfred Noyes put it: 'Mr Barry Pain seems to have avoided self-advertisement as others have all too often sold their souls for it.'

But then I'm not an evangelist for Barry Pain but for these five books that he wrote and that you are now holding: *The Eliza Stories*.

This is how *The Times* described them in 1928:

'In 1900 appeared a tiny green volume with a cover design by Tom Browne, entitled *Eliza*, depicting scenes from the life of a City clerk and his wife in a suburban villa. It had been refused by many publishers, even by those who were producing his other books, but the public quickly recognised in the character of Eliza's husband, the narrator of the stories, a brilliant new comic creation. The pompous and fussy little home despot reflected so much of the universal weakness of humanity that Mr Pain could not supply enough of him. *Eliza* was followed by *Eliza's Husband, Eliza Getting On, Exit Eliza* (alas!), and finally *Eliza's Son*, a priggish youth who might, had he grown up, have proved as amusing as his father.' (*The Times*, 7 May 1928)

I've just been looking at the original editions of the Eliza books, and quite honestly I'm not surprised that nobody took them seriously at the time. The first two appeared as rather scruffy little miniature volumes that looked as if they were apologising for not being real books. There then followed a gap of eight years, and the last three appeared sandwiched between advertisements for Pears' soap and 'Plantol' (a toilet soap made from fruit and flowers) as one shilling paperbacks, described by the publishers as 'a popular form at a price which places them within the reach of all who appreciate good stories.'

They were not dignified books. They were not Literature. Their place was the railway bookstall, not the library shelf. Little wonder that an institution such as The London Library never bothered to own a copy, or that Sir Alfred Noyes should avoid referring to them by name.

But, perhaps, across the chasm of eighty years you will look at them with different eyes. To mine, they seem valuable now not only for their humour but for the glimpses they provide of everyday life at the turn of the century. They may, at first sight, seem to be covering the same ground as George and Weedon Grossmith's *Diary of a Nobody* (1892), but for my money the Eliza books are funnier and truer. In fact they are in a different class.

Eliza's husband (whose name, by the way, is never revealed) is a comic creation of the same calibre as John Cleese's Basil Fawlty – a character who is as exasperating and infuriating as he is funny.

Eliza herself emerges as an intelligent, humourous, compassionate woman of almost saint-like tolerance. Their son, on the other hand, is different again.

Eliza's son is a creation beyond the realm of comedy. He has all the faults of his father, but instead of being gullible and foolish, he is almost demoniacally clever. The laughable foibles of the father become disturbingly dangerous flaws of character in the son. He perceives the world solely in terms of profit-making. For example, he reduces all his Christmas presents to their cash value and then works out a profit and loss account for each year; he regards a scholarship to Oxford as 'really a cash discount offered by a college to its best customer'; and at school he only understands friendship in terms of whom he has lent money to and at what percentage return. He is a chilling epitome of a society whose only ethic is monetary gain, and of a breed of businessman that was familiar in Barry Pain's day, but had still not wrested the reins of power from the old land-owning establishment. The Eliza saga ends with an almost prophetic note of warning – ostensibly to the parents who had bred this cold, calculating monster – but perhaps to all of us.

Finally, I would like to thank my friend, Tom Parkinson, who many years ago first introduced me to the Eliza books of Barry Pain, and without whose enthusiasm *then* you would not be holding this book in your hand *now*.

Terry Jones

ELIZA

Eliza's Husband

'SUPPOSE,' I said to one of the junior clerks at our office the other day, 'you were asked to describe yourself in a few words, could you do it?'

His answer that he could describe me in two was no answer at all. Also the two words were not a description, and were so offensive that I did not continue the conversation.

I believe there are but few people who could give you an accurate description of themselves. Often in the train to and from the City, or while walking in the street, I think over myself – what I have been, what I am, what I might be if, financially speaking, it would run to it. I imagine how I should act under different circumstances – on the receipt of a large legacy, or if for some specially clever action I were taken into partnership, or if a mad bull came down the street. I may say that I make a regular study of myself. I have from time to time recorded on paper some of the more important incidents of our married life, affecting Eliza and myself, and I present them to you, gentle reader, in this little volume. I think they show how with a very limited income – and but for occasional assistance from Eliza's mother I do not know how we should have got along – a man may to a great extent preserve respectability, show taste and judgment, and manage his wife and home.

The more I think about myself, the more – I say it in all modesty – the subject seems to grow. I should call myself many-sided, and in many respects unlike ordinary men. Take, for instance, the question of taste. Some people would hardly think it worth while to mention a little thing like taste; but I do. I am not rich, but what I have I like to have ornamental, though not loud. Only the other day the question of glass-cloths for the

1

kitchen turned up, and though those with the red border were threepence a dozen dearer than the plain, I ordered them without hesitation. Eliza changed them next day, contrary to my wishes, and we had a few words about it, but that is not the point. The real point is that if your taste comes out in a matter of glass-cloths for the kitchen, it will also come out in antimacassars for the drawing-room and higher things.

Again, ordinary men – men that might possibly call themselves my equals – are not careful enough about respectability. Everywhere around me I see betting on horse-races, check trousers on Sunday, the wash hung out in the front garden, whisky and soda, front steps not properly whitened, and the door-handle not up to the mark. I could point to houses where late hours on Sunday are so much the rule that the lady of the house comes down in her dressing-gown to take in the milk – which, I am sure, Eliza would sooner die than do. There are families – in my own neighbourhood, I am sorry to say – where the chimneys are not swept regularly, beer is fetched in broad daylight, and attendance at a place of worship on Sunday is rather the exception than the rule. Then, again, language is an important point; to my mind nothing marks a respectable man more than the use of genteel language. There may have been occasions when excessive provocation has led me to the use of regrettable expressions, but they have been few. As a rule I avoid not only what is profane, but also anything that is slangy. I fail to understand this habit which the present generation has formed of picking up some meaningless phrase and using it in season and out of season. For some weeks I have been greatly annoyed by the way some of the clerks use the phrase 'What, ho, she bumps!' If you ask them who bumps, or how, or why, they have no answer but fits of silly laughter. Probably, before these words appear in print, that phrase will have been forgotten and another, equally ridiculous, will have taken its place. It is not sensible; what is worse, it is not, to my mind, respectable. Do not imagine that I object to humour in conversation. That is a very different thing. I have made humorous remarks myself before now, mostly of rather a cynical and sarcastic kind.

I am fond of my home, and any little addition to its furniture or decorations gives me sincere pleasure. Both in the home and in our manner of life there are many improvements which I am prevented by financial considerations from carrying out. If I were a rich man I would have the drawing-room walls a perfect mass of pictures. If I had money, I could spend it judiciously and without absurdity. I should have the address stamped in gold on the note-paper, and use boot-trees, and never be without a cake in the house in case a friend dropped in to tea. Nor should I think twice about putting on an extra clean pair of cuffs in the week if wanted. We should keep two servants. I am interested in the drama, if serious, and two or three times every month I should take Eliza to the dress-circle. Our suburb has a train service which is particularly convenient for the theatres. Eliza would wear a dressy blouse – she shares my objections to anything cut out at the neck – a mackintosh and a sailor hat, the two latter to be removed before entering. I should carry her evening shoes in a pretty crewel-worked bag. We have often discussed it. Curiously enough, she already has the bag, though we seldom have an opportunity to use it in this way. Doubtless there are many other innovations which, with appropriate means, I could suggest. But I have said enough to show that they would all be in the direction of refinement and elegance, and the money would not be spent in foolishness or vice.

As Eliza's husband, I should perhaps say a word or two about her. She is a lady of high principles and great activity. Owing to my absence every day in the exercise of my profession, she is called upon to settle many questions – as, for instance, the other day the question of what contribution, if any, should be given to the local Fire Brigade – where a word of advice from me would have been useful. If not actually independent, she is certainly not what would be described as a clinging woman. Indeed, she does occasionally take upon herself to enter on a line of action without consulting me, when my advice is perfectly at her disposal, and would perhaps save her from blunders. Last year she filled the coal-cellar (unusually large for the type of house) right up at summer prices. Undoubtedly, she thought that she was practising an economy. But she was dealing with a coal-merchant who does not give credit – a man who requires cash down and sees that he gets it. And – well, I need not go into details here, but it proved to be excessively inconvenient for me. She has lost the silly playfulness which was rather a mark of her character during the period of our engagement, and if this is due to the sobering effects of association with a steady and thoughtful character I am not displeased. She herself says it's the work, but the women do not always know. Possibly, too, her temper is more easily ruffled now than then when I point out things to her. I should say that she was less ambitious than myself. I do not mention these little matters at all by the way of finding fault. On the contrary, I have a very high opinion of Eliza.

We have no children living.

With these few prefatory words, gentle reader, I fling open the front door – to use a metaphorical expression – and invite you to witness a few scenes of our domestic life that I have from time to time recorded.

The Cards

ABOUT a year ago Eliza and myself had a little difference of opinion. I mentioned to her that we had no visiting cards.

'Of course not,' she said. 'The idea of such a thing!' She spoke rather hastily.

'Why do you say "of course not"?' I replied quietly. 'Visiting cards are, I believe, in common use among ladies and gentlemen.'

She said she did not see what that had to do with it.

'It has just this much to do with it,' I answered: 'that I do not intend to go without visiting cards another day!'

'What's the use?' she asked. 'We never call on anybody, and nobody ever calls on us.'

'Is Miss Sakers nobody?'

'Well, she's never left a card here, and she really is a lady by birth, and can prove it. She just asks the girl to say she's been, and it's nothing of importance, when she doesn't find me in. If she can do without cards, we can. You'd much better go by her.'

'Thank you, I have my own ideas of propriety, and I do not take them from Miss Sakers. I shall order fifty of each sort from Amrod's this morning.'

'Then that makes a hundred cards wasted.'

'Either you cannot count,' I said, 'or you have yet to learn that there are three sorts of cards used by married people – the husband's cards, the wife's cards, and the card with both names on it.'

'Go it!' said Eliza. 'Get a card for the cat as well. She knows a lot more cats than we know people!'

I could have given a fairly sharp retort to that, but I preferred to remain absolutely silent. I thought it might show Eliza that she was becoming rather vulgar. Silence is often the best rebuke. However, Eliza went on:

'Mother would hate it, I know that. To talk about cards, with the last lot of coals not paid for – I call it wickedness.'

I simply walked out of the house, went straight down to Amrod's, and ordered those cards. When the time comes for me to put my foot down, I can generally put it down as well as most people. No one could be easier to live with than I am, and I am sure Eliza has found it so; but what I say is, if a man is not master in his own house, then where is he?

* * *

Amrod printed the cards while I waited. I had them done in the Old English character. I suggested some little decoration to give them a tone – an ivy leaf in the corner, or a little flourish under the name – but Amrod was opposed to this. He seemed to think it was not essential, and it would have been charged extra, and also he had nothing of the kind in stock. So I let that pass. The cards looked very well as they were, a little plain and formal, perhaps, but very clean (except in the case of a few where the ink had rubbed), and very gratifying to one's natural self-respect.

That evening I took a small cardboard box that had contained candles, and packed in it a few carefully selected flowers from the garden, and one of our cards. On the card I wrote, 'with kindest love from' just above the names, and posted it to Eliza's mother.

So far was Eliza's mother from being offended that she sent Eliza a present of a postal order for five shillings, three pounds of pressed beef, and a nicely-worked apron.

On glancing over that sentence, I see that it is, perhaps, a little ambiguous. The postal order was for the shillings alone – not for the beef or the apron.

I only mention the incident to show whether, in this case, Eliza or I was right.

* * *

I put a few of my cards in my letter-case, and the rest were packed away in a drawer. A few weeks afterwards I was annoyed to find Eliza using some of her cards for winding silks. She said that it did not prevent them from being used again, if they were ever wanted.

'Pardon me,' I said, 'but cards for social purposes should not be bent or frayed at the edge, and can hardly be too clean. Oblige me by not doing that again!'

That evening Eliza told me that No. 14 in the Crescent had been taken by some people called Popworth.

'That must be young Popworth, who used to be in our office,' I said. 'I heard that he was going to be married this year. You must certainly call and leave cards.'

'Which sort, and how many?'

'Without referring to a book, I can hardly say precisely. These things are very much a matter of taste. Leave enough – say one of each sort for each person in the house. There should be no stint.'

'How am I to know how many persons there are?'

'Ask the butcher with whom they deal.'

On the following day I remarked that Popworth must have come in for money, to be taking so large a house, and I hoped she had left the cards.

'I asked the butcher, and he said there was Popworth, his wife, two sisters, a German friend, and eleven children. That was sixteen persons, and made forty-eight cards altogether. You see, I remembered your rule.'

'My dear Eliza,' I said, 'I told you as plainly as possible that it was a matter of taste. You ought not to have left forty-eight at once.'

'Oh, I couldn't keep running backwards and forwards leaving a few at a time. I've got something else to do. There's three pair of your socks in the basket waiting to be darned, as it is.'

'And, good heavens! That Popworth can't be my Popworth. If he's only married this year, he can't in the nature of things, have got eleven children. And a house like this can't call on a house like that without a something to justify it.'

'That's what I thought.'

'Then what on earth did you call for?'

'I didn't. Who said I did?'

* * *

I gave a sigh of relief. Later in the evening, when Eliza took a card, notched a bit out of each side, and began winding silk on it, I thought it wiser to say nothing. It is better sometimes to pretend not to see things.

Eliza's Mother

I GENERALLY send Eliza to spend a day with her mother early in December, and try to cheer her up a little. I dare say the old lady is very lonely, and appreciates the kindly thought. The return ticket is four-and-two, and Eliza generally buys a few flowers to take with her. That does not leave much change out of five shillings when the day is over, but I don't grudge the money. Eliza's mother generally tries to find out, without precisely asking, what we should like for a Christmas present. Eliza does not actually tell her, or even hint it – she would not care to do anything of that sort. But she manages, in a tactful sort of way, to let her know.

For instance, the year before last Eliza's mother happened to say, 'I wonder if you know what I am going to give you this Christmas?'

Eliza said, 'I can see in your eye, mother, and you shan't do it. It's much too expensive. If other people can do without silver salt-cellars, I suppose we can.'

Well, we got them; so that was all right. But last year it was more difficult.

* * *

You see, early in last December I went over my accounts, and I could see that I was short. For one thing, Eliza had had the measles. Then I had bought a bicycle, and though I sold it again, it did not, in that broken state, bring in enough to pay the compensation to the cabman. I was much annoyed about that. It was true I ran into the horse, but it was not my fault that it bolted and went into the lamp-post. As I said, rather sharply, to the man when I paid him, if his horse had been steady the thing would never have happened. He did not know what to answer, and made some silly remark about my not being fit to ride a mangle. Both then and at the time of the accident his language was disrespectful and profane.

However, I need not go further into that. It is enough to say that we had some unusual expenses, and were distinctly short.

'I don't blame you, Eliza,' I said. 'Anything you have had you are very welcome to.'

'I haven't had anything, except the measles,' she said; 'and I don't see how you can blame me for that.'

'But,' I said, 'I think it's high time you paid a visit to your mother, and showed her that we have not forgotten her. Take some Swiss roll – about sixpennyworth. Try to make things seem a little brighter to her. If she says anything about Christmas, and you saw your way to getting a cheque from her this year instead of her usual present, you might do that. But show her that we are really fond of her – remember she is your mother, and has few pleasures. A fiver just now would make a good deal of difference to me, and even a couple of sovereigns would be very handy.'

* * *

When Eliza came back, I saw by her face that it was all right.

'I didn't have to say anything,' she said. 'Mother told me of her own accord that she knew that you had money troubles, and that she was going to take advantage of the Christmas season to relieve you from them in a way which at another time you might be too proud to accept.'

'That,' I said warmly, 'is very thoughtful of her, and very delicate, and it can only mean one thing. It settles me. This year, Eliza, we will give your mother a present. Quite a trifle, of course – about two shillings. It will be a token, and she will value it.'

When I returned from the City I found that Eliza had purchased a small white vase for one-and-ten. The man in the shop had told her that it was alabaster. I had my doubts about that, but it was quite in my own taste – rather severe and classical. I complimented Eliza on her choice.

Three days before Christmas I got a letter from Eliza's mother. She said that she had been afraid that I was worrying about my debt to her of £4 13s. 9d. She took advantage of the Christmas season to return my IOU's and begged me to consider the debt as paid.

It was not at all what I had expected.

* * *

'No,' I said to Eliza at breakfast, 'I am not in the least like a bear with a sore head, and I will thank you not to use the expression. As for your mother's kindness, I am glad you think it kindness. I wouldn't have it otherwise. If you weren't a born idiot you wouldn't think so. My debt to your mother would have been discharged by – discharged in due course. By reminding me that I owed her money, she has practically dunned me for it, and forced me to pay her at a most inconvenient time. She comes badgering me for her dirty money at Christmas, and you call it "kindness"! Kindness! Hah! Oh, hah, hah!'

'Don't make those silly noises, and get on with your breakfast!' said Eliza.

Afterwards she asked me if I still meant to send her mother that little vase.

'Oh, yes!' I said. 'We can afford it; it's nothing to us.'

Eliza, entirely misunderstanding the word that I next used, got up and said that she would not stop in the room to hear her poor mother sworn at.

'The word I used,' I said calmly, 'was alabaster, and not what you suppose.'

'You pronounced it just like the other thing.'

'I pronounced it in an exclamatory manner,' I replied, 'from contempt! You seem to me very ready to think evil. This is not the first time!'

Eliza apologized. As a matter of fact, I really did say alabaster. But I said it emphatically, and I own that it relieved my feelings.

* * *

We keep the silver salt-cellars in the drawer of Eliza's wardrobe as a general rule. I should prefer to use them every day, or at any rate every Sunday. But Eliza says that they make work.

'Mother has written to me,' she said on the following day, 'to say that she will dine with us on Christmas Day. I had better get the silver salt-cellars down.'

'You'd better *put them up*,' I said meaningly. I know that sounds rather bitter, but I confess that I have always had a weakness for the wit that stings.

Well, it did not actually come to that. They allowed me to draw a couple of pounds in advance at the office. I suppose they know that when they have got a good man it is worth while to stretch a point to keep him. Not that I was at all dictatorial – apparently I asked it as a favour. But I fancy our manager saw that I was not a man to be played with.

Eliza's mother dined with us, and brought a couple of ducks. Conscience, I should say.

At the moment of writing my financial position is absolutely sound, and even if Eliza's mother forced me to use her present to me to pay my debt to her (£7 19s. 5d.), though I might think it dishonourable on her part, I should not be seriously inconvenienced. However, Eliza is going early in December to suggest sauce-boats (plated). That is to say, she may possibly mention them if any occasion arises.

Miss Sakers

ON Saturdays I always get back from the office early. This particular Saturday afternoon I looked at our chimneys as I came down the street. I thought it very queer, but, to make certain, as soon as I got into the house I opened the drawing-room door. It was just as I thought. I called upstairs to Eliza, rather sharply.

She came down and said, 'Well, what's the matter?'

I said calmly, 'The matter? Jane has apparently gone mad, that's all.' (Jane is the name of our servant.)

Eliza said that she did not think so, and asked me what the girl had done.

I must say it made me feel rather sarcastic – it would have

made any man feel sarcastic. I said, 'Oh, nothing. Merely lit the fire in the drawing-room; and not only lit it, but piled coals on it. It is not Sunday, so far as I am aware.' It is our rule to have the drawing-room fire lit on Sundays only. We are rather exclusive, and some other people seem to be rather stuck-up, and between the two we do not have many callers. If anyone comes, it is always perfectly easy for Eliza to say, 'The housemaid has foolishly forgotten to light the fire here. Shall we not step into the dining-room?' I hate to see anything like waste.

'At this very moment,' I added, 'the drawing-room fire is flaming half-way up the chimney. It seems we can afford to burn half a ton of coals for nothing. I cannot say that I was aware of it.'

'You *are* satirical!' said Eliza. 'I always know when you are being satirical, because you move your eyebrows and say, "I am aware", instead of "I know". I told Jane to light the fire myself.'

'May I ask why?'

'Miss Sakers is coming in. She sent me a note this morning to say so.'

'That puts a different complexion on the affair. Very tactful of her to have announced the intention. I do not grudge a handful of firing when there is a reason. I only ask that there shall be a reason.' Miss Sakers is the vicar's daughter. Strictly speaking, I suppose her social position is superior to our own. I know for a fact that she has been to county balls. She seemed anxious to cultivate an intimacy with us, so I gathered. I was not absurdly pleased about it. One has one's dignity. Besides, at the office we frequently see people far above Miss Sakers. A nobleman who had called to see one of the partners once remarked to me, 'Your office is a devilish long way from everywhere!' There was no particular reason why he should have spoken to me, but he seemed to wish it. After that, it was no very great thing that Miss Sakers seemed anxious to know us better. At the same time, I do not pretend that I was displeased. I went into the drawing-room and put some more coal on.

'Is it to be a party?' I asked.

'Not at all. She is coming quite as a friend.'

I went upstairs and changed all my clothes, and then purchased a few flowers, which I placed in vases in the drawing-room. Eliza had got two kinds of cake; I added a plate of mixed biscuits on my own responsibility. Beyond this, I did nothing in the way of preparation, wishing to keep the thing as simple and informal as possible.

* * *

The tea was quite a success. Miss Sakers was to have a stall at the bazaar in aid of the new church. I promised her five shillings at first, but afterwards made it seven-and-six. Though no longer young, Miss Sakers is very pleasant in her manner.

After tea Miss Sakers and Eliza both did needlework. Miss Sakers was doing a thing in crewels. I could not see what Eliza was doing. She kept it hidden, almost under the table.

To prevent the conversation from flagging, I said, 'Eliza, dear, what are you making?'

She frowned hard at me, shook her head slightly, and asked Miss Sakers about the special preacher for Epiphany Sunday.

I at once guessed that Eliza was doing something for Miss Sakers' stall at the bazaar, and had intended to keep it secret.

I smiled. 'Miss Sakers,' I said, 'I do not know what Eliza is making, but I am quite sure it is for you.'

There was a dead silence. Miss Sakers and Eliza both blushed. Then Miss Sakers said, without looking at me, 'I think you are mistaken.'

I felt so sure that I was mistaken that I blushed too.

Eliza hurriedly hid her work in the work-basket, and said, 'It is very close in here. Let me show you round our little garden.'

They both went out, without taking any notice of me. Not having had much tea, I cut myself another slice of cake. While I was in the middle of it, Miss Sakers and Eliza came back, and Miss Sakers said good-bye to me very coldly. I offered to raise my bazaar donation to ten shillings, but she did not seem to have heard me.

* * *

'How could you say that?' said Eliza, when Miss Sakers had gone. 'It was most tactless – and not very nice.'

'I thought you were doing something for the bazaar. What were you making, then?'

She did not actually tell me, but she implied it in a delicate way.

'Well,' I said, 'of course I wouldn't have called attention to it if I had known, but I don't think you ought to have been doing that work when Miss Sakers was here.'

'I've no time to waste, and I always make mine myself. I was most careful to keep them hidden. You are very tactless.'

'I don't think much of that Miss Sakers,' I said. 'Why should we go to this expense,' pointing to the cakes, 'for a woman of that kind?'

The Orchestrome

THE orchestrome was on Lady Sandlingbury's stall at the bazaar. Her ladyship came up to Eliza in the friendliest way, and said, 'My dear lady, I am convinced that you need an orchestrome. It's the sweetest instrument in the world, worth at least five pounds, and for one shilling you have a chance of getting it. It is to be raffled.' Eliza objects, on principle, to anything like gambling; but as this was for the Deserving Inebriates, which is a good cause, she paid her shilling. She won the orchestrome, and I carried it home for her.

* * *

Six tunes were given with the orchestrome; each tune was on a slip of perforated paper, and all you had to do was to put in a slip and touch the spring.

We tried it first with 'The Dandy Coloured Coon'. It certainly played something, but it was not right. There was no recognizable tune about it.

'This won't do at all,' I said.

'Perhaps that tune's got bent or something,' said Eliza. 'Put in another.'

I put in 'The Lost Chord' and 'The Old Folks at Home', and both were complete failures – a mere jumble of notes, with no tune in them at all. I confess that this exasperated me.

'You see what you've done?' I said. 'You've fooled away a shilling. Nothing is more idiotic than to buy a thing without trying it first.'

'Why didn't you say that before, then?' said Eliza. 'I don't believe there's anything really wrong with it – just some little thing that's got out of order, and can be put right again.'

'Wrong! Why, it's wrong all through. Not one scrap of any of the tunes comes out right. I shall take it back to Lady Sandlingbury at once.'

'Oh, don't do that!'

But my mind was made up, and I went back to the bazaar, and up to Lady Sandlingbury's stall. Eliza wouldn't come with me.

'I beg your ladyship's pardon,' I said, 'but your ladyship supplied me with this orchestrome, and your ladyship will have to take it back again.'

'Dear me! What's all the trouble?'

I started the instrument, and let her hear for herself. She smiled, and turned to another lady who was helping her. The

12

other lady was young, and very pretty, but with a scornful kind of amused expression, and a drawling way of speaking – both of which I disliked extremely.

'Edith,' said Lady Sandlingbury, 'here's this angry gentleman going to put us both in prison for selling him a bad orchestrome. He says it won't work.'

'Doesn't matter, does it?' said the other lady. 'I mean to say, as long as it will play, you know.' At this rather stupid remark they both laughed, without so much as looking at me.

'I don't want to make myself in any way unpleasant, your ladyship,' I said; 'but this instrument was offered for raffle as being worth five pounds, and it's not worth five shillings.'

'Come now,' said Lady Sandlingbury, 'I will give you five shillings for it. There you are! Now you can be happy, and go and spend your money.' I thanked her. She took the orchestrome and started it, and it played magnificently. Nothing could have been more perfect. 'These things do better,' she said, 'when you don't put the tunes in wrong end first, so that the instrument plays them backwards.'

'I think your ladyship might have told me that before,' I said.

'Oh! you were so angry, and you didn't ask me. Edith, dear, do go and be civil to some people, and make them take tickets for another raffle.'

'I call this sharp practice,' I said, 'if not worse, and – '

Here the other lady interrupted me.

'Could you, please, go away, unless you want to buy something? Thanks, so much!'

I went. I am rather sorry for it now. I think it would have been more dignified to have stopped and defied them.

Eliza appeared to think that I had made myself ridiculous. I do not agree with her. I do think, however, that when members of the aristocracy practise a common swindle in support of a charity, they go to show that rank is not everything. If Miss Sakers happens to ask us whether we are going to the bazaar in support of the Deserving Inebriates next year, I have instructed Eliza to reply: 'Not if Lady Sandlingbury and her friend have a stall.' I positively refuse to meet them, and I do not care twopence if they know it.

The Tonic Port

WE do a large export trade (that is, the firm does), and there are often samples lying about in the office. There was a bottle of

Tarret's Tonic Port, which had been there some time, and one of the partners told the head clerk that he could have it if he liked. Later in the day the head clerk said if a bottle of Tarret's Tonic Port was any use to me I might take it home. He said he had just opened it and tasted it, because he did not like to give anything away until he knew if it was all right.

I thanked him. 'Tastes,' I said, 'just like any ordinary port, I suppose?'

'Well,' he said, 'it's more a tonic port than an ordinary port. But that's only what you'd expect from the label.'

'Quite so,' I said – 'quite so.' I looked at the label, and saw that it said that the port was peculiarly rich in phosphates. I put the bottle in my bag that night and took it home.

'Eliza,' I said, 'I have brought you a little present. It is a bottle of port.' Eliza very rarely takes anything at all, but if she does it is a glass of port. In this respect I admire her taste. Port, as I have sometimes said to her, is the king of wines. We decided that we would have a glass after supper. That is really the best time to take anything of the kind; the wine soothes the nerves and prevents insomnia.

Eliza picked the bottle up and looked at the label. 'Why,' she said, 'you told me it was port!'

'So it is.'

'It says tonic port on the label.'

'Well, tonic port practically *is* port. That is to say it is port with the addition of – er – phosphates.'

'What are phosphates?'

'Oh, there are so many of them, you know. There is quinine, of course, and magnesium, and – and so on. Let me fill your glass.'

She took one very little sip. 'It isn't what I should call a pleasant wine,' she said. 'It stings so.'

'Ah!' I said, 'that's the phosphates. It would be a little like that. But that's not the way to judge a port. What you should do is to take a large mouthful and roll it round the tongue – then you get the aroma. Look: this is the way.'

I took a large mouthful.

When I had stopped coughing I said that I didn't know that there was anything absolutely wrong with the wine, but you wanted to be ready for it. It had come on me rather unexpectedly.

Eliza said that very likely that was it, and she asked me if I would care to finish my glass now that I knew what it was like.

I said that it was not quite a fair test to try a port just after it had been shaken about. I would let the bottle stand for a day or

14

two. Ultimately I took what was left in Eliza's glass and my own, and emptied it into the garden. I did this because I did not want our general servant to try it when she cleared away, and possibly acquire a taste for drink.

Next morning I found that two of our best geraniums had died during the night. I said that it was most inexplicable. Eliza said nothing.

* * *

A few nights afterwards, Eliza asked me if I thought that the tonic port had stood long enough.

'Yes,' I said; 'I will decant it for you, and then if Miss Sakers calls you might say carelessly that you were just going to have a glass of port, and would be glad if she would join you.'

'No, thank you,' she said; 'I don't want to deceive Miss Sakers.'

'You could mention that it was rich in phosphates. There need be no deception about it.'

'Well, then, I don't want to lose the few friends we've got.'

'As you please, Eliza. It seems a pity to waste more than half a bottle of good wine.'

'Bottle of what?'

'You heard what I said.'

'Well, drink it yourself, if you like it.'

* * *

Some weeks afterward I found the bottle of Tarret's Tonic Port still standing in the sideboard. I gave it to our servant, explaining to her that it would be best mixed with water. There was still the risk of her acquiring drinking habits, but I could think of no one else to give it to. That night Eliza found the girl crying in the kitchen. When Eliza asked what was the matter, she said that she would rather say nothing, but that she was wishful to leave at the end of her month.

Of course Eliza blamed me, but I had told the girl as distinctly as I could speak that it was a wine which required dilution. However, Eliza persuaded her to stay on. The girl took the pledge on the following day, and seemed changed in many ways. She put the bottle back in the sideboard; there was still more than half of it left.

* * *

After that nothing happened with reference to the tonic port, until one day I noticed that our cat (who had recently lost her kittens), seemed in a poor state of health. I gave it a few spoonfuls of the tonic port in a little milk. It drank it with avidity, somewhat to my surprise. I had one or two little things to do in the garden after that, and when I came back Eliza said that the cat had become so very strange in its manner that she had thought it best to lock it in the coal-cellar.

I went to look at it, and found it lying on its back, dead. It had a singularly happy expression on its face. Both Eliza and myself were very sorry to lose it.

I judged it best to say nothing about the port. But the bottle had gone from the sideboard. Eliza said that she had removed it, to prevent further accidents.

I told the head clerk about it, but he only laughed in the silliest way. He is a most ill-bred man, in my opinion.

The Gentleman of Title

ONE of our younger clerks, a man of the name of Perkins, is said to be very well connected. He certainly spends more than his salary, and rarely wears the same trousers on two consecutive days. But I am not a snob, nor one who thinks much of these things, and I have never cultivated young Perkins. Consequently it rather surprised me when he introduced me to his friend, the Hon. Eugene Clerrimount. Then I remembered what had been said about Perkins's connections.

* * *

The Hon. Eugene Clerrimount was a handsome young man, though apparently troubled with pimples. His manner had in it what I should call dash. There was not an ounce of affectation about him; but then high rank does not need affectations – I have always noticed that. He appeared to take rather a liking to me, and insisted that we must all three go out and have a drink together. This is a thing which I really never do, but on this occasion I allowed myself to be persuaded. Not liking to mention beer, I said that I would take a glass of sherry wine. Nothing could have been more friendly and pleasing than his behaviour towards me; there was nothing at all stuck-up about him. It turned out that, after all, the Hon. Eugene Clerrimount had forgotten his purse, and Perkins happened to have no money on him; I therefore paid for the drinks, and also lent the Hon. Eugene Clerrimount half a crown for his cab; it was, indeed, quite a pleasure to do so. He thanked me warmly, and said that he should like to know me better. Might he call at my house on the following Saturday afternoon? As luck would have it, I happened to have a card on me, and presented it to him, saying that it would indeed be an honour. 'Thanks,' he replied, 'and then I can repay you this half-sovereign, or whatever it is.' 'Only four shillings,' I replied, 'and pray do not mention it.'

* * *

Eliza was certainly less pleased than myself when she heard that the Hon. Eugene Clerrimount was coming. She said that he might be all right, or he might not, and we did not know anything about him. I replied: 'One does not know anything about anybody in that rank of life. It is not necessary.'

'Oh!' she said. 'Isn't it? Well, I don't happen to be an earl myself.'

And, really, on the Saturday morning I had the greatest difficulty to get Eliza to take a little trouble with the drawing-room, though I asked for nothing more than a thorough dusting, chrysanthemums, and the blinds up. For the tea I offered to make myself entirely responsible. There was some doubt as to whether the girl should announce him as the Hon. Mr Clerrimount, or the Hon. Eugene Clerrimount, or Mr Hon. Clerrimount. 'She'd better do all three, one after the other,' said Eliza snappishly. I obviated the difficulty by telling the girl, as she opened the drawing-room door merely to say, 'A gentleman to see you.' I am rather one for thinking of these little ways out of difficulties.

Eliza wanted to know what time he was coming. I replied that he could not come before three or after six, because that would be against etiquette.

'Suppose he came at five minutes to three by accident,' said Eliza. 'Would he sit on our doorstep until the clock struck, and then ring the bell?' I was really beginning to lose patience with Eliza.

However, by three o'clock I had Eliza in the drawing-room, with a magazine and paper-knife by her side as if she had been reading. She was really darning socks, but they could easily be concealed in an empty art flower-pot when the front bell rang.

* * *

We sat in the drawing-room until six, but, strangely enough, the Hon. Eugene Clerrimount never came. The trifle that I had spent on the Madeira cake and macaroons was nothing, but it did wound my feelings that he had not even thought it worth while to explain his inability to keep his appointment.

And on the Monday I said to Perkins, rather sharply: 'There

was that matter of four shillings with your friend. I've not received my money, and I should thank you to see about it.'

'What?' said Perkins. 'You ask my friend and me to come and drink with you, and then want me to dun him for the money to pay for it. Well, I *am* blowed!'

Oh, the whole thing was most unsatisfactory and incomprehensible!

The Hat

I HAD long believed that all was not right with my hat. I could prove nothing, but I had no doubt in my own mind that the girl took liberties with it. It is very easy to brush a silk hat the wrong way, for instance, but silk hats do not brush themselves the wrong way; if it is done, someone must have done it. Morning after morning I found marks on my hat which I could not account for. Well, I said nothing, but I made up my mind to keep my eyes open. It was not only the injury to the hat – it was the impertinence to myself that affected me.

One Saturday afternoon, while I was at home, a costermonger came to the door with walnuts. The girl answered the bell, and presently I saw the coster and his cart go past the dining-room window. I don't know why it was, or how it was but a suspicion came over me. I stepped sharply to the door, and looked out into the passage. There was no one there. The front door was open, and the kitchen door was open, and in a position between the two, against the umbrella-stand, was – something worse than ever I had expected.

I picked that hat up just as it was, with the walnuts inside it, and placed it on the dining-room table. Then I called Eliza to come downstairs.

'What is it?' she asked, as she entered the dining-room.

I pointed to the hat. 'This kind of thing,' I said, 'has been going on for years!'

'Oh, do talk sense!' she said. 'What do you mean?'

'Sense!' I said. 'You ask me to talk sense, when I find my own hat standing on the floor in the hall, and used as a – a receptacle for walnuts!'

She smiled. 'I can explain all that,' she said.

'I've no doubt you can. I'm sick to death of explanations. I give ten or eleven shillings for a hat, and find it ruined. I know those explanations. You told the girl to buy the walnuts, and she had got nothing else to put them in, and the hat was handy;

18

but if you think I take that as an excuse, you make a mistake.'

'I wasn't going to say that at all.'

'Or else you'll tell me that you can paste in a piece of white paper, so that the stains on the lining won't show. Explanations, indeed!'

'And I wasn't going to say that either.'

'I don't care what you were going to say. I won't hear it. There's no explanation possible. For once I mean to take a strong line. You see that hat? I shall never wear it again!'

'I know that.'

'No one shall wear it! I don't care for the expense! If you choose to let that servant-girl ruin my hat, then that hat shall be ruined, and no mistake about it!'

I picked the hat up, and gave it one sound, savage kick. My foot went through it, and the walnuts flew all over the room. At the same moment I heard from the drawing-room a faint tink-tink-tink on the piano.

'Yes,' said Eliza. 'That's the piano-tuner. He came at the same time as the walnut-man, and bought those walnuts. And he put them in his hat. *His* hat, mind you, not *your* hat. Your hat's hanging up in the usual place. You might have seen it if you'd looked. Only you're –'

'Eliza,' I said, 'you need say no more. If that is so, the servant-girl is much less to blame than I had supposed. I have to go out now, but perhaps you'd drop into the drawing-room and explain to the tuner that there's been some slight misunderstanding with his hat. And, I say, a glass of beer and two shillings is as much as you need offer.'

My Fortune

THE girl had just removed the supper-things. We have supper rather early, because I like a long evening. 'Now, Eliza,' I said, 'you take your work – your sewing, or whatever it may be, and I will take my work. Yes, I've brought it with me, and it's to be paid as overtime. I dare say it mayn't seem much to you – a lot of trouble, and only a few shillings to show for it, when all's said and done – but that is the way fortunes are made, by sticking at it, by plugging into it, if I may use the term.'

'The table's clear, if you want to start,' said Eliza.

'Very well,' I replied, and fetched my black bag from the passage to get the accounts on which I was working. I always hang the bag on the peg in the passage, just under my hat. Then it is there in the morning when and where it is wanted. Method in little things has always been rather a motto of mine.

'It has sometimes struck me, Eliza,' I said, as I came back into the dining-room, with the bag in my hand, 'that you do not read so much as I should like to see you read.'

'Well, you asked me to take my work, and these socks are for you, and I never know what you do want.'

'I did not mean that I wanted you to read at this moment. But there is one book – I cannot say exactly what the title is, and the name of the author has slipped my memory, which I should like to see in your hands occasionally, because it deals with the making of fortunes. It practically shows you how to do it.'

'Did the man who wrote it make one?' asked Eliza.

'That – not knowing the name of the man – I cannot say for certain.'

'Well, I should want to know that first. And aren't you going to start?'

'I can hardly start until I have unlocked my bag, and I cannot unlock my bag until I have the keys, and I cannot have the keys until I have fetched them from the bedroom. Try and be a little more reasonable.'

I could not find the keys in the bedroom. Then Eliza went up, and she could not find them either. By a sort of oversight they were in my pocket all the time. I laughingly remarked that I knew I should find them first. Eliza seemed rather pettish, the joke being against herself.

'The reason why I mentioned that book,' I said, as I unlocked the bag, 'is because it points out that there are two ways of making a fortune. One is, if I may say so, my own way – by method in little things, economy of time, doing all the work that one can get to do, and –'

'You won't get much done to-night, if you don't start soon,' said Eliza.

'I do not like to be interrupted in the middle of a sentence. The other way by which you may make a fortune – well, it's not making a fortune. It's that the fortune makes you, if you understand me.'

'I don't,' said Eliza.

'I mean that the fortune may come of itself by luck. Luck is a very curious thing. We cannot understand it. It's of no use to talk about it, because it is quite impossible to understand it.'

'Then don't let's talk about it, especially when you've got something else to do.'

'Temper, temper, Eliza! You must guard against that. I was not going to talk about luck. I was going to give you an instance of luck, which happened to come within my own personal experience. It is the case of a man of the name of Chumpleigh, in our office, and would probably interest and amuse you. I do not know if I have ever mentioned Chumpleigh to you.'

'Yes, you've told me all about him several times.'

I might have mentioned Chumpleigh to Eliza, but I am sure that I have never told her all about him. However, I was not going to sulk, and so I told her the story again. The story would not have been so long if she hadn't interrupted me so frequently.

When I had finished, she said that it was time to go to bed, and I had wasted the evening.

I owned that possibly I had been chatting rather longer than I had intended, but I would still get those accounts done, and sit up to do them.

'And that means extra gas,' she said. 'That's the way money gets wasted.'

'There are many men in my place,' I said, 'who would refuse to sit down to work as late as this. I don't. Why? On principle. Because it's through the cultivation of the sort of thing that I cultivate one arrives at fortune. Think what fortune would mean to us. Big house, large garden, servants, carriages. I should come in from a day with the hounds, and perhaps say I felt rather done up, and would like a glass of champagne. No question of expense – not a word about it – money no object. You'd just get the bottle out of the sideboard, and I should have my glass, and they'd finish it in the kitchen, and –'

'*Are* you going to begin, or are you not?' asked Eliza.

'This minute,' I replied, opening the black bag. I examined the contents carefully.

'Well,' I said, 'this is a very strange occurrence indeed – most unaccountable! I don't remember ever to have done anything of the kind before, but I seem to have forgotten to bring that work from the City. Dear me! I shall be forgetting my head next.'

Eliza's reply that this would be no great loss did not seem to me to be either funny, or polite, or even true. 'You strangely forget yourself,' I replied, and turned the gas out sharply.

Shakespeare

I LED up to it, saying to Eliza, not at all in a complaining way, 'Does it not seem to you a pity to let these long winter evenings run to waste?'

'Yes, dear,' she replied; 'I think you ought to do something.'

'And you too. Is it not so, darling?'

'There's generally some sewing, or the accounts.'

'Yes; but these things do not exercise the mind.'

'Accounts do.'

'Not in the way I mean.' I had now reached my point. 'How would it be if I were to read aloud to you? I don't think you have ever heard me read aloud. You are fond of the theatre, and we cannot often afford to go. This would make up for it. There are many men who would tell you that they would sooner have a play read aloud to them than see it acted in the finest theatre in the world.'

'Would they? Well – perhaps – if I were only sewing it wouldn't interrupt me much.'

I said, 'That is not very graciously put, Eliza. There is a certain art in reading aloud. Some have it, and some have not. I do not know if I have ever told you, but when I was a boy of twelve I won a prize for recitation, though several older boys were competing against me.'

She said that I had told her several times.

I continued: 'And I suppose that I have developed since then. A man in our office once told me that he thought I should have done well on the stage. I don't know whether I ever mentioned it.'

She said that I had mentioned it once or twice.

'I should have thought that you would have been glad of a little pleasure – innocent, profitable, and entertaining. However, if you think I am not capable of –'

'What do you want to read?'

'What would you like me to read?'

'Miss Sakers lent me this.' She handed me a paper-covered volume, entitled, 'The Murglow Mystery; or, The Stain on the Staircase'.

'Trash like this is not literature,' I said. However, to please her, I glanced at the first page. Half an hour later I said that I should be very sorry to read a book of that stamp out loud.

'Then why do you go on reading it to yourself?'

'Strictly speaking, I am not reading it. I am glancing at it.'

When Eliza got up to go to bed, an hour afterwards, she asked me if I was still glancing. I kept my temper.

'Try not to be so infernally unreasonable,' I said. 'If Miss Sakers lends us a book, it is discourteous not to look at it.'

* * *

On the following night Eliza said that she hoped I was not going to sit up until three in the morning, wasting the gas and ruining my health, over a book that I myself had said –

'And who pays for the gas?'

'Nobody's paid last quarter's yet. Mother can't do everything, and –'

'Well, we can talk about that some other time. To-night I am going to read aloud to you a play of Shakespeare's. I wonder if you even know who Shakespeare was?'

'Of course I do.'

'Could you honestly say that you have ever read one – only one – of his tragedies?'

'No. Could you?'

'I am going to read *Macbeth* to you, trying to indicate by changes in my voice which character is speaking.' I opened the book.

Eliza said that she couldn't think who it was took her scissors.

'I can't begin till you keep quiet,' I said.

'It's the second pair that's gone this week.'

'Very well, then,' I said, shutting up the book with a bang, 'I will not read aloud to you to-night at all. You may get along as you can without it.'

'You're sure you didn't take those scissors for anything?' she replied meditatively.

* * *

'Now then,' I said, on the next night, 'I am ready to begin. The tragedy is entitled *Macbeth*. This is the first scene.'

'What is the first scene?'

'A blasted heath.'

'Well, I think you might give a civil answer to a civil question. There was no occasion to use that word.'

'I didn't.'

'You did. I heard it distinctly.'

'Do let me explain. It's Shakespeare uses the word. I was only quoting it. It merely means –'

'Oh, if it's Shakespeare I suppose it's all right. Nobody seems to mind what *he* says. You can go on.'

I read for some time. Eliza, in reply to my question, owned that she had enjoyed it, but she went to bed before her usual time.

* * *

When I was preparing to read aloud on the following evening, I was unable to find our copy of Shakespeare. This was very annoying, as it had been a wedding present. Eliza said that she had found her scissors, and very likely I should find the Shakespeare some other night.

But I never did. I have half thought of buying another copy, or I dare say Eliza's mother would like to give us it. Eliza thinks not.

The Unsolved Problem

'ELIZA,' I said one evening, 'do you think that you are fonder of me than I am of you, or that I am fonder of you than you are of me?'

She answered, 'What is thirteen from twenty-eight?' without looking up from the account-book.

'I do think,' I said, 'that when I speak to you you might have the civility to pay some little attention.'

She replied, 'One pound fifteen and two, and I hope you know where we are to get it from, for I don't. And don't bang on the table in that silly way, or you'll spill the ink.'

'I did not bang. I tapped slightly from a pardonable impatience. I put a plain question to you some time ago, and I should like a plain answer to it.'

'Well, what do you want to talk for when you see I am counting? Now, what is it?'

'What I asked was this. Do I think – I mean, do you think – that I am fonder of me – no, you are fonder of I – well, I'll begin again. Which of us two would you say was fonder of the other than the other was of the – dash it all, you know what I mean!'

'No, I don't, but it's nothing to swear about.'

'I was not swearing. If you don't know what I mean, I'll try to put it more simply. Are you fonder than I am? There.'

'Fonder of what?'

'Fonder of each other.'

'You mean is each of us fonder of the other than the other is of – of the each?'

'I mean nothing of the kind. Until you muddled it the thing was perfectly clear. Well, we two are two, are we not?'

'Of course I know that, but —'

'Wait a minute. I intend that you shall understand me this time. Which of those two would you say was fonder of the other than the other was of the other, or would you say that each was

24

as fond of the other as the other one was? Now you see it.'

'Almost. Say it again.'

'Would you say that in your opinion neither of us were fonder of the other than both were of each, or that one was fonder of the other than the other was of the first, and if so, which?'

'Now you've made it worse than ever. I don't believe you know what you mean yourself. Do come to supper and talk sense.'

* * *

I smiled cynically as I sat down to supper. 'This doesn't surprise me in the least,' I remarked. 'I never yet knew a woman who could argue, or even understand the first step in an argument, and I don't suppose I ever shall.'

'Well,' said Eliza, 'you can't argue until you know what you are talking about, and I don't know what you're talking about, and you don't seem to know yourself, or, if you do, you're too muddled to tell anybody. If you want to argue, argue about one pound fifteen and two. It's Griffiths, and been sent in three times already.'

'Don't shirk it, Eliza. Don't try to get away from it. I asked you which of us you thought was the fonder of the other, and you couldn't understand it.'

'Why, of course I understand *that*. Why didn't you say so before?'

'As far as I remember, those were my precise words.'

'But they weren't! What you said was, "If neither of us was fonder of both than each is of either, which of the two would it be?" or something of the kind.'

'Now, how could I talk such absolute nonsense?'

'Ah!' she said; 'when men lose their temper they never know what they're saying!'

I had a very good answer to that, but just at the moment the girl brought in the last post. There was a letter from Eliza's mother. There was also an enclosure in postal orders quite beyond anything I had expected, and she expressed a hope that they might enable us 'to defray some of the expenses incidental to the season'. As far as my own personal feeling is concerned, I should have returned them at once. In some ways I dare say that I am a proud man. I have been told so. But the poor old lady takes such pleasure in giving, and she has so little other enjoyment, that I should have been reluctant to check her. In fact, taking the money as evidence of her affection, I was pleased. So was Eliza.

'Pay Griffiths's twopenny-halfpenny account to-morrow,' I said, 'and tell him that he has lost our patronage for ever.'

* * *

We did not recur to the original question. Personally, I should say that, in the case of two people it might very well happen that, though at one time the affection of one for the other might be greater than the affection which the other had for the one which I originally mentioned at the same time, yet at some other time the affection which the other one had for the other might be just as much greater than the affection which the first one had for the second, as the difference was in the first instance between the two. At least, that is the general drift of what I mean. Eliza would never see it, of course.

The Day Off

ON the occasion of the marriage of our junior partner to Ethel Mary, only surviving daughter of William Hubblestead, Esq., J.P., of Banlingbury, by the Canon of Blockminster, assisted by the Rev. Eugene Hubblestead, cousin of the bride – on this occasion the office was closed for the whole of one day, and the staff had a holiday without deduction of salary.

The staff had presented six silver (hall-marked) nutcrackers and a handsomely-bound volume of Cowper's Poetical Works. The latter was my own suggestion; there was a sum of eight shillings over after the purchase of the nutcrackers, and I have always had a partiality for Cowper. The junior partner thanked us personally, and in very warm terms; at the same time he announced that the following Thursday was to be treated as a holiday.

* * *

The weather was glorious, and I have never had a more enjoyable day. The girl laid breakfast overnight, and we rose at half-past five. By half-past six Eliza had cut some mutton sandwiches, and placed them in a basket with a bottle of milk – the milkman having obliged with a specially early call by appointment. A brief journey by train, and by a quarter-past seven we were at Danstow for our day off in the country.

Danstow is a picturesque little village, and looked beautiful in the hot sunlight. I was wearing a fairly new summer suit, with brown boots. As I remarked to Eliza, it would probably have created a feeling of surprise among the villagers if they had learned that, as a rule, my professional duties took me to the City in the morning.

Eliza said: 'All right. What do we do here?'

'Why,' I said, 'there's the old church. We mustn't miss that.'

We went and examined the old church. Then we went twice up and down the village street, and examined that.

'Well,' said Eliza, 'what next?'

'Now,' I replied, 'we just stroll about and amuse ourselves. I feel particularly light-hearted.'

'That's breakfasting at six, that is,' said Eliza. 'If you could find a quiet place, we might have a sandwich.'

We went a little way along the road, and I espied a field which seemed to me to look likely. I said to a passer-by: 'I am a stranger here. Can you tell me whether there would be any objection to our sitting in that field?' He said, in rather an offensive and sarcastic way, that he believed the field was open for sitting in about that hour. I did not give him any reply, but just opened the gate for Eliza.

We sat down under the hedge, and finished our sandwiches and milk. The church clock struck nine.

'What train do we go back by?' asked Eliza.

'Not until half-past nine to-night. There's a day for you!'

'Twelve hours and a half,' said Eliza. 'And we've done the sandwiches, and done the milk, and done the church, and there's nothing else to do.'

'Except amuse ourselves,' I added, as I took off my boots, which had pained me slightly. I then dozed off.

* * *

Eliza woke me to say that she had read all the newspaper the sandwiches were wrapped in, and picked some wild flowers, and the flowers had died, and she wanted to know what the time was. It was just past eleven.

She said: 'Oh, lor!'

I soon dropped off again.

When I woke, at half-past twelve, Eliza was not there. She returned in a few minutes, and said that she had been doing the church over again.

'That was hardly necessary,' I observed.

'Oh, one must do something, and there's nothing else to do.'

'On the contrary, there's luncheon. We'll have that at once, so as to give us a good long afternoon.'

'The afternoon will be long enough,' she said. If I had not

known that she was having a day's enjoyment, I should have thought that she seemed rather dejected in her manner.

* * *

The luncheon at the village inn was not expensive. Eliza said that their idea of chops was not her idea; but all the same she seemed inclined to spin the thing out and make it last as long as possible. I deprecated this, as I felt that I could not very well take my boots off again until I had returned to the field.

'Very well, then,' she said. 'Only let's go back slowly.'

'As slowly as you like,' I replied. 'It's the right boot principally; but I prefer to walk slowly.'

When we had resumed our old position under the hedge, and I had removed my boots, I said:

'Now, then, I think I've earned a pipe and a short nap. You amuse yourself in any way you like.'

'Do *what* with myself?' she asked rather sharply.

She walked twice round the field and then I fell off to sleep. It turned out afterwards that she also did the picturesque old church for the third time, and went over a house which was to let, refusing to take it on the ground that there was no bathroom. This was rather dishonest, as she would not have taken it if there had been a bathroom, or even two bathrooms. I would not do that kind of thing myself. I awoke about tea-time. The charge for tea at the inn was very moderate, though Eliza said that there was tea which was tea, and tea which was an insult.

Eliza found that there was a train back at half-past six, and said she was going by it, whether I did or not, because it was a pity to have too much of a good thing, and she hadn't the face to ask for the keys of that church again. I accompanied her. I fancy that the brown leather is liable to shrink in the sun, and I was not unwilling to get back to my slippers and stretch myself out on the sofa.

There is nothing like a long day in the country; quite apart from the enjoyment, you feel that it is doing you so much good. I am sorry that Eliza did not seem to enter into the spirit of the thing more.

The Mushroom

WE were at breakfast one morning in the summer when the girl entered rather excitedly and said that to the best of her belief there was a mushroom coming in the little lawn in the front of the house. It seemed a most extraordinary thing, and Eliza and I both went out to look at it. There was certainly something white coming through the turf; the only question was, whether or not it was a mushroom. The girl seemed certain about it. 'Why,' she said, 'in my last place mushrooms was frequent. You see, being wealthy, they had anything they fancied. If I didn't know about mushrooms, I ought to!' There is a familiarity in that girl's manner which to my mind is highly objectionable. The establishment where she was formerly employed was apparently on a scale that we do not attempt. That does not justify her, however, in continually drawing comparisons. I shall certainly have something to say to her about it.

* * *

However, it was not about Jane that I intended to speak, but about the mushroom.

Eliza said that I ought to put a flower-pot over the mushroom, because, being visible from the road, someone might be tempted to come in and steal it. But I was too deep for that. 'No,' I replied, 'if you put an inverted plant-pot there everybody will guess that you are hiding a mushroom underneath it. Just put a scrap of newspaper over it.'

'But that might get blown away!'

'Fasten down one corner of it with a hairpin.'

Eliza said that I was certainly one to think of things. I believe there is truth in that. On my way to the station I happened to meet Mr Bungwall's gardener (a most obliging and respectful man), and had a word with him about the mushroom. He said that he would come round in the evening and have a look at it.

* * *

I was pleased to find (on my return) that the mushroom was still in the garden under the newspaper, and had increased slightly in size.

'This,' I said to Eliza, 'is very satisfactory.'

'It would make a nice little present to send to mother,' Eliza observed.

There I could not entirely agree with her. I pointed out that in a week's time I should probably be applying to her mother for a small temporary loan. I did not think it an honourable thing to attempt to influence her mind beforehand by sending a present. I wished her to approach the question of the loan purely in a business spirit. I added that I thought we would leave the mushroom to grow for one more day, and then have it for breakfast. That ultimately was decided upon.

Then Mr Bungwall's gardener arrived, and said he was sorry to disappoint us in any way, and it was not his fault, but the mushroom was a toadstool.

'This,' I said to Eliza, 'is something of a blow.'

'Perhaps,' she said, 'Mr Bungwall's gardener is mistaken.'

'I fear not. But, however, I happened to mention about that mushroom to our head clerk this morning, and he said that he thoroughly understood mushrooms, and had made a small profit by growing them. To-morrow morning I will pick that toadstool or mushroom, as the case may be, take it up to the City, and ask him about it.'

Eliza agreed that this would be the best way.

* * *

But at breakfast next morning she seemed thoughtful and somewhat depressed. I asked her what she was thinking about.

'It's like this,' she said. 'If your head clerk says that our toadstool is a mushroom, while Mr Bungwall's gardener says that our mushroom is a toadstool, we shan't like to eat it because of Mr Bungwall's gardener, and we shan't like to throw it away because of your head clerk, and I don't see what to do with it.'

'You forget, my dear. We have a third opinion. Jane says the mushroom is a mushroom.'

'Jane will say anything.'

'Well, we might put her to the test. We might ask her if she'd like to eat the mushroom herself, and then if she says yes and seems pleased, why, of course we'd eat it. I'll go and pick it now.'

And when I went to do so I found that the mushroom had gone.

* * *

Eliza said that Mr Bungwall's gardener told us it was a toadstool to keep us from picking it, and then stole it himself, because he knew that it was a mushroom.

That may be. I should be sorry to believe it, because I have always found Mr Bungwall's gardener such a very respectful man. To my mind there is an air of mystery over the whole affair.

The Pleasant Surprise

I HAD got the money by work done at home, out of office hours. It came to four pounds altogether. At first I thought I would use it to discharge a part of our debt to Eliza's mother. But it was very possible that she would send it back again, in which case the pence spent on the postal orders would be wasted, and I am not a man that wastes pennies. Also, it was not absolutely certain that she would send it back. I sent her a long letter instead – my long letters are almost her only intellectual pleasure. As for the four pounds, I reserved two for myself, for any incidental expenses, and decided to give two to Eliza. I did not mean simply to hand them to her, but to get up something in the way of a pleasant surprise.

I had tried something of the kind before. Eliza once asked me for six shillings for a new tea-tray that she had seen. I went and stood behind her chair, and said, 'No, dear, I couldn't think of it,' at the same time dropping the six shillings down the back of her neck. Eliza said it was a pity I couldn't give her six shillings for a tea-tray without compelling her to go upstairs and undress at nine o'clock in the morning. It was not a success.

However, I have more than one idea in my head. This time I thought I would first find out if there was anything else wanted.

So on Sunday at tea-time I said, not as if I were meaning anything in particular, 'Is there anything you want, Eliza?'

'Yes,' she said; 'I want a general who'll go to bed at half-past nine and get up at half-past five. If they'd only do that, that's all I ask.'

'You will pardon me, Eliza,' I said, 'but you are not speaking correctly. You said that was all that you asked. What you meant —'

'Do you know what I meant?'

'I flatter myself that I know precisely —'

'Then if you know precisely what I meant, I must have spoken accurately.'

But as we went to church I discovered that she wanted a new jacket. Her own was trimmed rabbit, and had been good, but the fur had gone bald in places.

*   *   *

Next morning I wrote on a sheet of notepaper, 'To buy a new jacket. With your husband's love.' I folded the two sovereigns up in this, and dropped the packet into the pocket of Eliza's old jacket, as it hung in the wardrobe, not telling her what I had done. My idea was that she would put on the jacket to go out shopping in the morning, and putting her hand in the pocket, get a pleasant surprise. As I was leaving for Town, she asked me why I kept on smiling so mysteriously. I replied, 'Perhaps you, too, will smile before the day is over.'

On my return I found Eliza at the front door. 'Come and look,' she said cheerfully. 'I have got a pleasant surprise for you.' She flung open the drawing-room door, and pointed. In the middle of the table stood a *spiræa*, a most handsome and graceful plant. It stood in one of the best saucers, with some coloured paper round the pot, and the general effect was very good. I at once guessed that she had bought it for me with the change from my present to her, and thought it showed very good feeling in her.

'I hope you have not given too much for this,' I said.

'I didn't give any money for it.'

'I don't understand.'

'Well, you must know I had a present this morning.'

'Of course I know.'

'Did mother tell you? Yes, she has sent me a beautiful new jacket. Then a man came round with a barrow of plants, and he said he didn't want money if I had any clothes to spare. So I gave him my old worn-out jacket for this *spiræa*, and —'

I remembered that I had seen the man with the barrow farther down the street.

'Excuse me for one moment, Eliza,' I said, and dashed out after him.

* * *

He was a big, red-faced man, and he made no difficulty about it at all.

'Yes,' he said, 'I bought that jacket, gov'ner, and I don't deny it. There it is at the bottom of my bundle, and I ain't even looked at it since. Nor I ain't goin' to look now. You says there was two suvreigns in the pocket. A gent like you don't want to swindle a common man like me. If you says the two suvreigns was there, then they're there now, and I can return yer two pound out o' my own, in a suttunty of gettin' 'em back out o' the jacket-pocket. Bless yer! I knows an honest man when I sees one.'

With these words he drew the money from his own waistcoat pocket, and handed it to me. I took it with some reluctance.

'Hadn't you better make quite certain —'

'Not a bit,' says he. 'If them suvreigns was there when the jacket were 'anded to me, they is there now. I could see as you was a man to be trusted, otherwise I'd 'ave undone the bundle and searched long afore this.'

* * *

'What have you been doing?' said Eliza, on my return.

'Never mind. Your mother has given you a new jacket. Let me have the pleasure of giving you a new hat.' I pressed the two coins into her palm.

She looked at them, and said, 'You can't get a hat for a half-penny, you know, dear. What did you rush out for just now? And why did you have these two farthings gilded? You'll be mistaking them for sovereigns, if you're not careful. Were you trying to take me in?'

I did not quite see what to say for the moment, and so I took her suggestion. I explained that it was a joke.

'You don't look much as if you were joking.'

'But I was. I suppose I ought to know if any man does. However, Eliza, if you want a new hat, anything up to half a sovereign, you've only to say it.'

She said it, thanked me, and asked me to come and help her water the *spiræa*.

'It's such a shapely *spiræa*,' she said.

'Yes,' I answered sadly, 'it's a regular plant.' And so it was, though I had not been intending what the French call a *double entendre* at the time.

The Mopworths

I MUST say that both Eliza and myself felt a good deal of contempt for the Mopworths. We had known them for three years, and that gave us a claim; Peter Mopworth was a connection of Eliza's by marriage, and that also gave us a claim; further, our social position gave us a claim. Nevertheless, the Mopworths were to have their annual party on the following Wednesday, and they had not invited us.

'Upon my soul,' I exclaimed, 'I never in my life heard of anything so absolutely paltry.'

'I can't think why it is,' said Eliza.

'Oh, we're not good enough for them. We all know who his father was, and we all know what he is – a petty provincial shopkeeper! A gentleman holding important employment in one of the principal mercantile firms in the City isn't good enough for him. If I'm permitted to clean his boots I'm sure I ought to be thankful. Oh, yes! Of course! No doubt!'

'You do get so sarcastic,' observed Eliza.

'That's nothing – nothing to what I should be if I let myself go. But I don't choose to let myself go. I don't think he's worth it, and I don't think she's worth it either. It's a pity, perhaps, that they don't know that they're making themselves ridiculous, but it can't be helped. Personally, I shan't give the thing another thought.'

'That's the best thing to do,' said Eliza.

'Of course it is. Why trouble one's head about people of that class? And, I say, Eliza, if you meet that Mopworth woman in the street, there's no occasion for you to recognize her.'

'That would look as if we were terribly cut up because we hadn't been asked to their party.'

'Possibly. Whereas, I don't even consider it worth talking about.'

We discussed the Mopworths and their party for another hour and a half, and then went to bed.

* * *

'Lying awake last night,' I said at breakfast next morning, 'I couldn't help thinking over the different things we have done for those serpents.'

'What serpents?'

'Those contemptible Mopworths. I wonder if they have any feelings of shame? If they have, they must blush when they think of the way they have treated us.'

'I can't think why they've left us out. Perhaps it's a mistake.'

'Not a bit of it. I've been expecting this for some time. Of course he has made money. I don't say – I would rather *not* say – how he has made it. But it seems to have turned his head. However, after this I shall probably never mention him again.'

Eliza began to talk about the weather. I told her that Mopworth had done things which, personally, I should have been very sorry to do, and that I should be reluctant to adopt his loud style of dress.

'But, of course,' I added, 'no gentleman ever does dress like that.'

Eliza said that if I intended to catch my train I had better start. I started.

* * *

On my return I said to Eliza that, though the whole subject was distasteful to me, there was one point to which I had given a few moments' consideration. Reluctant though I was to sully my lips with the name of Mopworth, I felt it a duty to myself to say that even if the Mopworths had asked us to their annual party, I should have refused point blank.

'Really?' said Eliza. This annoyed me slightly. She ought to have seen, without being told, that it was impossible for people like us to continue to know people like them.

'I am accustomed,' I replied, 'to say just exactly what I mean. As far as I can remember, I have lately more than once asked you to drop the Mopworths. If I have not actually done it, it has been in my mind to do so. They are connected to us by marriage, and I am not unduly proud, but still I feel that we must draw the line somewhere. I do not care to have Mopworth bragging about the place that he is on intimate terms with us.'

'Well,' said Eliza, 'there aren't such a lot of people who ever ask us to anything. Miss Sakers is friendly, of course, especially when there are subscriptions on for the bazaar or the new organ, but she doesn't carry it to that point.'

'Quite so,' I said, 'and I'm by no means certain about Miss Sakers. She may be all right. I hope she is. But I candidly confess that I by no means like her manner.'

At this moment the girl brought in a note, delivered by hand, from Mrs Mopworth. It said that she had sent an invitation to Eliza but had had no reply. She felt so certain that the invitation must have been delayed in the post (which was not surprising, considering the season) that she had ventured to write again, though it might be against etiquette. She hoped that we should both be able to come, and said that on the previous occasion I had been the life and soul of the party.

'Well,' I said, 'Eliza, what would you like to do?'

'Oh, I'm going!' she replied.

'Then if you insist, I shall go with you. I've never had a word to say against Mrs Mopworth. It is true that *he* is not in every particular what – well, what I should care to be myself. Possibly he has not had my advantages. I do not want to judge him too harshly. My dress clothes are put away with my summer suit in the second drawer in the box-room. Just put them to the fire to get the creases out. And, Eliza, write a friendly note to Mrs Mopworth, implying that we had never heard of the party. I saw from the first that the omission was a mistake.'

Eliza went away smiling. Women are so variable.

The Pen-wiper

ELIZA always works me some little pretty trifle for my birthday, and always has done so since the day when I led her to the hymeneal altar. But it is not done at all as a matter of course. During the days before my birthday, when she is working at the present, she keeps a clean handkerchief by her side, and flings it over the work to hide it when I enter the room. This makes it more of a surprise when the day comes. As a rule, I whistle a few bars in a careless way before entering the room, so as to give her plenty of time to get the work under the handkerchief. There is no definite arrangement about this; I merely do what good taste dictates. Last year, instead of the handkerchief, she kept a large table-napkin by her side when she was working. However, though I did not tell her so, this let the secret out. I knew that she must be doing me a pair of slippers.

* * *

This year, on my birthday, when I came down to breakfast, I found placed before me the hot-water plate with the tin cover to it – a very useful article when there happens to be an invalid in the house.

Eliza, bending down behind the tea-cosy to hide her smile, told me to be quick with my breakfast, in rather a censorious voice. I lifted the tin cover, and there on the plate was the pen-wiper which Eliza had made for me.

This rather graceful and amusing way of giving a present is not really Eliza's own invention. I did it some years ago when I gave her a pin-cushion. As the pin-cushion was made to imitate a poached egg (and really very like), perhaps the humour in that instance had rather more point. However, I do not say this at all to find fault with Eliza. I am rather one to think of novelties, and if Eliza cares to copy any of them, so much the better.

* * *

The top and bottom of the pen-wiper which Eliza had made for me were of black velvet, which always had a handsome look to my mind. On the top was worked in gold beads, 'Kindly clean the pen.' The interior was composed of several folds of very pale shades of art muslin. Only the day before Messrs. Howlett & Bast had refused to send any more patterns, as the last lot sent had not been returned, though twice applied for. I understood that now.

However, it made a very good pen-wiper, in pleasant, simple taste, and I thanked Eliza for it several times more warmly. At my suggestion it was placed on the centre table in the drawing-room. One never wrote there, but it seemed naturally to belong to the drawing-room.

* * *

So far, my birthday had gone happily enough. In the evening, when I returned from the City, I sat down to write a short, sharp note to Messrs. Howlett & Bast. I explained to them that by their impertinence they were running a grave risk of entirely losing my custom, and suggested to them that the lot of patterns to which they referred might possibly have been lost in the post.

When I had finished the letter, I wiped my pen on the inside of my coat. This is my general custom. Some men wipe their pens on their hair – not a very cleanly habit, in my opinion – besides, unless the colour of the hair is exceptionally dark, the ink shows.

I had no sooner wiped my pen on the inside of my coat than I remembered Eliza's present. Determined to show her that I appreciated it, I took a full dip of the ink, stepped into the drawing-room, and wiped the pen on the new pen-wiper. Then I called upstairs: 'Eliza, I have just found your present very useful. Would you like to come and look?' She happened to be fastening something up the back at the time, but she came down a minute afterwards.

She picked up the pen-wiper, looked at it, exclaimed 'Ruined!' and then walked rapidly out of the room. I followed her, and asked what was the matter.

It appeared that the words, 'Kindly clean the pen', meant that the pen was to be cleaned on a scrap of paper before the pen-wiper was used. Eliza said that I might have known that the pretty muslin was not intended to be a perfect mess of ink.

'Well,' I said, 'I didn't know. That's all there is to say about it.'

But it was not, apparently, all that there was to say about it. In fact, the whole thing cast an unpleasant shade over the evening of my birthday. Finally, I took a strong line, and refused to speak at all.

The 9.43

IN the course of conversation on Saturday evening it had transpired that Eliza had never been in St. Paul's Cathedral.

'Then,' I said, 'you shall go there to-morrow morning; I will take you.'

'I'm sure I'm agreeable,' said Eliza.

On the Sunday morning one or two little things had happened to put me out. At breakfast I had occasion to say that the eggs were stone-cold, and Eliza contradicted me. It was very absurd of her. As I pointed out to her, what earthly motive could I have for saying that an egg was cold if it was not? What should I gain by it? Of course she had no answer – that is, no reasonable answer. Then after breakfast I broke my boot-lace in two places. No, I was not angry. I hope I can keep my temper as well as most men. But I was in a state of mind bordering on the irritable.

* * *

Eliza came downstairs, dressed for going out, asked me why I was not ready, and said we should miss the 9.43.

'Indeed!' said I. 'And what, precisely, might you mean by the 9.43?'

'I mean, precisely, the train which leaves here for the City at seventeen minutes to ten.'

'One of your usual mistakes,' I replied. 'The train is 9.53, and not 9.43.'

'Have you a time-table?' she asked.

'No.'

'Because if you had a time-table I could show you that you are wrong. Why, I *know* it's the 9.43.'

'If I had a time-table I could show you most certainly that it is the 9.53. Not that you'd believe it, even then. You're too obstinate, Eliza – too certain of yourself!'

* * *

'Look here!' I observed, after she had argued that point at some length, 'let us come back to the original subject of discussion. Which of us travels most to and from London? That is the reasonable way to settle it.'

'You do, on week-days. But you never go on Sundays, and the Sunday trains are different.'

'I am fully aware of the difference. Every day I am thrown into constant contact with the time-tables. Only last night I was looking at them at the station. As far as I know, my memory is not going.'

'No more is mine.'

'Really? A week ago I purchased and brought home six new collars. They are not marked. Why? Because you forgot them! At

38

this very moment that I am speaking to you I am wearing an unmarked collar.'

'Yes; but I only forgot them one day.'

'Then why did you not mark them on the other days?'

'Because on the other days you forgot to bring home the marking-ink.'

'M, yes,' I said. 'In a sense that is true. I have my own business to attend to in the City, without always thinking about marking-ink. But what has that got to do with it? And why bring it in? We are not talking about marking-ink; we are talking about trains!'

She said that I began it, and of course I pointed out to her that I had done nothing of the kind.

* * *

We argued for some little time as to which of us had begun it, and then Eliza said, in her spiteful way:

'We are not talking about which of us began it; we are talking about trains!'

'It's very little use talking to you about trains. I know you're wrong! I would stake my life, cheerfully, that it is 9.53, and not 9.43. But you'd never own you're wrong; you're too obstinate for that!'

'Of course I don't own I'm wrong, because I'm not wrong! That would be silly!' she added reflectively. 'Even if it was 9.53, I shouldn't be wrong. All I said was, that we should miss the 9.43. Well, if there is no 9.43, we cannot catch it; and what you don't catch, you miss!'

'Absurd nonsense! If you do not catch scarlet fever, you do not say that you miss it!'

She replied: 'We are not talking about scarlet fever; we are talking about trains!'

'Bah!' I exclaimed. I should have added more, but at this moment the clock on the dining-room mantelpiece struck ten.

The Conundrums

I HAD bought the little book at the station stall, and it seemed to be very well worth the sixpence which I paid for it. It was entitled 'Everybody's Book of Bright and Original Conundrums'. Of course I had an idea in my head in buying the book; I am not the man to throw away my money to no purpose. I thought that these conundrums would be not only a pleasant amusement, but also a valuable intellectual exercise to Eliza and myself during the winter evenings. Then we could use them for social purposes during the Christmas party season. I do not know how it may be with others, but I have often found, when introduced to a lady, that I have said, 'Good evening,' and then had absolutely nothing else to say. With the help of the conundrum book I would fill in any awkward pause by asking her who was the most amiable king in history. That would break the ice. Besides, if we kept the book reasonably clean, it might afterwards make a very serviceable and acceptable present to Eliza's mother. I generally know pretty well what I am doing, I think. I looked at two or three of the conundrums on the way home. There was one which I do not remember precisely, but remarkably clever – something about training the shoot and shooting the train. I often wonder who it is who thinks of these things.

* * *

I was, perhaps, rather unfortunate in the evening when I brought the book home. Something may have occurred to put Eliza out; she was inclined to be quite sharp with me. I asked her, gaily, in the passage when I came in, 'Can you tell me, dearest, the difference between a camel and a corkscrew? If not, here is a little volume which will inform you.'

'Oh, yes! One's used for drawing corks, and the other isn't. You needn't have wasted sixpence on a rubbishy book to tell me that.'

'But your answer is not the correct one,' I replied. 'The correct answer contains a joke. Think again.'

'Well, I can't, then. I've got the wash to count.'

I said that the wash could wait, but she did not appear to hear me, and went off upstairs.

* * *

At supper I took occasion to say:

'You answered me very tartly when I asked you this afternoon for the difference between a camel and a corkscrew. Perhaps you would not have done so had you known that I bought that book with the intention of sending it as a present to your mother.'

'Do you think ma would care about it?'

'I think it would cheer her lonely hours. There are upwards of a thousand conundrums in the book. I have only read twelve, but I found them all exceedingly amusing, and, at the same time, perfectly refined.'

'Well, I don't see the good of them.'

'They are an intellectual exercise, if you try to guess the right answer.'

'I don't believe anybody ever did or ever will guess the right answer.'

'If I had time,' I said, 'I believe I could generally think out a witty answer myself. I do not want to boast, but I believe so.'

'Very well, then,' said Eliza, snatching up the book and opening it at random, 'here's one for you. "If a lady slipped down the steps of St. Paul's Cathedral, what would she say?" Give me the answer to that.'

'I will try to,' I replied.

* * *

Now, just at the moment when Eliza put the question I felt that I had really got the answer, and then it seemed to pass away from me. Later in the evening I was certainly on the right track, when Eliza dropped her scissors, and the noise again put me off. I spent a very poor night; the answer kept sort of coming and going. Just as I was dropping off to sleep, I seemed to have thought of the answer, and then I would wake up to be sure of it, and find it had slipped me again.

As I was leaving the office, in the evening, after thinking till my head ached without arriving at any result, I put the question to one of our clerks. I thought he might possibly know.

'No,' he said, 'I don't know what a lady would say if she slipped down those steps. I could make a fair guess at what a man would say, if that's any good to you.' Of course it was not.

So, on my return home, I told Eliza that I had not had enough time to spare to think of the answer, and I should be glad to know where she had put the book.

'Oh, I sent that to mother!' she said. 'I thought you wanted it sent.'

'You might have waited until you knew whether I had finished with it. But, however, what was the answer to that silly riddle?'

'The one about St. Paul's Cathedral? That wasn't in the book at all. I made up the question out of my own head for fun.'

'Then,' I replied, 'all I can say is, that your idea of fun is not mine. It seems to me to be acting a lie. It was not a conundrum at all.'

'It would have been if you could have thought of an answer.'

'Say no more,' I replied coldly. 'I prefer to drop the subject.'

The Ink

THE ink-pot contained a shallow sediment, with short hairs, grit, and a little moisture in it. It came out on the pen in chunks. When I had spoiled the second postcard, Eliza said I was not to talk like that.

'Very well then,' I said, 'why don't you have the ink-pot refilled? I'm not made of postcards, and I hate waste.'

She replied that anybody would think I was made of something to hear me talk. I thought I have never heard a poorer retort, and told her so. I did not stay to argue it further, as I had to be off to the City. On my return I found the ink-pot full. 'This,' I thought to myself, 'is very nice of Eliza.' I had a letter I wanted to write, and sat down to it.

I wrote one word, and it came out a delicate pale grey. I called Eliza at once. I was never quieter in my manner, and it was absurd of her to say that I needn't howl the house down.

'We will not discuss that,' I replied. 'Just now I sat down to write a letter —'

'What do you want to write letters for now? You might just as well have done them at the office.'

I shrugged my shoulders in a Continental manner. 'You are probably not aware that I was writing to your own mother. She has so few pleasures. If you do not feel rebuked now —'

'I don't think mamma will lend you any more if you do write.'

'We will not enter into that. Why did you fill the ink-pot with water?'

'I didn't.'

'Then who did?'

'Nobody did. I didn't think of it until tea-time, and then – well, the tea was there.'

I once read a story where a man laughed a low, mirthless laugh. That laugh came to me quite naturally on this occasion.

'Say no more,' I said. 'This is contemptible. Now I forbid you to get the ink – I will get it myself.'

* * *

On the following night she asked me if I had bought that ink. I replied, 'No, Eliza; it has been an exceptionally busy day, and I have not had the time.'

'I thought you had forgotten it, perhaps.'

'I supposed you would say that,' I said. 'In you it does not surprise me.'

* * *

A week later Eliza said that she wanted to do her accounts. 'I am glad of that,' I said. 'Now you will know the misery of living without ink in the house.'

'No, I shan't,' she said, 'because I always do my accounts in pencil.'

'About three months ago I asked you to fill that ink-pot with ink. Why is it not done?'

'Because you also definitely forbade me to get any ink to fill it with. And you said you'd get it yourself. And it wasn't three months ago.'

'I always knew you could not argue, Eliza,' I replied. 'But I am sorry to see that your memory is failing you as well.'

* * *

On the next day I bought a penny bottle of ink and left it behind me in an omnibus. There was another bottle (this must have been a week later) which I bought, but dropped on the pavement, where it broke. I did not mention these things to Eliza, but I asked her how much longer she was going to cast a shade over our married life by neglecting to fill the ink-pot.

'Why,' she said, 'that has been done days and days ago! How can you be so unjust?'

* * *

It was as she had said. I made up my mind at once to write to Eliza's mother – who, rightly or wrongly, considers that I have a talent for letter-writing. I felt happier now than I had done for some time, and made up my mind to tell Eliza that I had forgiven her. I wrote a long, cheerful letter to her mother, and thought I would show it to Eliza before I posted it. I called upstairs to her, 'Come down, darling, and see what I've done.'

Then I sat down again, and knocked the ink-pot over. The ink covered the letter, the table, my clothes, and the carpet; a black stream of it wandered away looking for something else to spoil.

Then Eliza came down and saw what I had done. To this day she cannot see that it was partly her own fault. The bottle, of course, was too full.

The Public Scandal

I AM not a landlord. It suits my purpose better, and is in every way more convenient, to rent a small house on a yearly agreement. But if I were a landlord, I would not allow any tenant of mine to do anything that tended to undermine and honeycomb the gentility of the district. I should take a very short method with such a tenant. I should say to him or her: 'Now then, either this stops, or you go out this instant.' That would settle it. However, I am not a landlord.

Even as a tenant, I take a very natural interest in the district in which I live. I chose the district carefully, because it was residential, and not commercial. The houses are not very large, and they might be more solidly built, but they are not shops. They have electric bells, and small strips of garden, and a generally genteel appearance. Two of the houses in Arthur Street are occupied by piano-tuners, and bear brass plates. I do not object to that. Piano-tuning is a profession, and I suppose that, in a way, I should be considered a professional man myself. Nor do I object to the letting of apartments, as long as it is done modestly, and without large, vulgar notice-boards. But the general tone of the district is good, and I do most strongly object to anything which would tend to lower it.

* * *

It was, as far as I remember, on the Tuesday evening that Eliza rather lost her temper about the hair-pins, and said that if I kept on taking them and taking them she did not see how she was to do her hair at all.

This seemed to me rather unjust. I had not taken the hair-pins for my own pleasure. The fact is that the waste-pipe from the kitchen sink frequently gets blocked, and a hair-pin will often do it when nothing else will. I replied coldly, but without temper, that in future I would have hair-pins of my own.

She said: 'What nonsense!'

At this I rose, and went upstairs to bed.

I think that most people who know me know that I am a man of my word. On the following morning, before breakfast, I went into the High Street to buy a pennyworth of hair-pins. The short cut from our road into the High Street is down Bloodstone Terrace.

It was in Bloodstone Terrace that I witnessed a sight which pained and surprised me very much. It disgusted me. It was a disgrace to the district, and amounted to a public scandal. St. Augustine's – which is the third house in the terrace – had taken in washing, and not only had taken in washing, but were using their front garden as a drying ground! An offensive thing of that kinds makes my blood boil.

* * *

44

'Eliza,' I said, as I brushed my hat preparatory to leaving for the City, 'I intend to write to Mr Hamilton to-day.'

'Have you got the money, then?' asked Eliza eagerly.

'If you refer to last quarter's rent, I do not mean to forward it immediately. A certain amount of credit is usual between landlord and tenant. An established firm of agents like Hamilton & Bland must know that.'

'Yesterday was the third time they've written for the money, anyhow, and you can say what you like. What are you writing for, then?'

'I have a complaint to make.'

'Well, I wouldn't make any complaints until I'd paid last quarter, if I were you. They'll only turn you out.'

'I think not. I make the complaint in their interest. When a tenant in Bloodstone Terrace is acting in a way calculated to bring the whole neighbourhood into disrepute, and depreciate the value of house property, the agents would probably be glad to hear of it.'

'Well, you're missing your train. You run off, and don't write any letters until to-night. Then you can talk about it, if you like.'

*　*　*

In the evening, at supper, Eliza said she had been down Bloodstone Terrace, and could not see what I was making all the fuss about.

'It is simply this,' I said. 'St. Augustine's is converted into a laundry, and the front garden used as a drying-ground in a way that to my mind is not decent.'

'Yes,' said Eliza, 'that's Mrs Pedder. The poor woman has to do something for her living. She's just started, and only got one job at present. It would be cruel —'

'Not at all. Let her wash, if she must wash, but let her wash somewhere else. I cannot have these offensive rags flapping in my face when I walk down the street.'

'They're not offensive rags. I'm most particular about your things.'

'What do you mean?'

'It's your things that she washes. I thought I'd give her a start.'

I dashed off half a glass of beer, put the glass down with a bang, and flung myself back in the chair without a word.

'Don't behave in that silly way,' said Eliza. 'She's a halfpenny cheaper on the shirt than the last woman.'

'You need not mention that,' I replied. 'In any case I shall not complain now. I must bear the burden of any mistakes that you make. I am well aware of it.'

'I'll tell her to hang them out at the back in future.'

'She can hang them where she pleases. I suppose I can bear it. It's only one more trial to bear. One thing goes after another.'

'On the contrary,' said Eliza, 'she's never lost as much as a collar. There's a smut on your nose.'

'It can stop there,' I said moodily, and went out into the garden.

The 'Christian Martyr'

THE 'Christian Martyr' was what is called an engraving, and a very tasteful thing too, besides being the largest picture we had. It represented a young woman, drowned, floating down a river by night, with her hands tied, and a very pleasing expression on her face. With the frame (maple, and a gilt border inside) it came to three-and-six. I bought it in the Edgware Road on my own responsibility, and took it home. I thought Eliza would like it, and she did.

'Poor thing!' she said. 'You can see she must have been a lady too. But frightfully dusty!'

'You can't get everything for three-and-six. If you'd been under the counter in a dirty little —'

'Well, all right! I wasn't complaining; but I like things clean.' And she took the 'Christian Martyr' into the kitchen.

* * *

'Where did you mean to put it?' asked Eliza.

'The only good place would be between "The Charge of the Light Brigade" and "The Stag at Bay".'

'What! In the dining-room?'

'Certainly.'

'Well, I shouldn't,' said Eliza. 'It's a sacred subject, and we use the drawing-room on Sundays. That's the place.'

'I think I can trust my own taste,' I said. I got a brass-headed nail and a hammer, and began. Eliza said afterwards that she had known the chair would break before ever I stood on it.

'Then you might have mentioned it,' I said coldly. 'However, you shall learn that when I have made up my mind to do a thing, I do it.' I rang the bell, and told the girl to fetch the steps.

I hung the 'Christian Martyr', and was very pleased with the effect. The whole room looked brighter and more cheerful. I asked Eliza what she thought, and she answered, as I expected, that the picture ought to have been in the drawing-room.

'Eliza,' I said, 'there is one little fault which you should try to correct. It is pig headedness.'

* * *

At breakfast next morning the picture was all crooked. I put it straight. Then the girl brought in the bacon, rubbed against the picture, and put it crooked again. I put it straight again, and sat down. The girl, in passing out, put it crooked once more.

'Really,' I said to Eliza, 'this is a little too much!'

'Then put some of it back.'

'I was not referring to what I have on my plate, but to that girl's conduct. I don't buy "Christian Martyrs" for her to treat them in that way, and I think you should speak about it.'

'She can't get past without rubbing against it. You've put it so low. I said it would be better in the drawing-room.'

As usual, I kept my temper.

'Eliza,' I said, 'have you already forgotten what I told you last night? We all of us – even the best of us – have our faults, but surely —'

'While you're talking you're missing your train,' she said.

* * *

On my return from the City I went into the dining-room and found the picture gone. Eliza was sitting there as calmly as if nothing had happened.

'Where is the "Christian Martyr"?' I asked.

'On the sofa in the drawing-room. You said yourself that it was only in the way in here. I thought you might like to hang it there.'

'I am not angry,' I said, 'but I am pained.' Then I fetched the 'Christian Martyr' and put it in its old place.

'You are a funny man,' said Eliza; 'I never know what you want.'

* * *

As we were going up to bed that night we heard a loud bang in the dining-room. The 'Christian Martyr' was lying on the floor with the glass broken. It had also smashed a Japanese teapot.

'I wish you'd never bought any "Christian Martyr",' said Eliza. 'If we'd had a mad bull in the place it couldn't have been worse. I'm sure I'm not going to buy a new glass for it.'

* * *

So next day I bought a new glass myself in the City, and brought it back with me. But apparently Eliza had changed her mind, for a new glass had already been fitted in, and it was hanging in the dining-room, just where it had been before.

As a reward to Eliza I took it down and put it up in the drawing-room. She smiled in a curious sort of way that I did not quite like. But I thought it best to say nothing more about it.

The Pagrams

PROPERLY speaking, we had quarrelled with the Pagrams.

We both live in the same street, and Pagram is in the same office as myself. For some time we were on terms. Then one night they looked in to borrow – well, I forget now precisely what it was, but they looked in to borrow something. A month afterwards, as they had not returned it, we sent round to ask. Mrs Pagram replied that it had already been returned, and Pagram – this was the damning thing – told me at the office in so many words that they had never borrowed it. Now, I hate anything like deception. So does Eliza. For two years or more Eliza and Mrs Pagram have met in the street without taking the least notice of each other. I speak to Pagram in the office – being, as you might say, more or less paid to speak to him. But outside we have nothing to do with each other.

* * *

It was on Wednesday morning, I think, at breakfast, that Eliza said:

'I've just heard from Jane, who had it from the milkman – Mrs Pagram had a baby born last night.'

'Well, that,' I observed, 'is of no earthly interest to us.'

'Of course it isn't. I only just mentioned it.'

'Is it a boy or girl?'

'A girl. I only hope she will bring it up to speak the truth.'

I replied that she might hope what we did not expect. So far Eliza had taken just exactly the tone that I wanted. But as I watched her, I saw her expression change and her underlip pulled down on one side, as it were.

'Well,' I said rather sharply, 'what is it? These people are nothing to us.'

'No. But – it reminded me – our little girl – my baby – that died. And I —'

Here she put down her knife and fork, got up, and walked to the window. There she stood, with her back to me.

I had a mind to speak to her about the foolishness of recalling what must be very upsetting to her. But I said nothing, and began to brush my silk hat briskly. It was about time that I was starting for the City.

I went out.

Then I came back, kissed Eliza, and went out again.

* * *

I was a little surprised to find Pagram at the office.

'I should have thought you'd have taken a day off,' I said.

'Can't afford that just now,' he replied, in rather a surly way.

'All well at home?'

'No.'

'By my watch,' I said, 'that office clock's five minutes slow. What do you make it?'

'Don't know. Left my watch at home.'

I had noticed that he was not wearing his watch. Later in the day, I had some more conversation with him. He is quite my subordinate at the office, and I really don't know why I should have taken so much notice of him.

* * *

When I came back that night I was in two minds whether to tell Eliza or not. She hates anything like extravagance, and if I told her I felt sure she would be displeased. At the same time, if I did not tell her, and she found it out afterwards, she would be still more displeased. However, I decided to say nothing about it. I was a little nervous on the point, and I own that my conscience reproached me.

As I came into the hall, Eliza came down the staircase. She was dressed for going out, and had a basket in her hand. She said: 'I want you to let me go over to the Pagrams to see if I can do anything. She and the baby are both very ill – the nurse has had no sleep – they've no one else to help them. And – and I'm going!'

'Now, do you think this is necessary, Eliza?' I began. 'When you come to consider the position we've taken up with regard to the Pagrams for two years, and the scandalous way in which they —'

Here I stopped. The hall door was shut, and Eliza had gone, and it was not worth while to continue.

'Now,' I thought to myself, 'it's ten to one that Eliza finds me out, and if she does, she'll probably make herself unpleasant.'

However, I determined not to trouble myself about it. If it came to that, I flattered myself that I could make myself as unpleasant as most people when any occasion arose.

* * *

It was hours before Eliza returned. She burst into the room and said, 'They're both better, and the baby's a beauty, and I'm to go back to-morrow afternoon.'

'Indeed!' I said. 'I don't know that you're not going a little too far with these people.'

'Do you think so? I've found you out. You didn't tell me, but Pagram did. You lent him three pounds this morning. We can't afford that.'

'Well, well,' I said; 'I've managed to get some overtime work, to begin next week. That – that'll come out all right. You ought to leave these business matters to me. Anyhow, it's no good finding fault, and —'

'Does Pagram generally return what's lent?'

I lost my temper and said that I didn't care a damn! And then – just then – I saw that she was not really displeased about it.

'Why,' she said, 'you silly! I'm glad you did it. The poor things were at their wit's end, and had got – they'd got nothing! You've saved them, and I never have liked anything you've done half as much as this.'

Here Eliza burst into tears – which is really very unusual with her.

Promotion

HOW true it is, as one of our English poets has remarked, that it is always darkest before the silver lining!

While this little work was actually in the hands of the printers, an incident occurred of such great and far-reaching importance that I cannot refrain from making it the subject of an additional paper. I can give it in one word – promotion.

It came at a time when I was suffering from great depression and considerable irritation, as I have already indicated in my opening remark. It was on a Wednesday morning, and those who know me know that invariably on Sunday, Wednesday, and Friday I put on a clean shirt. The number may seem excessive, and perhaps out of proportion to my income, but I own without shame that I am careful as to my personal appearance. I must also add that I am very particularly careful –

and, I think, rightly – on the question of the airing of linen.

All I said was that I should put on that shirt, whether Eliza liked it or not, and that it would probably give me my death; but that it did not matter, and perhaps the sooner it was all over the better. There were circumstances under which life was hardly worth living, and when one's express injunctions were continually disregarded one began to despair.

Eliza spoke quite snappishly, and said that my linen was always properly aired, and that I was too fussy.

I replied, without losing my temper, that there was airing and airing. Even now I cannot think that Eliza was either just or accurate.

* * *

At breakfast-time one or two other little circumstances occurred to put me out. A teacup which is filled so full tht it overflows into the saucer is a perfect thorn in the flesh to me. So is bacon which is burnt to a cinder. I hardly did more than mention it, but Eliza seemed put out; she said I did nothing but find fault, and as for the bacon, I had better go into the kitchen and find fault with the girl, for it was the girl who had cooked it.

'On the contrary,' I said, 'in ninety-nine cases out of a hundred when a servant does wrong it is her mistress who deserves the censure.'

'Go it!' said Eliza, an expression which I do not think to be quite ladylike. 'And if a hansom-cab runs over you in Oxford Street, you go and get the damages out of the Shah of Persia. That's the line to take.'

This answer exasperated me by its silliness, and I had quite made up my mind not to say another word of any kind during breakfast. Indeed, but for the fact that I had not quite finished my bacon and that I hate waste, I should have got up and walked out of the room there and then.

A little later I happened to look up, and it struck me from Eliza's face that she might be going to cry. I therefore made a point of saying that the butter was better than we had been having lately, and that it looked like being a fine day after all. Anything like weakness is repellent to me, but still, when one sees that one's words have gone home one is justified in not pressing the matter further.

Still, I am prepared to own that I started for the City in but low spirits, and with no inclination to join in the frivolous conversation that was going on in the railway carriage. On arriving at the office I was surprised to find that Figgis, our head clerk, was not there. He gave me the tonic port, and was inclined to be dictatorial, but I must confess that he was always a most punctual man. I was very much surprised.

* * *

Our senior partner, Mr Bagshawe, came much earlier than usual – 10.30, to be precise – and sent for me at once. He is a big, fat man; he speaks in short sentences, and breathes hard in between them. At the moment of entering his room I was as certain that I was about to be sacked as I have ever been of anything that I did not really know. I was wrong.

He made me sit down, glared at me, and began:

'Yesterday evening we detained Mr Figgis for a few minutes. At the end of our interview with him he left this office for ever, never to return – never!'

I said that I was very much astonished.

'We weren't. We've know there was a leakage. People knew what we were doing – people who oughtn't to know. He sold information. We put on detectives. They proved it. See?'

I said that I saw.

'So you've got Figgis's place for the future. See?'

At that moment you might have knocked me down with a feather; it was so absolutely unexpected. Give me time, and I think I can provide a few well-chosen words suitable to the occasion as well as any man. But now I could think of nothing to say but 'Thank you'.

He went on to explain that this would mean an immediate rise of £75, and a prospective rise of a further £75 at the end of a year if my work was satisfactory. He said that I had not Figgis's abilities, of course, but that a very close eye had been kept on me lately, and I had shown myself to be honest, methodical, and careful in details. It was also believed that I should realize the importance of a responsible and confidential position, and that I should keep the men under me up to the mark.

The rest of our conversation was concerned with my new duties, and at the close of it he handed me Figgis's keys – my own name and the office address had been already put on the label.

I should not be fair to myself if I did not make some reference to Mr Bagshawe's comparison of Figgis's abilities and my own. I will merely state the fact that on more than one occasion Figgis had gained success or avoided failure from suggestions made to him by myself. That he did not give me the credit for this with the firm is precisely what I should have expected from a man of that character. However, I have my opportunity now, and the firm will see.

* * *

When I returned to the clerks' office I found one of the juniors playing the fool.

'I wish you'd stop that, please,' I said, 'and get on with your work.'

'Who gave you the right to give orders here?' he asked me rudely.

Fortunately, that was what I had expected he would say, and therefore I had my answer ready.

'Mr Bagshawe did, three minutes ago, when he made me head of this department in place of Mr Figgis.'

And without another word I went calmly to Mr Figgis's desk and unlocked it. The effect was remarkable, and gave me great pleasure. During the luncheon hour I received several congratulations, and was pressed to partake of liquor. But I had long ago made up my mind that if the firm did ever place me in a good and responsible position, I would give up alcohol during business hours altogether. I carried out that resolution, and shall continue to do so; Figgis, with all his so-called abilities, was frequently drowsy in the afternoon. Apart from that, I hope I was not wanting in geniality. I snatched a few moments to telegraph to Eliza: 'Meet train to-night. Very good news for you.'

* * *

On my way to the station I purchased a small bottle of champagne – it cost half a crown, but the price for this wine is always pretty stiff. I also took back with me in my bag a tinned tongue and some pears.

Eliza was waiting for me, and was obviously excited. She had guessed what had happened.

'Got Figgis's berth?' she said.

'Yes. Let's get off the platform as soon as we can. Everybody's looking at us.'

We walked home very quickly, Eliza asking questions all the way, and looking, as I noticed, quite five years younger. After what I have said as to my purchases, I need not add that supper that night was a perfect banquet.

We had a long discussion as to our future, and did not get to bed until past eleven. I was at first in favour of taking a rather better house, but Eliza thought we should do more wisely to spend the money over making ourselves more comfortable generally. When she came to go into it in detail, I found that on the whole hers was the preferable course. New curtains for the drawing-room are to be put in hand at once. The charwoman is to come regularly once a week. We raised the girl's wages a pound, and she went into hysterics. Eliza has insisted that I am to have a first-class season ticket in future. There is much can be done with £75.

On the whole, about the happiest evening of my life.

ELIZA'S HUSBAND

His Prefatory Note

SOME time ago I published a little work called 'Eliza'. It
consisted of scenes from my home-life and incidents in my
career. I pointed out the importance of little things, only too
often disregarded. To my mind, the mere arrangement of a few
biscuits on a plate may show the kind of man that is master of
the house. I gave instances of proper retorts that I had made in
the course of conversation, and showed how in other cases I
had relied rather on the expression of my face, or some simple
gesture, or walking straight out of the room. I illustrated the
way in which I managed Eliza, and the girl, and the home
generally; in fact, I showed what could be done by a man of
small income, though in a more or less semi-professional
position socially, simply by the exercise of good taste and
thoughtfulness.

I am far from being a vain man. I do not ask others to model
themselves upon me exactly. I may have my faults, and I ask
nobody to imitate them. I am quite well aware that there have
been occasions when, after some differences of opinion between
myself and Eliza, I have found out that her views, after all, were
the more correct. It was so only the other day, when the
question of the choice of a dust-bin came up. My selection was
'The Sanitary Refuse Receptacle', which had brass handles, and
a very pretty scroll pattern round the top. It was expensive, I
admit, and I am by no means blind to the question of expense,
but the style of it was quite beyond mistake. Compared to the
others we inspected, it simply stood in a class by itself – and,
mark this, a dust-bin is not a thing that in the ordinary course
of suburban life you can keep entirely to yourself. It is the one
piece of furniture of the house which must at regular intervals

be brought into the public eye, so to speak. When the dustmen call, there it is in full sight of every passer-by as well as neighbours who may be at their doors and windows, and naturally they form their own conclusions. However, Eliza was very strongly in favour of a much cheaper article, so strongly, in fact, that I gave way in order that the man in the shop might not think there was any disagreement between us. I just raised my eyebrows, and said: 'Oh, have your own way as usual; it's enough for me to want one thing to make you want another.' She had her own way. She said money was always useful, and you never knew what might happen. Afterwards, when the lamentable incident of the horse occurred – narrated at length in my subsequent pages – I felt that she had been right.

And possibly there are one or two points about me that it would not be altogether easy for just anybody to catch. I have been told that I have a manner of my own. There may be something in that, and manner is not easy to describe. You know that it is there, and that is all you can say about it. This book may contain useful hints to family men in similar circumstances to myself if it is read properly and seriously, but I cannot promise they will be able to acquire my manner. It is not stand-offish exactly, and I don't think it would be called free-and-easy. It's – well, it's either born with you or it's not. Let me give you one or two little illustrations as to manner.

On one occasion a gentleman entered the office when I had occasion to reprimand the boy most severely for an irregularity in his petty-cash account. 'Here,' said the gentleman to me, 'you seem to own this place. Can you tell me if Mr Bagshawe's in?'

On another occasion a beggar, who told me that he had been a valet in titled families, and should therefore have been in a position to judge, touched his hat and said, 'Thank you, m' lord,' though I had never even hinted at the possibility of my being a peer of the realm.

Once when I had been attracted by the cheapness of some gun-metal watches in a shop-window, and asked to see them, the man behind the counter said: 'It would be no good to show them to you, sir; they're only meant for clerks and people of that kind. You wouldn't like the quality. But I've got a superior article that might suit you.' And ultimately he sold me one at 12s. 6d., though it was more than I had intended to give.

Another time, on returning from the seaside with Eliza, I was getting our luggage together at the London terminus. My porter pulled out of the van a portmanteau which was clearly labelled 'Count von Popoff', and said, 'That one of yours, sir?'

These are only a few instances, and I could give others. Why is it that I am so frequently mistaken for a man of considerable means, or even for a nobleman of high position? I was turning it over the other night.

'Do you think,' I said to Eliza, 'that there is anything remarkable in my personal appearance?'

'Well,' she said, 'your right eye still shows where you fetched up against the dresser in the dark the other night, but there's nothing else very much out of the way.'

Nor do I think that there is anything in my attire to account for it. I dress in as gentlemanly a way as my means will allow. But these mistakes have never been made on Sunday morning, when, if attire had anything to do with it, they would be more easily comprehensible. No, I can only assign them to my manner; there is a something about it, apparently.

Possibly the gentle reader will form some estimate of it when he reads the further scenes and incidents of my domestic life. They belong to a year which, quite contrary to my expectation, was somewhat overcast by a financial misfortune. It was due to no fault whatever of mine, as every just reader of the pages which relate the affair of the horse will allow. And it is the more pathetic because it followed close on my advancement and increase of salary; hardly had I mounted one rung higher on the ladder before the balloon collapsed.

Readers will be glad to know that at the end of the year it rose like the Phœnix from its ashes. The commercial firm – one of the finest in the City – in which I hold a most important position, gave me the further advance in salary that had been promised if my appointment proved satisfactory. They might have done it more graciously, and it seemed to me a singularly ill-chosen time for pointing out to me supposed defects in the working of my department; but, still, they did it. In fact, I am writing of troubles which are now definitely past.

My financial position is at present perfectly sound. I do not wish to brag – there is nothing I dislike more – but we do things on quite a different scale now. If Eliza goes up to see her mother now, and it happens to be a very wet and dirty day, and there is no room inside the trams, I tell her just to take a shilling cab, and not think twice about it; and, what is more, I have known her on some occasions to do so. And if Mr Sidney Gorles and Mr Percy Jennings were not members of the Batrick Park Lawn Tennis Club I should join tomorrow. It is not the subscription which stops me; it is merely that I am rather particular about the kind of company I keep. This being so, I even feel some pleasure in going over the days when the pressure was far more severe.

And I hope that this book may fall into the hands of many young couples who will read it seriously and try to get some useful lessons from it.

First-Class

WHEN you are travelling from our suburb to the City in the morning and back again in the evening, you cannot always pick and choose your company. The trains are too crowded. I have written twice to the company about it, and on both occasions I received a polite and well-worded reply, but the evil has not been remedied.

I felt this very much at the time when I had a second-class season ticket. I was frequently obliged to enter a compartment with Sidney Gorles and his friends. They are not at all my kind of people, and they are not up to my standard. Wit, when it is really wit, I can appreciate – no man more so; but the senseless questions which Sidney Gorles was in the habit of addressing to me were the merest buffoonery, and I have told him so pretty sharply more than once. I wonder that even his friends could smile at them. Nor was that all. Sometimes they would play a game of cards called, I believe, Napoleon. More than once Sidney Gorles himself, if not actually intoxicated, had obviously exceeded the bounds.

He would frequently begin by asking if the hens were laying nicely now. He is perfectly well aware that I do not keep fowls. Sometimes he would ask if the Virginia creeper was creeping as well as could be expected. He would also put a question with regard to a tortoiseshell cat which I shall not sully this page by repeating. When I treated his remarks with silent contempt, he would tell me not to be so coy and cold, or to come out from under that hat, or to give him just one loving smile; sometimes he would simulate paroxysms of sobs, and say that I had broken his heart.

That was the kind of man Sidney Gorles was – vulgarity itself; most offensive. I am at a loss to understand why a respectable insurance company continued to employ him. If I were in their place I should make very short work of Mr Gorles.

When I was raised to be the head of a department, with an increase of £75 for the first year, Eliza and I decided – it was almost, in fact, at her suggestion – that I should now take a first-class season ticket. Had we known then what was to happen in the matter of the horse (of which I shall speak later), we might have decided differently. I should certainly have disputed the advisability of settling with Eliza's mother, who had obliged with temporary loans during a period of pressure. It was a real pleasure to the old lady to assist us, and we might have looked at it from her point of view. In any case, I think thirty or thirty-five shillings on account would have been ample. However, Eliza was particularly hot at the time on being out of debt. Most women, I have found, are too impulsive. They mean well, but they need the guiding hand.

Perhaps I was wrong. I am not one of those who pretend that they never made a mistake. But on my last second-class journey Sidney Gorles was particularly troublesome, and I just said to him:

'To-morrow I shall not have the pleasure of your company. And,' I added rather bitterly, 'it is, perhaps, worth while to pay for the privilege of avoiding it.'

He dropped back in his seat as if he had been shot.

'He's going first-class!' he exclaimed to his friends. 'Hold my hand, somebody, and loosen my corsage. It's His Majesty the King of Siam, and we never knew it.' He then begged me to spare his life, and made other senseless observations of which I took no notice.

Next morning when I appeared on the station platform Gorles and his friends all took off their hats to me. When I got into my carriage, Gorles came up to the door and said loudly enough for everybody to hear:

'Beg pardon, but is your Majesty about to return to Siam?'

'Don't be a fool, Gorles!' I said peremptorily.

'Sorry you take it like that,' said Sidney Gorles. 'If you *had* been returning, I wanted to send my love to the Siamese twins – that's all.' Then he made a rush for his second-class carriage.

In the evening at Broad Street, I had no sooner taken my seat in the train than Gorles once more came up. He touched his hat.

'Beg pardon, my lord,' he said, 'but her ladyship desired me to say that the roans would be unable to meet you at the station to-night. One of them is suffering from a family bereavement, and is not going out just now. Her ladyship is sending the – er – perambulator.'

After that for some time I took a strong line. I went up to town a train earlier than Gorles, and I came back one train later.

Eliza said that if I would only take a joke as a joke, and join in it, Sidney Gorles would soon let me alone.

'You will permit me, my dear,' I said, 'to be the best judge in this matter. There are some of Mr Gorles's so-called jokes –

notably one with reference to a tortoiseshell cat – in which no man with a sense of propriety would wish to join.'

Eliza went on with her work in silence for some minutes and I certainly thought that my words had gone home. Then she said:

'What was it exactly that Gorles said about the tortoiseshell cat?'

'I am surprised at you, Eliza! If you knew what it was, I am sure you would not wish to ask.'

'Of course not. Who wants to be told what they know already?'

'I could explain my remark. What I meant was —'

'Oh, never mind what you meant. You shouldn't have begun about it if you didn't mean to finish it. Now I shall be lying awake half the night trying to think what it was. And that'll be your fault.'

Not quite just, I thought. I merely recommended her to take some good book, and in this way to turn her mind to other subjects.

* * *

But Sidney Gorles was not the only trouble in connection with my first-class season ticket – not by any manner of means. It has been, I believe, observed by a well-known writer that at the very moment when our highest expectations appear to be fulfilled, something frequently occurs to take the gilt off the gingerbread.

It was so in the matter of my increased salary; this was followed by the regrettable incident of the horse, which (for the instruction it conveys) I shall narrate subsequently. It was so again in the matter of my first-class ticket. A man of my kind of mind notices these things and thinks about them. They are a mystery. We cannot understand them.

The firm (highly respected in the City) in whose employment I hold an honourable and practically semi-professional position would tell you that I am an honest man. I will go further: I will say that dishonesty in any form, and more especially when it is dishonesty at my expense, awakens in me a disgust which it is difficult to express in language suitable for general circulation.

Briefly, I noticed – I could not help noticing – that those who entered my first-class carriage were frequently people who quite obviously had not paid the first-class fare. Where were the inspectors? That was what I asked myself.

On one occasion – and one only – did I in my second-class days travel first-class. It was through hurry and inadvertence. Even when I discovered my mistake my conscience was perfectly clear, for I held a return half which I had paid for and been unable to use between two stations on another line. Between myself, therefore, and railway companies in general the account was fairly balanced. But on that occasion an inspector did enter the carriage, demanded to see my ticket, and – not too politely – compelled me to pay the difference. Where were the inspectors now – now when I really required them?

One day a man entered who smelled of gas and train-oil and carried a bag of tools; he was apparently a plumber. He put his feet up on the cushions, and said to me:

'Bit of all right for us, ain't it?'

As he seemed to be under a mistaken impression about me, I said that I held a first-class season ticket.

'Ah!' he said, 'I 'as my private Pullman car as a rule, but they've forgot to 'itch it on to-day. Careless beggars!'

As soon as I got home I wrote a long letter to the company relating this incident, and asking if – speaking as man to man – they could pretend that this kind of thing was satisfactory. I again received a polite and well-worded reply thanking me for calling their attention to the matter.

But I was still subjected to similar annoyances, and I saw that there was nothing for it but to take the matter into my own hands, to mark down some habitual offender, and to make an example of him.

I had no difficulty in selecting my case. It was a grubby old man with a furtive look and a shabby brown overcoat. I frequently found him in the compartment that I entered in the morning, and I also observed him on the return journey. He always travelled first-class. And this was going on right under the noses of the railway officials.

The guard of my evening train was a very civil and intelligent fellow. I had once given him a shilling. He always smiles and touches his hat when he sees me. I waited for my opportunity, and then one night I spoke to him at Broad Street.

'Guard,' I said, 'there is a man in that first-class compartment with the door open. He's just got in, and he's the only man there. He makes a practice of travelling first, and I wish you would just ask to look at his ticket. It would not surprise me very much to find that he had no ticket at all; certainly he is not a first-class passenger.'

'I'll put that right,' said the guard, and went up the platform to the compartment which I had indicated. He looked in, touched his hat most respectfully, and came back to me.

'There must be some mistake, sir,' he said. 'That's Sir William, the director, you know.'

Fortunately I kept my presence of mind. I said:

'I'll just see for myself.'

It was – as I knew it was – the grubby old man in the shabby brown overcoat. After all, I suppose that gentlemen of title and position can, if they choose, neglect their personal appearance and show a disregard for the things that we think important.

I went back to the guard.

'That's Sir William right enough,' I said. 'He and I are – well, there's no mistake about that. The man I meant very likely hopped out again, seeing that I had my eye on him.'

'Nothing more likely,' said the guard.

I gave him another shilling and took my seat.

Since that time I have once or twice spoken to Sir William as a director, though, of course, I had too much tact to let him know that I knew it. I thought he might be glad to have my favourable opinion of the admirable way in which the line is conducted. But I should say that he is a man who does not much care for conversation in trains – it may be, of course, that he is slightly deaf. Sometimes he did not seem to hear when I spoke to him. But he once asked me for a match, and thanked me most affably.

'The Hag of Haverstone'

'I THOUGHT,' said Eliza, 'that you weren't one for reading these trashy novels. I've spoken twice to you about the sweep not having come, and got no answer. There you sit.'

I put the book down. I had just finished it.

'Pardon me,' I said, 'but this book is not, strictly speaking, a novel at all.'

She picked the book up and read the title-page, ' "The Hag of Haverstone: a Story of the Old Days. By Margaret Ratton." And here's a picture on the cover of a gentleman in armour jumping into a ditch with a bath towel under his arm. And that is not a novel! Oh well, we live and learn.'

Satire is not Eliza's strong point; perhaps she would do better to leave that to me. However, I replied quietly:

'I said that it was not, strictly speaking, a novel. It might perhaps be called an historical novel – a work which contains under the attractive guise of a story much useful information, and gives a vivid account of the old days. And you have misunderstood the picture. The gentleman in armour is Sir Guy Redheart. He is carrying despatches – and not a bath towel – for

Prince Rupert. He is not leaping into a ditch. He is plunging into a fathomless abyss to save the despatches from falling into the hands of the enemy. You are liable to jump to hasty conclusions, Eliza.'

'Same as him,' said Eliza. 'What did he want to take and do a silly thing like that for?'

'You do not understand. The despatches contained a complete key to the enemy's position. It was of the utmost importance that they should not learn that this information was being conveyed to the prince. It was a noble, a self-sacrificing, an heroic action.'

Eliza looked at the picture meditatively.

'Pity he went out without his mother. Nice-looking man, too. But that weakness in the intellect don't always show.'

'I imagine that you are saying this to annoy me, Eliza. Sir Guy Redheart was not in the least a weak-minded man. I have read the story, and I ought to know. It says of him in his boyhood, when he did not know who he really was —'

'There you are,' said Eliza. 'A woman that washed for mother had a son went the same way – ten years old and couldn't have told you his name were it ever so. Still, they used to send him errands just like the man in the book.'

'Will you kindly permit me to finish my sentences instead of talking nonsense?'

'You weren't talking nonsense exactly. At least, I never said so.'

I controlled myself.

'Sir Guy Redheart in his boyhood did not know who he really was. His own mother did not know.'

'It often runs in families,' said Eliza.

'And they did not know, because in his infancy he had been lost, and was brought up as the son of a simple woodcutter. Only the Hag of Haverstone herself was at that time acquainted with the secret of his noble birth. And the authoress distinctly states that in his boyhood he was astute beyond his years. Astute beyond his years, Eliza; and you will at least permit the authoress, Margaret Ratton, to know what she is talking about. At a further point he is specially chosen to carry these despatches because, as the general says, "There we have cunning and courage combined, the wit to plan, and the spirit to carry through the enterprise!" '

'Ah!' said Eliza. 'And had he gone far with these despatches?'

'He had ridden till his horse dropped under him, and then proceeded on foot.'

'And the roads dusty and the pubs frequent,' said Eliza. 'That would be it. Well, it's a good temperance lesson, anyhow, and that's more than you can say for some of these books.'

'The man,' I said, 'was a brave, true-hearted hero, neither a fool nor a drunkard, and I am at a loss to understand why you should —'

'I am only going by what you've told me.'

'We will put the matter to a simple test. Hand me the book, please. Thank you. Now we shall see. Sir Guy Redheart was pursued, you will remember. It says here: "He could hear their galloping steeds. In a few moments they would be round the corner. To fly was impossible, and no place of concealment presented itself. Stay! Close to his feet yawned the Devil's Pit. There in its black and limitless depths – and there alone – the despatches would be safe. What though it meant instant death to him? With a loud cry of 'For the Prince and the Cause!' he leaped into the abyss. The troopers heard that cry as they swept into the open. 'Baffled, by God!' exclaimed the foremost of them." But I have read enough.'

'If I were Margaret Ratton's mother,' said Eliza, 'I should want to know where she learned all that swearing from.'

'We will stick to the point, please. You say that Sir Guy Redheart did a foolish thing. You have heard the circumstances. What ought he to have done? What would you have done?'

Eliza threaded a needle very carefully.

'Let's hear what you'd have done first.'

'Well,' I said, 'you may possibly think that I speak in a spirit of braggadocio.'

'Bag of what?'

'Not bag. Braggadocio. But, as it happens, I have been in an almost similar position to Sir Guy Redheart. When I was in a subordinate position to that which I now hold, I was given important letters to post for the firm. In order to catch the post I had to cross a City street thronged with traffic as fast as I could run. I went, of course, at the imminent risk of my life —'

Eliza here interrupted me in a way that I dislike extremely. For some reason or other she seemed bent on making herself unpleasant.

'No,' I said, 'not at the imminent risk of my grandmother's ducks, but at the imminent risk of my own life, as those who know the dangers of our crowded London thoroughfares best would tell you. I said little or nothing about it at the time, but the facts remain; and that being so, I think I have a right to say that I should have done exactly what Sir Guy Redheart did.'

'Finished?' asked Eliza.

'I have.'

'Then perhaps you'll let me get a word in. When you posted those letters, did you post yourself as well?'

'Of course not. The question is absurd. Why?'

'Because that's exactly what Sir Guy Redheart did. Anybody would think he and the blessed despatches were all made in one piece or they were screwed on to him. What he ought to have done – and what a common-sense man would have done – was to pitch the despatches down the abyss and then walk back to the pursuers with his eyes on the ground as if he'd dropped something and were looking for it. Ten to one that dodge would have kidded them. Time enough to jump down fathomless precipices when you can't help it or there's something to be got by it. But what can you expect of a chap like that? He doesn't want people to know he's got despatches, so he has them written large on a roll big enough to paper our passage and leave a bit over for mending, and then carries it under his arm for everybody to see. The likelihood is he might have got it all on a half-sheet, folded it small, and tucked it into the lining of his helmet. Or if it really wanted all that paper, why didn't he slip it into a fish-basket with a bit of green stuff on the top, so that nobody could see what he was getting at? No; he's got to go flourishing it about so as there can't be any mistake. And that's a true-hearted hero, is it? All I can say is that if you set him down in our street to-day he'd have to scratch pretty hard to get a living, and the police would likely run him in for a wandering idiot before he ever got started.'

'I think, Eliza, you would do better not to interfere with literary questions which you do not understand. You want to make a clean sweep —'

'Yes; and talking about sweeps, you'll have that kitchen chimney alight, and so I tell you. Why, the girl can't get on for the soot falling. I sent her round to say Packham was to be here at six this morning, and he as good as told her he wasn't coming till he was paid for last time. And that's three shillings; and what are you going to do about it?'

I handed her two-and-eightpence and told her she would find four stamps in the drawer of the ink-stand.

I sometimes wonder what Sir Guy Redheart would do in my position. It is a curious fact, but he seems never to have had any petty annoyances.

The Horse That Did No Wrong

I HAD formed my own plan for the Easter Monday immediately following my promotion. I had a long talk over the matter weeks before with Mr Percy Jennings, who teaches riding and driving, and lets out horses and vehicles.

He heard what I had got to say, and seemed respectful, but doubtful.

'Well, sir,' he said, 'things being as you say, if I might advise, I should think you'd better change your mind. Let me send you a nice comfortable victoria and one of my men to drive you, and then there can't be any mistake.'

'I think not, Mr Jennings,' I said. 'I want to drive myself and my wife in a dogcart to the Lion at Winthorpe; it would give me no pleasure to be driven. I know that my limited experience with – er – the humbler animal does not amount to very much, but I feel that I should be all right with a safe horse. You understand, a perfectly safe horse. I mean one that has no vice of any kind under any provocation, that does not require any looking after, and, if possible, an animal that is in the habit of going to and from the Lion, and knows the road thoroughly.'

Mr Percy Jennings sucked a straw thoughtfully.

'You're asking for miracles,' he said, 'but as it happens I've got just that miracle. Young horse – Tommy we call him. He's worth £60 of any man's money, and he's worth £80 to me in my business. In fact, if you offered me £80 for him now, I'd tell you to put your money back in your pocket. You see, I get gents here to learn, and when the beginners are beginning I take them out with Tommy to get confidence. Say it's an oldish gent who's never seen a horse before, and has been told to ride by his doctor – first few times I put him up on Tommy. Say it's a nervous lady wants to start a governess cart, and don't know how to drive – I starts her with Tommy. That horse has never done anything wrong, and never thought of doing anything wrong, since the day he was foaled. He couldn't do wrong if you asked him, and he'll do anything else you ask. Why, the blooming horse would climb a tree if he thought I expected it of him. The very first day he was in the shafts I drove him straight to Winthorpe – and that's a fact. No work comes amiss to him, nor nothing else, either. He'll stand like a statue with his nose over a buzzing motor, or he'll draw you twelve miles an hour without a whip. You can stop him with a thread, and turn him with just thinking about it. And he's as pretty as he's good. But –'

Mr Jennings stopped short and shook his head.

'Well?' I said.

'But I don't let that horse out to every chance comer to knock about as he pleases on the high-roads on an Easter Monday.'

'Now, Mr Jennings,' I said, 'do I look like a man who would knock a horse about?'

'No,' he said, 'you don't. If I may say it without offence, you're the ignorant, nervous sort. And I've known them bring the horse and cart back safe when one of the rowdy lot, that think they know something, will get three-parts screwed, start racing, and go to glory. If I'd thought that you were one of the rowdy lot, I shouldn't so much as have mentioned him to you. However, we can't stop here talking all day. Set that horse towards Winthorpe, and he'll go there and stop at the Lion – he's used to it – if he's not interfered with. Let him take his own pace up hill and down; he knows his business. And at night he'll take you home all right if you let him alone. You taking all responsibility up to ten fivers, I might think about it.'

Business was subsequently arranged on these terms.

* * *

Eliza has not, perhaps, what would be called a sunny disposition. I said in my nonchalant way that evening, as I stirred my cocoa:

'I've arranged about the Bank Holiday, Eliza. I'm going to tool you over in a high dogcart to Winthorpe. I understand they give you a decent dinner at the Lion. Then I shall tool you back at night – moonlight, you know. Best horse in Jennings's stables – not let out as a general rule.'

All she would say at first was that extravagance was never any pleasure to her, and she wondered what mother would say if she knew. But after a certain amount of argument on both sides, I said that of course I should expect to make up for it in other ways as far as possible, and she admitted that she might enjoy it.

'If,' she added, 'we ever get home alive.'

'That will be all right,' I said. 'I shall not ask you to drive. That will be my province, and I am not entirely without experience.'

During the next few days I talked over the details frequently. There is nothing like a thorough preparation for making a success. I also kept my eye open in the streets and made some useful notes with reference to —

(a) Getting into the dogcart;

(b) Position of the hands and expression of face when driving;

(c) Arrangement of the rug;

(d) Getting out of the dogcart.

I also read carefully in our public reading-room an interesting and instructive article on 'How Race-horses are Trained'. Its bearing on the subject was somewhat indirect, but I gathered from it the meaning of several phrases which had previously been something of a difficulty to me.

* * *

I may say at once that we reached the Lion at Winthorpe without any accident. There was one little contretemps, as the French would say. We happened to meet Miss Sakers – for which, in itself, I was not sorry. She bowed, and in raising my hat I fancy the reins got caught – I never quite understood how it happened – but the horse turned round. However, I got down, and put him back in the required direction. It was merely a mistake on the horse's part, and he showed no trace of obstinacy. I also dropped my whip once or twice, but there is always some boy to pick that up for you and glad to earn a few coppers. I could not, considering the circumstances, agree with Eliza that a halfpenny would have been sufficient. However, I was quite good-tempered about it – indeed, I felt in particularly high spirits. I was wearing a straw hat for the first time that season – it was a last year's hat, but Eliza had cleaned it with salts of lemon, so that really it was quite presentable. I also wore a black diagonal frock-coat and vest that I reserved for Sundays and similar occasions, and a pair of white flannel trousers and brown boots. The trousers were new and almost unnecessarily long and roomy. However, as Eliza pointed out at the time, that, of course, allows for shrinkage in the wash. My necktie was of white satin with sprigs of flowers embroidered in the natural colours – tasteful and, I think, uncommon. Eliza wore her mackintosh – rather against my wishes, as the day was quite fine. The general appearance of our turn-out gave me great satisfaction. I cannot help thinking that we made some impression on people that we met, and I amused myself with wondering what they thought I was.

The dinner at the Lion was good, though Eliza rather kicked at the price. I drank one pint of bitter at dinner, and no more. In the light of subsequent events the necessity of mentioning this will be apparent. The place was, unfortunately, rather crowded, and not entirely with the best class of people. There were too many Bank Holiday cyclists there for my taste. One gentleman entered into conversation with me on the subject of horses. He was an elderly man, and Eliza said afterwards that she did not like his eye. Personally I found him most civil, quite ready to listen to me and to take a word of advice. He said that he had seen me drive up, and had said to the landlord: 'That man knows what he's doing, anyhow.' He seemed quite surprised to hear that it was not my own horse, and said he supposed I was trying it.

'Well,' I said, 'under certain circumstances I might buy him.'

Here Eliza drew in her breath hard and long through her nose. It is an unpleasant habit. She does it whenever I say or do anything that she dislikes. Yet I had kept strictly within the limits of truth. I have no doubt that if my income had justified it I should have bought that horse. Indeed, as things turned out, I practically – but do not let me anticipate.

There is not very much to do at Winthorpe. We obtained permission from the proprietor to walk round the garden, but that took only three or four minutes. Then Eliza found out that there was a coconut shy in the village, and insisted on going to it. It was, perhaps, a little *infra dig.* (as they say), but I was in an easy temper after dinner, and let myself be persuaded; also, there was nowhere else to go. Eliza won four coconuts, and seemed to enjoy it. I had rather the feeling of having left all that kind of thing behind me, myself, and said so.

Eliza and I decided almost unanimously for an early tea and a pleasant drive home to a quiet evening. The elderly gentleman joined us at tea and offered me brandy and soda-water at his expense.

'Thank you,' I said, 'but when I am going to handle the ribbons I like to keep my head as clear as possible.'

He said that he thought I was right. He really made himself most useful and obliging when we were leaving. There was a good deal of confusion through so many vehicles being drawn up outside at the same time.

The return journey was a great surprise. I had expected that the horse going home would fly like the wind, and that I should have difficulty in holding him. It was not so at all. He seemed reluctant to start, and I could never get him beyond a very slow trot; three or four times he seemed on the point of stopping altogether. Mr Percy Jennings had told me that I should never want the whip, but I felt constrained to make a moderate use of it, and, really, it seemed to cause no improvement at all. The farther we went the worse the horse got, till it seemed to be less trouble to let him walk, which I did. About a mile from home

Eliza pointed out to me that the horse was going very much down on one side, and very much up on the other.

'Ah!' I said, 'then he's gone lame. That accounts for everything. I shall have to blow Jennings up about this. Still, as it is a valuable animal, we perhaps had better get out and lead him the rest of the way. Personally, I shall be glad to stretch my legs.'

Eliza, who is, perhaps, a little inclined to grumble at every trifle, said that anything was better than some kinds of driving, and joined me in the road. We walked slowly back, and had to put up with many silly, and even personal, remarks from those who met us. Some of them whistled the 'Dead March', which was not only quite inappropriate, but, in my opinion, actually blasphemous. I suppose one must not expect the best taste from these Bank Holiday crowds. I made no reply. I could have said a good deal, but, being with a lady, I wished to avoid any fracas.

Eliza left me when we reached our house. She said that I could take the horse and cart back to the yard while she went in and helped the girl to get supper.

Mr Percy Jennings was standing in the yard when I led the horse in.

'What's all this?' he said.

'That's what I want to know,' I replied rather sharply. 'This horse that you made so much fuss about was not fit for work. He's dead lame. No fault of ours. I can assure you we —'

'Oh, shut up!' he said offensively. Then he called 'Jim!' and some kind of ostler person appeared.

He gave Jim some orders, and I heard enough to realize what had happened. Jim was to ride off at once to the Lion at Winthorpe and bring Tommy back if he was still in the stables there. If not, he was to find out where the horse had gone and follow him up, let the police know, and not come back without him. Neither of them took the least notice of me. I did put in a question once or twice, but they went on just as if I had never spoken at all. I am not the man to put up with disrespect. I was much annoyed. As soon as Jim had gone off, I said:

'And now, perhaps, you can give me a few minutes of your attention, Mr Jennings. It seems through some mistake on the part of the stable people at the Lion I have brought back the wrong horse. Naturally, I disclaim all responsibility for their blunder.'

'Oh, go away!' said Mr Jennings. 'I'll talk to you when you're sober.'

'I am perfectly sober, and I'll thank you not to venture to dare to —'

'Then, if you're sober – and I don't say you are, but *if* you are – you must be a bigger fool than ever I took you for. You drive out my best horse, worth a hundred and twenty to me, and you bring back this dying cripple, worth what the knacker will give for him to-morrow. I tell you if I don't get my own horse back you'll have to pay that fifty. I've got your name and address, and your employer's name and address; and that won't half make it up to me. Worst day's work I've ever done, this is. Oh, don't stand gaping there! Get out of the yard! Get out of my sight!'

I have not reported this speech exactly as it was spoken. Before every noun a certain adjective – always the same – was inserted. I have omitted that adjective.

'I am extremely sorry for the error,' I said with dignity.

He said that he didn't want my (same adjective) sorrow.

'But in future,' I continued, 'all communication between us must be through our respective solicitors.'

I rather wish now that I had not said that. The horse was never recovered, and my solicitor could only get the claim down to £34 (£10 cash, and the rest in weeky instalments). I feel that I could have done as much as that myself; and as it was I had to pay the solicitor.

But at the time by blood was up, and I did not very much care what I said – as long as it showed him that I was not to be played with.

Mr Jennings then made a remark about our respective solicitors which cannot be further particularized.

I, personally, simply swung round on my heel and walked right out of the yard.

* * *

I am willing to admit that I had some apprehensions as to the way in which Eliza would take this. In one way she took it far better than I expected.

Let me take an instance. A few days before, being in a playful mood, I sprang out at her from behind a door in order to make her jump. She did jump – and so far I suppose the thing was a success. But she also dropped and broke a vase – a pretty little thing, representing a boot, with maidenhair fern growing over it. She quite lost her temper, and said things which I trust and believe she regretted afterwards.

But now, when the loss was far more considerable, she was much quieter. It would be idle to say that she was cheerful about it, but she never once said it was all my fault. On the contrary, she said it was all her own fault – because she had known all along I had got the wrong horse, but she said nothing about it because she knew that she knew nothing about horses.

I thought she was wrong in saying that the man who stole our horse was the elderly man who had entered into conversation with me, and made himself so pleasant, and that he had done his utmost to bustle us and confuse us when we were leaving the hotel.

But I did not argue the point. I did not feel much like arguing about anything. One of my favourite hymns points out that the roseate hues of early dawn vanish far more quickly than a beginner might suppose. So it had been with my increasing income. What with the extra expenses that we had already incurred and this serious blow, we were now in much the same position that we had been the year before.

I paid the £10 in cash to Mr Jennings at once. The solicitor thought it would be better. Fortunately, I had some money in hand at the time. And the balance, £8 15s., I borrowed from Eliza's mother. There is one drop of sugar in the darkest cloud – I found an opportunity to sell the flannel trousers at very little under cost.

The Burglar

ELIZA'S mother having written to us that she was confined to the house with a severe cold, Eliza said that she would go up the London and spend the day with her, sleeping there that night. There was, of course, the railway fare to be considered, and I did not forget it, but Eliza's mother had just obliged with the £8 15s. required to make up the first payment to Jennings. Besides, she is a lonely old woman, and I know what severe colds are myself, so I raised no objections. On the contrary, I went out and bought an ounce and a half of liquorice ju-jubes – which frequently give relief to the throat – and sent them to Eliza as a present from me. I felt sure she would appreciate the kindly thought.

Left alone, I spent the evening in going round the house polishing the brass door-handles. Our girl habitually neglects them, and I hoped in this way to make her ashamed of herself. I also cut and folded a few paper spills. It is difficult to get Eliza to use them, but I think them a wise economy myself.

The girl went up to bed at half-past nine. I then drew myself a glass of beer and made myself comfortable in the dining-room. I sat in the easy-chair with one leg thrown over the arm, and smoked my pipe and read the evening paper. It quite brought back to my mind my gay bachelor days. One went the pace rather then. It has been well observed that young men are thoughtless. At ten I saw that the front and back were properly secured and the windows fastened, and was soon in bed and asleep.

An hour later I was awakened by a sound. It was the sound of a man's laugh, and it appeared to me to come from the kitchen. I realized at once that something must be wrong – that a burglar had forced an entrance. I did not for one moment lose my presence of mind. Stealthily and on tip-toe I crept to the window and peeped out. There was a light coming from the kitchen below, and my suspicions were confirmed. Undoubtedly my best and wisest course would then have been to have locked and barricaded the door of my room, opened the window, and called loudly for the police, who are the proper people to deal with cases of this kind. But I saw that this might be misunderstood, and I determined on taking pretty vigorous action at once, come what might, so I slipped on some warmer and more adequate clothing, knocked over the fire-irons to attract the attention of the burglar below, and then opened my door and called sharply:

'Who's there?'

The sounds in the kitchen ceased.

I shouted again.

'I must request an answer, please.'

There was a sound of a chair being pushed back and of quick footsteps. Then the back door slammed. The burglar had evidently gone. I went to the top of the stairs, and then I fancied I still heard someone moving in the kitchen.

'Who's there?' I called once more. 'Reply instantly, please.'

'Only me, sir,' said the girl's voice.

'Has the burglar gone?'

'What burglar? Oh yes, he's gone, sir. I heard him, and came down to catch him, and while I was making up my mind you called, sir, and that frightened him. He's gone all right.'

I went down at once. It was evident that two people had had supper there. A piece of cold bacon that we generally have at breakfast had been shamefully cut into. Bread and butter had been used simply *ad libitum*. There were also two empty beer-bottles which the men must have brought with them, as we have no bottled beer in the house.

'Why, then,' I said, 'there must have been two burglars!'

'It do seem like it,' she said.

She appeared very stupid and confused and slightly hysterical.

I was pleased to find that the burglars had taken nothing except the food they had eaten. A careful examination of the back door did not show that the lock had been forced in any way. But a skeleton key would probably do its work without leaving any trace. Nor could I discover by what ingenious process the bolts had been drawn back from the outside. Burglars are extremely clever in these things. A well-known London magistrate once observed that if they would only use their cleverness for some honest work it would be more satisfactory; the same thought has often occurred to me.

'Well,' I said to the girl, 'it is a pity that when you heard the noise and came down you had not the courage to dash into the kitchen and to secure one of the men. By waiting until I was practically on my way down you have allowed them both to escape. What you must do now is to go out at once and fetch a policeman.'

She said that she dared not for the life of her, as the burglars might be still hanging round the house. I had almost decided to go for the police myself, but it seemed cruel to leave the girl alone in the house in her present condition, and as nothing of value had been taken I thought I would leave it until I could have a word or two with Eliza, who was coming back in time for breakfast in the morning. However, I made a note of the address on the beer-bottles and took careful measurements of a footprint that I found just outside the back door. When I got back to bed the excitement still kept me awake. It was not till it grew light that I dropped off for an hour.

* * *

Eliza said very little when I told her the story. She said it was a funny thing for burglars to come to a house of our kind, where there was nothing to get, and that they couldn't have known much. She also said that putting your head outside the door and shouting was not the best way to catch burglars, according to her ideas.

'Well,' I said, when I had finished the story, 'what do you make of it? What would be the right course to take now?'

For a few moments Eliza said nothing, and seemed to be thinking. Then she asked me how the girl was dressed. 'Had she just put on the first thing that came handy?'

'No; she was most properly and decently dressed. She probably had guessed that I should come down. I thought that showed a certain amount of presence of mind in her.'

'Blue dress?'

'Yes, I believe it was.'

74

'Curl-papers in her hair?'

'No.'

'Right. It's just as well you've got somebody with sense in her head to look after you. I'll step into the kitchen and sack that girl at once.'

'But she did her best. The burglar —'

'There never was any burglar. That blue's her best Sunday dress, and she'd got her hair done. And if I can't leave the place for a single night but what she must have her young man in to supper at all hours of the night, she and me had better part. Why, it ain't respectable.'

Eliza went into the kitchen. She was angry, and so, apparently, was the girl. In fact, the noise in the kitchen was much in excess of what I can approve. From what I overheard, it appeared that Eliza's surmise was correct. The girl said she didn't see why she shouldn't enjoy herself the same as others, and the sooner she went the better she would like it; and that anybody would have thought the rotten bacon was pearls and diamonds, for the fuss that was made about it.

The girl left that morning. We had some difficulty in replacing her, and for some days it was necessary for me to clean the boots myself, which went rather against the grain with me. However, we are now suited.

The surprising thing to me is that I did not see the truth of the matter before. The mere fact of the loud laugh should have convinced me that it could not have been a burglar. I was a little too much the man of action. Another time I shall make a point of reflecting before taking any strong measures.

By Arrangement

WHEN Jollibut at the corner shop was sold up – which I had seen long before was bound to come – I attended the sale. It was Saturday afternoon, and there was nothing else to do. I asked Eliza to come with me, and I asked her more than once, but she said she had only one pair of hands, and no time for gaieties. If she had been there, I should certainly have consulted her before bidding for the music-stool. Also, it was never my intention to buy the music-stool at all. Thirdly, if not necessary, the music-stool was useful. And, lastly, it was exceedingly cheap; and, as I told Eliza, if I had walked into a London shop and even attempted to buy a walnut music-stool, upholstered in old-gold velveteen, with the screw in working order, at that price, the man behind the counter would simply have laughed in my face. And this being so, I cannot think that Eliza was justified in saying all that she did. But there, what woman is strictly logical? Very few are, I am afraid. I have often noticed that men seem to see things that women don't.

I went there because, in a way, I was sorry for Jollibut. The corner shop had failed twice previously, both times in the general and fancy. When Jollibut had the front painted white, and started a boot and shoe emporium, with one corner curtained off in peacock blue to ensure privacy for customers who were trying on, I could see for myself that he was flying too high for the neighbourhood. And then the girls – three of them – dressed far beyond their station, and beyond their father's means. I was not surprised when the blow fell.

My bid for the music-stool was made from conscientiousness and good feeling. It seems to me that a man who attends an auction and never makes a bid is there under false pretences. I made two bids. The first was for a set of four oleographs, practically indistinguishable from oil paintings, in massive gilt frames. One of them, I remember, was a marvellously life-like study of a large slice of Dutch cheese on an Oriental plate, with some walnuts and a knot of pink ribbon in the foreground. I should not have been sorry to have purchased these pictures, but they went far beyond my limit. I did not make another bid until almost at the end, when few people were left. Then the music-stool came on, and I said two shillings. I said it to justify my presence, and to encourage the auctioneer. I was greatly surprised that no other bid was made. However, no great harm was done.

But Eliza was very short about it, and said it was wicked folly, when we had one music-stool already, and no use for another, and coals at the price they were. I said that I was, unfortunately, unable to alter the price of coals, and that we would defer the discussion until she was in another temper. She persisted, however, in keeping on at it, and at supper I had to refuse to speak at all, merely pointing at the butter when I wished her to pass it. She then said she didn't understand the deaf-and-dumb alphabet, and I had to get up and get it myself. It was a most unpleasant evening.

'And now you've got the blessed thing,' said Eliza, when the music-stool came home, 'you don't know what to do with it. You'd better go off to another auction and buy a hundred-guinea grand piano. Go on. We can afford it.'

'Pardon me,' I said. 'I know perfectly well what to do with it.'

'Then what do you sit staring at it for?'

'I was merely thinking how to use it in the most artistic and effective manner. I am going to show you what can be done by arrangement – simply by a little arrangement. And I think it will please you. Kindly refrain from entering the drawing-room until I call.'

I carried the music-stool into the drawing-room and shut the door. I placed the stool in the window overlooking the street. This window has lace curtains joined at the top and caught back below, leaving a space which had always seemed to me to want something. On the stool I placed our large atlas, to which we seldom have occasion to refer. I completely covered the atlas and the top of the stool with a handsome Turkish antimacassar that had been a present from Miss Sakers, and on the table thus formed I put a large geranium, the pot standing in a pretty saucer with a view of Cromer on it.

Then I opened the door and called to Eliza. 'Now, if you will step in,' I said, 'I think you will admit that a considerable improvement has been effected in your drawing-room. The stool now has exactly the appearance of one of the low occasional tables that you find in the art furniture shops. I do not suppose I could have bought such a table under a guinea.'

She admitted that it seemed all right, and turned up the Turkish antimacassar.

'But it don't bear looking into,' she added.

'And,' I said, 'it is not the custom for visitors to a house to look into things. It would be exceedingly ill-bred of them to do so. So that argument falls to the ground. The geranium shows now as it never did before, and it has all been effected by a little talent for arrangement. I wish you had more of it, Eliza.'

* * *

As I said to Eliza after the accident had happened, she had only herself to thank. I had merely arranged the things; it was, naturally, for her to see that the arrangement was made permanent, and that the atlas was firmly secured to the top of the stool by string or some other suitable manner. At least, the girl might have been warned about it; as it was, when she began dusting in her rough-and-ready way, of course the whole thing went over. I still fail to see why she put her foot on the geranium and broke it in two. She said it was all done before she knew what had happened.

'However,' I added, 'I will take the music-stool and try some other kind of arrangement which will, perhaps, be more successful.'

'Well, you can't have it,' said Eliza.

'And why not?'

'She's done —'

'Who's done?'

'The girl. She's done nothing but complain about there being no chair in her bedroom. She says she was never in a place before where there was no chair. So I just took and gave her that music-stool.'

'So a polished walnut music-stool, upholstered in old-gold velveteen, and worth, perhaps, thirty or forty shillings if purchased in the usual channels, is a suitable object of furniture for a servant's bedroom, especially when by her own act of carelessness she has just occasioned us a serious pecuniary loss. I will only say that I was not aware of it. I will merely point out that —'

At this moment we were startled by a scream and the sound of something falling heavily in the room above us.

'Here! I must see what that is,' said Eliza.

She came back in a minute or two.

'It was the girl,' she said. 'She's not much hurt. She was hanging an illuminated text on the wall of her room, and got up on the stool to do it; only the jerk she gave it in getting up sent the top round, and she fell off. She might have known that it worked on a screw.'

'Yes, yes,' I said, 'but is the music-stool injured?'

'Music-stool! Death-trap, I call it! No, that's not hurt. One of the silliest things you ever bought, that was.'

* * *

I said no more about it until the following evening, and then I asked pleasantly:

'Well, Eliza, do you think still that a handsome music-stool is quite in its place in a servant's bedroom?'

'Never did think so. Only what were you to do with it?'

'If you will bring it down to the drawing-room, I will show you what can be done with it by arrangement. No, I am not thinking about an occasional table again. It is something quite different. I propose to treat it as a pedestal – to put it on the top of the piano, draped with, say, a Turkish antimacassar, and have the bust of Beethoven that we got from your Uncle Hector on the top of it; and I think that the general appearance will —'

'Oh, well, you can't have it.'

'And why not?'

'I was out this afternoon, and I came on a second-hand shop where they'll take anything.'

'Well?'

'Well, they've taken the music-stool. I got an old chair for it – good enough for the girl's room – and a bit of linoleum that'll come in for the upstairs passage.'

'Then, Eliza, I can only say that you have very much exceeded your prerogative.'

'I knew it would make you swear. But the girl said she wouldn't stop in a place with a thing that worked round under you like that. To my mind, you ought to be thankful we've come out of it no worse. Just you come along upstairs and help me put that bit of lino down.'

Miss Jerningham

I ADMIT that I was not displeased when Eliza told me that Miss Sakers wished to bring her friend Miss Jerningham to call on us one afternoon. But I did not like the way Eliza smiled and said we were getting on in the world. It seemed to me so undignified.

'Very well,' I said; 'I suppose we must take Miss Sakers' word for it that her friend is a lady, and a fit person for us to receive in our social circle.'

'Don't you be too rash about it,' said Eliza in rather a nasty way. 'I'll write for her pedigree and a reference from two clergymen, and you run up to the police-station and see if they know anything about her. Can't be too careful about that social circle, you know.'

'There is no occasion for any remarks of that kind,' I said. 'It may be that I have a certain amount of pride. Possibly I am a little particular about the people whom I choose to know. If it is so, I am not ashamed of it.'

'Well, I think it's silly. Here's Miss Sakers trying to act in a friendly way, and you go setting yourself up. You've not got any social circle, and you know it. And you might be more grateful for kindness.'

'Why should I be grateful? I have not the least doubt that I have met many people far higher in position than this Miss Jerningham. At the same time, if she comes I will do my best to entertain her in a proper manner. I suppose it will be a case of tea?'

'No, not a case. Extra spoonful. That's if they stop for it. Don't you worry.'

It seemed to me a mere waste of time to continue the discussion while Eliza was in this frame of mind. I went up to the bedroom and employed myself far more profitably in tacking up a couple of Japanese fans to hide the spots where the damp had come through the wallpaper.

* * *

At breakfast next morning I said cheerfully:

'And on what day are we to have the pleasure of welcoming Miss Jerningham to this neighbourhood?'

'Miss Sakers didn't say any particular day.'

'That is a little thoughtless of Miss Sakers. She must be perfectly well aware that a certain amount of preparation is required if the thing is to be a success.'

'They'll just drop in – unless they happen to think better of it. You are such a born worrier.'

'But they cannot think better of it. I quite understood from you that it was a definite agreement.'

'Miss Sakers said she would like to bring her friend, and I said we should be glad to see her. But this Miss Jerningham may not care about it. It's easy enough to say she had a cold, or felt too tired. This house isn't much of a place to look at.'

'This house is small, and does not represent the summit of my tastes and ambitions, but there is nothing repellent about it. The venetians are not broken in our drawing-room window, as they are at "St. Mildred's", nor are our steps in the disgraceful condition which is apparently habitual at "Daisy Mead". At least we compare favourably with our neighbours.'

'Well, you never know. It seems this Miss Jerningham is connected with a titled family. Very likely she won't think it worth while. Anyhow, you needn't worry about it. The chances are that, if they do come, it will be one day when you are away in the City.'

'I should regret that, because I wish to show you that I am not so stand-offish as you supposed yesterday. As things stand, you must be prepared any day. I should suggest one of Stodger and Sands' "ever-ready fruit cakes". You can tell the girl not to take it out of the tinfoil until the moment comes. The fire in the drawing-room must, I fear, be lit every day, but three in the afternoon will be soon enough. It would have been more reasonable of Miss Sakers to have fixed a day. A few chrysanthemums, I think; they last a long time if proper attention is given. And —'

'Do you know what the time is?' asked Eliza.

I glanced at the clock, and dashed off at once. I just caught the train.

All day in the City I had the impression that Miss Jerningham would call that day. We were very slack in the office, and I managed to return home rather earlier than usual.

As I entered the house I saw the girl in the passage, and said in a whisper:

'Any ladies called?'

'No,' said the girl.

'Anything come from Stodger and Sands'?'

'Yes, sir – this.'

She gave me an envelope. It was merely a trifling account for some articles that we had purchased there at different times, accompanied by a very uncivil letter.

'Fire lit in the drawing-room?'

'No, sir. And none ordered.'

I went straight into the drawing-room and lit the fire myself. Then I went into the passage and called sharply up to Eliza.

'What's the matter now?' she said as she came down the stairs.

'The matter is that Miss Jerningham may be here any minute, and I find the fire in the drawing-room not lit – I have just lit it myself – no flowers in the vases, and apparently no preparation of any kind made. I take the trouble to order definitely what is required and yet I find nothing done.'

'I'd a card from Miss Sakers by the second post to say that she and Miss Jerningham would come on Saturday. Next Saturday, you know. Three days on ahead. And you've lit the fire in the drawing-room!'

'Yes,' I said. 'I've just time to remove the coals before they catch.'

I went into the drawing-room and did so. If I had burned the whole place down, Eliza could hardly have said more than she did.

* * *

The tea was fairly satisfactory. Miss Jerningham seemed to me to be a pleasant person of about forty, but not exactly beautiful. The pince-nez which she wore to correct her squint was not entirely successful in that respect, but it certainly gave her a distinguished appearance. Both she and Miss Sakers talked principally to Eliza, and I had rather the feeling that I was being left out of it.

Also a slight accident happened to me, which I took with a smile at the time, though it might have been dangerous. When our visitors had gone, I took another cress sandwich, and said:

'I have no wish to make myself unpleasant, Eliza, but unless you can speak very seriously to that girl I must do it myself. I might have injured myself severely.'

'It was nothing to do with the girl. You took that chair, and, of course, it went down.'

'The chair was not in its proper place. It's proper place is in the corner behind the wickerwork fern-stand, where nobody can sit on it.'

'Well, you would have the whole room turned out this morning, and, of course, the girl got it mixed up with the others. It looks just like the rest. It's only when you sit on it that the leg comes off. My word! I never saw Miss Sakers laugh so much in my life before.'

'Possibly it would have been in better taste if she had laughed less. People have been crippled for life by similar accidents. Miss Jerningham's behaviour was much quieter. There's a certain style about that lady. I think I could have guessed, even if you had not told me, that she belonged to a titled family.'

'I said she was connected with a titled family. Pugley the name is; he was Mayor of somewhere or other, and got knighted, and Miss Jerningham is governess to the children. But he's taken to drink to such an extent now that she's leaving.'

I did not pursue the subject. It has been very well and truly observed that rank without moral worth is dross.

The Gloves

WE had talked about it before church and afterwards, and had really got no further. When I brought it down to the plain question, 'If it was not the girl, who was it?' Eliza would give no answer and turned obstinate.

At dinner I flung myself back in my chair.

'It simply comes to this,' I said: 'You are asking me to believe that a pair of practically new dogskin gloves have wings and can fly away.'

'Pass the mustard, please,' said Eliza moodily.

'That's nothing at all to do with it.'

'Never said it had, did I? (And I said "pass the mustard", not "chuck" it.) You've gone and put them somewhere.'

'Thank you,' I said. 'I'm not the kind of man that goes and puts things somewhere.'

'Yes, you do. You've just put your sleeve in the gravy.'

* * *

This changed the conversation for the time. I was much irritated, and with good reason, it being a new coat and the first time on. I did what could be done at the moment with warm water, and subsequently a little benzine put the matter right. Still, it was just one more annoyance.

'Now,' I said, 'let us return to the subject of those gloves. You say I put them somewhere. I did. I put them where I always put them, at the back of the top left-hand drawer of the chest on which the looking-glass stands. That is where they were put last Sunday; this Sunday they are not there. Why?'

'Perhaps you took them out during the week.'

'You ought to know me well enough by this time, Eliza, to know that never in my wildest moments should I dream of wearing my Sunday gloves on a week-day. I do not lay claim to much, but I do think I have method in small things. And if I did not take them, and you did not take them, the girl must have taken them.'

'Well, why should she?'

'Why should she take a number of the *Home Helper*, a copy that had been lent to us, and that I had not finished reading, and use it for the kitchen fire? Yet we know that she did that. It was proved, and she confessed it. If you sit there and refuse to act, I must.'

I rose and rang the bell sharply.

'I want you,' I said to the girl, 'to bring me the gloves that you wear when you do the grates in the morning.'

She stood blinking and staring at me as if she did not know what I meant.

'You understand?' I said. 'The gloves that you wear when you do the grates in the morning. I wish to see them.'

'I don't wear none.'

'Ah!' I said. 'Then, that's all.'

* * *

Eliza said it was difficult enough to get a girl to stop anyhow, and that if I went upsetting and interfering and messing about like that she really didn't know what she would do.

'I have no wish,' I said, 'to upset, nor to interfere, nor to mess about. But I paid one and elevenpence for those gloves and have only worn them a few times, and I choose to regard their disappearance as a serious matter.'

'Well, you see the girl hadn't got them.'

'I am by no means so sure of that. She looked guilty, and she looked frightened.'

'Well, when a man acts as if he'd gone clean off his head it's no wonder —'

'Excuse me, but the order I gave her was a perfectly reasonable one, and I am not going to let the matter stop here. You may think that a sum of nearly two shillings is a mere nothing, and that we can afford to throw it in the gutter, but I don't agree with you. I was compelled to go to church this morning in a pair that was quite out of keeping and entirely spoiled my appreciation of the service.'

'I noticed that it hadn't done you much good,' said Eliza.

'And,' I continued, 'that kind of thing cannot go on. I will have my things treated with proper respect, and – mark my words – if gloves are taken one day, and nothing is done about it, something else will be taken the next. You say that the girl is honest. I say that in houses where the girl is honest new pairs of dogskin gloves do not suddenly vanish in this fashion. If she has not taken them for her work, she has taken them to sell or to give away. You can't stop me, Eliza. I'm determined to get to the bottom of this mystery. Apart from mere personal feelings, it is my plain duty as master of this house to —'

Here I suddenly observed that Eliza had left the room. It was not too polite, considering that I was speaking.

She returned in a minute with the gloves in her hand.

'There you are,' she said. 'Left in the pocket of the coat you wore last Sunday and put away for the summer.'

'You astonish me,' I said. 'Did I really leave them there?'

'Oh no!' she said bitterly. 'Of course not! The King of Timbuctoo left them on the grand piano. Another time, before you accuse people of stealing your precious gloves, you might –'

'Come, Eliza,' I said, 'this is Sunday, and there is no occasion for you to lose your temper. I must say that I am surprised I can have left them there, and I am very glad you found them. It was quite a happy idea of yours. As the girl will be coming in to clear, shall we step into the drawing-room and try over a few hymns?'

The Invitation

I HAD bought Eliza as a present a packet of pale green correspondence cards with envelopes to match, the envelopes being stamped with the initial 'E' in bronze on the flap. She said it was kind of me, and thanked me and asked what she was to use them for.

'You will use them, as their name implies, for correspondence.'

'I never write to anybody except to mother, and she wouldn't half like it if I sent her one of those.'

'And why not?'

'Looks too showy. Looks as if we're spending money on luxuries; and, of course, when she has to lend the money – well, that's how it is.'

'I cannot admit,' I said, 'that because your mother has occasionally obliged us, as you say, she is therefore free to dictate to us what style we are to adopt in writing materials. But, however, there are other letters which you might write. It would be no bad thing if you practised the art of letter-writing a little more than you do; in fact, that was in my mind when I bought these cards.'

'Still, when you've got nobody to write to and nothing to say.'

'I can tell you at once off-hand a letter which I wish you to write. Pagram is alone at present, his wife and children being at his mother's. It would be a kindness to ask him to come in to supper next Sunday.'

'All right. Certainly ask him. But what's that got to do with letter-writing?'

'Merely that I wish you to write the invitation. That is simple enough.'

'But why don't you ask him yourself? You see him every day at the station. That doesn't want any letter.'

'There is a right way and a wrong way of doing everything, Eliza. Invitations to dinner should be written, and should be written by the hostess. Strictly speaking, three weeks' notice should be given.'

'His wife and the kids will be back before then. Besides, you said next Sunday.'

'Quite so. I don't press the point about the notice. But you must certainly write the invitation.'

'And what am I to say?'

'The correct form would be to say that you will be pleased to have the pleasure of his company at supper on Sunday next.'

'All right. It beats me how you ever came to know these things, seeing what you are and always have been.'

'Then, you will take one of those cards at once and —'

'I can't do it now. I was going through the wash when you called me down, and I like to finish one job before I begin another. And the way that steam-laundry tears everything to rags is something wicked. I do believe I shall have to give them up.'

However, she promised to write the invitation first thing the next morning, and with that I had to be satisfied.

* * *

On my return from the City next day I called up the stairs:

'What about that letter, Eliza? Have you done it?'

'What do you want to ask for? I said I would, didn't I? Of course I've done it.'

I stepped into the dining-room, and there on the table by the ink-stand lay Eliza's letter, unstamped, the envelope not even addressed. A little thing like that often makes me mad. It seemed as if the only way to get anything done was to do it myself. I addressed the letter, stamped it, and posted it, and then went up to have it out with Eliza.

'Look here, Eliza,' I said: 'I've got to speak to you rather seriously. It seems to me you're going beyond the limit; there's more than one way of telling a lie.'

'Don't you dare to use that language to me,' said Eliza. 'Why, what are you talking about?'

'I asked you if you'd written that letter to Pagram. You said you had.'

'So I did.'

'But you'd not posted it. You'd not even addressed the envelope. You might just as well not have written it.'

'Then it's you and not me that's telling the lies. Why, I dropped that letter into the box with my own hands before you'd been gone from the house an hour this morning.'

'Dear me!' I said. 'Then I'm afraid there's been a mistake somewhere; I saw one of those green envelopes with the initial lying on the dining-room table. It was fastened up, and I naturally concluded that it was the invitation. What was it then?'

'None of your business; it was for the manageress at the laundry. They've torn a lot of embroidery off – well, never mind – something of mine, and I wrote to ask her what she was going to do about it.'

'I'm really extremely sorry, Eliza. I'm afraid I've been rather too hasty. I took it for granted it was the letter to Pagram, and I addressed and posted it.'

'What?'

'I'm afraid I posted it.'

Eliza sat down.

'That's all right,' she said. 'I write a letter to a laundry about a particularly private thing, and you go and post it off to one of your men friends. Go it! Don't ask me to look him in the face again, though, because I won't. Now go and get yourself shut up in an asylum before you do any more harm.'

Making every allowance for her irritation, which was, perhaps, not unnatural, and even in a sense did her credit, that was not the way to speak to me, and I said so. She was asking me in rather a loud tone of voice if I would kindly hold my silly tongue, when the front bell rang.

It was Pagram. He had got Eliza's note, and said that, as he happened to be passing, he thought he would look in to thank us and say he'd be glad to wag a knife and fork with us on Sunday. In strict etiquette he should have replied in writing, and I do not quite like his familiar way of speaking, but, still, I was very glad he called. I explained to him my mistake, and asked him to return the letter unopened. 'As a matter of fact,' I said, 'it was a letter of Eliza's that simply had to deal —'

'Dealing with the character of a servant,' interrupted Eliza.

It was a direct falsehood, but under the circumstances I let it pass.

The Funeral

THE late Mrs Arthur Magsworth died at the age of one hundred and two. She was – with the exception of false teeth – in full possession of her faculties until the last. For the last twenty years she had lived at Bellevue, 13 Gladstone Villas, Plumley Heath, and on her decease the *Plumley Heath Advertiser*, in commenting on her great age, rather raised the question whether human life is not showing a tendency towards prolongation. There were only a few lines, but thoughtful and well expressed.

Neither Eliza nor I had the pleasure of knowing Mrs Arthur Magsworth, but she had been for many years an intimate friend of Eliza's mother. They had much the same tastes, and they suffered from the same complaints, which is in itself a kind of bond. Indeed, one of Eliza's first observations on hearing of this said affair was, 'Mother will feel this.' I understood from Eliza that everything was to go to the nephew, George Magsworth, and there might be some small memento for her mother.

On the same day we had a letter from Eliza's mother, regretting that her precarious health prevented her from attending the funeral, and saying that she had sent an anchor composed of white geraniums on moss. She wished Eliza to go in her place, and had spoken to George Magsworth about it. She added in a postscript: 'This being on my account, I should insist on paying second return Plumley Heath.'

'Nothing seems to be said about my accompanying you,' I observed. 'I don't know how far that's taken for granted.'

'If mother had meant two second returns, I think she'd have said so,' said Eliza. 'But I don't think she'd stick at that, and, I suppose, being Saturday morning, you could get off all right. I think you ought to come. It's not often you get any little – well, any little outing.'

'I agree with you, Eliza,' I said. 'I think it is natural and right for a man to accompany his wife on these melancholy and trying occasions. She feels then that she has something to lean upon.'

Eliza said that she didn't suppose she would want much propping, but that it would be more social if we went together. I reminded her that it was not the time for flippant expressions.

It is an understood thing at the office that I can have Saturday morning every now and then, and I made no bones about asking for it on this occasion, seeing what the cause was. Mr Bagshawe gave me permission at once, and was kind enough to say that he hoped it was no near relation.

'Not very near,' I said. 'It's more on my wife's side.'

I also settled the question of the ticket by writing to Eliza's mother to say that I wished to show my respect for the deceased by accompanying Eliza in the rendering of this last tribute, but that I should, of course, expect to pay for my own ticket. On Saturday morning, just as we were starting, we got her reply, which was quite satisfactory on the question of the ticket, and expressed a hope that we would share her midday meal with her on our way back through town. That also was all to the good.

We had some time to wait at Waterloo. In fact, our train was nearly half an hour late in starting. I fancy there must have been some race-meeting on, for there was quite a crowd on the platforms, and field-glasses and sporting papers seemed to be everywhere. However, we got off at last, and I said to Eliza that I was afraid we should miss the first part of the service. However, as Eliza pointed out, it was not our fault, and we could not control the trains. It was a beautiful sunny morning, and had we been on a less melancholy errand it might have seemed enjoyable. Eliza wore a black sailor hat, black skirt, and her black mackintosh. She is a little too inclined to wear that mackintosh on all occasions, but it served to hide the fact that her blouse was of a pale pink colour. My own mourning hat-band and my black gloves I had by me from a previous funeral.

As far as clothes went, we neither of us had to spend a penny. This was satisfactory.

'I wonder,' I said, 'if, when I am laid to my last rest, there will be many to pay one final —'

Here Eliza, who had been looking out of the window – I had not noticed that when I began to speak – drew in her head, and said, if she lived right close to the line like that, she would be ashamed to have her back-yard in the state those were.

At this moment the train stopped for ten minutes. Then it went on for a little and stopped again. After that stoppages became frequent, and I saw how it would be. We arrived at Plumley Heath long after the funeral was over, and only just in time to catch our tain back.

We explained it all to Eliza's mother, and she was most reasonable about it. She said she would write to George Magsworth about it, and he must at any rate give us credit for our good intentions. He had sent her, in accordance with the deceased lady's wishes, a handsome and massive silver cream-jug and a pair of opera-glasses with bag and strap complete. I have seldom seen Eliza's mother in better spirits or showing to better advantage than she did that day. She insisted on handing me a sovereign for our expenses, though I told her that they had not nearly amounted to that, and she made Eliza a present of the opera-glasses. We then sat down to an elegant and substantial repast, and I asked one or two riddles which were well received.

We left about half-past three to walk to the station. I had removed my hat-band, and was carrying Eliza's mackintosh over my arm. The funeral being now over, there seemed to be no occasion to keep the thing on.

Eliza said she would rather like to try her new opera-glasses. We happened to be passing the Frivolity at the time. I said that, if she cared to look in for an hour, there would be enough change from the sovereign to pay for cheap seats.

It was a good performance. I was especially struck with the Bartini Brothers, who did several things on the high trapeze that (as I remarked to Eliza) I should have been very sorry to have attempted myself. On her return home Eliza said that she had thoroughly enjoyed her day.

'That may be so in a kind of a sense,' I answered; 'but we must not and cannot forget its melancholy associations.'

* * *

On the Monday morning a message was brought me that Mr Bagshawe wished to see me in his private room. I went in at once.

'I saw you on your way back from the funeral yesterday,' he said.

'Yes, sir? I had not the pleasure of seeing you.'

'No. You were going into a music-hall with a lady in pink, and you were still wearing your race-glasses.'

The race-glasses were, of course, Eliza's opera-glasses. Appearances must have been rather against me.

'I think,' I said, 'that I can explain what must have looked like –'

'Don't you trouble. That don't want any explanation. Next time, though, that you want to go to a funeral I'll ask you to put a sovereign on for me. Now get back to your work.'

And under this thoroughly unjust imputation I labour till this day.

The Leak

'I HAVE a nose,' I said coldly, 'and it is not merely ornamental.'

'Nobody says that you haven't got a nose,' replied Eliza snappishly, 'and nobody would call it ornamental, either. But if it was any use to you, you'd know that the leak isn't here, but upstairs.'

'My dear Eliza, do let us talk common sense.'

'That's what I've been trying to get you to do this last half-hour. You go and get the plumber to come and stop the leak in the bedroom. Then that'll be all right.'

'If I did, he would waste an hour – time for which I should be charged – trying to find a leak which was not there. That is not my idea of common sense. I shall instruct him that the leak is here in the dining-room, and direct his attention particularly to the gas-bracket on the left of the fireplace.'

'You go on. You do as much instructing and directing as you like. But as soon as the man comes he'll be sent straight to the bedroom. It smells worse there, so that's where the leak is; and I'm not going to have my wall-paper spoilt in here for no rhyme or reason.'

'It may be true that the smell is worst in the bedroom, but that happens to be another proof of my words. The gas, being lighter than air, rises and collects in the room overhead. I am sorry to say that the floors and ceilings in this house admit of such a thing easily happening. Perhaps you will explain how, when gas rises – you must remember that fact – we get the smell downstairs if the leak's upstairs.'

'That's the down-draught in the chimney brings the gas down. If we had fires, now, you wouldn't get any smell of gas here at all; it would be all upstairs. Of course, as it comes down the chimney, it's strongest near the fireplace, and that's what sets you thinking about that bracket.'

'Pardon me, Eliza; that is not what sets me thinking about the bracket. Long before there was any actual leak that bracket was in my mind. It was in my mind when we took the house. I saw then that it was a cheap and bungling piece of work, and I knew we should get this trouble sooner or later in consequence. What I maintain is —'

'Oh, don't you go on arguing and maintaining,' said Eliza, 'or you won't have time to look in at Timson's on your way to the station. We'll just leave it like this. You can tell him the leak's in the scullery, or in the back-garden, or anywhere you like; and if I give this man a hint when he comes as to where the leak really is – well, that's nothing to do with you, is it?'

'Yes, it has. I do not choose to be made a fool of in the eyes of Timson's man. If I am not master in my own house, and it's not for me to say where a gas leak is, at any rate I don't wish every Tom, Dick, and Harry in the place to know it. But I'll tell you what I will do. We will neither of us say anything to Timson or his man. We will leave them to find the leak, and I'll bet you ten shillings it's not in the bedroom.'

'I'm not going betting and gambling, for I know what it leads to, and I've heard you tell mother that you never bet, either, else I'd like to take that ten shillings from you.'

'Well, if you wish it, we will not bet; we will have a simple arrangement that if the gas leak is in the bedroom I will make you a present, and if it is in the dining-room I shall have a present from you.'

'There can't be any harm in that,' said Eliza.

'There may, on the contrary, be great good in it: it may give you a sharp lesson against obstinate contradictoriness.'

'You mean, it may teach you not to be so silly. Now I'll tell you what I want if I win.'

She named certain articles of wearing apparel, the total cost of which would be nine shillings. In the event of my winning, I decided upon a box of a hundred cigars at the same price. To my mind, no pipe, not even a meerschaum, has as good an appearance as a cigar. Unfortunately, cigars are not cheap, and never can be.

On my way to the station I looked in at Timson's. I merely said: 'There's a gas leak up at my house – I wish you'd look into it for me.'

He said the matter should be put in hand that morning. Timson is a very civil fellow, and should do well. He never presses for money until the thing has run three months, and even then does it in a most delicate and gentlemanly way. And he always touches his hat.

* * *

When I returned from the City in the evening, I found Eliza looking very tired and depressed. The unpleasant smell had entirely disappeared.

'Ah!' I said playfully. 'I'm afraid I shall not have the pleasure of presenting you with those – well, those articles of apparel to which I have already alluded.'

'No,' she said. 'And you won't get your cigars, either.'

'What do you mean? Hasn't Timson's man —'

'Timson's man! Been here all day. Only just gone. The mess that room's in upstairs! The girl's cleaning it down now.'

'Where was the leak, then?'

'There wasn't any. But how that old rat managed to get in between those joists is what beats me. He had the floor up, and I've had the carbolic down.'

'What! You mean it was a dead rat?'

'Yes. Oh, don't talk about it! Timson's man isn't particular, but even he – well, I sent him up a jug of beer, and couldn't do less. And he said to me when he was going that he didn't know what money he'd made, but he'd swear he earned it.'

It was rather a curious thing that it should turn out like that. However, I happened to find a shilling in a bus the other day, and treated myself to ten of those cigars. I lit one up last Sunday night, and Eliza said suddenly that she couldn't help thinking of that old rat. It reminded her, I suppose, of the present that she was to have made to me.

The Thermometer

ELIZA said that we did not want a thermometer.

'No,' I said, 'we do not want a thermometer in the sense that we want bread to eat and clothes to wear, but it is an object generally to be found in the hall of a gentleman's house, and is extremely useful besides. I think you are a little too prone to grumble and find fault.'

'I don't grumble. I know that every now and then you've got to go out and buy some foolish thing that we don't want any more than we want the moon. You're like that, and it always happens some week when we're short. If it hadn't been a thermometer, it would have been something else. If you're nailing it up in the passage, mind it's somewhere where the girl can't fetch up against it.'

'It is already nailed up, and it would be impossible to knock against it without first of all removing the umbrella-stand. Kindly instruct the girl that she is not to dust it. I will take entire charge of that myself. Her rough-and-ready way is not suitable for a scientific instrument.'

Eliza was about to reply, when there came a knock at the front door. It was merely Miss Sakers, who had called to see if we had anything for a jumble sale which she was organizing. She was unable to stay to tea – a little unfortunate, as there were crumpets in the house.

* * *

'If you had to buy something,' said Eliza, 'it seems a pity you didn't get one of those things that tells you what the weather's going to be when you rap it.'

'You mean a barometer. That may come.'

'Oh, I don't want you to buy anything else!'

'I had no such intention. I was only thinking that, if your mother was at all undecided what to do about Christmas, you might see your way. However, I could not have purchased a really good barometer for one shilling, which was all I paid for the thermometer. Nor do I see why a barometer would have been preferable.'

'Well, that's simple enough. One tells you what you don't know, and the other tells you what you do know. I don't know what the weather's going to be, but I know whether I'm warm enough without going and asking a thermometer.'

'But do you know what the temperature is on the grass outside at midnight or later?'

'No,' she said, 'nor want. I don't sleep on the grass outside.'

'Well, that,' I said, 'is not the right spirit in which to look at it. I may add that the use of a thermometer in cases of illness is often absolutely essential.'

* * *

I little thought when I said those words that the very next Sunday would give me an opportunity to apply them. But so it happened. I awoke in the morning with a slight cold in the head.

'I shall remain in one room all day,' I said at breakfast, 'and that room must be maintained at a temperature of sixty degrees. The best doctors are agreed as to that.'

'Well,' Eliza said, 'this room's more than sixty now.'

'You cannot possibly know,' I replied, and directed the girl to bring me the thermometer, and to handle it carefully.

After a minute or two I consulted it.

'The temperature of this room,' I said, 'is not sixty; it is a shade under forty-five.'

'I know better,' said Eliza.

'Do you seriously mean to tell me that you are a better judge of the temperature of this room than that thermometer is?'

'Yes, if it says this room's forty-five.'

'Then,' I replied, 'I must decline to discuss the matter with you.'

I put on more coal at once. Eliza said she wished she could have foreseen all that thermometer would lead to. She then went up to get ready for church – not, I fear, in a very suitable frame of mind.

The thermometer still remained at forty-five, and it occurred to me that it might be in a position where a draught of cold air was playing on the bulb. I put it on the other side of the room. Certainly my own impression was that the room was almost uncomfortably warm. But thinking that this was an erroneous idea due to my indisposition, I again made the fire up. Perhaps I slightly overdid it, for I noticed that the mantelpiece, which is of iron and painted light blue, was beginning to turn brown. By this time I was in a proper perspiration, and the thermometer still stood at forty-five.

A careful examination explained the whole mystery. The tube had been wantonly broken at the extreme end. It was therefore of little use as an accurate recorder of the temperature. I was very much put out about it, and rang for the girl at once. She was sulky and irritated, and obstinately refused to confess that it was she who had broken it. Eliza was perfectly furious at the state of the mantelpiece when she came in. Altogether it was far from being one of the happiest Sundays of my married life.

* * *

We gave the thermometer to Miss Sakers for her jumble sale, but she did not seem very enthusiastic. She said it was old clothes she was thinking of mostly.

The landlord in his penny-wise-and-pound-foolish way refuses to repaint the mantelpiece. That man will get a pretty sharp lesson from me one of these days.

A Gloomy Sunday

'ELIZA,' I said, 'I am going to put to you rather a curious question. What would you do if I fell overpoweringly in love with another woman?'

'That's a nice sort of thing to ask,' said Eliza – 'Sunday afternoon, too! What next? I wish you'd get on with your tea, for the girl's waiting to clear, and can't get out till she's done it.'

'And I am to choke myself to oblige my own servant! Very well; I require nothing more, and if I did I should certainly refuse to take it. Perhaps you would wish me to black her boots also.'

'Don't be so silly! I promised her she should go to her married sister's this afternoon. When you're asked to do anything, why can't you give a civil answer?'

At this moment the girl came in. When she had retired with the tea-things, I turned to Eliza.

'You say that I cannot give a civil answer. I will not go into that. But I should like to remind you that a few minutes ago I put a question to you and could get no answer whatever.'

'Oh! What was that?'

'I asked you what you would do in the event of my falling overpoweringly in love with —'

'That nonsense? There was nothing to answer. It couldn't happen.'

'It is true that my principles are strict. Perhaps I might also lay claim to a strong will. But I should hesitate to say that such a thing couldn't happen. There are storms that sweep away all – everything, in fact.'

'I dare say. But you're not the stormy sort, you know.'

'What right have you to say that?'

'I've been married to you long enough to have found out if you had been. You're the quiet and respectable kind, and be thankful you are.'

'Under a quiet and respectable exterior there may be a good deal hidden. At the office, for instance, I am supposed to have rather a remarkable control over my temper —'

'Ah!' interrupted Eliza. 'They should have heard you at dinner to-day.'

'If you mean what I said about the way in which the sprouts were cooked – or, to be more accurate, ruined – there are times when a man must speak out if he calls himself a man at all.'

'Yes, but he needn't go slopping the gravy all over the —'

'Stick to the point, Eliza. Try to stick to the point. Just as I can and do break out in the matter of temper when I think it right and necessary, so it is quite possible I might break out in other ways. I am only human. I have never pretended to be more than that. It is quite possible that I might form some mad and overpowering passion for another woman.'

Eliza seemed to think it over. And then, greatly to my surprise and annoyance, she smiled.

'All right,' she said. 'You tell me when that happens. If ever I did die of laughing it would be then. I'd have to have a few friends in to see it.'

'I fail to see,' I replied rather sternly, 'that the wreck of three lives is any matter for amusement.'

'Wreck of your grandmother's ducks!' exclaimed Eliza. I think this rather a vulgar kind of expression, and have repeatedly asked her not to use it. At times it seems as if my wishes went for nothing. 'Where's the wreck coming in?' she went on. 'You seem to think that if you made a fool of yourself about some woman she'd be certain to make a fool of herself about you. That's where my fun would come in, because she wouldn't. Why, think what you are – think what your age is. Why, look at yourself in the glass. And don't talk such silliness.'

'That will do, Eliza; you have said quite enough. Possibly, when you are quieter, even you will think that you have said a little too much. And this,' I continued in a bitter way, but quite patient – 'this is Sunday! The day of rest. Ha! And peace. Oh, ha, ha! I come home after a hard week's work. My favourite dish of vegetables is ruined by what I call criminal carelessness, but I am not even allowed to make a few remarks about it. My tea is cut to suit the convenience of a mere domestic servant. That's all right. The master of the house is of no importance, of course. Keeping my temper, I try to start an interesting subject of conversation. What is my reward? I get a string of insults, ending with a rude and offensive insinuation as to my personal appearance. And I am supposed to stand it.' (Here, I will admit, I grew rather warmer.) 'I am expected to put up with it. There you're mistaken. I am damned if I —'

'Hold on!' said Eliza, picking up the book she had been reading; 'you can finish that by yourself. I'm not going to stop in the room to be sworn at.'

'Mistaken again,' I said, getting a little quieter. 'I never said that you were; I said that I was. To speak more correctly, I said that I should be if —'

But Eliza had already gone into the drawing-room. I followed her, and said:

'Kindly permit me to explain. So far was I from —'

Eliza rose, and went back to the dining-room again. I followed, being quite determined that she should hear me out.

'This is childish,' I said. 'But even under circumstances of extreme provocation I am determined to —'

Eliza then put her book under her arm and went upstairs to the bedroom. I followed, saying on the stairs:

'I wish to make my position perfectly clear. You have chosen to accuse me of —'

She went into the bedroom, shut the door and locked it.

'Eliza,' I said through the keyhole, 'I must ask you to control your temper and —'

At this moment the front door bell rang, and Eliza immediately opened the bedroom door again.

'That's Miss Sakers,' she said, 'and the girl's gone to her married sister's. And what are we going to do? Are you going to open the door to her, or am I?'

'Neither,' I said; 'I am going out for a short walk. Naturally, if I find Miss Sakers on the doorstep, I shall ask her in and escort her to the drawing-room.'

Having said that I was going out for a walk, I had naturally to be as good as my word. Although I was back ten minutes before church-time, they had already left. This annoyed me so much that I went straight to bed.

It was one of those gloomy, trying days that you get sometimes.

Two Letters

IT is possible that some of my readers may regard me as one of the rather reckless sort, open-handed, and never thinking twice how the money goes. They would be mistaken. My tastes may be slightly on the luxurious side, and in consequence I may sometimes have purchased articles beyond what Eliza would approve. But value for money has ever been a motto of mine, and I am strongly in favour of what I call wise economies. Doing away with something you do not care about is a wise economy; getting the same thing cheaper elsewhere is another. Any gentleman like myself, with an income that is moderate, or rather less, and with an interest in the management of his home, will know at once what I mean. I had this question of a wise economy in my head when I asked Eliza where her mother was intending to spend her holidays.

The fact was that the eminent City firm with which I am

professionally connected had arranged my holiday for the first fortnight in September. That is always a bad month, the quarter's rent coming at the end of it. I suggested that I should prefer some other fortnight, but it was not entertained. In fact, Mr Bagshawe, who was a little upset that morning, said I could take that fortnight or leave it, but it would be that or none. I turned it off with a smile, but it rather annoyed me; it looked as if he had forgotten my position.

The expense of living at the seaside is always considerable and sometimes outrageous. At a first glance it looked to me rather as if either the holiday or that quarter's rent would have to go. I had allowed the last quarter to hang on a little, and my landlord's agents had made themselves as nasty as they could about it, and this time it would be difficult, or even impossible, to postpone it later than the end of October. At the same time, I did not like to abandon the idea of a holiday. So, turning my attention to the chance of any wise economy, I hit on something in the co-operative way.

Eliza said that she did not know where her mother was going. 'In fact, it wouldn't surprise me if she didn't go at all this year. Troubled as she is with that shortness of breath, any kind of moving about comes as a trial to her.'

'It certainly is my opinion that she ought not to be allowed to go alone. If she came with us, we could look after her a little. She would pay a share, which we could arrange, and I fancy it would work out as a wise economy for us.'

'Yes,' said Eliza, as she sucked the end of her cotton before threading the needle – an objectionable practice, and, as I have proved to her by actual experiment, quite unnecessary. 'Yes, that would make a big difference to us. Whitstable's where she always goes – Mrs Bunn's – and I dare say we should find it all right. Still, mother's no fool, you know.'

'No, indeed. Your mother is an intelligent woman; anybody has only to look at her to see that. I think these jokes about mothers-in-law are silly. She may have moods in which she is what might be called self-willed, but as a rule I find her company most enjoyable. The arrangement which I propose will be best for her and best for us, and I'll sit down to-night and write —'

'Hold on a second,' said Eliza. 'When I said she was no fool, what I meant was that she's pretty sharp to see when anybody is trying to get at her, and then she doesn't like it. And when she doesn't like anything – well, you know what she is yourself. She'll part with money as freely as anybody when she wants, but she can't stand being done out of anything – and I don't blame her, either. Suppose we did make a sovereign out of it – which is the most we could do in the fortnight – she might think we were on the job, and then —'

'Eliza, I do think you might be a little more choice in your expressions. It's a mystery to me how you pick them up.'

'Talking to the girl, I suppose. Most of the day there's no one else to talk to, and I wasn't born with my mouth sewed up. But, be that as it may, you'd better leave this notion of yours about mother. If she suggested it, that would be all right; but if you suggest it she'll begin to smell a rat. Besides, she is one of the independent sort, and she won't like any interfering. You see, she's older than we are.'

'Seeing that she is your mother,' I said, 'that is only to be expected. I fully see the force of your arguments, but, to my mind, it's a case for tact – that is to say, it depends a good deal on the way it's put. If we share with your mother, I think I can show you by figures that we save at least £2 – with proper management, of course – and I am not disposed to throw £2 in the ditch for want of a little tact. The moment this table's cleared I sit down and write that letter.'

'Well, anyhow, mind you don't send it before I've seen it.'

'You shall certainly see it, and when you have seen it, I have no doubt you will come to my way of thinking.'

*   *   *

I found, when I sat down to write the letter, that the dining-room ink had been taken off into the kitchen. That is a thing I have always set my face against. As I said to Eliza, it was becoming a question whether my wishes were to be considered or whether I was to be made a living sacrifice to my own servant.

Eliza said the girl had asked if she could spare it, as she was writing to her married sister; and what was a drop of ink?

'A drop of ink is a drop of ink,' I said pointedly, 'but discipline is discipline.'

Eliza then said I was a holy terror, and I went on with my letter. The letter began by saying that Eliza had asked me to take my pen in hand to make a little suggestion.

'The fact is,' I went on, 'that when we were arranging our own little holiday, we could not help thinking how much pleasanter it would be if we could have you with us. Perhaps you would enjoy it more, too, than dreary solitude. We were thinking of Whitstable, but we would leave that entirely with you. All the trouble of ordering would be taken off your hands, and it would be a real rest for you. In the evening, or on wet days, I could read out, and it would be a pleasure to me. And if your health was not quite the thing, Eliza would be at hand to give you every attention. I fear it would be useless for me to propose that you should be our guest, though that is what I should like best, so you could either pay a lump sum or so much by the week, as preferred.'

I ended by saying that our little garden was looking nice and fresh after the rain, and we both sent our best love. Then I read it all out to Eliza.

'Well, you've wasted your time and your notepaper,' said Eliza, 'for I shan't let you send it.'

'If I choose to send it, it will be sent. Make no mistake about that. What's your objection to it?'

'To start with, what do you mean by sticking it all on to me, and saying it's my suggestion? That is as barefaced a one as ever I heard. And what nonsense about her being lonely! That Mrs Bunn's more like a friend than a landlady to her, she always says. Then, fancy your saying that what you want most is to pay all her expenses! Go it! Why didn't you say you'd have the Prince of Wales down to meet her at once? There'd have been just as much sense in it. Do you think she doesn't know to a penny what we owe her at this moment? Why, it's as good as calling her a fool to her face. That letter won't go. I won't have it.'

I had seen for some time back that it would become necessary for me to put my foot down. The occasion had arrived. I kept my temper perfectly, and said quietly, though emphatically:

'It is useless to argue with you in your present frame of mind, and I shall not attempt it. That letter will go. It is my letter, and I take the entire responsibility.'

'Yes, but it's my mother,' said Eliza.

'I utterly decline to enter into it. That letter will go. But for the accident that I have removed my boots, the right foot of which was causing me considerable pain, I should take it out and post it this moment. As it is, I shall post it on my way to the station to-morrow. I have nothing more to say except that I could wish you had some common sense and self-control, and – er – good night.'

I went straight up to bed. She called after me that if I sent that letter she would send one herself. She added that the fat would then be in the fire. This was said in a regrettably loud tone of voice, and, the partition walls being thin, must have been perfectly audible to the servant.

I rose early next morning, as there were sundry little matters in the garden that needed my attention. When I came in, Eliza said:

'Are you still determined to post that letter?'

'I am.'

'Sure?'

'Quite sure. It is idle to reopen that subject. I should be glad to know whether the dish before me is intended for poached eggs or for bullets, because —'

'Wait a bit. I had a letter from mother this morning. Like to look at it?'

The letter began by saying that she was in fairly good health, but for the shortness of breath after meals, and hoped we were the same. Then came the important part.

'I've made up my mind not to go away this year; I can't stand those trains. Only yesterday I got on the Underground to go to the Exhibition, and whether it was what I had taken for my dinner or not I can't say.'

Then followed a few lines of purely medical interest. The letter went on:

'I told Mrs Bunn I should take my usual fortnight, and don't want to disappoint her, for she is a good woman, if ever there was one, and I make no doubt the money's something to her. So I'll take the rooms, and you two must spend your holiday there. Of course, there will be nothing for you to pay, and you must look on it as your birthday present.'

'Well?' said Eliza. 'Hurry up and post that letter of yours now.'

'Ah!' I said. 'This is good. This is very good indeed. I will say this – your mother can do a handsome thing with a better grace than anybody I know.' I pulled the letter which I had written out of my pocket, and began to tear it up. 'Of course, this puts an entirely different complexion on things.'

Eliza came over and kissed me. 'You old silly! why, you nearly made a real bust-up between us. Don't you do that again!'

'Well, well,' I said, 'that's over, anyhow. Now, what about the question of shoes for the beach, my dear?'

The Entertainment

'Miss Sakers looked in this afternoon,' said Eliza. 'They're getting up some kind of an entertainment, so as to pay off the debt from the last bazaar.'

'And if my advice had been taken there would have been no debt. On the contrary, there would have been a substantial balance for the Organ fund. As it is, I wash my hands of the whole thing.'

'Miss Sakers said she wanted you to help.'

'Oh! Indeed? Did she say whether it was a song or a recitation?'

'No; she just said she wanted you to help.'

'I suppose she would leave the choice to me. If I did anything, I think it would be a recitation – or possibly a reading: "Enoch Arden" makes a very good reading, especially if accompanied by dissolving views. Of course, dissolving views means a certain outlay, but if you're going to do a thing at all, I always say that —'

'Here, hold on,' said Eliza, 'I thought you washed your hands of the whole thing.'

'So I do. Quite true. I absolutely disclaim any responsibility whatever for the failure of that bazaar. That's my position, and I won't shift from it one hair's-breadth. But the entertainment is a different matter altogether. Miss Sakers apparently thinks that a performance by myself would add to the attraction. Very likely she overrates my abilities. But, at the same time, I should be behaving like a sulky child if I refused her. No, no, Eliza! I'm not going to make myself ridiculous.'

'Ain't you?' said Eliza.

And I didn't quite like the way she said it. But I was just starting for our greengrocer (to ask him if he would care to eat a lettuce like that himself), and for the time the subject dropped.

* * *

'Now, Eliza,' I said after supper, 'suppose I left it to you to settle what I was to do at this entertainment, would you advise a song or a recitation?'

'Certainly not a song, and if you try to recite you may forget the words.'

'I see. You think a reading would be better.'

'That might do. You don't want it too long. What's that bit about the garden – the thing you wanted a magic-lantern for?'

'Not garden. "Enoch Arden" is the name of it. It's about a man who comes back after being away a long time and finds his wife has married somebody else.'

'That's not bad,' said Eliza. 'It would make 'em laugh, anyhow.'

'I trust it would do nothing of the kind. It is a long and beautiful poem by the late Lord Tennyson. I might get it into half an hour if I cut some of it out. And it never fails to bring tears to the eyes.'

'Then that's off,' said Eliza. 'Supposing everybody wanted to last half an hour, where'd the entertainment be? Besides, we're quite in a small way, and it's more than ever I expected for you to be asked to help at all. I can't think why she said she wanted you.'

'If you mean that you think me incapable of reading a short poem with appropriate gestures and facial expressions, you are welcome to say so. You have seen but little of the artistic side of my nature. But there was a time when, as a boy, I won a prize for recitation. Had I seen an opening I should probably have taken to the stage. Miss Sakers is not the first who had credited me with some little gift in that direction.'

'Of course, I know you can read, and write too. I suppose you were taught the same as others. All I say is, that if you do anything for that entertainment it oughtn't (seeing what we are) to go beyond five minutes.'

'Very well. I do not know why social position should settle these matters, but it shall be as you wish. The recitation which in my boyhood won me a copy of "The May Queen", cloth gilt, with numerous illustrations, took less than five minutes. It told how "the Assyrian came down like the wolf on the fold, and his cohorts were gleaming with purple and gold, and the sheen of their spears was like —" '

'Hold on,' said Eliza. 'That's poetry.'

'It is.'

'Poetry always gives me the hump. I shouldn't do any poetry if I were you. Why don't you look out one or two things, and then ask Miss Sakers to choose? She'll be in here again on Saturday, she said, to see you about it.'

I spent the entire evening in trying to find something which would be suitable.

'How would it be,' I asked Eliza, as I went through our little collection of books – 'how would it be if I did something in character?'

'What do you mean? Dressed up? It would be pretty serious. I'll tell you what it is – you seem to me to be losing your head over this entertainment.'

Eliza has absolutely no artistic side to her character. I cannot blame her for what is a natural deficiency, but I felt justified in pointing it out.

'And it is just that,' I said, 'which prevents you from entering more fully into what you might have entered into more fully than you now do enter into it.'

'What's all that mean?' asked Eliza.
'Rats!' I said, and went up to bed.
I admit that I was much put out.

* * *

Finding nothing in our own small library that quite pleased my taste, I purchased next day in the City a copy of 'Haverford's Giant Reciter' – a remarkably large book for a shilling. I selected two pieces – 'Won by a Head' and 'Two by Tricks'. Business being slack, I was enabled to devote some of my time at the office to studying these. I worked at them also in the luncheon hour, and in the train going home.

Eliza said later that evening that it wasn't much fun sitting with a man who hadn't a word to say to you, and just put his head back and screwed his eyes up and whispered.

'I was committing a piece to memory. I will repeat it to you, if you like.'

'All right. What's it called?'

' "Won by a Head".'

'I didn't ask whom it was by. I asked what it was called.'

'Just as I said. It's "Won by a Head".'

'I don't care if it's one by him or one by somebody else. What's the name of it?'

'It seems hopeless to make you understand.'

'Then what's the good of reciting a thing when nobody can understand it? You don't seem to know where you are.'

However, that was soon cleared up.

* * *

Miss Sakers called, as arranged, on Saturday afternoon. She was very smiling and affable.

'I hear,' she said, 'that you're going to be good enough to help us with the entertainment.'

'Certainly – with pleasure. I'm afraid that I can't do much.'

'But I don't ask for much. If you and the others that we've asked give a shilling each, that will cover the rent and lighting of the hall, and then we shan't have the fiasco that we had with the bazaar. And it will be quite a good entertainment. Mr Stapleby's getting it up.'

By an adroit movement I managed to slip the copy of 'Haverford's Giant Reciter' out of sight. I also paid over the shilling – a sum which was at the time a consideration to me.

Eliza, interpreting my frown correctly, saw that she was not to say anything about my mistake as to the nature of the help required of me. And to this day Miss Sakers is none the wiser.

But I shall not go to that entertainment. Why should I pay money to see Stapleby and his friends make fools of themselves?

The Remarkable Fog

IT is the custom of the partners of the firm which has secured my services to give a dinner once a year to a few of those who hold the highest positions in their employ. The dinner is given at a first-class restaurant, and on quite an unlimited scale.

When I received my invitation I took the matter in hand at once. My reply was based on the model given in 'The Perfect Gentleman', and was, I think, in the best taste. I insisted that Eliza should go over my evening clothes with a little benzine at least one week before they were required – if this is left till the very last, the smell is often only too noticeable. I also purchased a new pair of good patent-leather boots. Eliza said, in rather a nasty way, that it was just as well that these dinners only came once in a year. I answered, with a smile:

'The boots will still remain when the dinner is over, my dear; and if I can judge by appearances, I have seldom had better value for half a guinea.'

The only possible objection that could be taken to them was that they creaked, the very best boots are liable to do this, and it can be neither foreseen nor prevented. However, Eliza said that she did not care to be awakened in the middle of the night, and I promised that on my return I would remove my boots in the passage downstairs. As a matter of fact, Eliza is a singularly heavy sleeper.

The dinner was a great success, and although champagne was served *ad libitum*, the bounds of sobriety were never actually exceeded. The only person who at all approached the border was a man of the name of Watson, whose inclusion among the invited guests seemed to me a matter of doubtful policy. He has been with the firm for many years, but he is not my idea of a gentleman. Personally, I kept a very close watch on myself, not wishing to incur the slightest risk of the merest suspicion of anything not being as it should be. Very few men when invited, and even pressed, to take so much, would have taken so little; but, with me, self-control is a second nature.

I took the last train back, and found, on my arrival, that a dense fog had set in. However, I walked home without thinking much about it, humming a tune as I went. I let myself in with my latch-key, groped for the chair by the umbrella-stand, sat down, and took off my boots. I placed these under the chair, wound up my watch, and then struck a match. The first thing that struck me was that our stair-carpet had been taken up; then I noticed that the furniture and wall-paper were strange to me. In the fog I had missed my right turning and taken the next. By an accident my latch-key had fitted, and I was in the wrong house – a house very much like my own, but not my own. And just as this dawned on me, a dog began to bark most savagely.

I did not lose my head. I rather flatter myself that under no possible circumstances should I lose my head. If I had lost my head, I should have stopped and explained. I might have shown that my latch-key happened to fit the lock, and my appearance would have helped to prove that I was no burglar. But I was in evening-dress in the wrong house with my boots off, and with my face slightly flushed from fast walking, and no explanation could have avoided a most unjust suspicion on the part of the occupants as to my sobriety. So, keeping my head, I left at once, closing the door behind me.

If I did make a mistake at all, it was that I forgot to take my boots with me. Mind, I discovered it almost immediately, but it was a mistake, and I did not see my way to put it right. I might have gone back, but I did not know whereabouts the dog would be; and if the occupants of the house were already roused, I should be merely incurring the absurd suspicion to which I have already alluded. So I walked, or, more accurately, ran home in my socks. You may be sure that I got the right house this time, and that I was particularly careful to avoid waking Eliza.

Next morning she asked when I had returned. I told her. I mentioned also that I had noticed that the clock in the passage was four minutes slow, and had put it right; and that I had folded up my evening things and put them away.

Eliza said:

'What for?'

'Nothing in particular,' I replied.

The fact was that I had wished to have some evidence, in case Eliza discovered that I had come home without my boots, that the loss was not due to any – well, say any lapse on my part. I also gave her a very clear account of the dinner, and expressed my regret that Watson had taken just that second whisky and soda after dinner which makes all the difference.

'Personally,' I added, 'I never touch anything after dinner.'

This was Sunday morning. For some reason or other the firm always gives its annual dinner on a Saturday evening. I had a very hearty breakfast; in fact, Eliza remarked upon it, and said it was no compliment to the dinner of the night before.

'Ah!' I said, 'I expect it's very different with Watson. It would never surprise me if he were not asked next year.'

Just then the girl came in to say that she had hunted everywhere for the boots I wore the night before, and how was she to clean them while she didn't know where they were?

I said:

'The boots in question are patent-leather and valuable, and require to be cleaned in a special manner. I prefer to undertake them myself, and have put them aside for that purpose.'

Eliza then thought it her business to strike in.

'What nonsense!' she said. 'She's done patent-leather of mine.'

The girl said that it was all the same to her, but it had got to be one way or the other.

I said sternly that it and everything else had got to be just exactly as I said. I then took my hat and went for a little stroll before church. I had some idea that if the discussion were prolonged Eliza might become suspicious. If she had once found out that I had after that dinner left my boots in the wrong house, talking would have been of little use.

There are some things we shall never understand. I shall probably never know what moved me to go back to the street which, owing to the fog, I had mistaken for my own last night. Once there, I had no difficulty in locating the house – the eleventh on the left. I had no thought of getting the boots back; I was only hoping that when the people of the house found a pair of practically new boots under the chair in their passage they would have the sense to say nothing about it; any talk on that subject in the neighbourhood might have been most prejudicial. I just took one glance at the house, and saw in the window this notice:

TO LET.
Keys at No. 12.

It all came over me in a flash. I had left the boots in an empty house! I was carrying out my plan before some men would have had the time to form a plan at all. In five seconds I was knocking at the door of the next house, asking for the keys of No. 11, which I wished to see on behalf of a friend, and apologizing for troubling them on a Sunday. The woman who gave me the keys apologized too for the noise her dog was making. But she said that he was a good watch-dog, and when he had heard some drunken brute trying the door of the next house the night before, he had barked like anything. I had reason to know that this was in part true.

The first thing I saw when I entered that fatal house was my copy of the menu. I must have pulled it out with my handkerchief, or by some other accident. I caught the words *Blé vert à l'Allemande*, which would appear to be the French for soup, and *Pommes naturelles*, which I had not been able to identify. The chair was still there – owing to some little misunderstanding with the landlord the previous tenants had not got all their furniture out – and the boots were still under it. In another moment they were in the tail-pockets of my frock-coat.

I confess that I look back on this incident with no little pleasure. It may seem absurd at first sight, but I believe there are men in the diplomatic service who could not have taken that situation up and dealt with it as I did. Everything passed off well.

At the same time, if I am invited (as I have reason to expect) next year, I shall make no bones about ordering a cab to meet me at the station on my return and saying nothing to Eliza about it. In these fogs anything may happen. I have had the menu suitably framed, and it makes quite an addition to our drawing-room.

ELIZA GETTING ON

The Move

WHEN Eliza's poor dear mother was called to her rest, the actual money which Eliza received worked out at much less than had been expected, and was tied up in a way that I personally – and I suppose I am a man of business if I am anything – thought totally unnecessary. However, the poor old lady had allowed herself to be guided entirely by the advice of Eliza's brother Frank, a man of whom I have no very high opinion. (I have myself seen him drinking sherry wine at half-past eleven in the morning, and shaking hands with the barmaid afterwards in a way that was simply derogatory.) I take it that it was entirely due to Frank that my name was not so much as mentioned in the will.

I had always been on the best of terms with Eliza's mother. She occasionally obliged me with a little temporary financial advance in times of pressure, and refused interest, though offered. I frequently wrote to her, always including any witticism (if suitable) that I might have heard in the City.

I also sent her presents – sometimes a few flowers from our garden, sometimes plums, sometimes a cucumber – yes, and at times of the year when cucumbers meant money. I must say I was disappointed. If ever there was a case of undue influence, that was one.

I must add a few words on the subject of Eliza's mother's funeral. All Frank had got to do was to come to me and say, 'This sad event puts me in rather a responsible position, and I should be glad of a few words of advice from a man with your knowledge of the world.' That would have been the natural thing for him to have done. I should imagine that, though not an executor, as son-in-law of the deceased I had some claim to be consulted. I should have said politely, 'By all means. Let us go into the question thoroughly.'

Nothing of the kind happened. He did not come to me in that way, and I am far from being the sort of man that sticks himself forward. So far as the funeral was concerned, I am in a position to say that he did not even consult Mr Bullock, who was the other executor.

The inevitable consequences followed, as they so often do.

It seems to me now a providential blessing that Eliza was down with the influenza at the time, and unable to attend the funeral. Not to mince matters, it was not so much a funeral as a fiasco, bungled from the very start, as I knew it would be. It all happened three years ago or more, and even now it gives me no sort of pleasure to dwell upon it. I would sooner drop the subject.

What else could be expected? The undertaker employed was quite in a small way, had to hire everything, and, so far as I could see, took no sort of personal interest in his work. We were twenty minutes late in getting away, which shows what the organization was like; and whatever else the driver of the second coach may have been on the way back, he certainly was not sober. I was not the only one who noticed it, and Mr and Mrs Bullock would tell you the same thing. But it is a painful thing, and the less said about it the better.

But, in quitting the topic, I should like to say just one word as to the actual fittings. When my time comes, whether the plate on my coffin is silver or brass, I do hope, at any rate, that my name will be engraved on it straight, and not cock-eyed. That is all I have to say.

Well, there is just one more point, though I hate this raking up of old sores. I refer to Eliza's brother's *faux pas* as regards Mr Dadling. He is an old friend of the family, was for many years a traveller to a well-known firm of wine and spirit merchants, and has now retired. During the illness of the deceased he left at the house a bottle of brandy of a quality that simply cannot be procured for money; in fact, it was only his close connection with the trade and a little special favour that enabled him to obtain it. He subsequently sent a floral tribute, consisting of an anchor of violets on a heart-shaped background of white geranium. I have the gravest doubts if that could have been procured from any shop for less than thirty-five shillings. But was Mr Dadling invited to the funeral? He was not. He was forgotten – simply forgotten, as if he had been so much dirt. Of course, the only safe way is to make a list, and that is one of the first things I should have told Frank if I had been asked.

However, he is, after all, Eliza's brother; and, in any case, as I have already implied, I prefer to draw the veil over the whole affair. Otherwise I should have had a word to say on the subject of refreshments. I do not pretend to be an expert in these matters, but in a case of doubt I should have thought it best to err on the safe side. The funeral started nominally at the very inconvenient hour of half-past twelve. I presume it was arranged to suit the undertaker, for certainly it suited nobody else. As a matter of fact, it started at ten minutes to one. I took it for granted that wine and sandwiches, or at the very least biscuits, would have been handed. It was not so much a question of etiquette as of common humanity. But they were not handed and not even suggested. It may have been a simple want of foresight, or there may have been another reason. It is of no use to dwell on these things. We cannot recall the past.

After all, there are pleasanter things to talk about, and if I linger one moment on the question of the trousers worn by Frank at the funeral, it is merely to show the reader that I do not grumble without cause. I had my doubts about them as soon as I came into the room, and later I had an opportunity to get a closer look at them in a better light. Dark grey they may have been, and if he likes to say that they were very dark grey, I shall not deny it. My point is that they were not black. Personally, I wore the trousers of my dress suit at the funeral and for many a long day afterwards, and it was quite open to Frank to have done the same – well, what I mean is, that it was quite open to him to have worn his own dress trousers. It all resolves itself in my mind into a question of respect for the deceased. And that is my last word about it.

Fortunately, it is not necessary for me to say anything as to the near-side horse in the second coach, because everything I have said about Frank's trousers applies to that horse equally. There is no getting away from it. The horse simply was not of a suitable colour for the sacred and solemn function that it was called upon to perform. I may not be a great judge of horses, but I am not colour-blind. That horse was dark brown, and it was only too painfully obvious that much of its tail was not genuine. I am quite reasonable about the point. I do not blame the horse, and I do not blame the undertaker. Being quite in a small way, he probably had to take what he could get. But I must, and I do, blame the man who selected that undertaker on his own initiative, without asking for the advice that an older and wiser man was quite ready to give him. I will not pursue the subject further. I prefer to wipe the whole thing out of my mind.

The one thing I must add is a matter of personal explanation.

Eliza and I sent a wreath. I know what I paid for it, and I know that Mrs Bullock said it was a perfect picture; but never mind about that. To that wreath a card was attached bearing the name of the donors and a suitable inscription in my own handwriting; and I had not grudged time in the composition of that inscription. If these things are not done in exquisite taste, they had better not be done at all. During the whole of the ceremony that card was kept face downwards. I will try to believe that this was accidental, but I must say that it was an accident that should not have happened. I managed in a tactful way to mention to Mrs Bullock that it was our wreath, but I have no doubt that some people thought we had sent nothing, and were surprised at the omission.

I am not at all sure that one of these days I shall not make out a list of all the different things that were wrong at the funeral of Eliza's mother – simply as a matter of curiosity.

* * *

Still, so far as things went, there was an improvement in our circumstances. And at about the same time I received the further advance in salary that had been promised me. This might very well have been made the occasion for a few graceful words of compliment and thanks for my services. What my employer, Mr Bagshawe, actually said was:

'Well, I suppose you'll have to have the rise, but it's the last you'll get, and it's more than you're worth.'

This shows that a man may be senior partner in a City firm of the first importance, and yet be wanting in the feelings and manners of a gentleman. The idea of telling him that he could keep his money did occur to me. However, I contented myself with saying that I did my best to give satisfaction.

'That's what every incompetent fool says when he is sacked,' said Mr Bagshawe.

I had either to keep silence or to tell him that he need not go out of his way to be rude. I kept silence – I have, perhaps, as much self-control as most men – and the interview then terminated.

It was evident to me from the first that, with our pecuniary position going upward by leaps and bounds like this, we should have to move into a new house – something more appropriate to our class of life. But I doubt if Eliza would ever have seen it had it not been for the question of the furniture. Her mother's furniture was to be divided equally between Eliza and Frank, and a day was fixed for them to meet and make their selection.

'I shall not accompany you, Eliza,' I said. 'As I have been left out, I wish to remain out. I shall not even offer a word of advice. You know as well as I do that tablespoons are what we have always been short of, and that sheets which have been turned sides to middle no longer look the same thing. But I want you to do quite as you like about it. Make your own selection. Otherwise, I might have mentioned that the bureau, being old, is probably more valuable than it looks, and would be useful for my papers. As it is, I would sooner not give so much as a hint.'

However, Eliza asked me a few questions as to bedsteads, clock for the dining-room mantelpiece, and so on, and it would have been mere ill-temper not to have replied. She came back from the division slightly flushed, and said that she had kept her end up, and that Frank had told her she ought to have been a pawnbroker. She showed me her list, and really I had no idea there would have been so much.

As there was no room for our new acquisitions in the little house we then occupied, Eliza agreed, rather reluctantly, to a move.

The house which I originally had my eye upon was 'Soulsrest' (241 London Road). Not being an architect, I find it difficult to give much idea of the place, but one side of the roof came down much lower than the other side, and there was a sort of turret in one corner. Eliza thought it looked cock-eyed, but it seemed to me to be distinctly artistic.

It had corner fireplaces and windows where you would least have expected them. Over the fireplace in the drawing-room was carved the motto 'Stet Domus', but this, unfortunately, had cracked across owing to a settlement. The landlord, who was also the builder, told me that every house was bound to settle if it was properly built, but these large cracks do certainly detract from the appearance. There was a veranda at the back, and a copper knocker on the front door gave the thing a finish. Anybody who passed that house was bound to look at it.

I admit the rent was twenty pounds more than we wished to give, but then there was a sundial in the garden and everything was in the best taste. Besides, the landlord said he would be only too glad to meet me, as it was not everybody's house. I could see, though, that Eliza was set against it from the first, and on looking into it we found that most of the doors would not shut and the windows would not open. It may have been, as the landlord said, simply a matter for a little adjustment, but it rather gave Eliza an argument. And when the landlord refused to have the drains tested on the ground that it would be equivalent to calling him a liar, I could see that the thing was hopeless.

The house which we finally decided upon was 'Meadow-sweet', and more Eliza's choice than mine. It was described on the agent's list as a desirable gentleman's residence, exceptionally well built, with lovely old-world gardens, extending to upwards of a quarter of an acre, but that does not really give you much of an idea of the place.

It was a semi-detached house, and, as compared with 'Soulsrest', it seemed remarkably solid, though it had not the same art character. The previous tenant had made rather a hobby of the bit of garden at the back, but the agent over-did it in calling it old-world. It was a little bit too ordinary to be quite my ideal, but I suppose that even for forty pounds a year – and we had some difficulty in getting it down to that – you cannot have everything.

The hot-water supply to the bathroom keeps me constantly wondering how we did without it for so long. We have bigger rooms than before, and two extra rooms. The landlord went far beyond what we had expected in the matter of wallpapers. In fact, taking one thing with another, I am not sure that Eliza was not right.

Once the thing was settled I began to get to work in earnest. As I said to Eliza, a move is almost always associated with mess, and worry, and confusion. There is no reason on earth why this should be so. All that is wanted is a certain amount of system.

'Yes,' said Eliza rather doubtfully, 'of course, you've got to think what you're doing.'

'Not enough,' I said. 'Too vague. You've got to go further than that. By my system mistakes are impossible. Every piece of furniture goes automatically into its right place in the new house, and before evening on the day of removal the whole thing is as much in order as if you had lived there all your life.'

'It sounds a deal too good to be true,' said Eliza. 'What is it?'

'Perfectly simple. To every piece of furniture is attached a gummed label with a number on it. That number is entered in a book, and against it is written the room in which it is to be placed, and, where necessary, its place in the room. For instance, I number this bureau 14. I enter that number in my registration book, and against it I write "Dining-room, left of fireplace". Very well. On the day of the removal I stand at the door of the new house. The bureau is brought out of the van. I look at the number on it, refer to my book, and am able to say at once exactly where it is to go.'

'Sounds all right; but these patent ideas never do come off.'

'We shall see,' I said.

And I cannot say too strongly that, however much Eliza may

try to turn the thing into a joke, the system did not fail. Accidents are things that no man on earth can guard against. I admit that it gave me a good deal of work, but it was work that I enjoyed. For over a week I spent most of my leisure in measuring up the new house to see where things would fit in, in gumming labels on the furniture, and in making the necessary entries in my registration book. Many a night I was sitting at my bureau (Eliza secured the bureau all right) until after eleven. I wanted to show how very easily a move could be arranged where the master of the house showed intelligence, and some little talent for organization.

We employed Mr Bunn to move us, and I have since regretted it. I should have preferred Crampton and Stubbs. They have the best vans, and move the best people, and all their men have the name of the firm in gold on their caps. But there was really no comparison between the two estimates, and Crampton and Stubbs rather implied to me that, unless it was a ready-money matter, they would not care to undertake it. Mr Bunn, on the other hand, said that half down and the rest in three months would suit him perfectly. I had just paid out for getting Eliza's mother's furniture up from London, and – well, I was hardly free to choose as I should have wished.

Mr Bunn's men were one hour and a half late in starting. I remained to supervise the loading up of the van. Eliza said I was only in the way, but if I had not been there to give them a word of warning, Mr Bunn's men would have damaged valuable property in getting it round the angle of the staircase. Just as they were finishing, I dashed off to 'Meadowsweet', in order to be ready for them on their arrival.

As it happened, I need not have dashed. Mr Bunn's men stopped on the way to mend a broken trace, so they told me. And, if breath is any criterion, they mended it at a public-house.

As soon as I saw the van come into sight, I felt for my registration book, that I might check each piece of furniture on its arrival and tell the men where to put it. It sounds hardly credible, but that registration book was not in my pockets. It was not lost. On the contrary, on thinking it over I knew perfectly well where it was. It was in a drawer of the bureau, where I had left it the night before.

I described the bureau to the foreman, and said that I should like to have that taken out first.

He said that he was sorry, but it was impossible. The bureau was right at the end of the van, behind everything else, and it would be about the last thing they would be able to get at.

That being so, I did the best I could from memory, and it is ridiculous of Eliza to say that I lost my head. What really happened was that, while I was trying to think where one piece of furniture was to go, the men would remove three other pieces and put them just anywhere.

* * *

We had supper in the bathroom that night. It was the only room where there was a clear table, and that table ought never to have been there. However, in about a week's time we were comparatively clear.

'Oof-pa'

I THOUGHT and said, when we moved into 'Meadowsweet', that it would be more in accordance with that class of house if we kept two servants.

'Call it three,' said Eliza. 'Three girls, besides the butler, of course. The chauffeur will have to sleep in the orchard-house, but that can be arranged. Right away. Toot-toot!'

'If you wish to be funny,' I said, 'I simply decline to continue the conversation. All I ask for is one fair cook and one house-parlourmaid.'

'Then, if we have the cook fair, we'd better pick a dark house-parlourer, so that we shan't get 'em mixed. No, you don't. All you'll get is one general, and occasional help if wanted. You're the sort of man that's used to elevenpence, gets a shilling, and wants to spend half a crown on the strength of it.'

We had some further discussion, but I did not press the point. I very rarely interfere in these domestic matters, my mind having rather a wider scope; perhaps it would be better if I took a more active part. With all her merits I should never have engaged Parker. I can lay my hand on my heart and affirm that positively. And I have told Eliza so.

I always call her Parker, and have made a point of doing so. It is the best style, and where no extra expense is involved this should be preferred. Besides, Parker is her actual name; and her first name, Victorine, is quite unsuited to the purposes of domestic service. But if you think I can persuade Eliza to call her Parker, you are much mistaken. Eliza calls her Jane, and speaks of her either as 'the girl', which comes a little too near vulgarity for my taste, or else 'our general', which might create confusion with Lords Kitchener and Roberts, and, in any case, gives away the secrets of the prison-house in an unnecessary manner.

Parker came in on a Friday. Her appearance did not seem to me to be greatly in her favour, being somewhat on the bulky side. She looked melancholy, and was getting on in life. Forty-three, I should say. On Saturday Eliza told me that she was a demon to work, and wasted nothing. This seemed satisfactory so far, but Sunday dinner is always the test that I go by.

We had, I remember, a stewed breast of veal, and peas of our own growing. The cooking was quite satisfactory. At least two of the potatoes I should have been ashamed to offer to a pig, but that was not Parker's fault. Our greengrocer was leaving the neighbourhood, and no longer cared what he sent out. But the waiting at table was not quite up to my level.

'Hand me the peas again, Parker,' I said. 'And another time don't need to be asked.'

To my great surprise, Parker drew a deep breath, and then exhaled it sharply, producing a sound somewhat like 'oof-pa'. Upon my word, I thought at first that it was intended for insolence. But immediately afterwards she handed the peas with every appearance of respect, and even of fear.

When she had gone out of the room I asked Eliza, 'Why does she make that curious sort of "oof-pa" sound?'

'Oh, that's nothing!' said Eliza. 'I asked her about it. She hurt her right knee-cap, and every now and then it gives a twinge. That's what makes her say "oof-pa". It will pass off.'

'I sincerely hope so,' I said, and at once changed the conversation from what I felt to be a delicate topic.

As Parker placed the fruit tart in front of me, I asked her what she was giving us. She said it was apple, 'oof-pa', and cranberry. And so it went on all day, and very unpleasant it was for me.

You see, it is impossible to say 'oof-pa' without seeming to express contempt and disgust. For instance, I called her in to tell her the way I liked her to do my boots in the morning. It is a point I am rather particular about, and so far Parker had not quite satisfied me. It has always been a motto of mine that if you get good boots and treat them properly, it is an economy in the end. 'If,' I said to her, 'you slosh a lot of blacking over the laces just to save time for yourself, you waste time for your employer by making him wash his hands unnecessarily.'

'Yes, sir,' she said. Quite correctly.

And then, just as I was explaining to her that, if she used the blacking brushes for brown boots, she was practically throwing twelve shillings into the gutter, she interrupted me by saying

117

'oof-pa' loudly. And, whether she meant it or whether she did not, it seemed as much as to say that I was making a silly fool of myself, and she had no patience to hear any more of it.

All this was on the Sunday. Monday, at breakfast, there was much less 'oof-pa', and in the evening Eliza said that she thought the worst was over.

On Tuesday that view seemed to be what you might call confirmed. No 'oof-pa' was heard all day, and we were both glad that Parker's knee-cap was all right again.

And on Wednesday it was 'oof-pa' here and 'oof-pa' there, and 'oof-pa' all over the house – worse than ever.

'Eliza,' I said, 'something will have to be done about this. I pay forty pounds for this house, and, in spite of that, here's our servant goes about saying "oof-pa"! The thing's quite out of keeping, and might very easily frighten a visitor.'

'Well,' said Eliza, 'if we ever get a visitor, you can explain how it happens.'

'Pardon me,' I said, 'but I can do nothing of the kind. Parker's knee-cap happens to be one of the things to which no self-respecting man can allude.'

'Anyhow, it's only in the damp weather that she gets these twinges, and we had a lot of rain last night. That's what has done it.'

'That may be,' I said pointedly, 'but what safeguard have we got against rain?'

'Ordinary umbrellas,' said Eliza, foolishly trying to turn it off.

However, that was no use. The thing had got on my nerves, and I stuck to the subject. I told Eliza that, in her place, I should go to the girl and say quite quietly, 'You suffer from a slight infirmity. I do not blame you for it; on the contrary, you have my sympathy. But you must be aware that it constitutes a total disqualification for service in a house of this class.'

'Why, if I talked to her that way, she'd think I'd gone clean off my burner.'

'Head, Eliza – head!'

'Besides, it's almost like giving her notice.'

'It is quite like it,' I said, 'and intended to be like it. It may be better expressed than is usual with —'

'Oh, well,' said Eliza, 'when I give a girl the sack I like her to know what I mean. But I'm not going to sack this one. She's a good worker, and they don't grow on gooseberry bushes.'

'Then there is only one alternative, and upon that I shall insist. A proper medical opinion must be taken, and these twinges, with the accompanying "oof-pa", must be cured.'

Somewhat to my surprise, Eliza did not disagree. I have given my words to the best of my recollection. Eliza says that she is perfectly certain I added 'whatever the expense'.

If I did – and I have the gravest doubts about it – I must naturally have meant, whatever the expense to Parker. Any thoughtful woman would have seen that for herself. But Eliza, in her reckless slap-dash way, sent out for the doctor the very next day. He came twice, and I suppose that sooner or later I shall have to pay him for it. Parker was then sent off to her married sister, rest being what it was alleged she required.

There she lay in bed for eleven days – feeding, I make no doubt, on the fat of the land, doing no work whatever, and being paid by me for it all the time. And I had to pay the occasional help to do Parker's work into the bargain. As I said to Eliza, in that case what are the hospitals for?

It happened at a most unfortunate time, too. It is, I believe, a general experience, shared by highest and lowest alike, that a move into a new house leaves you a bit short. You pay for a tenant's fixtures – about twice what they are worth – and you pay for the van. You pay for mending what the men break, and you tip them for doing it. I don't know what it may be like in other parts of the world, but in our neighbourhood they simply sniff at sixpence apiece. The money just leaks away. It's a new piece of curtains here, and a strip of linoleum there, and the old-oak stain for the dining-room floor, and brass-headed nails used like water. It takes a Rothschild to do that kind of thing without feeling it. And that is most emphatically not the time when you want to pay two servants to do the work of one.

I pointed out these things to Eliza at breakfast on the Saturday that Parker was to return, and Eliza said that she was sick and tired of hearing about it – I may possibly have mentioned the subject once before or at the most three times – and that anyhow the girl was cured and there was an end of it.

When I got back from the City that day I strolled into the garden, and found Parker there cutting cress – which, by the way, had been allowed to go long past its prime. I told her not to give us quite so much stalk with it, and then, in a genial way, added that I was glad she had recovered. In my experience, a kind word to one's inferiors is never thrown away.

'Thank you, sir,' she said. ' "Oof-pa!" "oof-pa!" I am quite well again, and glad to get back to my "oof-pa" work.'

Well, what was I to do? What is any man to do under circumstances like that? Knee-caps are no subject for discussion between a married man and an unmarried woman, and I doubt if there is any gentleman in England who is more careful about what he says in the presence of a woman than I am, but I made no bones about it. An explanation of some kind I was determined to have.

'If your knee is better,' I said, 'why do you keep on saying "oof-pa", as if you were in pain?'

She said that her knee was quite well, and that she had no pain at all. But she had got into the habit of saying 'oof-pa' now, and habit was a thing you could not do away with, and she supposed she would carry it to the grave with her. She then burst into tears and went into the house.

Presently Eliza came out, looking rather worried. She said:

'I don't know what you've been doing to upset that poor girl, but I do wish you wouldn't interfere with her. She talks about leaving at the end of her month, and, after all the money we've spent on her, she wouldn't say that for nothing. If you wouldn't go sticking your oar in, I could manage a deal better.'

I admit that I lost my temper, but there are some provocations that go past the limit. 'Very well, Eliza,' I said, 'from henceforward I shall say nothing to you or to her, or to anybody else about anything.'

I walked straight away from her and into the house. As I passed the scullery window I distinctly heard Parker stop sobbing for a moment to say 'oof-pa'!

I did not carry out my threat in actual practice. As a matter of fact, I had to speak to Parker twice that same night – once to tell her how to pour out a bottle of beer, information which I had given her before, and once to say that she had forgotten to put the chain on the front door as usual.

We had an explanation at breakfast next morning, when Eliza showed herself rather more reasonable, and said she would speak to the girl about it. Parker is still with us, and by dint of much patient work on our part is almost broken of the 'oof-pa' habit. But there is no absolute certainty about it. I am sure that when visitors are present I often feel almost as if I were walking on a volcano.

Flies

I SELDOM let a day pass without taking a glance at our thermometer, though it now means going round by the back to do it. I fixed that thermometer at first outside the front porch, and in a civilized country that would have been the proper place for it. But as the street boys made a cock-shy of it, and the police could or would do nothing, I simply took the law into my own hands and drove in a nail on the shady side of the scullery window. A little more security of property is what I should like to see.

However, be that as it may, neither my reading of the thermometer nor my own personal feelings led me to believe that the weather during the early part of August was specially hot. You might have called it normal, or, perhaps, not even that.

And, in spite of that, the flies at 'Meadowsweet' were absolutely beyond measure. I am sure, one Sunday morning, the way they came buzzing round our bacon was like nothing in my experience. As I fished the third in five minutes out of my teacup, I said to Eliza:

'These flies cannot be allowed to go on. They must be stopped.'

'Well,' said Eliza, 'I don't want 'em. You can stop 'em as far as I'm concerned.'

'Don't be silly, Eliza. We all have our duties to do in this life, and it ought not to be necessary for me to mention everything. What are the facts? In five minutes by that clock I've taken three dead flies out of my tea, and —'

'It'll take you a long time to finish 'em that way.'

'You miss the point, as usual. What I want you to see – in fact, what I want you to grasp – is that if a house of this class is properly managed, an incident of that kind does not happen and cannot happen. Why? Simply because things are looked after. As it is, I suppose I'm either to be eaten alive by flies in a house I pay forty pounds a year for, or I'm to see to it myself. It's the same thing all round. I buy a thermometer and I put that up – who'd look at it if I didn't?'

'Nobody,' said Eliza. 'Nor want.'

'Just what I knew you'd say. You take no intelligent interest in things. With the income we now enjoy I presume that the purchase of a few fly-strings or fly-papers would be nothing out of the way, but instead of that —'

'Hold on. Is it fly-strings you want?'

'What else have I been saying all this time?'

'Never even mentioned 'em. And you needn't make a face as if you'd just sat down on a tin-tack, for —'

'One moment, please. The fact remains that though these flies are amounting to an epidemic, you have never thought about fly-strings, never ordered them, never —'

'Why, I ordered them yesterday. And that's the second time Binns has disappointed me this last week. That boy of his has got a head like a sieve.'

'In that case,' I said, 'the fault lies entirely with Binns. He is not the only grocer in the neighbourhood, and one of these days I may have to give him a sharp lesson. We may now drop the subject.'

Eliza, unfortunately, is not quite so quick to see when a topic is exhausted. In fact, she went on and on.

At midday it seemed to me that the flies were, if possible, worse. We dined on roast beef and flies, with a fly-tart to follow. A bottle of Embridge's light dinner ale (rather a favourite beverage of mine, as it produces no drowsy after-effects) was converted into fly-soup almost as soon as opened. The meal was simply a mockery, and I said so. Afterwards, Eliza thought she would go for a turn, and said that Mrs Bast (who was down with another of her bilious attacks) had asked her to look in.

Under these circumstances I could not with propriety accompany Eliza, but I made no objection to her programme, and said that she would find me in the drawing-room on her return. Mrs Bast lives in quite a small way, but is said to be well connected. I have it from her own lips that her first husband was an officer in the army.

There seemed at first to be far fewer flies in the drawing-room. I congratulated myself that the smell of our furniture polish, which is, perhaps, a little too decided, was keeping them off. It was so very marked that, before stretching myself on the sofa, I opened one of the windows.

And then the invasion began. Flies streamed in through the window. Fourteen crawled in under the door. I should imagine that this last is a very unusual phenomenon, but I saw and counted them myself.

I hit on a happy expedient to protect myself against them. I wrapped my head, hands and ankles in newspaper, securing it with pins where necessary. This rendered me unable to read the book I had brought in with me – Pinching's 'Formation of Character' – but I could pursue my own meditations undisturbed. These periods of quiet thought are not without their value.

I was awakened by a sound of silly giggling, and, removing the newspaper from my face, I was somewhat startled to see Eliza and Miss Sakers. They had met by chance, and Eliza had asked Miss Sakers to step in.

A more annoying contretemps could hardly happen to a gentleman, and, with a little tact on Eliza's part, it might easily have been avoided. But, while determining to speak to Eliza about it afterwards, I showed no sign of irritation at the time. It should be a rule with every gentleman never to display irritation in the presence of a visitor. When Miss Sakers said that this was quite a surprise, I answered smilingly that the surprise was entirely mine.

It was intended as a compliment, and spoken in the tone of voice I generally use for that purpose. Also, as nobody took any notice of it, it probably did not matter. But on thinking it over I doubt if it quite did me justice. I was removing a newspaper from my ankles at the time, and was somewhat flurried, as any man would have been under the circumstances.

Eliza said that I looked like a parcel that had come undone in the post. To change the subject, I began to apologize for the flies, and to explain that the fault really lay with Binns.

When they had stopped laughing – and I think Miss Sakers would have shown better taste if she had stopped rather sooner – they decided to have tea in the garden. And, of course, I could only acquiesce, though I had my own opinions on the subject.

Nobody enjoys a little *al fresco*, as the French say, more than I do, and anybody who thinks that I am a narrow-minded man simply proves that he does not know me; but, all the same, one must have a certain regard for what the neighbours are going to think.

Our garden is overlooked by 'Burnside', and, to a lesser extent, by 'The Nest', and there are people who consider that tea in the garden comes too near a picnic to be suitable for a Sunday afternoon. I was surprised that Miss Sakers, with her vicarage upbringing, should have suggested it. But possibly the flies had something to do with it.

The tea was fairly satisfactory. Eliza would have hardly been mad enough to ask Miss Sakers in, if she had not known that there was a cake in the house. But cress sandwiches would have been a pleasant addition, and I mention them because, with a very little thought, we might have had them. There was the cress actually growing in that very garden at the moment. And for want of just that little thought I suppose cress is to be left till it rots in the ground. It is the kind of thing to make any man angry.

I mentioned it to Eliza afterwards, and all she said was this, 'If you wanted your beastly cress' – I am sorry to say that I give her exact words – 'why couldn't you open your silly mouth and ask for it?' The answer to that is that, with one provocation after another, I simply preferred to let everything go.

I had a few words, too, to say on the subject of tact. What necessity was there for bringing Miss Sakers straight into the drawing-room? It is not, as a rule, three times in a month that I drop off for a few moments on a Sunday afternoon, but Eliza knew that there was just the bare possibility of it. All she had to do was to detain Miss Sakers in the passage for a minute or two, pointing out the illustrated almanac that hangs there, and taking care to raise her voice slightly. Or she might have given a loudish cough. Either would have been certain to wake me, and I should not have been discovered in that ridiculous and humiliating condition.

Of course, Eliza had to defend herself, instead of admitting her fault. She said that they could hear me snoring as soon as they turned the corner of the street, and so it was no good to try to make Miss Sakers believe I was not asleep. Exaggeration of that sort I simply treat with contempt. She also asked how she was to know that I had been dressing myself up in newspaper, like some old Guy Fawkes.

This also was quite beside the mark, and when I attempted to discuss it she said that she had never seen Miss Sakers laugh so much in her life before – as if that mended matters – and if she did not go in to lend a hand the girl would never get out that night. Parker, I may mention, had obtained our permission to attend divine service that evening.

I preferred to remain in the garden. There were certainly fewer flies there, and there seemed to be a chance that I might now be able to snatch a few moments' rest.

When I looked at my watch again it was nearly supper-time. I folded up my garden-chair – these things being ruined in no time if left out – and carried it through with me into the scullery. I had no conception that anything unusual was about to happen. I went calmly in, whistling a hymn-tune as I went.

Eliza said afterwards that, if I had only looked where I was going, it would never have happened. The truth is that if Eliza had only had the sense to tell me that she had borrowed some of those filthy, sticky fly-strings from Mrs Bast, and hung them up in the scullery, I should naturally have kept my eye open for them.

As it was, I ran my face right into one of them, and before I knew where I was I had got a mouthful of dying flies and fish-glue. Naturally, I made a snatch at it with my hand, and then it stuck to my hand. It also stuck to my hair, and wound round my neck. I made an infuriated dash for the sink, and knocked against another of the abominations. One fly-string would have been ample in that small scullery, as I pointed out afterwards.

Eliza heard what I was saying, and came in to see what was the matter. She said that worse language for a Sunday evening she had never heard in her life before. I may certainly have been betrayed into a few hasty expressions, but I know many men who would have said more. I seemed to have got the filthy stuff all over me; I was all gum and buzz. Even with Eliza's assistance it was twenty-five minutes before I was in a condition to sit down to supper. A collar, which was clean on only that morning, had simply to be sacrificed; and it is quite an open question whether benzine will do anything for the stain on the necktie.

It has always been a bit of a problem to me why our inventors and so-called men of science do not devote more attention to improvements in the home, instead of wasting their time on flying-machines and other extraneous matters. Take, for instance, the ordinary 'catch 'em-alive-oh', as vulgar people call it. All that is wanted is some simple substance which will stick to flies, but will not stick to anything else. If I only had the leisure to think that thing out for myself, I am convinced there would be money in it.

A Game of Bowls

ELIZA met me in the passage as I came in.

'I say,' she said, 'has Mr Minting gone mad, or have you?'

I was not surprised. I had quite expected there would be a fuss.

'If,' I said, 'you refer to Mr Minting, of the glass and china shop, he was sane when I saw him this morning and gave him some directions. What is the matter?'

'Oh, well, six sugar-basins were delivered here this morning, and we've got one extra already that we never use. So I told the boy he'd come to the wrong house, and he said it was all right, and your order. I had hoped it was Minting had gone off his head. But if you say it's yourself, I dare say you know best.'

I pointed to the kitchen door, which was ajar, and then placed two fingers on my lips. I may be peculiar, but I do not think servants should be permitted to overhear anything in the nature of a domestic altercation. I dislike it extremely. I beckoned Eliza into the sitting-room.

'Now, Eliza,' I said, 'let this be a lesson to you once for all against hastiness in forming an opinion. Strange though it may seem to you, not one single sugar-basin has been delivered at this house to-day.'

'I suppose I can believe my own eyes, can't I?' said Eliza.

'On this occasion you cannot. What you, rather absurdly, mistook for sugar-basins are, as a matter of fact, finger-bowls. We need them. It surprises me that we have done without them for so long. Suppose we gave a dinner-party, we should look very foolish without finger-bowls.'

But Eliza was in one of her obstinate moods. She said that when we had the Prince of Wales and the Shah of Persia coming to dinner, it would be time enough to think about finger-bowls. Meanwhile, a set of new pie-dishes was what was really wanted in the house, and I had better take those finger-bowls back and change them.

I remained firm.

'Well,' she said, 'I call it stupid, with the expense of the move still hanging round our necks, to go and throw your money away on stuff that we shall never use as long as we live.'

'On the contrary,' I said, 'we shall use them on the dinner-table every night.'

'Well,' said Eliza, 'you've managed to eat your supper without them for a good many years, and I don't see the sense of it.'

'Quite so,' I said. 'In our early days, when we were comparatively low down in the world, it was supper. At present, in this house, for which I am paying no less than forty pounds a year, it is dinner. And other things should be in keeping. Kindly remember that.'

That night finger-bowls did not appear on the dinner-table, and Eliza said she had forgotten them.

'There is such a thing as forgetting on purpose,' I observed sarcastically.

'There couldn't be,' said Eliza. 'Because it you remember to forget a particular thing, you must remember the thing. You can remember on purpose, but you can't forget on purpose.'

'But,' I said, after thinking it over, 'you have just proved the opposite. Because if you would naturally forget something that you decide to remind yourself not to forget, then you are intentionally remembering not to forget something that you would otherwise have forgotten. And, conversely, if you decide not to remind yourself not to forget something that you would have forgotten if you had not been reminded, then you are in the position of —'

'Leave it, leave it,' said Eliza wearily.

'It's all very well to say leave it,' I replied. 'Logic was always a weak point with you, Eliza. The fact is that you have not the intelligence to understand my argument.'

'I can understand most things,' said Eliza, 'as long as you don't try to explain them. That's what sews anybody up.'

I asked Eliza to be a little more careful in her choice of expressions, but I made no further reference to the finger-bowls. However, after dinner I took an opportunity to say a few words to our maid, Parker, on the subject, and she said that she would be sure to remember in future.

Eliza says that whatever else people may say about that girl, at any rate she is thorough. I suppose she is. At any rate, she always makes a point of doing more than you say, and it frequently works out all wrong. For instance, I told her that I must have breakfast sharp at eight, and she sometimes has it ready from ten to twenty minutes earlier than that. Eggs and bacon won't stand it. By the time I come down the food is ruined. The same sort of thing happened with the finger-bowls. I told her as plainly as I could that I wanted her to place a finger-bowl before me after dinner. Next morning, when I came down to breakfast, I found not only a finger-bowl, filled with water of a heat that might have cracked it, but also a towel, and a soap-dish with a new cake of carbolic.

And, of course, if a servant sees that a blunder is treated as a joke, that is simply the beginning of the end. After that, she thinks that she can do what she likes, and that it will simply be passed off with a smile. Eliza behaved most foolishly. I can take a joke if I see a real necessity for it, and I can enjoy it afterwards. But when a servant exceeds orders, and does a foolish thing, that is not a joke. Eliza's mirth was simply misplaced, and I cannot see that she made it any better by saying that it was the way I looked that amused her. A short reprimand, seriously given, is what was wanted.

However, once I set my teeth and make up my mind to carry a thing through, I take some stopping. I had nothing whatever to reproach myself with. I had studied economy. If I had simply followed my own taste, I should have bought the finger-bowls with the gilt rim and the ivy-leaf pattern, and eighteenpence more is what they would have cost. With the material advance in income that we had recently experienced, finger-bowls were by no means out of the way.

I stuck to my point, and I must confess that I met with less opposition than I had expected from Eliza's original attitude towards the question. She said that, if I really wanted the blessed things, of course I could have them, as they weren't worth making a fuss about, but that I had better not buy the solid gold epergne with the diamond trimmings until I had paid off what was owing on the removal.

That was rather unreasonable, as credit had been arranged for and willingly granted. There is a great difference between owing money which you simply must pay now, and owing money which you will pay when the time comes.

But I said nothing at the time, having gained my point, and after this two finger-bowls appeared on the table every evening simply as a matter of course. And that was as it should be. Very nice the table looked – quite a West-End air about it.

As Eliza had met my views in this way, I made a point of consulting her before I purchased a coloured engraving of the King which had caught my eye in a shop window, and would, in my opinion, have made a beautiful picture for the hall. And, as she seemed to feel strongly about it, I left it alone.

This being so, I did not consult her as to my purchase of bulbs in the autumn. However, I kept within limits, buying cheaply at a sale, and she did not appear dissatisfied. On the contrary, she said she hoped the things would grow.

* * *

About two months later she had a note from her brother Frank saying that he had to come to town for a day, and would run down to see us about tea-time.

'Very good,' I said. 'When you write back, you may say that we hope he will do us the honour of remaining to partake of dinner.'

'If I wrote to him like that, he'd laugh. But, I say, I thought you didn't like Frank.'

'If he were not your brother, I should say that he was a bumptious, lying, unprincipled cad. As he is, I prefer not to say or imply anything to his discredit; but to you I may admit that I dislike him extremely.'

'Then why do you ask him to dinner?'

'Precisely because I do dislike him. No, Eliza, it is not ridiculous in the least. When he visited us at our old house he was very sniffy and superior. I should like to show him that the boot is now on the other leg, and that we live quite as well as he does. And better.'

'Well, if it's going to run us into a lot of expense —'

'But it need not do that. We still have one of the two bottles of sherry wine that I received for a Christmas present from my uncle last year. As for the dinner itself, we might begin with a few oysters. You have no objection?'

'Frank never eats them, and I hate them, and they always upset you, and they cost too much. Otherwise they'd do nicely.'

'Well, well, I must think out the question of dinner. Apart from that there is nothing to buy. Our table equipage is perfect. Yes, Eliza, I have never regretted that I bought those finger-bowls, and now I am glad of it.'

Eliza seemed thoughtful. 'Well, yes,' she said. 'Frank could have mine. I was never particularly keen about it.'

'What do you mean? We should have six finger-bowls. I bought six. It was precisely because I had some such crisis in my mind that I did so. If Parker has broken the other four, then Parker —'

'Oh, keep your hair on. Your blessed finger-bowls are all right. It's only that they can't be used just now.'

'And may I ask why?'

'It's your own fault principally. You went and bought that lot of bulbs, and made so much fuss about having hyacinths in the house, and where else was I to plant them? It's not as if the bowls were ever being used.'

'You need say no more. The whole thing is ruined. Do not ask Frank. Never ask anybody to anything. I give up.'

'I knew you'd get nasty about it,' said Eliza.

So Frank was not invited. However, he said when he came that he thought of stopping on and having a snack with us, and there was no getting away from it. We were quite unprepared, chops had to be sent for at the last minute, and a more unpleasant evening I think I never spent. Amongst other things, he asked me why I didn't buy some finger-bowls.

The Recitation

'ELIZA,' I said, 'I want you to look at me.'

She seemed surprised, but she did as I requested.

'Now, then,' I said, 'I want you to pay particular attention to the expression of face which I am about to assume, and tell me frankly what you think it indicates.'

I assumed the expression, and Eliza at once said indigestion.

'Not quite right. It was wistful melancholy. I will now change the expression. Try again, and take a little more time to it.'

She looked at me rather doubtfully.

'Same as the other one?' she suggested.

'Now, Eliza, that is simply thoughtless. I told you distinctly that I was going to change the expression. You must know what the word "change" means. That last one was suppressed rage. Once more now. And this time make an effort to —'

'What's the use? It's only guessing. You see, you don't look like what you think you look like.'

'No,' I said; 'the real trouble is that you don't think I look like

129

what I do. As it happens, I have made a special study of this subject. Here I have a copy of Mrs Bewlay's "Home Reciter". It is a handsome volume, and the man from whom I bought it assured me that it was acknowledged to be the standard authority.'

'Bought it, did you?' said Eliza. 'Oh, well, I suppose every now and then you've got to go out and buy something rotten. Else it wouldn't be you.'

'The book is in no sense rotten. It contains many extracts in prose and verse from the best authors, and Mrs Bewlay says in her preface that she has taken particular care to exclude anything at all bordering on what it shouldn't be. Its hints and directions have been most useful to me. The binding makes it an ornament to any drawing-room. And the two shillings I paid for it is a mere flea-bite. Then look at the illustrations. No less than twenty of them, all taken from actual photographs of the editor's daughter, Miss Agnes Bewlay, herself a talented reciter. Each illustration shows a different expression. All one has to do is to study them with a looking-glass. I spent upwards of twenty minutes on studying three of those expressions – wistful melancholy, suppressed rage, and adoration. And yet when I give you the first two you fail to recognize them. I can't think what's the matter with you.'

'Well,' said Eliza, 'if it comes to that, what's the matter with yourself? What are you doing it for?'

'Simply and solely because I have been asked to give a recitation at a public entertainment.'

Eliza dropped her teacup and broke it – one of the best set, of course – and then said I ought not to go saying things like that suddenly. 'You're joking, of course?'

'I am not joking, and I fail to see any reason why I should joke on such a subject.'

'And what did you say when you refused?'

'Your one idea seems to be to annoy me. I did not refuse. Why should I? More than one man has told me I ought to have gone on the stage. Of course, it's not a thing you'd appreciate. You know nothing about the drama.'

'If you've done it, you've done it,' said Eliza dejectedly. 'All I can do is to see that you do really know the words by heart. The rest we must just leave to Providence. Who asked you, and when is it, and where?'

'It is a smoking concert to be given at the Borstal Rooms, Drury Lane, on Saturday week, at eight p.m. The man who asked me was a clerk in our office of the name of Cobbold. He is getting the thing up, and the proceeds are to go to the widow of an old friend of his. Herbert Benjadale, who lost his life while orchid-hunting in British Guiana.'

'Sounds rum. I thought you'd got Cobbold the sack.'

'He is leaving at the end of the month in consequence of a report which I felt it my duty to make. He would persist in playing the fool in the office, and would not take a warning. The fact is, the man is a born comedian, not fitted for office work at all. I should not be surprised if he went on the halls. That man imitates Mr Bagshawe to the life; he'd make a cat laugh.'

'Does he imitate you, too?'

'Not so well. In fact, that was one of the things I had to speak about. But he bears no malice. He says I only did my duty, and he may live to be thankful to me. He's doing a couple of comic songs himself at this concert. He wants a serious reciter as a contrast, and, looking over the men he knew, with a view to voice and facial expression and so on, he picked upon me. It seems to me all simple enough. The only thing I regret is that I shall not be able to take you with me. You see, it's a smoking concert; only intended for men. I might ask Cobbold to make a special exception.'

'Don't do that,' said Eliza. 'I couldn't go if there were no other women. Besides, Miss Sakers may be coming round that night.'

* * *

The piece selected by me for recitation was 'Incident of the French Camp'. This is a poem by Robert Browning, an author of the highest class; now, unfortunately, dead. This piece is specially recommended by Mrs Bewlay in her admirable work for three reasons; it begins quietly, and then works up; it gives the reciter an opportunity to imitate Napoleon, a great general, though of doubtful morality; it provides a fine dramatic climax.

In fact, the frontispiece is an actual photograph of Miss Agnes Bewlay in this piece, giving her imitation of Napoleon, with the words underneath:

> With neck out-thrust, you fancy how,
> Legs wide, arms locked behind,
> As if to balance the prone brow
> Oppressive with its mind.

A very curious phenomenon of the human memory occurred in connection with this piece. On Monday night I repeated it to Eliza, and had every word perfect. To make assurance doubly sure, I studied it again in the train going to and from the City on Tuesday. On the evening of that day I tried to repeat it again, and the only line I got right was the last one, 'Smiling the boy fell dead'. Some scientific gentleman may like to give an explanation of this. Cobbold said definitely that every great actor had suffered from it at one time or another.

I had some difference of opinion with Eliza as to this last line. It was a question of facial expression.

She said, 'Why do you grin when you say the last line?'

'Because it says, as distinctly as words can speak, "Smiling the boy fell dead". I do it on purpose. It's a sort of illustration. I smile because the boy smiled.'

'Then I suppose you'll fall dead too, because that's what the boy did?'

'Enough of that,' I said. 'If you merely wish to play the fool I will take it into the garden and study it there.'

'I won't say anything else,' said Eliza. 'But don't go and do it in the garden. We are so overlooked.'

She seemed oblivious of the fact that recitations are practically made to be overlooked.

I do not know if other reciters have noticed it, but there is one line in this poem which is specially catchy. It is, 'To see your flag-bird flap his vans'. You want to watch yourself over that line. Once you've made the mistake of saying, 'To see your flap-bird flag his vans', you go on doing it, and it gives you hard work to break yourself of it.

Cobbold told me that the chair would be taken by a Mr Parkhurst, who had a large place in the Isle of Wight, and that full evening dress would be worn by performers, but not by the audience. This being so, I purchased very inexpensively a ready-made white waistcoat. I had to give Eliza to understand that one point on which I would not permit any interference whatever was my wardrobe.

I dressed very early on Saturday, that giving me time to go through the words of the recitation once more before taking the train. In the train I tested my memory and found everything satisfactory, except that I said flap-bird by mistake. As it was a fine night, and I had plenty of time, I walked from the station to Drury Lane. Cobbold had told me that I should easily find the Borstal Rooms, as there would be bills outside announcing the concert. However, I walked all the way down Drury Lane without seeing anything of the kind.

I said to a policeman: 'Could you kindly inform me where the Borstal Rooms are?'

He shook his head, and smiled in a kindly way. 'Don't know of any place of that name, sir – not nearer than Rochester.'

I took it that he was newly up from the country, and

addressed myself next to an old man who was leaning against the wall of a public-house. He was a disreputable-looking old man, and for some reason my innocent question made him very angry.

'Jest you say that agen,' he said – 'jest once more, and you'll get the front of your ugly fice punched in! I ain't goin' ter be insulted by no cock-eyed restyrong waiter like you. Clear art of it!'

It was now past eight, and there was no more time to lose. I took a cab, and even the cabman didn't know where the place was. There was nothing else that I could do. I went home, and I can tell you I was pretty furious.

* * *

Eliza said that the whole thing was a sell, got up by Cobbold to pay me out for reporting him, and she had had her suspicions of it all along. 'However,' she said, 'you can take it out of him on Monday.'

The difficulty about that was that Saturday had been his last day at the office. And on Monday I got a letter from him which was as civil as could be. It said: 'So sorry that you were unable to be with us at the Dartmoor Assembly Hall, Piccadilly, on Saturday night. I presume that the cause was some indisposition, and I hope it may prove but trifling. You were much missed. Mr Parkhurst had hoped to ask you down to his place at the Isle of Wight.'

I am perfectly certain that the address he gives in that letter is not the address he gave me before. But there may have been a mistake somewhere. Perhaps they were unable to get the Borstal Rooms, and he forgot to tell me.

Eliza points out that Borstal is the name of a penal settlement near Rochester, and that Parkhurst is the name of another in the Isle of Wight, and that Dartmoor speaks for itself. Very likely. But these coincidences do happen; we see them every day.

It has a queer look, too, that there is no such place as the Dartmoor Assembly Hall in Piccadilly. But that may be only carelessness.

The one thing I cannot explain is why all the clerks burst out laughing when I walked into the office on Monday morning; and, if Cobbold had only given me his address, I should certainly write and inquire.

* * *

But of one thing I am quite certain. I am not the kind of man that puts his hand to the plough and then throws up the

133

sponge. I have spent time and money on that recitation, and I mean to recite it. And if Eliza won't lead up to it one afternoon when Miss Sakers is here, I shall lead up to it myself. And if they don't like it they can lump it.

The Tyrolese Exercises

MY grey flannel trousers had been put away for the winter with some of Pigley's Patent Preservative. This is sold in penny packets; and so little is needed that one packet might very well last a man a life-time. Quite a small pinch of it will not only keep moth away, but will destroy any moth that already happens to be there. Eliza, who is quite enthusiastic about it, says that it would suffocate an elephant. The only real trouble about it is that the smell does undoubtedly cling. My system, with clothes that have been put away with the preservative, is to hang them on a line in the garden for twenty-four hours. This removes the worst of the smell, and the rest passes off slowly in use. In about a week or ten days it becomes hardly noticeable. It is a case where tact helps, as it does in so many things in life. For instance, Miss Sakers surprised us once by a call when the suit I was wearing still carried a considerable reminder of the patent preservative. I simply turned to Eliza and said carelessly: 'My dear, I am afraid the plumber has not made quite a success of that gas-leak.' Of course, Eliza had to mess the whole thing up by saying that we had not got any gas-leak, and she didn't know what I was talking about. But otherwise it would have passed off very nicely.

However, it was about those grey flannel trousers that I wished to speak. They had been made to my order by a fair-price tailor two years before, and were still distinctly good. They had been worn only on my annual holidays, and occasionally on a fine Saturday afternoon. Light flannel trousers on a Sunday are things I have always set my face against, whatever the opinion of the majority may be. This spring I had given them twenty-four hours on a clothes-line in the garden – naturally in a secluded spot where they could not possibly be overlooked – and, Saturday afternoon being fine and sunny, I took them up to my room to put on. And a very sharp disappointment I got.

I joined Eliza in the garden. 'Hullo,' she said, 'I thought you were going to put on those grey flannel trousers?'

'That had been my intention,' I said. 'However, I find that my express orders have been disregarded. Those trousers have been washed. Washed, mark you. And, as was inevitable, they have shrunk. It is impossible to make them meet at the waist without causing me great physical discomfort. There's twelve-and-six thrown on the dust-heap, sacrificed to your obstinacy. Why couldn't they have been dry-cleaned at home by our own simple process, as I directed?'

'They were,' said Eliza.

'Not washed?'

'No.'

'But could a chemical preservative in the form of a dry powder cause material to shrink?'

'No,' said Eliza, 'but a man getting fatter might cause his clothes to get too tight for him.'

I must admit that the idea had already crossed my mind once or twice, but I had shut my eyes to it. I was now very seriously disturbed. I went to the station and weighed myself on one of those penny-in-the-slot machines. I have been told that these are often inaccurate, and I could only hope that this was the case now.

I talked it over with Eliza on my return from the station, and she said that, of course, the only thing for it was more exercise. So I mowed the lawn twice and rolled the paths. And what was the result? At dinner I had an appetite that it was hopeless to fight against. The thing is what is called, I believe, a vicious circle.

On Sunday, Eliza, finding me slightly depressed, said that, as a rule, men did not get any thinner as they got older, and there was no use in getting snappy about it. If I really wanted to deal with it, a good twenty-mile walk was what she would —

'Thank you,' I said. 'I am not snappy. Far from it. Nothing of the kind. But I had some of your advice yesterday, and what did it lead to? The matter may not be of the first importance, but I propose to take it in hand myself and deal with it scientifically.'

'As how?' she asked doubtfully.

'As I say. You will see to-morrow.'

I felt sure that there must be some literature dealing with the subject, and on the following day in the City I made inquiries, during the luncheon hour, at three bookshops, explaining that I was doing it on behalf of a friend who was rather sensitive in the matter. Finally, I purchased a copy of Mossop's 'Tyrolese Exercises', with Chart. Considering the size of the book, the price (five shillings net) seemed to me a bit stiff. But there were numerous illustrations of Mr and Mrs Mossop engaged in the

Tyrolese exercises, and the price of these scientific works always runs high. I should be very sorry to see Eliza photographed in the costume that Mrs Mossop was represented as wearing, of which I will only say that it omitted much which should have been present. But perhaps I am specially particular.

The idea of Mr Mossop's system is both admirable and simple. Noticing that in nations where much climbing was done obesity was of rare occurrence, Mr Mossop devised a series of exercises, calling into play exactly the same muscles that would be required in, say, an ascent of the Matterhorn. The regular use of these exercises for the absurdly short period of fifteen minutes per diem is practically guaranteed to prevent any undesirable frontal extension, and ultimately produces a harmonious development of the entire frame.

I showed the book to Eliza. 'Here,' I said, 'is not only the means of dealing scientifically with my little trouble —'

'Your little what?' said Eliza.

'Not only the means of dealing scientifically with my little trouble,' I repeated firmly, 'but also another interesting addition to our library.'

She happened to open it at the picture which represents Mrs Mossop doing the back-stretch in the third position, which was not the one I should have selected. She sniffed.

'I shouldn't leave this book lying about,' she said.

'Well,' I said, 'of course, for the purpose of gymnastic exercises anything like constriction of clothing is to be avoided. That is well known.'

'Very likely. All the same, Parker has been strictly brought up, and I don't want her to give us notice just as she's getting into our ways.'

She went on turning over the pages, and seemed to get more and more despondent. 'I hope you understand the way these things go,' she said. 'They'd fairly flummox me. Here's a picture of a man with twelve arms in convict's dress.'

'Nothing of the kind,' I said. 'The man is not a convict. Those arrows are simply intended to show the direction in which the arms are to be moved. And the man has not got twelve arms. He has only two, and the others are put in with dotted lines to show the different positions in which they go in the course of the exercise. I have studied that one particularly. You begin like this. See.'

I gave her a demonstration, and if the vase had not been put on the very edge of the mantelpiece it would never have been knocked off. I said that I hoped this would be a lesson to Parker to use her brains when dusting. Incidentally, too, this demonstration proved the truth of what Mr Mossop says as to constriction of the clothing. Eliza had two buttons to sew on for me, but why she should have been so upset about it is more than I can imagine.

Thoroughness has always been rather a motto of mine. Mr Mossop, in the book, only demands fifteen minutes a day for the Tyrolese exercises, but I gave thirty – fifteen before breakfast and fifteen on going to bed. And once one had realized the necessity for a clear space and properly adjusted clothing, no further damage was done. I also cut down (considerably) my consumption of Embridge's light dinner ale. I may add that it had never been in any way excessive.

At the end of the week I felt that I had derived so much benefit that I might safely appeal once more to the verdict of the weighing machine on the station platform. I did so, and it registered an increase in weight of five stone eleven pounds, and then returned my penny. It was so obvious that the thing had got completely out of order that I thought it my duty to mention it to the station-master. He said that boys would get tampering with those machines, and if I liked to leave the penny with him he would hand it to the collector when he next came round. He seemed to have missed my point absolutely, and so I told him.

After that I lost all feeling of confidence in public weighing machines, and decided to expend no more money on them. But I continued to persevere with the Tyrolese exercises. I could now do them all without reference to the chart, and I told Eliza that if she cared to invite a few friends I might be persuaded to give a demonstration which would be interesting to them. I thought she seemed rather to fall in with the idea at the time. Her one objection was that the harmonious development of the entire frame had better be carried a little further first. However, in the end nothing came of it.

After I had continued with the exercises for about a fortnight it occurred to me that, after all, there was a very simple test that I might make to show the effect of the Tyrolese exercises. I went upstairs and once more tried on my grey flannel trousers. If I had found them an inch short round the waist I should have been amply satisfied. It would have shown that progress had been made. But to my surprise and delight I found that those trousers were now, if anything, too large. I could have done Tyrolese exercises in them without the slightest risk.

Eliza was in the garden, and I hurried out to her.

'Eliza,' I said, 'I will ask you to observe what I am wearing. A fortnight ago they were too small round the waist by three inches. To-day I wear them with comfort. I know it is not what you have expected —'

'Yes, it is,' Eliza interrupted.

'I think not,' I said, with a smile. 'You were prejudiced against Mr Mossop. You never believed in the Tyrolese exercises. You showed it in several little ways. And now you see that you were wrong and I was right. This is a triumph for Mr Mossop's system. This is what comes of dealing with a thing scientifically.'

'Funny,' said Eliza. 'I knew I'd made a pretty neat job of it, but I thought you'd have noticed it, all the same.'

'Noticed what? I don't know what you're talking about.'

'About the piece I let into the back of those trousers. You can't say that I don't look after your clothes properly now, can you?'

'Perhaps I can't. But you ought to have told me. I don't like things to be done behind my back.'

'Well,' said Eliza, 'it was just there where it was wanted.'

* * *

I have by no means lost faith in the Tyrolese exercises, and I am going on with them. But in future I shall use a tape-measure. Nobody will let a piece into the back of that.

The Circle Club

ON Eliza's birthday I presented her with a plated sauce-boat and six (best quality) handkerchiefs, and, in spite of her playful accusation of extravagance, I could see that she was pleased. That is how I fix the date of my invitation to become a member of the Circle Club. It was on the morning after Eliza's birthday at breakfast-time that I received a prospectus of the club and a letter from the secretary. The latter was written on the club notepaper and at the request of the committee. I admit I was gratified.

The possibility that I might one day become a member of a London club had already occurred to me. I had, in fact, mentioned it to Eliza as one of the things which might naturally be expected to follow on our advance in position and income. (She at that time seemed rather to pooh-pooh it.) But in the matter of modesty I am, perhaps, inclined to overdo it. I had never expected to be singled out by a West End club for a special invitation. Such, however, was the case. And the terms used were most flattering. I may say frankly that I was pleased.

The printed prospectus informed me that the club had been established for the benefit of gentlemen who, while resident in the more fashionable suburbs, were in the habit of coming to town frequently for the purpose of pleasure or business. 'Such,' said the prospectus, 'will find in the Circle Club a *pied-à-terre* of the most *recherché* description. The support of many noblemen and gentlemen of the highest position has already been secured, and it is confidently expected that the Circle Club will speedily take rank with the most exclusive and desirable of those historical associations for which London is so justly celebrated. The cellar and cuisine are of the finest class.'

There were illustrations of two of the rooms showing palms, electric lights, and furniture on a most lavish scale. The entrance fee was to be ten guineas and the annual subscription five.

This last item would, I admit, have definitely put me off. One may be ambitious, but one does not throw large sums of money about like that. However, the secretary's letter put quite a different complexion upon it. It ran as follows:

'DEAR SIR, – In consequence of the great success which has attended the inauguration of the Circle Club, particulars of which are enclosed, an enlargement of the premises has been proposed. In view of this, the committee have decided to elect a few additional members. A selection has been made of the names of certain gentlemen of acknowledged character and position to whom this offer may be made, and I have very much pleasure in acquainting you that your name is upon the list. Should you accept membership, the usual entrance fee of ten guineas will be waived in your case, the annual subscription will be reduced to two and a half guineas, and you will be entitled to rank as a foundation member with the associated privileges. You will incur no further liability of any kind.'

A very nice letter and very well expressed, in my opinion. Happening to find myself in the same carriage as Mr Bunt on my way to the City that morning, I thought I would have a word with him about it. He is a man that knows the world, a chartered accountant, and, so far as mere money is concerned, my superior, I suppose. His wife drives her own pony, and he employs a regular gardener, and is rather inclined to treat everybody with contempt.

We are not exactly on social terms, nor even after my recent advance up the social ladder should I quite have expected it. Still, we speak when we meet in the train, though he always gives me the impression of not saying a word more than he can possibly help. I was not sorry to let him know of this rather flattering offer that I had received.

'Good morning, Mr Bunt,' I said. 'I wonder if you would spare me a word of advice. I've just had a communication, requiring an answer, from the secretary of the Circle Club, and —'

'So did I,' grunted Mr Bunt. 'No answer. Burn it. Bogus. Swindle.'

'You don't think —'

'No,' snapped Mr Bunt, and built up a newspaper like a stone wall between us.

I made some further observation on the subject, but he did not appear to have heard it.

It seemed to me a coincidence that Mr Bunt had also received an invitation. But it was a shock and a surprise when I found that another had been sent to Mr Avis of 'Birdmore'.

You have only to look at the facts. 'Birdmore' is a £30 house, and Avis, on his own admission, has already had the gas cut off once. His father was a french polisher who committed suicide, his wife's father failed in the greengrocery, and he never pays his rates until he gets the summons.

There is nothing of the snob about me, and I am affable enough with Avis when we happen to meet. Still, if Avis is to be described as a gentleman of acknowledged character and position, then words seem to me to have lost their meaning. Avis himself thought it must be a mistake. I put it down to a confusion of two similar names, myself.

At the office I had some talk with young Gillivant, who can generally be depended upon for good up-to-date information on social subjects. He is placed with us merely in order to learn business, his father being in reality a Justice of the Peace, and (I am informed) a man of great wealth. He keeps his son rather short, but that, perhaps, may be wisdom. Young Gillivant keeps in touch with the fashionable world. You would never guess it to look at him, but he goes into titled Society.

Gillivant distinctly advised me to join the Circle Club. He said that it was a new club, and every new club was a bit of a try-on, but not necessarily bogus. He said that if I passed the chance, and tried for one of the old-established clubs, I might have to wait for some time, and even then it might end in disappointment.

He told me things about one of them, the Athenæum, which quite surprised me. It may be all he says, but fancy an entrance fee of forty-two pounds! I should want some very satisfactory references from them before I even consented to think about it.

Gillivant gave me several hints on club etiquette and was most useful. Being a member of the National Liberal Club himself, he was in a position to speak with some authority. He certainly left me with the impression that a club was an essential, and that in my case it would probably be the Circle Club or none.

In the eye of the imagination I could already see 'Circle Club' engraved on the lower right-hand corner of my visiting card – Gillivant had told me about that. But I quite expected a considerable argument with Eliza. To my surprise, she now seemed in favour of it. Of course, she may have been influenced by my generosity (already mentioned) on the previous day. But the reason she gave was different:

'The money seems rather a lot,' she said, 'but, after all, it works out about a bob a week. And if it mixes you up with men a bit, it may do you good. You see, you don't do any of the things that other men do, and you don't seem to know any of the things that they know.'

'Perhaps, on the other hand,' I said, 'I know some things that they do not.'

'Of course,' she said. 'And it's been getting worse lately. Only the other day you were showing that girl the right way to clean knives, and that's not a thing I like to see. I don't say you should take to drink and gambling, but you might keep out of the kitchen and act more like an ordinary man.'

Well, I am not an ordinary man. I admit it. And I am far from being ashamed of it.

However, that settled the question. I sent my subscription, and received a few pleasant words of congratulation on my election from the secretary, together with a copy of the rules and a formal receipt.

* * *

Looking back at it now, I am inclined to think that Mr Bunt was right.

On the Saturday after my election I said to Eliza: 'I may be later than usual this afternoon. I shall probably look in at the club for a cup of tea and a glance at the magazines.'

'Do, dear,' said Eliza.

I did. The club was in Greenchurch Steet, and I found that Greenchurch Street was in Soho, which was not what I had hoped. It was a small street, too. After a time I found the Circle Club. It consisted of a number of rooms over Anginello's Restaurant, and you went upstairs to it. I do not know why I had expected an entrance-hall on the ground floor, paved with squares of black and white marble, but that had been my idea.

At the top of the stairs there was a small glass cupboard with a man in livery asleep in it. I woke him up, and (as directed by Gillivant) told him that I was a new member and gave him my name.

Though awake, he remained very meditative. After a time he said 'Yessir,' and closed his eyes again.

'And is the secretary, Mr Arbuthnot, in?'

He seemed to be thinking this over for a while. Then he opened his eyes again. 'Can't say as to that, sir; but Mr Johnson's in the library.'

'Well,' I said, 'perhaps you would come round with me yourself and point out the principal rooms.'

He shook his head. 'Not allowed to leave this box, sir. But you can't make any mistake. And Mr Johnson's in the library.'

The man seemed to me stupid. However, I left my hat and umbrella in the hall, and began my explorations. I found three rooms with their names painted on the doors. On the billiard-room door a notice was pinned, saying that it was closed during redecoration. The dining-room did not interest me for the moment, and I opened the card-room door a few inches and peered in. I just got a glimpse of four men seated at a table, and then a deep voice roared out: 'Shut that door!'

If I had not been taken by surprise, I should have asked the speaker who the devil he thought he was talking to. As it was, I just shut the door, leaving myself in the passage.

On the floor above I found two other rooms. One was marked 'Secretary's Room. No Admittance.' The other was the library. So I chose the library, and went in.

This, clearly, was one of the rooms illustrated in the prospectus. I recognized it by the tassels on the curtains. But it had looked much larger in the picture, and had contained many fine palms. I could only find one palm now; it was small, and it was not genuine. The furniture was rich, but dirty. There were finger-marks on the newspapers, and crumbs on the carpet, and cigar-ash everywhere.

At the writing-table a fat man in a frock coat sat, with a pile of letters before him. He seemed to be writing answers to them, and was swearing under his breath all the time. As there was no one else in the room, I gathered that this was Mr Johnson. I rang the bell for my tea, picked up a magazine at random, and took a chair which was comfortable but dusty.

I then found that I had inadvertently selected a copy of *The Osmic Inhaler: What it is and what it does.* As I had not come there to read advertisements, I got up, and this time was careful to choose a real magazine. I also rang the bell again.

A few minutes later I rang it a third time. The man at the table now said, 'Damn' out loud, went to the door, and shouted 'Frederick!' I recognized Frederick when he came in as the servant I had seen in the glass cupboard; I now noticed how much too big his livery was for him. He seemed afraid of Mr Johnson, who told him sternly to take my order.

The tea was nearly cold, and twopence more than it should have been, but otherwise satisfactory. What was curious was that on the cup and saucer the words 'Anginello's Restaurant' were imprinted. While I was drinking the tea, Mr Johnson said that if I cared for a game of piquet he could spare half an hour. I explained politely that I did not know the game. He then said that the club billiard-room was shut, but there was a table over the way if I liked to give him a beating. To this I returned a similar answer.

'Is there any game you do play?' he asked.

'Draughts occasionally,' I said. 'But far too much time, in my opinion, is wasted on —'

'Well,' he interrupted, 'we've got no draughts, and the spellicans are worn out. So I think I'll be off.'

'Before you go,' I said, 'you must permit me to thank you for interfering on my behalf just now. The waiting here is surely very bad, isn't it?'

'Beastly,' he said. 'I'm the proprietor.'

* * *

I do not know whether it was the proprietor, or Frederick, or one of the card-players who stole my umbrella, but it was stolen. A few days later I received a curt notice that the club would be closed for a month for the annual cleaning. It certainly looked as if it wanted it, though Gillivant says that it is unusual to close a club in the middle of the season. At the end of the month I got another notice that, owing to want of support from the members, the proprietor of the Circle Club had been compelled to discontinue it. And I was referred to Rule 67. This was to the effect that no annual subscription or part of an annual subscription was under any circumstances recoverable from the proprietor.

I very nearly consulted a solicitor about it, but there is such a thing as throwing good money after bad. Eliza was to blame for her advice, but I have said very little to her about it. However, I have fifty visiting cards, with the name of my club engraved in one corner, and I intend to use them. It will be something saved out of the wreck.

The Aquapen

I THINK I have mentioned that young Gillivant, who is learning business with our firm, receives an allowance which is hardly proportionate to his father's wealth. As he is not free from an occasional burst of extravagance, he sometimes finds himself pressed for ridiculously small sums of ready money.

The other day he produced a gold-mounted fountain-pen from his pocket. 'Look at that,' he said to me bitterly. 'Present from my Aunt Elizabeth. It's a new dodge, called the Aquapen. Like an ordinary fountain-pen, except that you fill it with water, and it comes out ink. Got chemicals of sorts in its inwards, I reckon. Well, that cost twenty-five bob. It's worth twelve, and I can't find a son of Attenborough in London who'll give me more than two bob for it. I'm not asking them to lend. If they'd give me three-and-six for it, I'd let them keep it. I've never used the thing, and never shall. And me without a cent until to-morrow morning!'

I examined it carefully, and glanced through the directions which were in the box with it. They seemed simple enough as long as you followed the diagram carefully and did not confuse the different parts. It was obviously a high-class article.

'Well, Mr Gillivant,' I said, 'I very rarely do anything of this kind, but, if you really do wish to dispose of this pen for three-and-sixpence, I am prepared to —'

'Say no more,' said Gillivant. 'It's yours, and I see my way clear to lunch. Fancy lunching on Aunt Elizabeth's fountain-pen! Golly, what a life!'

I had rather a triumph over Eliza with my Aquapen on my return home. 'I have often required a fountain-pen for business purposes, and to-day I have purchased one,' I said. 'How much do you think?'

'Might be worth five shillings,' said Eliza.

'The price new – and this pen is practically new – is twenty-five. But I can generally see an opportunity when one comes in my way, and I bought it for three-and-six. It is an absolute novelty, known as the Aquapen. You fill it with water, and the water is immediately converted into ink.'

'Will it work?' said Eliza doubtfully.

'I have no doubt that it will. At the back of the printed directions are various testimonials (one of them from a bishop) to the effect that it works perfectly. However, we will put it to a practical test.'

Eliza brought me a glass of water, but I said that I would just run through the directions again before filling the thing. They were a shade more complicated than they had seemed at first. There were fourteen different things you had to do in filling the Aquapen and getting it ready for work, and you had to do them all in the right order. There was also a list of ten special warnings against things which you might not do unless you wished to ruin the pen altogether, and they were nearly all of them things that you would naturally have done if you had not been warned. It was a very nervous business.

After about half an hour, Eliza said rather nastily that she hoped I would wake her when I was ready to start.

'I am ready to start now. This is not a toy, but a highly scientific patent, and one has to be quite certain that one gets it right the first time one tries it. After that it can be done in a moment. Now, then, if you will read out the directions one by one, I will carry them out with the pen.'

Eliza took the paper and read:

'Unscrew cap A.'

'Good!' I said. 'I have got that done. What next?'

'Depress perforated plate B on spiral spring C round tube D E until orifice F is exposed to view, taking care not to confuse this with orifice G, which is to be found on the —'

'One moment, Eliza. You are going too fast. First let me depress perforated plate B on spiral spring C.'

After a few minutes, Eliza said:

'Well, you must have done that now.'

'There's no must about it. I have not done it. And the reason is that I cannot find perforated plate B. I thought at first that this was it, but I can see that it is not.'

'Let me have a look,' said Eliza, and bent over me. 'How would it be,' she suggested, 'if I took a hair-pin and progged up that loose bit in —'

'Ruin the whole thing. I must think this out for myself.'

But, funnily enough, it was Eliza who discovered what was wrong. I had unscrewed the wrong cap at the other end of the pen – cap Q instead of cap A. After that everything went swimmingly. It was an anxious moment after I had squirted the water into it, for there was always the possibility that some mistake had been made. But as soon as I tried to write with it I was reassured. I have never in my life had a pen that wrote better; the ink was certainly pale, but still it was, beyond any possibility of doubt, ink.

As I handed it to Eliza to try, I observed that there seemed to be practically no limit to the marvels of modern science.

'Well,' she said, 'it took you two hours to get this thing

started, and you could have got an ordinary pen and ink going in two seconds. Don't see where the catch comes in, myself.'

'It took two hours only because I was new to it. It will not take ten minutes next time. Suppose I were in some place where I could get water but no ink, how useful this would be!'

'There isn't a village in England where you can't buy better ink for a penny than ever this silly old machine will make. Never mind. You can take it to the North Pole with you next time you go.'

As it happened, Eliza was quite wrong. I tried it after breakfast next morning, and the ink was already much darker. The oscillation in the train did it good, and within eleven hours of filling, the ink in that Aquapen could hardly have been distinguished from ink except by an expert.

I showed it to several men that day, and they all agreed that it was one of the most ingenious things they had seen. Young Gillivant said that if he had money to spare he did not know that he wouldn't think about offering to buy it back.

That was the only happy day I ever had with that Aquapen.

A week later I said to Gillivant, 'Look here, I've given that Aquapen of yours a pretty extended trial, and I find it is not as you represented it. I think, in common honesty, you ought to take it back.'

'What's the matter? Won't it work?'

'It did the first day. On the second day I lent it to Mr Bagshawe to sign the wages cheque, and – well, he was very angry about it – told me never to bring the infernal thing into his office again. I've overhauled it and refilled it, and for the last three days it has refused to make any mark of any kind. I bought it as a pen, and it is not a pen.'

'You must have done something rotten with it. Bet I'll spot what it is. Give me hold of it.'

I gave it him, and he tried to sign his name with it. It was precisely as I said – it refused to mark.

'Ah!' said Gillivant, 'I expect one wants to press a little harder –'

'On no account,' I said. 'That's what Mr Bagshawe did, and –'

But I was too late. The Aquapen simply streamed ink at him. I offered him a recipe which I had found useful myself for removing ink stains from linen, but the way in which it was received did not encourage me to resume the negotiations at that moment.

On the following morning, however, I said that he had seen for himself that the Aquapen was a complete failure, and I should like to know what he felt he ought to do about it.

'Well,' he said, 'you don't deserve it for ever letting me touch a dangerous thing like that, but I'll give you the straight tip. The most you could get out of me would be three-and-six, if I had it, which is not the case now. Take it to the makers in Holborn, and they're bound to give you a new pen or the cash price.'

I did not think that the makers were bound, but I thought it quite worth while to try it. I entered their shop with the air of a man who means to stand no nonsense, and showed an assistant the pen. 'Cost twenty-five shillings a few weeks ago, and is not worth twenty-five pence. What's the good of a pen that won't write? I call it an absolute —'

'Permit me,' interrupted the young man, taking the pen from my hand. He had smooth black hair, parted in the middle, and the air of a very patient nurse dealing with a fractious and partially imbecile child.

'Mind you,' I said, 'either I must have a new pen or my money back.'

'Twenty-five shillings?'

'Yes, that's what I said.'

As far as I could see, all that young man did was to unscrew one of the caps and then screw it on again. Then he drew a sheet of paper to him, and wrote a few lines. There was no reluctance in starting and no excessive flow of ink. It could not possibly have gone better.

'I don't think I understand, sir,' he said. 'What is it you are complaining about? The pen is in perfect order. Try it for yourself.'

I tried it. 'Seems all right now,' I had to admit. 'But it has given me a deal of trouble. If you press hard on the nib it —'

'Of course. But you are specially warned on the paper of directions not to press hard, and are told what will happen if you do. If you don't mind, I'll take the name and address of the retailer who charged you twenty-five shillings for this. It is our fifteen-shilling quality, and we do not allow it to be sold for more or less than that.'

'Well, strictly speaking, I did not buy it from a dealer. I got it from a friend of mine for three-and-sixpence, but twenty-five shillings was what he said his aunt paid for it.'

'Will there be anything else this morning?' said the young man.

He said it very patiently, but to my mind he was most offensive. What he ought to have said was that he quite understood how the mistake occurred. By omitting that, he practically called me a liar and a swindler. And what he did actually say was only another way of asking me to get out of the shop.

I said, 'Nothing more, thank you. Good morning.'

He never even answered me. I was much upset – angry, in fact. I did not see young Gillivant again that day, or he would have had the rough side of my tongue.

For two days the Aquapen worked as well as anybody could have wished, but my old confidence in it was entirely sapped. It always came as a surprise to me when I found that it really did write. One morning I had the happy idea that now was the time to sell it, either to Gillivant (who had explained to me that he must have mistaken the price pencilled on the bottom of the box) or to some other man in our office. If I waited till it struck work again, I might never get my money back on it at all. So when I started for my train I slipped my Aquapen into my pocket.

I should have hardly thought it possible that so small a thing could have held as much ink as it disgorged into my pocket on the way. The articles totally ruined or seriously injured by it were:

1 coat.

1 waistcoat.

1 shirt.

1 under-garment.

1 pair of Berkeley braces – the special Aquapen ink acting as a solvent of rubber.

1 handkerchief.

1 cigarette case of (imitation) lizard skin.

3 'Pride of the Harem' Turkish cigarettes.

4 halfpenny stamps.

When I discovered the disaster, I must have slightly lost my head. I took that Aquapen and hurled it out of the carriage window. For a few seconds it gave me a kind of savage satisfaction that I had got rid of the thing. But afterwards I reflected that the three-and-sixpence was now lost irretrievably.

At the office Gillivant came up to me, looking slightly worried. 'I say,' he said, 'I'll give you three-and-six for that old Aquapen.'

'I cannot do it,' I said coldly.

'Well, five bob, then. My Aunt Elizabeth's coming to see me – worse luck – and she's certain —'

'I repeat, I cannot do it.'

'Seven bob is my last, final offer, and you ought to take it. You know the pen's no good.'

'I do,' I said. 'And because I knew it was rubbish I threw it away. It is no longer in my possession.'

'Golly!' said young Gillivant 'I'm afraid I'll have to buy a new one, for the old girl's bound to ask about it. Fifteen shillings! I could do better with the money.'

'I can't pretend I'm sorry,' I said. 'You sold me a defective pen which has caused me much worry and actual financial loss. Now you have to pay fifteen shillings. This will be a lesson to you.'

'Hold on,' said Gillivant. 'I've got it. I'll tell her I've lent the pen to you. Oh, yes, that'll be all right.'

'Then,' I said, 'you will be making a most unwarrantable use of my name.'

But this did not appear to affect him.

Psychic Investigations

'ELIZA,' I said one evening, 'I do not say it at all by way of blame, but do you think that we two pay sufficient attention to developing the psychic side of our nature?'

'I've got about enough to do developing your psychic socks,' said Eliza. 'How you come to go through them as you do I can't think, unless you've got nails sticking up through the soles of your boots.'

'Had that been so, it would have caused me extreme pain, and I could hardly have failed to notice it. I admit that these repairs, necessary unfortunately, make some demands upon your time, but the psychic side of our nature is far more important.'

'Well, you never used to worry about it. Where did you hear about it? What is it?'

'It is – there is no way of putting it in a few words. Of course, I had known something of it before, but I heard more from a gentleman whom I happened to get into conversation with that day I lunched at the vegetarian restaurant. You remember?'

'Yes, I remember. You asked to have dinner put half an hour earlier. And what did he say?'

'He said that I might possibly have great psychic gifts lying hidden for want of cultivation. I might be a hypnotist, or clairvoyant, or medium, or automatic writer, and never know it for want of psychical development.'

'But he didn't happen to mention what that was?'

'Not in so many words. But, naturally, it's – well, it's doing the sort of thing that – er – brings that kind of thing out.'

'Doesn't tell you much. These mediums do table-rapping, don't they?'

'That might of course come into it.'

'I can do that myself.'

'Really? You surprise me. Why have you never told me?'

'Might have done if I'd happened to have thought of it. Why, it's years and years since I've done it. But I could do it when I was a girl and I expect I can do it now.

'Then you have in you, Eliza, the beginning of a great psychic gift. We must have a demonstration at once. This is most interesting. It must be gone into.'

'I don't mind,' said Eliza. 'Wait till I've finished this sock.'

I asked her if she preferred any particular table. She said any old table would do, and it would not be necessary to turn down the lights, or to have a musical-box playing, or to concentrate the mind.

'It's just a bit of fair heel-and-toe spiritualism,' said Eliza, which was not at all the kind of language that the gentleman at the vegetarian restaurant had used in discussing the subject.

She spread out her hands on the table. 'Now, then,' she said, 'one rap means "Yes", and two raps mean "No". Are there any spirits present?'

There was a loud and decided rap under the table. Yet I could see for myself Eliza had not moved.

'Wonderful,' I said.

'Will they answer questions?' Eliza went on; and again came the one rap for 'Yes'.

'Now,' said Eliza to me, 'you ask any questions you like.'

'Have I,' I said, 'any great psychical gifts unknown to myself?'

There came two sharp raps in quick succession, and then Eliza jumped up and burst out laughing. 'Why, you old silly, you needn't gape like that. It's just a trick. I learned that when I was working at Butterson's before I ever met you. It was a girl called Bella Ware taught me, and she got it from her father, who worked for Blackley's – one of those professional conjurers that they send out for parties. Look here, I'll show you how it's done, if you like. It's easy enough, if you've got the right kind of joints for it.'

She showed me how it was done, and it was certainly ingenious and most interesting. But, as I pointed out to Eliza, it did not affect the question. I knew, of course, that tricks and fraud were sometimes used, but it was the real genuine thing which interested me.

'In fact,' I said, 'it's something I've been reading in the local paper that has turned my mind to it again. I don't know if you remember the case of that Yorkshire manufacturer who was missing two years ago. Mordaunt his name was. The detectives hunted for a fortnight and failed to find him. And then a clairvoyante wrote to the family and told them the exact spot in which the body would be found; a search was made, and the clairvoyante was right. The man had drowned himself in a pool in a disused quarry.'

'Yes, I remember something about it,' said Eliza. 'Rum, wasn't it?'

'That same clairvoyante, Mrs Bunbury Peck, is going to lecture on psychic force in the small room of the Town Hall on Thursday night, and the lecture is to be accompanied by a series of experiments which, the advertisement says, have hitherto baffled explanation. Now that will be the real thing, and we must on no account miss it.'

'Don't know about that,' said Eliza. 'What's the least you can get in for?'

'The back seats are a shilling.'

'And you can go to the cinematograph for sixpence, and they've got a new programme there next Thursday.'

'We might go to the cinematograph next week.'

'Oh, well,' said Eliza, 'if you're really set on this lecture, we'll go. I've never met the lecture yet that I could keep awake through, but I may have better luck this time.'

* * *

The performance was to commence at eight-thirty, and the doors were opened at eight. At eight sharp Eliza and I were there, and so far nobody else had arrived, except a lady in full evening dress, with rather a shabby cloak over it. She was talking to the man who took the money, and examining the plan of the seats.

This lady looked at Eliza and Eliza looked at her, and next moment they were kissing one another. They both talked at once, and they both laughed while they were talking. They went on and on, and it appeared that they were old friends. I caught such phrases as, 'Well, this is an unexpected treat – surprise of my life – thought about you hundreds of times – should have known you anywhere – no, not changed a hair.'

Eliza seemed to have forgotten all about the entertainment. People were streaming past us into the room, and our chance of getting a decent seat seemed definitely gone. It really began to look doubtful whether we should get seats at all.

'Eliza, my dear,' I said, 'sorry to interrupt you, but —'

'This is my husband, Bella,' said Eliza. 'Miss Bella Ware, who's known professionally as Mrs Bunbury Peck.'

Miss Bella Ware shook my hand heartily, and said that she was delighted to know me, and that it was jolly good of us to come and see her little show. She looked delighted, too, which I've found unusual.

'Now, then,' she said to Eliza, 'give me your tickets.'

Immediately our money was returned to us, and we were given reserved seats (at five shillings each) in the front row of all. We both protested, but it was in vain.

'The idea!' exclaimed Miss Bella Ware. 'The best seats in the house are what you'll have, and I wish they were better still. And pay for them you shall not. So if you make any fuss about it, I won't come round to a whisky and soda with you afterwards. Here, Eliza, do write the address down, and then I must skip and do my face up.'

In another moment she had raced off.

'Eliza,' I said, 'what are we to do about it? We haven't got any –'

'I know,' said Eliza. 'But there's a quarter of an hour yet, and our tickets are reserved. We can get home and back in six minutes, and it won't take me two to tell Jane what to do.'

It was a most remarkable evening. From my place in the front I saw Mr Bunt, who was in the three shilling seats, and gave him a nod, which rather pleased me. Mrs Bunbury Peck had quite a colour when she was chatting with us, but on the stage she was very pale and had dark lines under her eyes which had certainly not been there before. Her whole manner was changed, and might have been described as being on the languorous side. I could not understand all she said about psychic force, and (from what I saw of her afterwards) I have some doubt if she understood it herself, but the experiments were really wonderful. The audience was most enthusiastic. I quite looked forward to seeing the lady again at 'Meadowsweet', and putting a few questions to her on psychical matters.

She had told Eliza that we were not to wait for her after the lecture. 'I've got to pack my traps and wash my face, and it will be a quarter of an hour before I can get away,' was what she said. However, after seeing Eliza home, we both agreed that the gentlemanly thing to do would be for me to return and offer my escort, and I did so.

Miss Ware appeared to be in the best of spirits and talked to me as if she had known me all her life. In the first three minutes she told me that she would clear eight pounds out of the show that night and make up for a frost at Surbiton the week before, and that when she was vaccinated she had it done just above the ankle, and sundry other matters of an intimate character.

She admired 'Meadowsweet', and was kind enough to say that she knew perfect taste when she saw it. She praised the whisky, and in this respect her actions confirmed her words. She found that the sandwiches were the very best she had yet struck, and she said that she had known at once from the look of me that I was a sportsman. Decidedly, a pleasant woman, though what I believe is called Bohemian. She had resumed her natural colour and manner, and she smoked four of my cigarettes – consecutively, of course.

'I say, Bella,' said Eliza, 'what made you take and call yourself Mrs Bunbury Peck?'

'Well, my dear, I go knocking about all over the place by myself, and if I say I'm a married woman, that saves me a lot of bother. I used to be "Saranatha: the Oriental Problem", but dad thought that fancy style was about played out. He said if I did the same business with the plainest name I could think of, it would be more of a novelty, and people would be more likely to believe it was genuine.'

'But isn't it genuine?' I asked.

'No, my old duck, it ain't. The things I did to-night were all kid, pure kid, and nothing but kid. And very well they went, too.'

'But the lecture – the things you said – don't you believe in it?'

'The gentleman who wrote that patter for me believed in it, and I believe in it when I'm saying it. But off the stage I don't think about it. You see, this is my business.'

'Still, you are really a clairvoyante, Miss Ware. I mean, you did discover where Mordaunt's body was.'

'Well, in a way I did, but it's not the way it got into the papers. I'd been talking about the missing man to dad, and I had a dream about it that night. Thought I saw a big stone cross by a roadside, turned off up a narrow path, and found a red-headed man lying asleep on a pile of stones on the right. I told dad about it, though I didn't think anything of it myself. But he said he would work it for what it was worth. If it didn't come off, it wouldn't matter, and if it did, it was an advertisement for life. He wrote the telegram and kept it pretty vague except that he put in a bit about bracken and heather. There was no stone cross in the neighbourhood where Mrs Mordaunt lived, but there was a stone monument with a cross carved on the bottom of it. There was a track leading up the hill all right, and they found the poor man in a quarry on the left of it – drowned in a pool. He had black hair, too. Still, Mrs Mordaunt swallowed it whole and sent me a fiver, and there was enough in it if it was properly worked up. Dad saw to that. Every place where I go to lecture that story – dad's edition of it – is sent to the local paper. It was a bit of a coincidence and a bit of luck, but it's done me a lot of good. Of course, you're a sportsman, old dear, and you won't say a word about this to anybody.'

I promised her. She apologized for leaving as early as 12.30, but she said she doubted if she would be able to get into her hotel if she stayed later. I escorted her to the hotel, and, of course, the place was shut up and the lights were out. But Miss Ware got in all right. The man who let her in was inclined to grumble, but she said that she could see he was a sportsman, and that seemed to soothe him.

I have decided to discontinue psychic investigations. They do me no harm – in fact, I had a very pleasant evening – but they seem to make other people so abominably dishonest.

Mellingham

I HAVE always considered August to be the best month for a holiday. So when Mr Bagshawe told me that my holiday would be the first fortnight in August, and that I could take it or leave it, he was really meeting my wishes in a way which, had he known it, would probably have pained him.

This gave us a clear month in which to make our plans. On going into my accounts, I found that the sum which could be reasonably allotted to holiday expenditure was quite satisfactory. In previous years our holidays had, by an unfortunate coincidence, generally fallen at a time of financial stringency. I have known what it was, after a holiday, to wait for a fortnight before I could send the requisite postal orders to Herne Bay and get my watch back. This year the general outlook was singularly bright.

There was plenty of time, as I have said, to settle which seaside place should receive our patronage. We generally talked it over in the garden after dinner. The way that garden had come on was something remarkable. And it would have looked still better but for the penny-wise-pound-foolish policy of the landlord in refusing to meet us three-quarters of the way in the matter of a small greenhouse. Perhaps the garden was not the best place for the discussion, but the weather was tempting. Eliza was always seeing things which wanted doing, and – well, a man may go into the question of Southend for the summer, or he may push a heavy lawn-mower; but, unless he is a man of quite exceptional physique, he cannot do both at once. We came in when it got dark; but when you have been up and at it all day, so to speak, the intelligence is not as fresh as it was before it began to – I mean, one may be tired. Eliza says that one night I fell asleep in the middle of saying the word 'prohibitive', in reference to the fares from London to Scarborough.

Anyhow, at the end of a fortnight, though we had practically talked our way through an A B C railway guide for the February before last, which I had borrowed from next door, we had come to no decision. It was just as if Eliza wanted to turn over the whole world before she picked a place; and she is just the same when she is choosing a hat. If I mentioned one seaside place, she asked questions about another. If I found the other would do very well, she said some of these little country vicarages went pretty cheap at this time of the year. And when I began to look over the advertisements for vicarages, she said that what she would love would be to get out of England, if it was only for ten minutes, so that she could say she had done it. The people in the house opposite once went to the Channel Islands, and have talked to Eliza about it.

And then one evening she made up her mind definitely. A catalogue of greenhouses had been sent me, and this rather put her out.

'We can't afford it,' she said. 'Besides, it's the law of this country that if you put up a greenhouse, and the landlord chucks you out, then the landlord sticks to the greenhouse. And a pretty rotten law I call it, too.'

I assured her that I had no intention of buying a greenhouse, and had merely applied for the catalogue because I took an interest in the subject, and that in any case I was not responsible for the laws of England. But, unfortunately, she was further annoyed by my suggestion that she should send round a card to our friends stating that she was at home on the first and third Saturdays.

'You'll make me cross in a minute,' said Eliza. 'Yes, you send out word that you'll be at home in the new vinery to all the dukes and duchesses on the hundred-and-oneth Monday after Advent. Do; and see what you'll look like. If I want to make my friends laugh, I'll take some other way of doing it. I never in all my days saw such a —'

'Pray calm yourself, Eliza,' I said. 'I was merely suggesting that you should conform to an ordinary social custom. There is no occasion for a fuss. In any case, you could not send out cards now, as we shall be away on our holiday, if you can make up your mind where you want to go.'

'I settled that this afternoon. Margate.'

'Margate?'

'Yes. You needn't sniff. Miss Sakers has been there, and says she can recommend rooms. A Mrs Widdicomb.'

Miss Sakers is a lady by birth, by education, and by natural refinement, and this had some weight with me. After a little talk, I directed Eliza to write to Mrs Widdicomb. It appeared that she had already done so, in order to save time.

In due course, Mrs Widdicomb's reply came on a post card. It ran as follows: 'Mrs W. regrets is full August but can recommend next door Mrs Pangrave clean reasonable bath no dogs.' The letter was without punctuation, and not what I should call well expressed. However, Eliza wrote to Mrs Pangrave.

Mrs Pangrave sent a post card, stating her terms. These made Eliza angry. She wrote back on another post card that there seemed to be some mistake, as she was asking for Mrs Pangrave's charge for furnished apartments, and not for the price of the freehold.

I said that, speaking generally, prices were pretty high in August.

'Then Margate won't do. We must get something that's not so much run after. Just take the newspaper, and if you see anything likely in the advertisements, read it out.'

Presently I read as follows: 'In the heart of sunny Surrey. Romantic, old-world farmhouse. Peaceful and retired. Good cooking and attendance. Fishing and golf in the vicinity. Terms very low to desirable visitors.'

'Now that does sound a bit of all right, don't it?'

'You need to be on your guard against slang expressions, Eliza. It certainly seems attractive. But I'm afraid it will be snapped up.'

'Don't you believe it. That's an evening paper, and by to-morrow morning I can be down there. It's not far to go. Ivy Farm, near Framlin. Where's that old A B C? If there's any snapping to be done, we'll do it.'

We breakfasted early next morning, and Eliza got away directly afterwards, so as not to miss a chance. If everything was satisfactory, she was to engage the rooms at once. There was a sharp shower in the course of the morning, and I hoped that Eliza was safe in the hospitable shelter of Ivy Farm.

On my return from the City, I found Eliza on the sofa, which is very unusual for her. She seemed tired and depressed.

'And what about Ivy Farm?' I asked at once.

'Off. Right off. So was part of the roof, and the rain coming in. "Romantic" was a misprint for "rheumatic". Name of the people's Smith. He failed in the grocery, before he took to farming and failed again. The whole of the garden's given up to growing stinging-nettles. The woman was drunk when I arrived. The butcher only calls once a week. They live principally on rabbit, and the rabbit they were cooking when I was there had been kept too long. It's four miles from Framlin, and I had to walk both ways in the rain. A two-year-old time-table ain't much good. That train had been altered, and I had to wait three-quarters of an hour. It's given me the hump. For goodness' sake let's talk about something else.'

I told her of a rather interesting conversation I had had with Pridgeon. He is much older than I am, but at the office he is my subordinate. We had happened, curiously enough, to be talking about greenhouses. He said that it was quite simple to put one up which would not become the property of the landlord. He had done it himself, and had built the greenhouse himself. He gave me a lot of details – prices of material, measurements, and so on – which I wrote down.

Eliza got up off the sofa and asked a lot of questions, and went over some rough drawings which I had made with the help of that catalogue. Suddenly she said she had got it.

'Got what?' I asked with some surprise.

'Got our holiday and our greenhouse and everything else. We don't go away. We stop here, and you build the greenhouse. You were always handy with carpenter's tools, and if Pridgeon could do it, you can. We can pay for the materials, go away for an excursion or a week-end, and still have money left over.'

'But people always go away for a holiday.'

'Don't you think so much about what people always do. We're not ill. We want a greenhouse a lot more than we want a change. I'm sure it goes to my heart to think of all those bedding-plants being wasted.'

There certainly seemed to be something in the idea. 'But what am I to say when I'm asked where I'm going for my holiday? It's all very well, but a man doesn't want to be looked down upon.'

'Well, if you feel like that, you can say you are going to Mellingham.'

'Where's that?'

'If asked, romantic, old-world village in Sussex, no railway station. Then nobody can look it up. As a matter of fact, I don't know that it's anywhere. I bought a bun at that rotten place Framlin this morning, and Mellingham was the name on the bag. That's how I came to think of it.'

'Well,' I said, 'there's a certain risk about it, but, by Jove, we'll do it!'

At the office next day young Gillivant asked me where I was going for my holiday.

'Mellingham,' I said, and he seemed quite satisfied.

Presently, old Pridgeon asked me where I was going for my fortnight in August.

'We shall run down to Mellingham.'

'Where's that?' said Pridgeon.

'In the heart of Sussex – just a peaceful, retired little village.'

'Beautiful county,' said Pridgeon. 'You couldn't do better.'

* * *

It was certainly the most successful holiday we ever spent. Eliza went into the greenhouse question with enthusiasm, and was most helpful. She bought a second-hand door for it at a sale for a price less than I had thought possible. She found a man who was quite a good carpenter, and willing to work half a day in exchange for old clothes – and they really were old, too. She did nearly all the painting herself. The total cost came considerably under our calculation.

And when that was done, Eliza saw the advertisement of a cheap day-trip to Calais and back. It would run into money, and, as I pointed out, the passage might mean inconvenience and even suffering for both of us; but Eliza seemed set upon it. As it happened, there was a complete calm. It had been calm for days. Nobody on board was ill at all. We had some hours in Calais, a most excellent luncheon at the station restaurant, and a stroll through the old town. I could dilate upon this topic, but I have since written at considerable length 'A Traveller's Impressions of Calais', and I am proposing to publish this separately, as soon as I can find an illustrated magazine with sufficient enterprise. I was pleased to note that English was understood at the restaurant and English money accepted. This should go far towards cementing what has been called the *entente cordiale*.

On the first day of my return to work, Mr Bagshawe, with a geniality which is unusual in him, asked me where I had spent my holiday.

'Well, sir,' I said. 'We were in France part of the time, but mostly at Mellingham, in Sussex.'

'Beautiful county,' he said absent-mindedly, and proceeded to another subject.

The Insult

MR WYSE was a partner in the firm, being a nephew of Mr Bagshawe's. But it was a very junior partnership, with limited powers. Mr Wyse had not been with us six weeks before I saw that he was not the man of business his uncle was. He had neither the knowledge nor the habits of it. Sometimes he'd not be at the office till the afternoon, and sometimes he would stop away altogether. He was much more affable than Mr Bagshawe, but not in a way I liked. Sometimes I would give him a perfectly serious answer to what seemed a perfectly serious question, and then he would burst out laughing. I dislike such goings-on.

One day one of our clerks, quite a young junior boy, came to me and said, 'Mr Wyse said I was to tell old stick-in-the-mud he wanted him.'

'Nobody of that name in the office,' I said. 'You'd better go back and tell him so.'

'Not me,' said the boy. 'He'd fire me out.'

'Very well,' I said. 'Get on with your work then.'

Presently in comes Mr Wyse, pretty furious. 'What are you doing?' he said. 'I want you – just sent for you.'

'For me, sir?' I said. 'Very sorry. That wasn't the name the boy gave.'

And then he chose to treat the whole thing as a joke. But I don't like such manners myself.

He had got a friend, a Mr Harnet, who was always in and out of the office. Often, passing through, he would have a few words of conversation with me on the subject of politics of the day and so on. He was friendly and pleasant enough, but there was a nasty flashy look about him that was not at all to my mind.

One day he overtook me as I was going out to lunch, and asked me in an airy way to come and have a drink with him. At the time I confess that I took it rather as an honour. I said that I would do so with pleasure. I had ginger-beer, beyond which I never go during business hours, and he had whisky and soda.

Presently, dropping his voice, he asked me if I knew anything about a certain bit of business. It was a Government thing, and we were tendering for it, and the figures of our tender had been through my hands that morning. I did not at the time think that he meant any harm, especially as he was a friend of Mr Wyse's. All the same, Mr Bagshawe had laid me down my rule, and I stuck to it.

'No, sir,' I said, 'I know nothing about it.'

'You don't know if your firm's tendering?'

'I can't say at all. Mr Wyse might be able to tell you.'

'Well,' said Mr Harnet, 'you've been with your people some time, and you hold an important post there – ought to be better paid, too. What you don't know you could easily get to know, I think. Suppose you did happen to get the figures for that tender, and happened to mention them over a friendly glass with me, nobody would be harmed, and it would be worth a fiver to you. It's done every day in the City, and nobody thinks –'

'You're no gentleman!' I said, 'and I don't want anything to do with you. There's the money for the ginger-beer, and I'm off.'

I had never had such a thing happen to me in the whole course of my experience. I was very much upset by it. I went back to the office – for any attempt to eat luncheon after that would have been a farce. As bad luck would have it, Mr Bagshawe was away at an arbitration, or I should have gone straight to him. He was to be back by four, and I determined to wait till then.

But soon after three in came Mr Wyse, and to my astonishment Mr Harnet was with him. I could hardly believe my own eyes. However, that being so, it was clearly my duty to let Mr Wyse know at once what kind of a man he was associating with, and in I went at once to his office.

Then came another surprise. As soon as they saw me they both burst out laughing.

'It's all right, old stick-in-the-mud,' Mr Wyse said. 'Don't look so woebegone. You're not hurt. You've been spoofed. Mr Harnet bet me there was not a man in our office he couldn't buy for a fiver. I took the bet and named you. It's all right. You've won me my bet, and there's a sovereign for you.'

I am afraid I rather lost my head then. I said, 'You can keep your dirty money. I don't want it. And I don't want any more tricks of this kind either. A plucky lot you'd have done for me if I'd lost my berth through your foolery.'

Mr Wyse began to get angry. 'People have been known to lose their berths before now for impertinence. Keep a civil tongue in your head and clear out.'

But I had quite lost control of myself. I went on talking. I reminded him how many years I had been with the firm, and what my character had been. I came there to do my work to the best of my ability, and not to be insulted; and I would sooner go than put up with it. Then I said he ought to be ashamed of himself, and banged the door as I went out.

And then came what I believe is called the reaction. I wished I had said rather less, and expressed it differently. Towards the end of the afternoon Mr Wyse and Mr Bagshawe were shut up together, and every moment I expected to be called in and given the sack. Under no circumstances did I wish to lose my place, and just at that time it was particularly necessary I should keep it. In a few months' time I should be having extra expenses in connection with an event to which I had been looking forward with considerable satisfaction – expenses for nurse and doctor and so on.

I thought of going and apologizing to Mr Wyse. But I was afraid that if I saw the man I should lose my temper again. It came to be time for me to go, and Mr Bagshawe and Mr Wyse were still shut up together, and they had not yet sent for me. This seemed to make it all the worse. I should have the thing hanging over my head all night.

In the train I made up my mind not to say a word to Eliza about it. There seemed to me just a chance that I might scrape through with an apology and promises for the future. And, naturally, just at that time I did not want Eliza to be worried at all. Of course, if the worst came to the worst, she would have to be told, but it would be better to wait till then.

So I went into the house whistling, and when I saw Eliza I smiled intentionally.

'What's happened?' she said. 'What's the matter?' It is really wonderful, the intuition some women have.

'Nothing,' I said. I should certainly have believed that I said it in an airy and light-hearted way but for Eliza's answer.

'Sit down at once and tell me about it.'

Well, things being so, I did tell her, and without attempting to defend myself. 'I blame myself for it,' I said.

'The only thing I blame you for,' said Eliza, 'is that you didn't say twice as much, and put it twice as strong. My word! if I had that precious Mr Wyse here, I'd talk to him. The idea of such a thing, with a man in your position in the office, and all! Why, I couldn't have respected you if you hadn't let out at him a bit. Do him good.'

It was indeed a day of surprises. It had never occurred to me that Eliza would take it like that.

'Yes,' I said, 'it may do him good, but it won't do us any good. It's pretty certain I shall get the sack, and I don't want to be out of work just when —'

'You're not going to get the sack, you old silly. Mr Bagshawe and Mr Wyse were shut up for an hour together, weren't they?'

'Rather more than that.'

'Well, if Mr Bagshawe were angry with you for being disrespectful, how long would it take him to fire you out? By all that you've told me, about two minutes. No, he's got a rough side to his tongue, and he don't take any trouble to make himself pleasant. But you always said he acted fairly and business was business with him. You're not going – you needn't fret about that. I dare say Mr Bagshawe will call you in and give you a bit of a dressing-down, for the sake of discipline, and if he does you'd better swallow it quietly. But that's the most there'll be to it.'

I was by no means sure that she was right, but somehow after that my spirits revived considerably.

'Still,' I said, 'there's the suspense. It's like that thing one's always reading about, the sword of – what was the man's name? – sword of Dam – something or other.'

'Even if you can't remember, you might behave yourself,' said Eliza.

'Sword of Damocles,' I exclaimed. 'Of course. Knew it as well as I know my own name.'

* * *

Mr Bagshawe sent for me as soon as he arrived at the office.

'Mr Wyse reported you for gross insolence yesterday afternoon. Said you would have to go. Got anything to say about it?'

'I am afraid I was insolent,' I said, 'but I had a great deal of provocation, sir. Perhaps Mr Wyse told you the circumstances?'

'Yes. What was your grievance? We can't know if a man's to be trusted if we never test him. I've tested you twice myself since you've been here, though you knew nothing about it. Want to be insolent to me about it?'

'No, sir. But it's not quite the same thing. A test made quietly in the office for a good reason is one thing. This was different. I don't think Mr Wyse had any doubt about me, or he would never have betted. And he allowed a stranger to make a very insulting proposal to me just for his fun. It – well, it upset me.'

'So you made a fool of yourself. If you'd come to me quietly with your complaint, you'd have been in the right – I'm not going to pretend I approve of what Mr Wyse did. As it is, you're in the wrong. Luckily for you, there's been nothing of this kind against you before. Also, Mr Wyse and myself didn't quite see eye-to-eye – well, we've agreed to separate, and he won't be here again. Bound to have happened. Here am I with the whole work thrown on my shoulders; one partner ill and another gone – and never any use when he was here. How am I to get through it? Tell me that.'

'Well, sir, if there were anything that I could do —'

'If there wasn't you'd be a fool. You've been here long enough to know the routine, haven't you? And it looks as if you were to be trusted, so long as you can keep your temper. You'll have to help me – Pridgeon can do your work. Here, take these letters. Dictate the answers as you think they should be. Let me see 'em as soon as they're typed. Work in Mr Wyse's room for the present. Quick as you can, please.'

I took great trouble with those letters, and I think they satisfied him. On only one did he make any comment, and that as it happened was a score for me.

'Your reply to Penworth Sons too civil by half. Couldn't you see it was a try-on of theirs?'

'Yes, sir. But – er – I thought it better in view of the other business we have with them just now, the —'

'Yes. I'd forgotten for the moment. Right.'

And so it went on for weeks. I had the most responsible things to do. People of importance who had come to see Mr Bagshawe were handed over to me instead. I did most of the work that Mr Wyse did, and I may fairly say I did it a deal better. There never was a word of praise from Mr Bagshawe. If there was the least little thing wrong, I heard from him about it. He made no bones of keeping me till seven or eight and never thanked me. Most days he repeated that he had not the faintest intention of making me a partner, and warned me to keep my tongue in check for the future.

I do not know what my new position is, for I have never been told. I once heard a clerk say to a visitor, 'Mr Bagshawe is out, but I have no doubt the manager could see you.' By the manager he meant me, and I did not correct him. Mr Bagshawe did not even speak of an advance in my salary. But he has paid me the advance – another fifty a year – and very welcome to Eliza and myself in view of the great occasion approaching. When I thanked him, all he said was, 'Try and earn it.'

Considering this change in my position and that I am now on many occasions practically representing the firm, I have been particularly careful in the matter of office dress. Everything very quiet. Coloured ties are quite a thing of the past. Neither Mr Bagshawe nor myself ever wear anything but black. At one time I was inclined to a bowler hat if the weather were bad, or to a straw hat if the weather were fine and hot. But that sort of thing would be quite out of place now. I always wear a silk hat in the City, and so does Mr Bagshawe.

If insults always turned out like this, I could put up with another two or three.

'Name This Child'

MR BAGSHAWE had received my telegram, explaining why I should be an hour late at the office that morning. His reply was handed to me just as I was starting for the train. It ran: 'Not wanted here to-day, nothing doing; congratulate.' This kind and thoughtful message was very welcome. The nurse seemed rather disappointed, though, when she saw me back in the house again. She said all that was wanted now was peace and no interference, and that it would be better for everybody concerned if I simply went to bed. And after some hesitation, and making one or two final suggestions, that was what I did.

The nurse was a capable woman – Eliza said she was perfect – and everything went as well as possible. But from the day she entered the house till the day she left it she seemed in a perpetual bad temper with me. If I pointed out the slightest thing that in my judgment ought to have been done, she always asked me if I wanted to kill the child.

I received many congratulations at the office, but old Pridgeon seemed a little annoyed at my manner. 'You shouldn't behave as if you had invented babies,' he said. 'If they hadn't been known before your time, you'd never have had any time.'

The birth of our child was duly announced in *The Times* newspaper. Mr Bagshawe reads *The Times* and a financial paper every morning. From things he has let drop, I believe he is profoundly dissatisfied with both journals, but he never changes. I doubt if he admits the existence of any other papers. The day the notice appeared, just as I was leaving the office, he surprised and pleased me by offering to be one of the godfathers to the child – 'to that brat of yours', was how he phrased it. 'Can't do ceremony,' he added. 'Get a proxy.'

I need hardly say that I accepted at once. I expressed my sincere gratitude, and said that this was indeed an honour. It is true that in making the offer his language was not what I should have called well chosen, but the way he carried the thing through subsequently was simply princely. He sent a cup, plate, knife, fork, and spoon, all in solid, hall-marked silver, and a five-pound note to start a bank account for the baby. Eliza's brother Frank, who was to be the other godfather, said, the other man having pretty well covered the field it looked as if he himself ought to get through on a shilling hymn-book – a remark that struck me as being in the worst possible taste. That man says things which revolt me.

If that boy had been a girl, there would have been no trouble whatever about his names – or perhaps I should say her names. But this not being so made it quite different. (The expression is a little faulty here, but I think the meaning can be grasped.)

The fact is that Eliza all along had a presentiment that it would be a girl, and this presentiment was confirmed by a remarkably life-like dream that she had, in which she started for Shoolbred's, but got into a crowded church by mistake, and the parson stopped his sermon to congratulate her on her daughter's success in the pole-climbing, upon which the whole congregation rose and cheered. After that dream she was so certain that it would be a daughter that she declined to consider any other possibility, and names were decided upon accordingly.

So if the boy had been a girl, he would have been called Gladys Kate – that is to say, she would have been called that. Gladys was a name to which Eliza and myself were both partial, and Kate was Eliza's mother's name. There was the whole thing cut and dried, and no further discussion was needed.

But the girl being a boy, her – I should say his – names had still to be settled. The first name was easy enough. It happened that Mr Bagshawe's first name is the same as my own – a coincidence which I take rather as a compliment – so in bestowing that name upon my son we were calling him after his father and after his godfather at one stroke.

It was the second name which made the trouble.

'I think,' said Eliza, 'that Frank will expect the boy to be named after him.'

'It does not seem to me necessary,' I said. 'I prefer Lionel.'

'If it comes to preference,' said Eliza, 'the name I should really like would be Algernon.'

Just then a note came in from Miss Sakers, to say that if as godmother she had the privilege of choosing one of dear baby's names she should like him to be called Anselm. To my mind, when a boy goes to school, and has to take the rough with the smooth, he is a good deal handicapped by such a name as Anselm.

I observed that it was impossible to please everybody.

'Well,' said Eliza, 'it's very worrying. Nurse says, "Why not take and call him William?" and seems rather set upon it. And it is natural, somehow, that she should have a voice in the matter.'

'Better give him three dozen names at once, and I'll step down and ask Parker what she would like to suggest.'

'Now,' said Eliza, 'it's no good getting cross about it. Here we are within twenty-four hours of the angel's christening, and nothing's settled. And it doesn't seem possible to settle anything without offending half the friends we've got.'

'They should mind their own business. It seems to me that people take a liberty in suggesting anything or expecting anything. There was old Pridgeon laying down the law at the office this morning. "If you intend your boy for the City," he said, "call him Whittington, and he'll be lucky." He's got nothing to do with it, and so I told him.'

'Still, Whittington isn't half a bad name,' said Eliza. I have never known her so vacillating about anything as she was about the choice of my son's second name. I admit that I had come to no absolute decision myself.

'Not quite such a good night,' the nurse reported next morning. 'I think she was too much worried yesterday about baby's second name. Late last night Miss Sakers wrote saying that if Anselm were not liked, either Constantine or Wilberforce might be substituted. Such nonsense I have never heard in my life. As I said, why can't you take and call him William, and be done with it?'

I had not the slightest idea why that nurse wanted my son to be called William, and I do not believe she had the slightest idea either. People go sticking their oar into another man's pie, and too many suggestions spoil the broth, as the proverb says. I was so irritated by it that I said to Eliza that for two pins I would cut out the second name altogether.

'Good idea!' exclaimed Eliza. 'Why on earth didn't you think of that before? The boy will have his father's Christian name and surname. And neither Frank, nor Miss Sakers, nor anybody else can be offended, because they will all be left out together. That's what we'll do.'

And that is what we did. But to Mr Bagshawe I put it rather differently. I said: 'After all your kindness, sir, we've been wishful to call the boy after you.' After a pause I added: 'It seems rather like taking a liberty, but I happen to have the same name myself.' He neither resented it nor seemed pleased about it. He said 'Ah', and then proceeded to matters of business.

The only difficulty that is likely to arise is from confusion between my son and myself. This has not caused much trouble so far, because Eliza never calls the boy by his name, but by anything which she happens to think of at the time, 'ducksi-woodlekin' predominating. Also her voice in addressing the boy is an octave higher than in addressing me.

But the other day I found at the house a cardboard box addressed to me by name, with the 'Esquire' properly added. I found inside it a soft ball of wool and a toy rabbit. I have asked Eliza to mention, in thanking Mrs Burbidge for her present to

the boy, that we should take it as a favour if, in any future
correspondence with him, she would be careful to add the word
'Junior' on the address.

* * *

The other evening I could not help contrasting in my mind our
position as it is now with our position a few years ago.
Increased income, better house and garden – the greenhouse is
our own – greatly improved position for myself at the office –
the room which was Mr Wyse's has been handed over to me
permanently – several notable advances in the social direction. I
thought over these things with a good deal of satisfaction.

'Eliza,' I said, 'there cannot be the least doubt about it. We
really are getting on.'

'I should think we are, indeed,' said Eliza. 'Why, everybody
who sees him admires him. I'm sure, when I take him out, it's
almost embarrassing, the way people turn round to look at him.
And clever? Cleverness is no word for it. I can tell you, if
everything isn't just as his majesty likes it, he soon lets you hear
about it.'

There was a row overhead which appeared to indicate that
everything was not just as he liked it at the moment.

'Yes, Eliza,' I said, 'but you don't quite see what I was
referring to. It was more —'

But Eliza had already run upstairs.

EXIT ELIZA

Reflections on the Child

I SAID a few words on this subject to Eliza, and she replied that if I only wanted to cast reflections on the child I had better hold my tongue altogether.

'On the contrary, and far from it,' I said. 'I want nothing of the kind. Any man who says I am deficient in the proper feelings of a father merely proves himself to be an ignorant fool. I wish to face the facts, Eliza – that's all, and there's no occasion to get short about it.'

The truth is that the arrival of a son and heir in a gentleman's family is not all skittles. I have found in business that the more a thing looks like being all skittles the more it isn't. It is just the same in the house. At first, of course, the congratulations of one's friends were welcome, and there were presentations to the child of a gratifying nature. After the notice (in the best newspapers) advertising the birth, a perfect deluge of samples and circulars descended upon us. Of different kinds of meat extracts alone so many samples were sent that for over a week clear soup at dinner became simply a matter of course. All satisfactory enough as far as it goes, but is it everything? What about character?

The fact of the case is there is absolutely no dependence to be placed on baby. I do not blame him. His is, perhaps, a common fault of infancy, and I am always ready to forgive and forget. But to me on more than one occasion he has been most disappointing. You never know where you are with him. I had, for instance, found out by repeated experiments that if I waved one finger slowly in front of his face at a distance of, say, eleven or twelve inches, he at once gave a particularly winning and sunny smile. Naturally, I was anxious to exhibit this small accomplishment. It seemed to me to indicate the early working of the mind.

An opportunity arrived when Miss Sakers asked of her own accord to have the child brought down. I mentioned this phenomenon to her.

'I will show you,' I said. 'I will wave my finger over the child's face, and you will see the result.'

I waved my finger over the child's face. The child was immediately sick.

The thing is a mystery to me. Here we have an infant in robust health. He sleeps well, has a hearty appetite, and rarely cries. But any attempt to exhibit him to a visitor only too frequently has the unpleasant result indicated. It almost seems as if he did it maliciously. At any rate, it is a course of action which is bound to create a totally wrong impression. Miss Sakers said that if she had known she would have stopped me, and that it was not right to treat a baby like that. I kept my temper, as I almost invariably do when speaking to a lady. But it is not pleasant to me to be accused of stupidity and cruelty, and that is what her observation comes to.

It seems to me that the stupidity lies principally with other people. Baby has at present five wool balls and two rabbits. One wool ball and one rabbit would have been ample, and the money spent on the others might have been more usefully employed. Before giving a present to a baby it is obviously wise to consult some responsible person, such as the father, to know what is required. Some slight addition to the child's wardrobe would have given it at least as much pleasure – both the rabbits and one of the wool balls cause it extreme terror – and would have saved me expense.

Then, again, though it may be less the fault of the baby than of Eliza herself, I have practically ceased to be master in my own house. A girl of seventeen has been engaged by us to assist Eliza in the care of the child. The other day, as I entered the room, that chit of a girl held up her finger at me, and said '*Hush!*' The word 'please' was not used. Eliza said that she was justified, the child being asleep at the time and the girl in a hurry. Am I nobody, then? However, I make no comment.

The same girl has practically forbidden me on one occasion to enter a room in my own house – 'You don't go in there, sir,' was the expression used – and has also told me to take off my boots, on the ground that they squeaked. One has to draw the line somewhere, and I did not take off the boots. In fact, I told the girl that I paid her wages to attend to the baby, and not to interfere with matters that were beyond her province.

The other day Eliza was talking to the baby, and I heard her say, *'You'll be a finer man than your father, won't you?'*

'I do not wish to use any strong expression, Eliza,' I said, 'but that remark of yours is absolutely idiotic, besides being offensive to me personally. You are speaking of what you cannot possibly know, and you are saying it to a child who cannot possibly understand it.'

'Then,' said Eliza, 'if baby can't understand, it don't matter if I'm wrong; and anyway, I'm right. A much finer man you'll be than your father, ducksey, won't you?'

It is hopeless to contend against this kind of thing. I will only say that it wounds me. We will pass to another point.

I like order in my house. I like my servants to do their work properly. I like punctuality at my meals. So far, I have insisted upon these three things, and been able to secure them. That is all quite a thing of the past now. It is of no use for me to say anything. If I do, the baby is always brought in as an excuse; and if I decline to accept the baby as an excuse, then I am considered to be a brute. The other morning my shaving water was not hot, and the eggs at breakfast were boiled as hard as a stone. When I ventured upon a word of reproof to Parker about this she looked injured and said that the baby had slept longer than usual that morning, and that it was not possible to do everything. I defy any man to prove any possible connection between the length of a baby's sleep and the length of time that an egg is boiled. They are two different things altogether. Here am I with one extra servant in the house, and with less comfort than I have ever had before. Is that disgraceful, or is it not? That is all that I ask.

Those of my readers who are acquainted with my previous volumes of domestic memoirs will probably have been struck by one strong characteristic of mine – I will now allow myself to be placed in an absurd and ignominious position. I have a sense of my own personal dignity, and I am not ashamed of it. It is something altogether distinct from vanity, a fault which I despise. This characteristic of mine has at any rate saved me in one respect. I may not be master in my own house, but I have definitely declined to wheel the perambulator.

I did it once, and once only. It was on a Saturday afternoon, and I noticed that I seemed to attract more than usual attention. Small boys in the street stared at me and then ran off and fetched other boys to have a look. Presently I caught a glimpse of myself in a mirror in a shop-window. It was enough. 'This,' I said to Eliza, 'will not happen again.'

Eliza was not pleased with my decision. She says that in asking me to wheel a perambulator she is really conferring an honour upon me. Into such extravagances may maternity lead a woman.

'There is a right way and a wrong way of doing everything,' I ventured to remind her. 'When we take our walk on Saturday or Sunday afternoon, the proper course is for the nursemaid to wheel the perambulator and for you and me to walk beside it.'

'Oughtn't the other girl to run behind and bark?' asked Eliza.

I declined to make any reply to foolishness of this kind. Here am I by my own unaided exertions practically in the position of manager to a city firm of the highest importance and respectability. Character is what has done it. Ability may have come in, but I assign it principally to character. A man in that position can *ipso facto* have nothing whatever to do with the wheeling of a perambulator. I was on the point of writing that I might as well be asked to clean my own boots. But, as a matter of fact, I have, since the arrival of the baby, twice been asked to clean my own boots. At any rate, I have been told that if I did not nobody else would.

The result is that Eliza generally wheels the perambulator herself. She insists upon speaking of it as 'the pram', although I have frequently told her that, to my mind, this abbreviation is a vulgarity.

One of our great national poets – I think it was Longfellow, but will not be certain – has said that a man who has children has given hostages to fortune. I am not absolutely clear of the meaning of this, but it seems quite likely. I should prefer to put it in another way myself, and to say that a man who has a baby has practically taken a back seat.

But I will not wheel the perambulator.

The Average Adjuster

THE other day, while I was wheeling the perambulator with one hand and reading a copy of *Home Hints* with the other, I came upon what might be described as a great thought.

To prevent misunderstanding, I may say that I was wheeling the perambulator in my own garden, and was particularly careful to keep to that part of the garden which is not overlooked by next door. The great thought to which I have referred was a quotation from a gentleman whose name I am unable to recall. He was, I believe, a Jesuit father. He said that if he was allowed to have the care of a child until the age of eight – or it may have been five – anybody else was welcome to take the child on afterwards. Such is the force of early associations, and so soon may an indelible stamp be set upon the human character.

At this moment Eliza from an upper window said that if I could not keep the perambulator on the path, and wanted to upset the whole thing and murder the child, I had better bring it in at once. I have said as plainly as words can speak that I object most strongly to being addressed from an upper window while I am in the garden. However fortunate one may be in one's neighbours, there is no necessity to tell them everything. But apparently what I want or do not want goes for very little nowadays. The observation also was quite beside the mark, because the perambulator-wheel had only just touched the box edging, and I should have been certain to have noticed it myself in another moment without any outside interference.

I do not permit myself to be spoken to twice in that manner, and so I took the perambulator back to the house immediately. I left that copy of *Home Hints* in the perambulator, for which I am now sorry.

After dinner that night (I think I have mentioned in a previous work that we always dine in the evening now), the baby being asleep and Eliza occupied with my socks, there seemed to me to be an opportunity for rational conversation based upon the statement which I had read that afternoon with reference to the opinion of the Jesuit father.

'Eliza,' I said, 'in the course of my reading to-day I have come upon an observation which to you may at first sight seem extraordinary.'

'Well?'

'A Jesuit father or priest – an extremely well-known man, whose name I do not remember to have heard before – has given it as his opinion that if he can have the care of a child until the age of five, or it may be eight, anybody may have that child afterwards.'

'Brute!' said Eliza. 'But that's just like so many men – get sick of a job before it's half done.'

'You totally misunderstand,' I said. 'What the Jesuit father wished to imply was that it was during these early years that the character is what might be called moulded.'

'Don't go on,' said Eliza. 'I've had Miss Sakers in here this afternoon talking about bismuth and dill-water as if she were my grandmother. That's about as much advice as I can stand for one day. And the funny thing is that the advice always comes from people who can't know anything about it. Miss Sakers has never had a baby of her own.'

'Careful, Eliza, careful!' I said, holding up a warning finger.

'What have I got to be careful about? Then look at your Jesuit priest, the man with the mouldy character that you were making so much fuss about. What can he know? I've always been told that these Jesuit priests aren't allowed to marry. People who want to try silly games with bismuth can try them on their own babies, and not interfere with mine.'

'Your temper, Eliza, leads you into a confusion of ideas. All I wish to point out is that, as the Jesuit father very justly observed, these early years are most important from the point of view of education. We do not know what our boy may become. The future of the Empire might quite conceivably turn on the way we handle that boy now.'

'Then don't go wheeling his pram into a brick wall while you're mooning over your rotten paper.'

'If you refer to what happened this afternoon, I was not within yards of a brick wall, and the paper was not rotten. But I have no wish to indulge in recriminations. All I want to do is to point out that now, if ever, you must begin to train that child towards the profession which he will ultimately adopt.'

'Ah!' said Eliza. 'And what is it you want him to be?'

'I have thought that question out very carefully. It must be something a little out of the way, because otherwise you'll get over-competition.'

'I'll bet he keeps his end up, anyway,' said Eliza.

'The profession must also be reasonably lucrative. I have not the least doubt that early financial anxieties have taken years off my life. Two professions struck me particularly – that of the Average Adjuster, and that of the Tea Taster.'

'If I catch you giving that child tea you'll hear from me, and that's all about it.'

'It was not my intention to give the child tea. I must say that on the whole I prefer the career of the Average Adjuster.'

'What's that?' asked Eliza.

'An Average Adjuster is, as the name implies, a man who adjusts averages. It has to do with insurances and shipping and that kind of thing. You wouldn't understand it.'

'Do you understand it yourself?'

'As far as is necessary.'

'Well, what is it you want me to do about it? Do you expect me to run up and wake that baby out of a nice sleep and tell him to adjust averages? It seems to me you get more unreasonable every day you live.'

'All I meant, as you perfectly well know, was that habits of accuracy and punctuality —'

'That's the first word you've said about them. You were talking about tea-adjusting, or some such nonsense.'

'Very well, Eliza. I have done my best to get you to take an intelligent view of this, and I have failed. I cannot find what is not there. Personally, I shall continue on the lines I have indicated. I intend to cut out that great thought of the Jesuit father from *Home Hints*, and to preserve it as my guiding principle. Kindly ring the bell.'

'Hands full,' said Eliza. 'Ring it yourself.'

I did so. Parker answered it, and she was wiping her hands on her apron as she came in. She is always doing this, and I have spoken about it until I am sick and tired of it.

'Parker,' I said, 'kindly bring me the copy of *Home Hints* which you will find in the perambulator.'

In about five minutes Parker returned to say that the paper in question had been used to re-light the nursery fire.

'That's it,' I said bitterly. 'Pray go on. Burn everything. Don't trouble to ask me first.'

Eliza said that if I talked like that she didn't see how I could expect servants to stop.

'I think,' I said, 'that I can show you that I did no more than –'

'Well,' said Eliza, as she put the last sock back into the basket, 'I can't wait to hear about it. I've got to go and see to that Average Adjuster.'

I think I understand why some men take to drink.

Sampson

ON Sunday morning I had gone out as usual to consult the thermometer (which I found to be in agreement with me as to the warmth of the day), when I saw on my lawn two things which annoyed me extremely. One was an empty mustard-tin, and the other was the cat from 'Burnside', next door. To pick up the mustard-tin and throw it at the cat was with me the work of a moment. Eliza then put her head out of the nursery window and said loudly, 'I wish you wouldn't do that.'

'Refrain from screaming,' I replied, and went indoors to have it out with her. She kept me waiting ten minutes on account of the baby, who, of course, has to be made an excuse for everything.

When I did at last succeed in asking her kindly to explain what she meant by such conduct, she produced a letter from

Mrs Epstein, who lived at 'Burnside'. The letter said that she and her husband had been called away into the country owing to the serious illness of Mr Epstein's mother, and asked if Eliza would kindly look after the cat and see that it was fed while she was away.

'And you can inform me why the Epsteins' servants cannot look after the cat, and why this burden is to be laid on us?'

'They haven't got any servants. They never had but the girl, and she bolted on Friday morning, leaving the breakfast things not washed up. And Mrs Epstein has always been obliging enough to me. She gave baby a wool ball, and she is making him another, and when the milkman disappointed us she —'

'Then I understand the Epsteins' cat is to live here indefinitely?'

'Not indefinitely. Until they come back. Why not? I can tell you baby is a lot fonder of Sampson than he is of his wool rabbit.'

'Sampson?'

'Yes; that's the cat's name.'

'Well, if he is to remain here there must be certain rules and regulations which —'

'Oh, it's not he – it's she. It was meant to be a tom-cat, and that's why they called it Sampson, and then it turned out differently, as cats so often will.'

'And,' I asked sarcastically, 'did Mrs Epstein ask you to take charge of the empty mustard-tin and feed that as well? Because, if not, it must have been thrown over the wall by the people at "The Nest". It is not the first time I've had to complain about that kind of thing from them, and I shall just write a pretty sharp letter —'

'Oh, you needn't trouble. It's our own mustard-tin. Baby had it there. He likes it. I don't know where you threw it, but you had better go and see if you can find it again. He won't like it if that mustard-tin's gone.'

I should have imagined that a live cat and a sharp-edged mustard-tin were both of them extremely improper playthings for a baby of thirteen months, and I said as much.

'Oh, I'm always there,' said Eliza. 'Don't you worry. It's no good laying down the laws to babies. You give them things you think they ought to like, and they scream themselves to death. And then they take up with something you think they ought to hate and regularly enjoy it. Gladys says that her youngest sister at baby's age would not play with anything except a large lump of coal she had found and used to kiss it every night before she went to sleep.'

Gladys is the name of our second servant. She is really a nursemaid, but does other things. She is the girl who deliberately told me to hush in my own house. The morbid eccentricities of the younger members of her family did not interest me in the least, and I told Eliza so. I disapprove *in toto*, for that matter, of the name Gladys for a girl in that position. Eliza says that if I didn't like it I ought to have forbidden the banns when she was baptized (a confusion of thought, of course), and that it's too late to interfere now. This is untrue. Other people would have taken and called the girl Emily, which is what I wished.

On the following morning I had a serious complaint to make to Eliza with reference to Sampson. A cat has no business to go to sleep on a staircase, especially when the staircase is not properly lit. A very serious accident might have happened. I might have broken my neck.

'Well, you haven't, anyhow,' said Eliza. 'I hope you didn't tread on the poor cat. She's so nervous just now. If you'll go out into the garden and bring her in we might give her her breakfast.'

I refused absolutely. I am not a self-assertive man but I am not going to play second fiddle to a next-door neighbour's cat, at any rate.

The cat continued to give trouble. It was always where it was not wanted. Having discovered that I positively disliked it, its favourite pastime was to rub its head against my legs.

'It will do that once too often,' I said to Eliza, who replied that she did not see how I could be so unkind to dumb animals.

On Tuesday morning Eliza said she had a post card to say that Mr Epstein's mother was much better.

'Mr Epstein's mother is nothing to me nor I to her, but if this means that the Epsteins are about to return and to take charge of their cat instead of saddling us with it, I am most happy to hear it.'

On Wednesday morning Eliza said to me that she was perfectly sure it was going to rain, and that I had better take my bowler hat.

'On the contrary,' I said. 'The barometer is rising and has been rising for the last two days. There it is in the hall, and if you would sometimes consult it you would not make these mistakes. Even if it were going to rain, I should not care to appear at the office except in a silk hat. Mr Bagshawe always wears one.'

'Seems a pity to spoil a good hat,' said Eliza.

'As a matter of fact, it is not a good hat. It is over a year old, and I was intending to procure a new one to-day.'

'Ah!' said Eliza. 'Then it doesn't matter so much. Of course, it's mostly your own fault. You left the hat on the chair in the hall instead of hanging it up, as usual, and you know what cats are. However, the Epsteins are coming back to-day, and I shouldn't wonder if they let baby have one of the kittens.'

No comment was possible. Nothing that any man could possibly say could have expressed my feelings. I maintained absolute silence, finished my breakfast hastily, and left for the City. I have definitely forbidden Eliza to accept that kitten, even if offered

I am heartily sorry now I ever told Eliza that it was an old hat.

Three Stamps

STRICTLY speaking, the bureau in the dining-room belongs to Eliza. It was part of the furniture bequeathed to her by her mother. In practice it has, as a matter of fact, become mine. I am the only person who uses it. It contains my papers. Even Eliza generally speaks of it as 'your bureau'. It is perfectly equipped with everything which I may require in the way of stationery. Eliza said that she thought I might have worried through life without buying sealing-wax of three different colours. The comment, of course, was absurd. It costs no more to buy three sticks of three colours than to buy three sticks of one colour. Nor is it true, as she alleged, that nobody uses sealing-wax except the chemist. I use it myself on suitable occasions.

I was going over my bureau one evening to see that everything was in order, and I was much annoyed by what I found – or, rather, did not find – in the stamp drawer.

'As usual,' I said to Eliza. 'This is the kind of thing I am subject to. A month ago precisely I bought and placed in this drawer twelve stamps. To-day there are only three. I have, perhaps, used one of them myself. I am utterly at my wits' end to know what to do to keep stamps.'

'Stick 'em on your face,' said Eliza. 'You don't buy stamps to keep. You buy them to use.'

'Don't argue,' I said. 'I have not used them – that is my point. Those stamps have been taken. What I want to know is, who has taken them?'

'I have,' said Eliza. 'I always do and always shall. I didn't take them to decorate the walls with. I took them to stick on letters. You can't send letters without a stamp. See? That reminds me. If you've got three of them you can hand one over to me now. I've got to send a recipe to Miss Sakers.'

I gave her a stamp. I said that I should imagine it was humanly possible for her to remember to buy stamps for herself in the future, and requested her to do so.

Just at this moment Mrs Epstein's little boy called to say that his mother would be obliged by the loan of a stamp. She may have sent a penny by the boy. If she did, the boy sneaked it. In any case, at the moment of writing the loan still remains a loan. As I said to Eliza, if there is anything the Epsteins do not get it will not be for the want of asking for it.

However, there is a way of dealing with these things. One of these nights I propose to see if Mrs Epstein cannot oblige me with the loan of a stamp.

But to continue. Later that evening the message was brought in that Mr Bunn had called, and wished very particularly to see me. I did not in the least wish to see Mr Bunn, knowing what it was about, but felt it to be more politic to have him shown into the dining-room. It was Mr Bunn who moved us when we came to this house, and his account has never been absolutely settled since. He does paper-hanging and decorating as well as removing, and is always full of suggestions. Eliza says that he twists me round his finger. The real truth is that where he has made suggestions which I believed to be useful I have occasionally adopted them, without, perhaps, taking sufficiently into consideration the question of expense. I was not at this moment quite prepared to settle Mr Bunn's account in full, and told him so fairly and frankly.

'That's all right, sir,' said Mr Bunn cheerfully. 'All I want is something to be going on with. I have my men to pay every week, and my credit with the wholesale has its limits. What do you say now to a cheque for a fiver on account?'

After some further conversation I wrote and gave him a cheque for three pounds ten and asked for a receipt.

'Certainly, sir,' said Mr Bunn. 'I'll make it out now. I'm afraid I shall have to trouble you for a stamp. But, after all, where it's two receipts instead of one it's only fair you should pay one of them.'

That was the last straw. A man might as well call at your house in order to cut your throat and steal a knife first to do it with. He told me he had got a new wall-paper just in which would make my hall look a very different thing. But I declined even to enter into the question.

And, of course, by the last post I had a letter requiring an immediate answer, and had no stamp for the answer. I was apparently to act as a free gratis post office to everybody except myself.

Eliza, who has rather queer notions of what constitutes a joke, seemed to be amused. I said very little myself, but I quite made up my mind as to the line which I would take. On my way to the City in the morning I looked in at Mr Bunn's. He employs a clever carpenter who can be trusted to handle a fine old piece of furniture. The bureau originally had a lock, but some time or other it had been removed, and I was now determined to replace it. It might be, of course, that Eliza had all the stamps, or it might not. To leave stamps about is equivalent to leaving money about. It puts temptation in the way of the servants, and is not right.

The man came next afternoon when Eliza was out, and did the job very neatly. It was a spring lock. The mere action of shutting the flap of the desk locked it. When Eliza returned I showed her what I had done.

'Paid Bunn's bill yet?' she asked.

'That is not what we are discussing. In future you must remember to buy stamps for yourself. You will be unable to get them from the bureau. I do not wish to encourage acts of thoughtlessness in you, or habits of dishonesty in the servants. You will observe, I place twelve stamps in the stamp drawer and I shut down the flap.'

'Don't shut it!' said Eliza quickly.

I do not take orders given in that way, and I did shut it. I then asked her what she meant.

'Oh, nothing much,' said Eliza. 'I happened to see that your keys were inside – that's all. Bad thing to get habits of thoughtlessness, isn't it?'

'If,' I said coldly, 'that girl Gladys is doing nothing, as usual, she can run round to Mr Bunn's and ask if he can send his man again.'

Bridge Abandoned

IT is my opinion that there is not very much in this game of bridge about which we hear so much talk. It is not an intellectual game, and for that reason alone, quite apart from what took place at the Epsteins', I shall not go on with it. In two evenings I practically made myself master of the whole thing. I do not mean that I can always say off-hand what I should score at the end of a game, or what the precise value of a trick in any suit is. But as that information is given in a very clear and concise form on the back of every bridge marker, it is hardly worth the while of a busy man to burden his mind with it.

I was introduced to the game by a Mr Spratt, who was staying with Mr Timson, the curate at St Augustine's. Though intended for the Church, Mr Spratt seemed rather bent on seeing life. He was always getting up tea-parties, going to bazaars, singing at concerts, and so on.

We did not, on the two occasions to which I have referred, play for points. Mr Timson only consented to learn on this condition, which I think is to his credit. I may add that I am myself opposed to gambling, and consider that any game which is not worth playing for its own sake is not worth playing at all.

One evening, on my return from the City, Eliza said to me that she would not mind betting that the Epsteins had got somebody coming to dinner that night.

'What makes you think so?' I asked.

'Mrs Epstein was buying tinned mulligatawny at the grocer's yesterday afternoon, and I saw the asparagus going in myself this morning. That speaks for itself.'

Eliza was perfectly correct. A little later, happening to be at one of our upstairs windows, I cast an eye into the Epsteins' garden. Mr Epstein had two strangers with him – both elderly men – and he was pointing out to them the place where the sweet-peas would be when they came up. I dismissed the subject from my mind. It was nothing to do with me, and I took no interest in it. All I said to Eliza was that if the Epsteins were going to give a dinner-party they might have remembered us, considering all the trouble we had had with their cat.

About nine o'clock that night Mrs Epstein's little boy brought a verbal message that Mr Epstein would be very glad if I would come in to make a four at bridge. My first impulse was to refuse. As I said to Eliza, if I am not good enough to be asked to dinner I am not good enough to be asked to anything. Eliza said that if she were me she would not be so silly.

The remark was as absurd as it was ungrammatical.

'If you were I,' I said to Eliza, 'you would be I. That is to say, you would be neither more silly nor less silly than I am. If you would only train yourself to look at things in a logical way, you would —'

'Are you going to keep that boy of the Epsteins' waiting all night while you make up your mind?'

If I must err, I would sooner err on the side of good nature. I sent word by the boy that I should be happy to oblige.

My observations from the window had shown me it would

not be necessary to assume evening dress. I changed my coat for something rather more recent, and went round.

Mr Epstein introduced me to Mr Horrocks and Mr Bird. We four were to play bridge while Mrs Epstein read the evening paper. Mr and Mrs Epstein, Mr Horrocks, and Mr Bird were all of them slightly flushed in the face, and there was more laughter than I could find any sufficient reason for.

We cut for partners, and I found I had to play with Mr Epstein. He asked me what kind of a game I played. I said that my game was average.

I then understood him to say, 'I am hearty and strong. What are you?' I replied politely that I was well myself. This perfectly inoffensive remark was the signal for a burst of laughter. Mr Horrocks said it was capital. Mr Bird said it was very good.

Then Mr Horrocks said 'Weak-and-weak' to Mr Bird, and Mr Bird nodded. I looked at the back of my marker, but I could find no reference to weak-and-weak. This evidently was not the game as I understood it.

Mr Epstein left the declaration to me, and although I had a very curious hand I was not in the least doubtful as to what I should do. I held ten clubs headed by the ace, king, queen, and my other three cards were the ace of the other suits. The preponderance of clubs was beyond any possibility of a mistake, and I declared clubs accordingly.

When I put down my hand Mr Horrocks and Mr Bird were once more convulsed with laughter, but Mr Epstein seemed far from pleased. He said he could appreciate a joke as much as any man, but that he thought I was really going too far.

'I do not see what you have to grumble at,' I said. 'It looks to me perfectly sound. Unless the other side have some remarkably good cards we must make nearly every trick.'

'We must make absolutely every trick. It scores twenty-eight. We should also have made every trick at no trumps, which would have scored eighty-four below the line and a hundred and forty above it.'

This particular hand was never played. They simply wrote down a score and the cards were dealt again. That is not bridge as I understand it. Even if you think that you can win, you should play the thing out. You never know what the other side may have.

Mr Bird then went hearts and made game. I followed with a no-trump declaration, and only succeeded in getting two tricks. I had imagined from the weakness of my own hand that my partner must be strong, but with the exception of two aces and two kings he had no cards of any value.

We lost the rubber, and Mr Epstein produced his purse. Fivepence a hundred had been suggested, and I had consented to this. But both Mr Horrocks and Mr Bird positively refused to receive money. They said that if they did they would be unable to sleep that night. It appeared that they both had trains to catch, and that they could not play another rubber. Both of them told me that it had been a most interesting and amusing game, and that they were delighted to have met me.

As we were leaving I overheard Mr Horrocks saying in a low voice to Mr Epstein, 'This will be a lesson to you, Epstein.' So quite evidently Epstein was not justified in trying to teach me how the game of bridge should be played. However, he received the reproof quite meekly, and merely said, 'You bet!'

At the moment of writing the Epsteins have not sent round again to ask me to make a four at bridge. But when they do I have made up my mind to refuse. I shall say that I am very sorry to seem disobliging, but that I have abandoned bridge. I prefer a game which gives a little more exercise to my mental faculties.

An Extraordinary Occurrence

SOME days ago, as I was walking down Chancery Lane on my way back from seeing our firm's solicitors, I was the actual eye-witness of a most extraordinary occurrence. The road was very slippery at the time, and a taxi-cab skidded, and ran with its front wheels right up on the kerb. I need hardly point out that this might have resulted in the loss of one or more human lives. As a matter of fact, no one was even hurt, and the cab itself was not damaged. The man inside the cab did not get out; the driver simply backed it away from the kerb and went straight on. This sensational incident made a great impression upon me.

On returning to the office I went into Mr Bagshawe's room to tell him what our solicitors had said. As a rule, I confine my conversation with him to business subjects. He prefers it and has said so. But I could not but suppose that he would be interested in the narrow escape which I had just witnessed. I described it to him in detail. When I had finished he asked me my age. The question surprised me, but I was able to answer it with complete accuracy, giving not only the year but the odd number of days. When I had finished, he said: 'Then don't talk like an infant of six. It wastes time and I don't like it.'

Mr Bagshawe rather prides himself on taking everything very calmly and quietly, and I always make an allowance for his manner. I dare say dyspepsia has something to do with it. As I was going out to lunch I remarked to young Gillivant:

'I witnessed this morning a most extraordinary occurrence.'

Gillivant looked at me rather suspiciously.

'Well?' he said.

I told him what I had seen in Chancery Lane. I pointed out that the front wheels of the cab were right upon the kerb, and that if a child had been standing there it would probably have been knocked down and killed. I also observed what a remarkable thing it was that the cab itself did not overturn. When I had finished he winked his eye and said: 'No good, old man.'

I inquired what he meant.

'I mean you can't catch me with that silly old sell. You want me to ask what there was wonderful in it. Try it on the office-boy, I'm too old for it.'

I assured him that nothing was further from my mind than any attempt to deceive or to play a joke upon him. What I had narrated was a simple fact. He again told me that it was no good, and quite evidently did not believe me.

Later in the day I said to old Pridgeon: 'I saw something to-day which seems almost incredible. In fact I told it to young Gillivant and he flatly refused to believe it. It happened in Chancery Lane. I was walking down the Lane when a taxi-cab passed me. I noticed that the surface of the road was greasy, but did not give it a second thought. No idea of an accident was in my mind. Suddenly the cab swerved round – skidded, I supposed.'

I continued the story to the end. Old Pridgeon then said rather gruffly that I ought to be ashamed of myself and walked away. It was a perfectly senseless comment. I had no reason whatever to be ashamed of myself. In telling him of the occurrence I had made use of no blasphemous or improper expression.

It is not every day that I have an item of exceptional interest to take home from the City, but this was an occasion, and I took advantage of it at dinner-time.

'Strange things happen in London,' I said to Eliza.

She said, 'Well?'

'I was walking down Chancery Lane this morning when I witnessed what might have been a most terrible disaster. One of those red taxi-cabs happened to pass me. The surface of the road at the time was extremely slippery, and I have no doubt that the man had to apply his brakes suddenly owing to some exigency of the traffic. Be that as it may, I can assure you —'

And I continued the story as before. 'I venture to say,' I added, 'that that is the most extraordinary occurrence.'

'I saw another extraordinary occurrence this morning,' said Eliza, 'when I was out with baby.'

'Ah,' I said, 'what was that?'

'I saw a man and he'd got two legs.'

'There's nothing extraordinary in that.'

'Oh, don't you see what a marvellous escape it was. If he'd had a hundred he'd have been a centipede.'

It was evidently of no use to discuss the matter with Eliza while she was in this frame of mind. I have, however, narrated the scene that I witnessed in Chancery Lane at length here, because I feel sure that it must interest my readers. I may add that the front wheels of that taxi-cab were at the very least half a foot upon the kerb.

The Garden Fête

ELIZA, who is far too much inclined to do things on her own responsibility, told me she had taken two tickets for a garden fête at Mr Buddilow's ('The Chestnuts') in aid of the new mission-room in Buxton Street. The tickets were a shilling each, but I am always willing to put my hand in my pocket for a good cause. I thought I should have been consulted – that was all – and said so.

'Besides,' I added, 'I am not personally acquainted with Mr Buddilow, and the whole thing is not in our parish.'

'No,' said Eliza. 'And I thought we might take baby. There is no charge for babies in arms. I could carry him some of the time, and you could —'

'If you knew anything whatever about garden fêtes, Eliza, you would know that they constitute a class of entertainment which is utterly and completely over the baby's head.'

As Eliza gave way on this point I raised no further objections. I understood from Eliza that there would be a band provided, and a *café chantant* in the Parisian manner, and various other attractions.

As it happened the weather was fine. I was a little in doubt as to the correct costume for the occasion. Eliza said I could go in anything and everybody else would. This was no help. Having regard to the fact that this was an entertainment for a religious object I went in a silk hat and frock-coat. Almost every man there was in a straw hat and flannels. If I had gone in a straw hat and flannels nobody else would have worn them. It seems to me sometimes as if everything I do is fated to be wrong.

Mr Buddilow is a Justice of the Peace, and a man of very considerable wealth. His garden is beautiful and extends, I should say, to upwards of three acres. Some of the paths were marked 'Private', with a rope stretched across them. It was a small matter, but it annoyed me. I had paid my money on the understanding that the grounds were thrown open to the public. Only part of them was thrown open. Several entertainments were provided, but one had to pay extra for all of them, with the exception of the band. In that case, I asked myself, what was the admission money paid for in the original instance? It looked to me like sharp practice, and I do not like sharp practice, even for a religious object. There was a coconut-shy, with which I definitely refused to have anything to do. It is not an amusement for a man of my age, intelligence, and position. Eliza, I am sorry to say, so far forgot herself as to have a shy, and I regret to add that she got a coconut. I had to carry it all the rest of the afternoon, and most inconvenient it was. The band on the lawn wanted a man over them who knew what work was. Their intervals were from ten minutes to a quarter of an hour by my watch between the pieces. And even so, before I left they had begun to play some of the old selections again. Tea was provided in a refreshment tent, and we were told we could pay ninepence each and have anything we liked. We paid ninepence each, and I hope Eliza had anything she liked. Personally, I did not. If there is one thing I dislike more than stewed tea it is a cake which has been made with bad eggs. If I had not constantly reminded myself of the real necessity for a mission-room in Buxton Street, a very low neighbourhood, I might have got rather irritable about it.

The *café chantant* (pronounced 'caffy shongtong') was also on the fraudulent side. Admission was threepence and the entertainment only lasted a quarter of an hour. After that you were turned out and a fresh batch came in. It was far less gay than I had expected. Somebody sang 'The Holy City', there was a performance on the pianola, and the choir boys sang 'Oh! who will o'er the downs so free?' It was the tenth time they had sung it that afternoon, and they appeared to be justifiably sick of it. It is almost impossible for me to avoid taking a businesslike view of a business transaction. The entertainment was not worth threepence. Eliza had refused to enter, on the ground that by standing outside the tent she could hear it all just as well as if she was inside. As I told her, that was a matter entirely for her own conscience, and I did not wish to dictate. Soon afterwards

Eliza said she had got tired of it and she should go home. I am glad to say that she took the coconut with her. I remained to see if there was any chance of my getting something approximating to my money's worth.

I was tired of walking about, and patent leather, though it gives a dressy appearance, has a tendency to draw the feet. Finding an unoccupied chair, I sat down. Almost immediately a cheerful old gentleman with a brown leather satchel stepped up to me and said: 'Twopence for the chair, please.' It was just a little beyond the limit. I asked bitterly how much I had to pay to be allowed to breathe. The satire was lost on him. He only laughed and said it was a jolly good idea; he would think about it.

I now come to the one thing in the afternoon that gave me any real satisfaction. I was passing a very small tent on which was a notice:

PROFESSOR RIENZI

Phrenologist

LEARN YOUR TRUE CHARACTER BY HIS
INFALLIBLE METHOD

As nothing was said about the price I should not have dreamed of entering. I had been caught out often enough and did not propose to be caught again that afternoon. But at the door of the tent a remarkably pretty girl, fashionably dressed, was standing, and she ran up to me in the friendliest way and caught me by the arm.

'Do come and see the phrenologist, sir,' she said. 'Most interesting. He tells you all about your gifts and abilities by the bumps on your head, and the charge is only a shilling.'

I have often wished to have an independent and impartial view of my character, and it was for that reason – and not in the least because the girl was pretty – that I parted with my shilling. Inside the tent was a man in a dressing-gown with a very long white beard and thick white hair. He made me sit down and passed his hand over my head. His description of my character, to my mind, showed extraordinary insight. He told me many things about myself which, so far as I know, are not generally suspected.

As I left I thanked him, and I said to the girl that it was a wonderful performance and well worth the money. She said: 'Then you might run about and get some more to come. We did awfully well the first part of the afternoon, but now things are getting slack again.'

I did not run about. I left at once because I did not wish to be involved in any further expenditure. I also wished on my return to 'Meadowsweet' to make a note of all the phrenologist had said about me. He had said nothing which was not in the highest degree gratifying.

After dinner, while Eliza was knitting wool socks for the baby, I said: 'I want a serious answer to a serious question, Eliza.'

'A funny thing you always want that when I'm counting stitches. What is it?'

'Would you say, Eliza, that I was a man of an iron will?'

'No,' said Eliza.

'Yet I have been assured to-day by an absolute stranger that such is the case.'

'Of course, if he did not know you, he might make the mistake.'

'I do not know that it was a mistake. The man was a professor of phrenology, which is a wonderful science. He had his own special means of finding out what my gifts and abilities might be.'

'What else did he say?'

'He said that I had the artistic temperament but kept within proper bounds. Many years ago I was told by a man who had no interest in making the remark that I ought to have gone on the stage. The phrenologist practically repeated that. He said I had the dramatic instinct.'

'What did you pay him?' asked Eliza.

'One shilling.'

'He earned his money,' said Eliza thoughtfully. 'That was at the fête this afternoon, wasn't it?'

'It was: after you had left. It is in my nature to tire quickly of gaiety and excitement. I was pleased to find one small tent devoted to the serious study of one's inner nature.'

'You knew it was all spoof, of course. Miss Sakers told me all about it. Professor Rienzi is just young Buddilow dressed up, and the girl outside the tent is the girl he is going to marry. She had a bet with another girl that they'd take two pounds before six o'clock, and I expect she's won it. Pretty girls can always do what they like, can't they?'

As I pointed out to Eliza, all her statements proved, even if they were correct, was that young Mr Buddilow happens to be a man with a most extraordinary insight into character.

The Letter to 'The Times'

I WAS talking over the subject the other day with one or two friends of mine, and we all agreed that dreams are very curious things. We cannot account for them.

My friends all had instances which happened within their own experience of dreams that had come true. These seem to be quite common, but they have never come my way.

'Why,' I said to Eliza that night, 'have I never had a dream that has come true? Men whom I cannot possibly think to be my superiors or even my equals seem to have dreams of this kind, or if they don't their wives do.'

'Don't seem to me the kind of thing I should worry about,' said Eliza.

'Look, for instance, at the dream that I had last night or early this morning. I was adding up an immensely long column of figures. The trouble was that I myself was one of the figures, so that when I got down to the bottom of the column to add them up, that put the addition all wrong. Mr Bagshawe came in at the moment, and I asked him what I should do about it, and he said the only thing to do was to wear larger boots in future. That is the kind of dream I get. It not only does not come true, but it cannot come true.'

'Last night,' said Eliza, 'I dreamt that some money came to me.'

'Seems to be much the same sort of dream as mine.'

'I don't know. We were sitting in this room together, and the girl knocked at the door, and brought in a letter, and the money was in the letter. That might happen.'

'I think not. Who's going to send you any money?'

At this moment a most singular and dramatic thing happened. Parker knocked at the door and brought in a letter for Eliza.

'Open it at once,' I said.

She did so. It contained a postal order for eighteenpence from the people at Grimsby who supply us with fish, and was accompanied by a letter apologizing for the mistake in the account which Eliza had pointed out to them.

'The first thing to do,' I said, 'is to make a note of the exact time at which the letter arrived.'

'Why?' said Eliza.

On second thoughts I could not exactly say why. All I could tell her was that it was usual. Whenever a dream comes true, people always make a note of the exact time. It seems to be one of the rules.

Eliza did not seem to attach much importance to the incident. She said that after all it was only eighteenpence, and it hardly seemed worth getting a supernatural warning about. At the same time, if those people at Grimsby tried anything of the kind on with her again, she would get her fish elsewhere. She then went up to see the baby, and I sat down at my bureau to prepare a careful and temperate statement of what had occurred for publication in the form of a letter in *The Times* newspaper.

I began as follows:

'DEAR SIR, It has been well observed by Shakespeare that there are more things in heaven and earth than are dreamed of –'

I stopped here, because I could not for the life of me remember the rest of the quotation. The memory is a very curious thing. You cannot explain it. That quotation is rather a favourite of mine. I use it constantly. And now it was gone.

However, I began again:

'DEAR SIR, – It is a question whether a supernatural premonition is required with reference to a small consideration which in this case was precisely the sum of eighteenpence, but may be conditioned by a further question of commercial morality, or, at any rate, accuracy, on which it may be fairly said that the fortunes of this empire do under Providence to some considerable extent —'

I read this over again. It was all right, and I could see the meaning precisely. But perhaps it was better after all to shut out abstract considerations for which *The Times* newspaper, in the event of any unusual pressure of news, might not be able to find space. I therefore began again:

'DEAR SIR, – A dream that came absolutely and literally true,' I wrote, 'although it merely involved the correction of a small sum in a tradesman's account, may perhaps be of some interest to those of your readers who are interested in such interesting subjects —'

The last phrase clearly needed to be recast. I was just going to recast it, when Eliza came in, and asked me what I was doing.

'I am preparing,' I said, 'a statement with reference to your dream and its fulfilment for publication in *The Times*. Our name of course will not be given, nor the address. It is customary to enclose these as evidence of one's bona fides, but they form no part of the matter to be published.'

'Well,' said Eliza. 'I'm blest if it doesn't beat me altogether.'

'The problem,' I said, 'is one upon which I myself would be glad to hear —'

'Oh, I'm not talking about that,' said Eliza. 'You go to

business in the City. You've got on pretty well. You've had your salary raised. And yet when you're at home you act just like a child. Do you mean to say you didn't know that I had never had any dream at all, and was just having a little game with you? I had written to complain about that account, and told them to put it right by return of post, or I should deal elsewhere. So of course I knew the money was coming.'

'In that case, Eliza, you made a statement to me which you must have known to be untrue. Conduct of that kind does not tend to increase my confidence in your character.'

'Oh, cheer up,' said Eliza. 'Everything's got to have a start. Even if the dream didn't come true, it would have come true if it had ever been a dream.'

'I want you to see the principle involved.'

'Yes,' said Eliza. 'And I want you to come and have a look at the waste pipe of the bath. I don't know what that girl's been doing to it, but the water won't run off. You had better bring a bit of cane with you or something of that kind.'

It seemed idle to pursue the subject further.

The Cockroach

THE other day, as I was leaving the office, old Pridgeon came up to me in a very free and easy way and said, 'What do you do about cockroaches?'

Now, I like Pridgeon very well, and in the matter of the greenhouse he certainly gave me some useful hints. But I should like to see him show a proper sense of the difference which has occurred in our relations. We are no longer on terms of equality. If I am not actually Pridgeon's master, I am at any rate approximate to that.

So I was rather stand-offish in my manner. I said, 'What do I do about cockroaches? I simply fail to understand you, Pridgeon.'

'Why,' said Pridgeon, 'what is the difficulty? What I mean is what do you do to get rid of cockroaches? It's simple enough, isn't it?'

'I do nothing to get rid of cockroaches, and have no need to do anything. In a house which is properly kept and looked after there are no cockroaches. We have none, and I cannot advise you.'

'Oh,' said Pridgeon, 'we've got them, and they're getting a bit too thick.'

I dismissed the subject from my mind at the moment, but when I got back, on my way up the High Street, I saw in an ironmonger's window a remarkably ingenious trap for cockroaches, acting electrically. The price, tenpence, was perhaps rather high for a thing of the kind, but scientific apparatus, as I found when I purchased the garden thermometer, nearly always runs into money. I determined that I would mention it to Pridgeon next day. The man himself is all right. It is merely that he has not the tact to adapt his manner to changed circumstances.

A few minutes later, in the course of casual conversation, Eliza said to me that Gladys rather believed that she had seen a black-beetle in the kitchen the night before. This naturally came to me as a bit of a shock.

'By black-beetle she means cockroach. They are an extremely annoying and disgusting thing to have in the house. May I inquire what she did about it?'

'Didn't do anything about it. Said it was too quick for her.'

'Well,' I said, 'after all, the very important thing is what you personally have done about it.'

'Nothing – same as Gladys. Have I got to pull my hair out every time the girl thinks she sees a black-beetle?'

'I never suggested that you should pull your hair out by the roots. I do suggest that in a house of this class, for which I pay forty sovereigns in rent every year, cockroaches should not be allowed to exist. However, it is the same old story. If anything has to be done, I must do it myself. Kindly give me my hat, please.'

I went out and purchased the cockroach trap which I had seen in the ironmonger's shop. Mr Pawling himself served me, and said that it was quite a new thing, for which he anticipated a great sale. I went over the directions with him and found the trap simple in construction and yet remarkably ingenious. The fact that the coackroach infallibly perished before it had ever reached the bait made it singularly economical in working. Also, as the trap reset itself automatically, it would destroy a million cockroaches with the same ease that it would destroy one. Science has always had a fascination for me, and I was really almost glad that we had a cockroach on which to experiment.

I showed Eliza the paper of directions and then explained the trap to her. As I had expected, she quite failed to appreciate the ingenuity of the mechanism.

'Unfortunately,' I said, 'I can ony give you an explanation. I cannot provide you with the intelligence to understand it. I shall now take the trap into the kitchen and set it myself, placing it, as directed, near the range.'

'While you are there,' said Eliza, 'you had better catch that cockroach and read the paper of directions to it. Otherwise it won't know which way it has got to go into the trap, and it may miss the second turning on the right, and nothing happen at all.'

I told her that intentional silliness did not appeal to me, and went into the kitchen. I examined the trap at 9.30, at 10, at 10.30 and at 10.45. The cockroach was not yet caught, but I believe it is a well-known fact in natural history that these insects are nocturnal in their habits. I examined the trap again at eight o'clock next morning, and the cockroach was still not to be found. As I said to Eliza, in things of this kind all that one wants is a little patience.

On the following morning and the day after the cockroach remained at large. I tried changing the position of the trap, I also altered the character of the bait provided. But I did not get the result I anticipated. Eliza, of course, had to regard it as rather a joke.

'On the contrary,' I said, 'it is a very serious matter. The cockroach lays a great number of eggs, and lays them continuously.'

'Pity it isn't a hen,' said Eliza.

'You will adopt a different tone,' I said, 'when you find the house swarming with cockroaches from cellar to roof.'

'Well,' she said, 'what did you want to buy that rotten old trap for? That will never catch anything except the mug who bought it. Tenpence for a thing like that! A penny-worth of beetle poison from the chemist was what you wanted.'

'I think not. We have a child in this house. It would be highly dangerous.'

'So it would, if I kept the child in the kitchen all night. But then I don't.'

'The poison might contaminate the milk.'

'So it would, if I put it in it. But I shouldn't.'

It was useless to continue the subject with her. Rather reluctantly I had recourse to Pridgeon. Unfortunately he was in a rather bad temper with me.

'Did you get rid of those cockroaches, Pridgeon?' I said, quite pleasantly.

'I thought we were not interested in cockroaches, not since we got our rise and took a larger size in hats.'

I passed this over. 'On the contrary,' I said, 'I should be interested to know how you got rid of them. I might find occasion to use the same method one day. We are only human, even the best of us.'

'Well,' said Pridgeon, 'I will tell you what I did. I got a paving-stone measuring six feet by three, and laid it down in the garden. I then placed the cockroaches on the paving-stone and passed the garden roller over it two or three times. After that they gave me no more trouble. You try it yourself.'

It ended, as it always does, in Eliza having her own way. She put down the poison and it killed nothing. Of course, however, it would be too much to expect her to confess that she was in the wrong. What she says now is that the cockroach was never seen before or since, and that it is her belief that Gladys imagined it.

If that is the case, all I have to say is that there is tenpence thrown in the gutter because Eliza chooses to employ hysterical servants.

The Duke of Coverdale

YOUNG Gillivant accompanied me to the station – not by my invitation, but with some idea of making himself agreeable. The reason for this subsequently transpired. I did not dream of lending him half a sovereign, and I told him so. I quoted him that excellent proverb which says that those who borrow come to sorrow. He said he was ready to take his chance. It was just then that he pointed out to me on the platform a tall gentleman of distinguished appearance with a grey beard.

'Know who that is?' said Gillivant.

I admitted that I did not.

'That's the Duke of Coverdale. Frightfully wealthy bug.'

I think I have already mentioned that Gillivant is extremely well connected and has a wide knowledge of society. His Grace entered a first-class smoking compartment in the train which I myself was about to patronize. I got rid of Gillivant by letting him have eighteenpence to be going on with, and I then entered the same compartment as the Duke. No man is less a snob than I am, but it struck me it would be interesting to say that night to Eliza: 'Whom do you think I travelled down with this evening? No less a person than the Duke of Coverdale, one of the wealthiest of our English aristocracy.'

I had hardly entered the carriage before the Duke bent forward towards me with a delightful old-world courtesy, and asked me if I could oblige him with a light.

I said, 'With pleasure, sir.' I did not say 'your Grace', because

I thought it quite possible that he did not wish for public recognition. At my suggestion he was condescending enough to put a few of my matches in his waistcoat pocket for purposes of reference.

The train was just starting when a ticket inspector entered the compartment. I said 'Season', and he nodded. The Duke produced a ticket which was not of the right colour. The inspector glanced at it and said, 'Ninepence excess, please.'

'The firsts on this rotten line are so like the thirds that anyone may make a mistake,' said the Duke.

'Ninepence excess, please.'

'Besides, there's no room in the thirds. Never is at this time of day.'

'Ninepence excess, please,' said the inspector.

The Duke then handed him a threepenny piece, a stamp, and fivepence in coppers, and told him to go to the devil.

'Thank you, sir,' said the inspector and got out.

I could not help smiling to myself, as I reflected how very different the manner of this underling would have been if he had had any idea of the rank of the person whom he was addressing. I was not in the least surprised that the Duke had a third-class ticket. Men of great wealth can afford to indulge in their little eccentricities.

A little later I ventured to call his Grace's attention to the fact that the sky now presented a threatening aspect. He said he believed the country wanted rain, and as he then resumed his evening paper I did not press the matter further. However, as I got out at my station I said, 'Good evening,' and he very graciously returned the salutation.

When I reached home I called Eliza's attention to my match-box.

'That's the ordinary twopence-a-dozen sort you always have, isn't it?'

'It is. What is rather interesting is that at this present moment some of the matches which were originally in that box are in the waistcoat pocket of one of our greatest land-owners, the Duke of Coverdale.'

'I wouldn't have stuck it, if I'd been you,' said Eliza. 'A man may borrow a match from you, but he has no business to pocket any.'

'He pocketed them by my express invitation. An extremely pleasant fellow. I had rather an interesting chat with him in the train coming down.'

'Duke of Coverdale,' said Eliza thoughtfully. 'I've come upon that name somewhere recently.'

'Nothing is more probable. His Grace is very much in the public eye. You have probably seen some reference to him in the newspaper.'

'May have done,' said Eliza. 'How do you know it was the Duke?'

'Gillivant pointed him out. He knows all those people.'

At dinner that night Eliza suddenly exclaimed, 'I've got it!'

'Got what?'

'I know where I came across the name of the Duke of Coverdale. His picture is in the fashionable weddings in this week's *Home Happiness*.'

'I'll trouble you for it.'

The picture was of a quite young man with an appearance of pimples on the face. The accompanying letterpress told me that he had been married a week previously, and was spending the honeymoon in the South of France.

'Is the picture like him?' asked Eliza.

'Not very,' I said. 'Photographs are so seldom satisfactory.'

I took that page of *Home Happiness* up to the office next morning, and confronted Gillivant with it.

'Ah,' he said. 'Somebody will get the sack over that. That's a bad blunder.'

I felt, and still feel, more inclined to believe the statements of *Home Happiness* than those of young Gillivant. However, I did not pursue the subject. I merely asked him if he had received the remittance that he expected, and if in that case he would kindly return me the small advance which I had made him.

It would certainly be a curious coincidence – and also highly unsatisfactory – if it turned out that the only time I ever had any conversation with a Duke, it was not a Duke at all.

A Failure in Economy

I HAD been struck – as I suppose almost every thinking man must at some time have been struck – by the vast amount of rhubarb which is every year allowed to go to waste. Many of us grow far more than we can use, and only a greengrocer can ever hope to sell it.

It is not even easy to give it away. I remember that once, when Eliza's mother had obliged with the water rate and last quarter's rent until better times, I twice sent her a bundle of our own home-grown rhubarb as a token of gratitude. The poor old lady asked me as tactfully as possible through Eliza to send no more, as she found it produced acidity, and her servant had now turned against it. Some men would dismiss such a subject from their minds at once as a mere trifle, but I am not of that type. It is not to me a trifle that the beautiful gifts of Nature should be squandered. It was, moreover, a question which was being peculiarly brought home to me. At my new house, 'Meadowsweet', the rhubarb bed is simply out of all proportion. It occupies space of which I could make better use, if the landlord were less difficult about it. He is one of these men who have to be humoured. Rhubarb jam was attempted on a small scale, but as Eliza dislikes it, and I cannot say that I am fond of it myself, and they refuse to touch it in the kitchen, it hardly seemed worth the trouble and expense. Consequently I was rather impressed when old Pridgeon – a practical man in his way, though he could never rise to my position in the office – happened to say that rhubarb wine, after two or three years in bottle, was indistinguishable even by experts from the finest Chablis.

Here I seemed to see a way out of my difficulty. It would be a pleasure to me naturally to place a bottle of good wine on my table which was of my own growing and manufacture. It was a still greater pleasure to feel that my rhubarb would not be wasted. The only trouble was that I was not acquainted with the standard process of the manufacture of rhubarb wine.

I first consulted the encyclopædia. Under the word 'rhubarb' I found that wine was one of the uses to which it might be put. I then turned up 'wine' and found that rhubarb was one of the substances from which wine might be made. Other information, of course, was given. I learned, for instance, that medicinal rhubarb is grown principally in Mongolia, and I picked up a thing or two about carbon dioxide. But not one word was said as to the process of manufacturing rhubarb wine. These encyclopædias need a deal of revision. I then wrote to the editor of *Home Happiness*, which we have every week, and asked him if he would kindly oblige me with a recipe for rhubarb wine in his 'Answers to Correspondents'. He kept me waiting for six weeks, and I then received this reply: 'The recipe for which "Constant Reader" asks is so well known that we do not think space could advantageously be given to it here.'

And then, as so often happens, a mere chance came to my assistance. It turned out that Parker's mother had made rhubarb wine, and that Parker thought she could remember how it was done. We got on to it at once. The process was much longer than I had expected, and Parker was far less certain about it than I could have wished. She was, for instance, not quite sure whether the bung should be put in the barrel or not.

However, one night the work was completed, and we went to bed at our usual hour. At about two in the morning we were awakened by a loud crash of glass. Eliza said there were burglars in the house. I was by no means sure of this myself, or I should probably have gone down, but I thought it best to take precautions. I keep a police whistle in our bedroom at night – a practice which I should recommend to every householder. I leaned out of the window and blew it sharply. Presently a policeman came along at a walking pace. A little more hurry would have shown a keener sense of duty.

'What's up?' he said.

'I have some reason to believe that this house has been broken into. We have just heard a crash of glass. It sounded as if it might be the scullery window.

'I'll go round and have a look,' said the policeman.

He was back in a minute and said it was the window of the scullery, and that I had better come down and let him in. There was no necessity for that at the moment, as he could easily put his arm through the broken pane and push the fastening back, and then get in at the scullery window.

This was what he did at my suggestion. We heard him moving about heavily downstairs, and then he called up that he could find nobody. I could not be quite sure that was right, so I went down.

'No sign of any burglar,' said the policeman cheerily, 'but you've got a rare old mess in your scullery.'

I looked in to see what had happened. It was a great pity that I ever allowed myself to be guided by Parker at all.

The bung had been blown out of the cask and had broken the window, and the whole place was swimming in rhubarb wine. When I mentioned it to Pridgeon some days afterwards he said that it was secondary fermentation, and all my foolishness in trying to do a thing without learning the way first.

At this moment a second policeman appeared, and he also got in at the scullery window. They inspected the coal-cellar with great care, and still seemed to linger. They were pleasant-spoken men, and said that these accidents would happen. I suggested a glass of beer, and they fell in with it at once. They finished the last two bottles in the house, and then decided that they must be getting on.

Of course, if there was any right or justice in the world, the price of that broken window, and of the materials used for the rhubarb wine, and of those two bottles of beer, would all be stopped out of Parker's salary. But under the present conditions of domestic service such a thing is not feasible.

However, an incident of this kind often gets one's blood up, and next morning I went round to the landlord's agent and practically held a pistol to his head.

'Either that rhubarb goes or I go,' I said. He took a note of what I proposed to put there in its place, and said that he would communicate with the landlord. Negotiations are still pending, but my position is a strong one, last quarter's rent having been paid down on the actual day, and I have reason to hope that my determined stand will meet with success.

In any case, there will be no more rhubarb wine in my house. Eliza is quite definite about it. I need hardly add that the noise of the explosion and the breaking glass woke everybody in the house except Parker. That is the way these things happen.

The Photograph

'ELIZA,' I said, 'it is part of your domestic duty to purchase such things as are required for use in our home. Could you tell me in a few simple words what principle guides you in making such purchases?'

'Principle? There's no principle about it. You just want to use common sense. As long as you get the best and see that you're not done in the eye —'

' "Done in the eye" is one of those expressions – one of many expressions, I am sorry to say – against which you need to be on your guard. Suppose, for instance, Miss Sakers had been present just now.'

'It wouldn't have mattered if she had been, and she wasn't, anyway.'

'Well, I will not argue that point. I will come back to the original subject of discussion. You first of all tell me that no principle is required in the matter of shopping, and you then proceed distinctly to enunciate a principle – to get the best quality possible, and to avoid anything in the way of an overcharge. Now that, like most feminine principles, is absolutely superficial.'

'Come on, then,' said Eliza. 'What's your own principle? You won't be happy till you've said it.'

'My own principle may be expressed in one word – compromise. I may buy things here, or I may buy them in

London. Often they are cheaper in London than if I buy them here. This is notably the case with fish. And yet I sometimes think it advisable to buy things here which I might have obtained at a more satisfactory price in London.'

'Glad you told me that,' said Eliza, 'because of course it will have to be stopped. We've got no money to throw away, and baby wants a lot of new things, and —'

'Just try and put that child out of your mind for one moment, and let me explain to you my reasons. I spoke just now about fish. As you are aware, I frequently bring fish back from the City in a basket. The difference is so considerable that it is worth while. But can you imagine what my feelings are when I step down from the station with that fish-basket in my hand and meet the cart of our own local fishmonger?'

'Well, if Harris don't like it, he should be more reasonable. So long as he behaves as if his blessed haddocks were gold-plated, he can't expect people to go on dealing with him. Getting it direct from Grimsby in the winter and from London in the hot weather saves a lot.'

'I am aware of it. Harris has entirely ceased to touch his hat to me, but I put up with that. Still, I feel it to be my duty, so far as I can, to encourage the industry and the enterprise of my humbler neighbours. Every week I smoke one ounce of tobacco, and I buy it from Smith at the corner – as pleasant-spoken and respectful a man as I could wish to meet. I could buy the same tobacco in London a halfpenny an ounce cheaper, which allowing for a fortnight's holiday, makes a difference of two shillings and a penny in a year. I sacrifice that willingly. Only yesterday I came upon an instance of enterprise here in the High Street which I thought it my duty to encourage.'

'Oh, go on,' said Eliza. 'Let's hear the worst.'

'When you have heard it, I think you will be sorry for the tone you have taken. As I passed the shop of the new photographer, Mr Higford, I saw an announcement in his window which led me to enter. I made a few inquiries, and I saw specimens. For the sum of eight shillings Mr Higford makes a photograph of you in the ordinary way. He enlarges this photograph on porcelain and tints it in the natural colours, giving very much the effect of a water-colour painting. He showed me one which he had just finished of the station-master's wife, and I can only say that I should have recognized it anywhere. What I am proposing, Eliza, is to make you a present of such a photograph.'

'It's very kind of you, of course,' said Eliza, 'but I don't think I want to be photographed at my time of life. Even when I was a girl I didn't use to photograph well – used to come out sort of peaky. I don't know how it was. Somehow when you know you're going to be photographed, your face seems to get stiff and your mouth goes crooked.'

'Well, Eliza,' I said, 'what I was intending was to give you a photograph, not of yourself, but of one who is even dearer to you than yourself.'

Eliza said, 'I should simply love it,' and kissed me violently.

'I think,' I said, 'that it would do very well over the mantelpiece in the dining-room, just above the clock. The space on the wall there has always looked to me as if it was asking for something.'

'Yes,' said Eliza. 'That's where we'll put it. We are more in the dining-room than we are in the drawing-room.'

I did not at the moment raise the question of the frame, but I had already seen something at Higford's which took my fancy. It was a very broad frame, stained dark green. In fact, there was more frame than picture. On the wood in the upper right-hand corner was a small bronze thing, which I took at first to be a spider. On further examination it turned out to be a medallion of Julius Cæsar. Higford said the registered name of it was the Art-in-the-Home frame.

I had already decided to be photographed in a sitting position by a table on which was a pile of correspondence. In one hand I should hold an open letter. I had decided on shepherd's plaid trousers, Higford having mentioned that these came out particularly well, and I also made a note of his hint to keep the feet as far back as possible. If protruded, these get out of focus and are unnecessarily enlarged.

My appointment for Higford was for three o'clock on Saturday afternoon. At 2.45 I was ready to start, feeling a little nervous, but not without some emotions of pleasurable antici- pation. Eliza came down the stairs carrying baby, and I could see at a glance that baby had his Sunday clothes on.

'Some people,' said Eliza, 'have babies taken with no clothes on at all, but I can't say that I think it's quite nice. It seems a pity, too, when the child has got really good things, not to put them in the picture. I shan't take the perambulator, I shall carry him. It's no distance to go, anyhow.'

I saw at once there had been a misunderstanding, and wondered whether it would not be better to clear it up at once. On the whole I decided to let it go. Fathers are sent into the world in order to be sacrificed.

Eliza looked at me wonderingly. 'What on earth has made you take and put on all your best clothes?' she said.

'Merely because I chose to do so. I had my reasons.'

'Well, you needn't get so short about it. Has anything happened to put you out?'

I was unable to check a sardonic laugh. Something had indeed happened to put me out. 'Nothing whatever,' I replied. 'Attend to your own business and I will attend to mine.'

The child was photographed crawling on the table. Higford said that this was a novelty. To speak more correctly, the child's clothes were photographed. Of the child you could see as much face as it then possessed and one fist. Babies cannot be expected to understand these things, and the fist had been thrust forward. In consequence it came out about twice the size of the face. For a production of this kind I did not think it worth while to go to the expense of the Art-in-the-Home frame. We had an old frame up in the attic which could be made to do. Eliza seemed perfectly satisfied.

Personally, whenever I see that photograph hanging in its appointed place, I confess to a slight feeling of disgust. It is not in the least like the child, and could never have expected to be like the child. Babies ought not to be photographed at all. Eight shillings thrown in the gutter – that's what I think about it.

Supply and Demand

THE Epsteins have gone, and on the whole I am not sorry, although we remained friends to the last. Eliza says that they were good-natured people and would have lent us anything they had got, and done anything in their power to oblige us. That is, I believe, true, as far as it goes. But they never had anything that we wanted, and there was never anything that they could do for us. On the other hand there was hardly an article in my house which the Epsteins had not borrowed at one time or another, and they were continually asking us to oblige them. I shall not lightly forget those black days when we had to take charge of the Epsteins' cat.

I remember one occasion when, as it seems to me, Mr Epstein was more than unusually unreasonable, and a good lot of tact was called for in dealing with the situation. I will narrate the circumstance.

For some time I had been in the habit of watering my garden with a can containing the water from the tap over the kitchen sink. Hearing through Pridgeon of an opportunity to acquire a short length of garden hose at what might be called a sacrificial price, I availed myself of it. This hose I was in the habit of fitting to the same tap. And then the water company, in their penny-wise-and-pound-foolish way, began to make themselves unpleasant about it. How they find these things out at all is what beats me. At any rate, after a considerable amount of argument on both sides (I pointing out that I was perfectly willing to utilize waste water from the bath, if they would provide the requisite fittings), I agreed to pay for a supply from a stand-pipe in the garden.

This was a great success and meant a considerable saving of labour. There were one or two trivial accidents, and, as I pointed out to Eliza, they might easily have been avoided. Anybody could see from the windows of the house that I was watering the garden, and it was only necessary to whistle before coming round the corner. Gladys neglected this simple precaution, and in consequence got it full in the face, and upset the perambulator which she was wheeling at the time. The girl simply loses her head in an emergency. The child was not injured in the least, and there was no occasion for Eliza to make any fuss about it. As I told her, the fault was not mine, and it was a thing which might have happened to anybody.

I must say I found the hose very convenient. The watering of the garden did not take half or a quarter of the time that it had once done. While engaged in the work, on more than one occasion I saw Mr Epstein watching me from his window. He has no stand-pipe and no hose, and his lawn is baked brown. I detected a look of admiration and envy on his face, which seemed to me satisfactory as far as it went. Knowing Epstein as I did, I might have known that it would not end there.

And then I received a letter from Mr Epstein. It was ill expressed and wrongly punctuated, and the man evidently had no notion how many 'r's' there are in 'embarrassed'. It contained slang expressions, such as 'I don't think' and 'Not half'. But the meaning of it was only too clear. It was a request that the next time I watered my garden I would water his as well, throwing the water over the intervening fence, and first of all 'singing out', as he expressed it, in order that any of the Epstein family who happened to be in the garden might have time to withdraw. I showed the letter to Eliza simply as an instance of the length to which atrocious impertinence might drive a man.

'Well,' said Eliza, 'you may just as well take and do it. You've got the water and they haven't. It wouldn't take more than ten minutes, and it does you good to be out in the garden. One must keep on friendly terms with one's neighbours. And by the way, you might be a bit more careful about that hose. It's principally when you are changing it from one hand to the other. You seem to forget that the water is going on all the time, and no one knows what it's going to hit next. That girl Gladys says she's positively afraid to go into the garden nowadays.'

'Thank you,' I said, 'but I do not think I have anything to learn in the management of a garden hose. If Gladys happens to have developed hysteria, that is not my fault. At the same time I do not propose to act as an unpaid jobbing gardener to Epstein. I wonder what he will ask next. He will expect me to go round after breakfast and black his boots before he starts for the City.'

'Well,' said Eliza, 'you have got to answer his letter, and I don't see what you can say.'

'I might, if I pleased, put it on the ground of simple commercial morality. I pay for the water supply for one garden, and not for the water supply for two gardens.'

'Yes. But what does Epstein care about that? For that matter, what do you care about it yourself? You diddled the water company as long as you could.'

'I do not agree with you, but it is all quite beside the point. I have no intention of telling Epstein anything of the sort.'

'Then what are you going to tell him?'

'If you will kindly wait a few minutes you shall see.'

I then stepped to my bureau and selected a sheet of our second-best notepaper. I wrote as follows:

'DEAR MR EPSTEIN, – Your favour of even date to hand. My own garden at this season claims very much of my time, but I shall be pleased to do what you request at the earliest opportunity.'

I showed this to Eliza.

'That seems all right,' she said. 'So you're going to do it after all.'

'I have said that I will do it at the earliest opportunity. But there is not going to be any opportunity. Mr Epstein will be quite satisfied with my letter, the water company will not be cheated, and I myself shall not be inconvenienced.'

'Well, of all the lies I ever heard —'

'Not lies, Eliza. Tact. Simply tact. Without it society could not exist.'

However, one day when I was in the City, Eliza herself deliberately watered the Epsteins' garden with our hose and our water. I was extremely annoyed about it, and told her plainly that she was beginning to take rather too much upon herself. It was simply a waste of time to be diplomatic if other people's gardens were watered behind your back in this way.

The Watch

ELIZA had a letter from her brother Frank by the first post in the morning. He had been to the Derby and had had his watch and chain stolen. It was a valuable watch.

'It does seem hard luck,' said Eliza.

'That,' I said, 'depends entirely on the way you look at it. I have no wish to pass any criticisms on your brother. Far from it. I myself do not attend race meetings. If he can reconcile it with his conscience, there is no more to be said on that head. Of course no intelligent man would take a valuable watch to a race meeting, and if he did, he would at any rate take particular care of it to see that it was not snatched. He has simply brought it on himself, and I hope it will be a lesson to him.'

'It's all jolly well to talk like that,' said Eliza. 'But you wouldn't like it if you had your own watch stolen, and it may happen to you one of these days.'

'I think not,' I said. 'For the last twenty years I have been going to and from the City. I have been in crowds where special warnings against pickpockets are issued. And I have never had my watch stolen. Why? Because I use ordinary care and intelligence.'

Nothing more was said on the subject at the time. On the following morning I had an appointment with a firm in Holborn before going to our office. I went there by the tube railway. There was a considerable crowd, as there generally is at this time in the morning, and I was hustled by two or three men in getting out of the lift. I thought nothing of it at the time.

My appointment was for ten sharp, and the clock was striking as I entered the office. I like habits of punctuality, and it annoyed me that I was kept waiting. After a few minutes my hand went somewhat impatiently to my watch.

My watch and chain were not there! Then I remembered that I had been hustled on leaving the lift. I do not exaggerate when I say that I broke into a cold perspiration. The loss of the watch was bad enough. It was a gold watch and had belonged to my grandfather. What was even worse was the thought of what people would say.

My first impulse was to go to Mr Bagshawe at once to tell him what had happened and to request his permission to go to Scotland Yard. I decided against this. The fact that I had lost my watch would not raise me in Mr Bagshawe's estimation. Far from it. It annoyed him to give anybody permission for anything. Reluctantly I came to the conclusion that I should have to leave it until the luncheon hour. It is very difficult to go through one's routine work when one's mind is distracted. All the time I was conscious that something was not in my waistcoat pocket which ought to have been there. I could picture to myself clever thieves removing all identification marks from that watch, or dropping the gold case into the melting pot, even while I sat dictating letters. It was a morning of the most absolute torture. I made one or two slight errors. I do not profess to be more than human.

I received very little consolation at Scotland Yard. I was asked for a description of the men who had hustled me. I said that they were short, and rather thick-set, and of a suspicious appearance. This did not seem to be enough, and I was not able to say more. However, thanks to methodical habits, I had the number of my watch and the address of the maker entered in my pocket-book, and these I was able to provide.

'Now do you think I shall get it back?' I asked eagerly.

'Can't say,' said the man, who showed no excitement and very little interest. 'We shall notify the pawnbrokers, of course, and if we hear anything we will let you know.'

We have in our office a young fellow named Gillivant, who is learning the business. He is well connected, and his parents would, I believe, be called opulent. But the allowance they make him is strictly limited, and he is naturally a man of very extravagant habits. He thinks nothing of losing fifteen shillings or a sovereign in an evening at bridge or some other game of chance. The consequence is that he is frequently pressed for small sums of ready money, and in order to obtain them he occasionally offers articles of his personal property for sale at sacrificial prices. It is not always safe to deal with him. I bought a fountain pen from him which did not turn out as expected. Still, as a general rule I can trust my own judgment, and when I heard Gillivant offering a new five-shilling watch in good going order for half a crown I pricked up my ears. The watch was right at the time, though, of course, that proved nothing. So far as I could judge the works were in good order. I subsequently bought it for two shillings and threepence.

The fact of the case is that I was a little shy about facing Eliza. It was most unfortunate that this should have occurred just after what I had said about Frank. Of course she would have to know sooner or later that I had lost my watch, but I thought that it would make for happiness in the home if I told her later. If she happened to ask me the time I could always tell it, keeping Gillivant's watch hidden from view in the palm of my hand. If she asked me where the chain was, I could say that I was not wearing it now, which would be perfectly true, and that I considered it a temptation to thieves, which would also be perfectly true. Later I might rather take back what I had said about Frank, and point out that I had known several able and competent men who had lost their watches. And then one day I could let it leak out. With a little forethought and management life's daily problems may be safely handled.

With my mind made easy by this resolution I was able to detect and remedy the slight errors which I had made in the morning. For instance, I wrote a letter to the firm I had been seeing in Holborn, commencing, 'Confirming our conversation of this morning,' and going on to represent myself as having said what as a matter of fact I did not say.

When I got home that evening I went straight into the garden, removed my coat and waistcoat, and began to mow the lawn. When you have no waistcoat on, the question of your watch is not likely to be raised.

While I was engaged in this occupation Eliza came out of the house.

'This is a funny thing,' she said. 'Why didn't you put your watch and chain on this morning? The first time in our married life I have ever known you to forget it.'

To deal with a situation like that requires a mind that works like lightning. I am perhaps rather fortunate in possessing that type of mind.

'There is no mistake at all about it,' I said. 'I have thought over what happened to your brother Frank. It is extremely improbable that any thieves would ever dare to treat me as they treated him, but I am determined to take no risks. That watch belonged to my grandfather, and when I am called to my rest I wish it to belong to my son. In future I shall wear a cheap watch in the City.'

'Have you just thought of that?' said Eliza.

'I have a complete answer to that question here,' I said, walking over to my waistcoat. 'I have already procured the cheap watch I desired. Two shillings and threepence was all I gave for it. There are plenty of chances for a smart man with his eyes open.'

And the next day I looked in at Scotland Yard and explained. And this closed one of the most satisfactory incidents in my domestic career.

Cigarettes and Ashes

THE spectacle of a closed shop in the midst of the busy traffic of the City is to me depressing. The shop which I have in my mind had for some time been occupied by a firm who seemed to be unaware that people who frequent the City are business men. It had offered gents' hosiery and underclothing at prices far in excess of the value supplied, and in the final instance I understand that the said clothing was seized for rent. Then for a time the shop remained closed. Every day my eye fell on those blank shutters, and they seemed to me absolutely pitiful. It was a splendid position, and, given requisite capital, I could have taken that shop over and made money with it.

However, one day I found the shutters down, and the windows half covered with notices announcing a great sale of bankrupt stock. Between the notices could be seen boxes of cigars, clocks, cases of cutlery, Dresden figures, all manner of things. I just peeped inside, and saw two men in frock coats, and a porter in a green baize apron. There was a background of packing cases. One of the men had curly black hair and a hooked nose, and may possibly have been of Spanish extraction. He jumped at me at once, and took me by the lapel of my coat.

'You was the man we were looking for,' he said. 'We want your opinion of a cigarette. Nothing to pay. You just try it, and tell us what you think.'

I was a little surprised, but on the whole I rather liked the man's manner.

'Well,' I said, 'I do not suppose that my opinion is worth much, but if you wish me to try a cigarette I have no objection.'

He handed me his own cigarette case, which was of gold, or looked like it, and at the same time told the porter severely to get the gentleman a match.

'The cigarette seems to me quite good,' I said.

The curly-haired young man waved his hand.

'There you are,' he said. 'I am much obliged to you. That confirms my judgment. We are selling bankrupt stuff here, and I had 1,300 of these cigarettes to sell. This brand fetches ten shillings a hundred in any tobacconist's. I am not a rich man, but I bought a thousand of them on my own account; that was all I could afford to take. I am very glad to find I have not done wrong. Much obliged to you, sir. Good morning.'

'Just half a minute,' I said. 'If you have kept a thousand yourself, you have still got three hundred to sell.'

'That is so,' he said. Then he turned to the porter, and changed his tone of voice.

'George, show this gentleman those boxes of Minaret cigarettes, and hurry up – don't keep him waiting.'

'And what price are you asking for them?'

'In boxes of fifty each at the rate of seven shillings a hundred. Look here – I'll tell you what I'll do. I have got to sell this stuff, and the sooner the better. Give me fifteen shillings for the lot, and they are yours.'

He opened one of the boxes and there seemed to be nothing wrong with it.

'I am afraid they will get too dry,' I said, 'buying so many at a time. I generally get packets of ten.'

'Well, what do you think?' said the young man. 'Do you think I would have bought a thousand for myself if there was any chance they were not all right? They are not packed in card boxes; they are in sealed tins. Look at those for yourself.'

'Well,' I said, 'it seems an advantageous offer. Fifteen shillings is a good deal of money; I should like to think about it.'

'Certainly, sir. By all means. Look in again about lunch-time, and if I have still got them —'

'You could not reserve them for me until then, I suppose?'

'I would with pleasure if I had my own way. The guv'nor won't have it. You see, he has only taken this shop for the inside of a week, and everything has to be sold to the first man who snatches at it. If I keep those back, I risk my place.'

I thought it over, and finally decided to make the purchase. It was true that at my rate of consumption there were enough cigarettes to last me a year and a half, and they were far more expensive than those I generally purchased. But I was getting them at half price, and it was an opportunity which might not occur again.

I told Eliza that I had taken advantage of a bankrupt sale, and that for some time to come my cigarettes would cost me only half the usual price. She quite approved. These things must be done tactfully. Of course, if I had simply told her that I had bought three hundred cigarettes she would have been angry.

I finished the first tin of fifty in six weeks – rather sooner than I had expected, but I suppose the truth is that if you have a large stock of a thing you use it more freely. I then opened the second tin, and found it filled with the sweepings of a grate. I was on the verge of opening another tin, but there was something else which I thought I might try first.

'Look here,' I said to old Pridgeon; 'I bought a few cigarettes the other day. You have seen me smoking them. The first box was A 1; the second was no good at all. I have told you everything quite frankly. Now, then, there are four boxes left; would you like to take your chance and make a sporting bid for them?'

'Yes,' said Pridgeon; 'I will give fourpence for the four.'

This, of course, was not to be thought of. I opened the other four boxes myself. All I need say is that if Pridgeon had given me fourpence for the four he would have lost money on it.

Naturally, I have been looking for the people who sold me those things, but they only had the shop for a week, and, of course, they cannot be traced. But if ever I do meet that young gentleman with the curly black hair and the hooked nose, I should not be at all surprised if I lost my temper.

The Wasps

LAST year we had great trouble with wasps. Some men would, no doubt, have grumbled at the time, and then would have let the thing slide. But I am not that sort. I do not allow the grass to grow under my feet, and I take Time by the forelock. This year, long before there was any talk about wasps, I told Eliza that I proposed to buy some cyanide of potassium, and to rid ourselves of the pests effectively.

'Be careful how you get playing about with it,' said Eliza; 'that is a poison, that is, and they think a lot of their cats next door.'

'I am acquainted with the law on the subject, Eliza, and I know what I am doing. If those cats come into our garden, that is an act of trespass, and they commit it entirely at their own risk.'

I purchased the cyanide of potassium at the local chemist's, going through the usual formalities, signing the book and stating the purpose for which I required it. I asked him if he believed it was suitable for the purpose, and he said that it was first class.

Just about this time some new people, of the name of Bodgers, had taken 'The Nest'. I was considering the propriety of advising Eliza to call upon them, when one morning I received a note from Mr Bodgers. It was in the third person, and was to the effect that if I wished to torture my dog or any other dumb animal, Mr Bodgers would be much obliged if I did not do it in the small hours of the morning, as the noise kept them awake.

I have no dog. I have tortured nothing. The only noises to which he could possibly refer were those made by baby, who on the night in question was suffering from some digestive trouble. I wrote a curt note in reply that I had received Mr Bodgers's note, and that I treated it with contempt, and I told Eliza at the same time that any possibility of social terms, or even of communication, between 'The Nest' and ourselves was now definitely at an end.

It may, at first sight, seem that this incident has nothing whatever to do with wasps. Every year added to my experience teaches me that lots of things have to do with lots of other things one would never have expected.

I waited with my bottle of cyanide of potassium with feelings of pleasurable anticipation. I think I should almost have been disappointed if it had not been a good wasp year.

I was not disappointed in that way.

One Sunday evening, as we sat at dinner, I was feeding myself with my fork, and waving my knife round my head at the same time. Eliza said, 'About time you got to work with that poisonous stuff of yours, isn't it?'

I replied that I had not forgotten it – that I already had the matter in hand.

On the following day the baby was stung; so was Gladys; so was Eliza; but providentially I escaped. Eliza said she did not see what I had bought that poison for if I did not mean to use it. She asked if I was saving it up in order to drink it myself.

'Talk about things that you understand,' I said; 'you appear to be under the impression that one first catches the wasp, and then forces the cyanide of potassium down its throat with a gun. It is not so. Even if such a method were efficacious, it would be too prolix, only one wasp being killed at a time. By watering the ground over and round their nests with this solution, I destroy the whole of the wasps; absolutely not one of them can possibly escape.'

'Well, I don't care how you do it,' said Eliza, 'so long as you do it. What is it you are stopping for?'

'So far, I have not been able to locate the nests.'

'They cannot be so difficult to see,' said Eliza. 'The dustman tells me that there are two nests at Bodgers's next door.'

'Ah!' I said. 'That explains much.'

A few days' studying of the habits of these insects showed me that the dustman had been perfectly correct. The wasps slept next door but boarded at my house. If I had been on social terms with Bodgers I should have called round and offered him the cyanide of potassium, with instructions how to use it. As things stood between us, this was, of course, out of the question. Etiquette is etiquette, it is what the Americans call the unwritten law. Finally, I sent a perfectly polite note to Mr Bodgers saying that I had observed that he had two wasps' nests in his garden, and that it would be to his own benefit, as well as to mine, if he got rid of them. His only reply was that the next time I started poking my nose over his garden wall he hoped those wasps would bite it.

And there, of course, the matter stood.

Four Quarts

'ELIZA,' I said one evening, 'I had to-day a little arithmetical problem of most extraordinary interest brought to me. I personally solved it almost at once, but perhaps I am something of an expert in such matters. I wonder if you would care to hear it.'

'There's an arithmetical thingamy that I can't solve, and that's the price they have the cheek to ask for cauliflowers. And no bigger than your fist when you've got them.'

'Well,' I said, 'this little puzzle has nothing to do with cauliflowers. A boy was sent to draw water. He was given a five-quart jug and a three-quart jug, and he was told to bring back four quarts exactly – neither more nor less.'

'Then all I can say is that I don't call that a fair and reasonable way to treat a boy, and a boy of any spirit would have told them so. There's enough trouble about a day's work, anyhow, without going out to make trouble. Why couldn't they have taken and given him just the five-quart jug, and then – if they wanted to be so nasty particular – they could have measured it off afterwards.'

'We are not concerned with the wisdom or otherwise of the parents who gave the boy those instructions. What we have to do is to find out how the boy did it. Perhaps the parents merely wished to test the boy's skill in arithmetic.'

'Then why send him half over the country on a fool's errand with those two great heavy jugs? They might just as well have told him to work out the sum in his head. That would have been the most sensible thing to do.'

'And that is precisely what I am doing. Work it out in your

head, Eliza, if you are capable of it. What would you have done in that boy's place?'

'Well, to start with, I should have left the three-quart jug at home. The less crockery is taken out of doors the better. It may only be luck, but I've never been at a picnic yet where there wasn't something broken.'

'Now come to the point, please. How would you get the four quarts?'

'Simple enough. I should fill the five-quart jug four-fifths full.'

'But how would you know that it was just four-fifths full?'

'Use my eyes, silly, same as anybody else. And I'll bet I wouldn't be wrong by half a pint either way.'

'That's not the right answer. The thing has got to be exact – four quarts, neither more nor less, as I told you.'

'Well, if you know how it's done, I don't need to worry about it. What's the catch?'

'There is no catch at all. The method adopted is somewhat complicated, but I think you'll admit that it is a masterpiece of ingenuity. Let me see now – one must get the different steps in the right order. Ah, yes; I think I recall it. You first of all fill the five-quart jug. Then you pour that away and —'

'Hold on,' said Eliza. 'You're coming out by the same hole you went in at. That can't be right.'

'True. An absurd slip – thank you for calling my attention to it. You first of all fill the five-quart jug. Then you fill the three-quart jug.'

'That's eight quarts you've got already. Full up. Turn off the tap.'

'I think, Eliza, that I should get on quicker if I were interrupted less. Yes, now I have it. You fill the big jug, and from that fill the small jug. You then empty the small jug, and — No; that's not it. Half a moment.'

'Take your own time,' said Eliza. 'And you needn't look so worried about it. It's only make-up. It isn't as if you'd ever have to do it.'

'I do not care to allow myself to be beaten by a thing of this kind – more especially as the first time I heard it I got the answer practically in a flash. Twenty-five minutes were the utmost that it took me. You fill the small jug. Then you fill the — No, again; that's not it. Perhaps you could oblige me with the back of an envelope?'

'I can give you a coal circular. These coal companies keep you fed up with waste paper.'

'It will do,' I said, producing my silver (hall-marked) pencil-case. Eliza went upstairs to put baby to bed. I had covered the back of that circular with figures before I arrived at what seemed to me the root of the difficulty.

'Well,' said Eliza, when she came down again, 'have you got it now?'

'Practically, yes. I have proved to my satisfaction that though my method of working was correct, I must have made some mistake in stating the question. It could not have been four quarts that the boy had to bring back. I am inclined to think that it should have been nine quarts.'

'Well, the two jugs together only held eight. How was he to bring back the odd quart? In his hat?'

'If it was not nine it must have been some other number, but it could not have been four. It is absolutely impossible with those two jugs to measure four quarts exactly.'

'Why, that it isn't. I hadn't meant to worry about it, but it rather stuck in my head while I was giving baby his bath. You can do it two ways.'

'One will be enough. Pray let me hear it.'

'Fill your big jug, measure off three quarts into the little one and pour them away. Then shift the two quarts that are left into the little jug, and fill the big one again. That gives you two quarts in the small jug and five in the big one. Fill up the small jug from the big one, and you've got three quarts in one and four in the other, and four's what you want, ain't it, silly?'

'Kindly repeat that slowly.'

'Four's what you want, ain't it, silly?'

'I meant, repeat the process.'

She did so. I suppose that in a sort of rough-and-ready makeshift way she was correct, though her solution by no means gave me the impression of ingenuity that I had noticed so much in my own.

'But I don't call that a problem,' said Eliza. 'It's only a silly old catch.'

'I admit that a greater problem lies in the working of the human mind. How was it that I had the solution this morning, but had not got it this afternoon?'

'Oh, that's nothing. I had my scissors half an hour ago, but I can't put my hand on them now. I wish you'd get up and see if you're sitting on them.'

I was. As I told Eliza rather sharply, her habit of leaving things about on chairs will, one of these days, lead to a serious accident.

Menial Work

'I DO not know if you are aware of it, Eliza,' I said, 'but I could simply write my name on top of the piano in the drawing-room.'

'Well, it ain't the place for it,' said Eliza. 'Go and write your name somewhere else.'

'Do not pretend to misunderstand me. You know perfectly well what I mean. There is a thick layer of dust on the top of that piano. What does that mean?'

'I should think it means that Jane forgot to dust the top of the piano. Don't look so worried about it. It won't kill anybody.'

'That is not the point. I insist upon decency and order in my house. Jane must dust that room at once.'

'Then you had better run out and tell her so. I sent her out to the fishmonger's. And the other girl can't do it, because she has got baby to look after. And I can't do it, because I have got to put my hat on so as to be ready for Miss Sakers. You had better do it yourself.'

'I will,' I said. 'If it is necessary for the master of the house to do the menial work of the house, I will do it. I trust it will make you ashamed of yourself, Eliza.'

She said that she trusted it would not, and went upstairs whistling. If I have told her once I have told her twenty times that I do not consider whistling a ladylike accomplishment.

I admit that I was angry, and I had a right to be. I pay forty pounds a year for my house, and I keep up a staff of two servants at a very considerable expense, and now I was told that if I wanted the piano dusted I must dust it myself. I went into the kitchen, snatched up a large blue duster from the table, and went back to the drawing-room. At that moment the front-door bell rang. As Eliza was putting on her hat, and Gladys was seeing to the baby, and Parker was out, there was only one thing to be done. I thrust the duster into my pocket and opened the door to Miss Sakers, passing the thing off with a few words of humorous apology.

While we were waiting for Eliza, I took Miss Sakers out to see one or two little improvements which I had been making in the garden. She was good enough to say that she only wished her own gardener could be present to see how things ought to be done. It is always pleasant to chat with a lady of intelligence, and by the time Eliza was ready I had recovered my good-humour. I had also completely forgotten, temporarily, the incident of the piano.

214

Eliza and Miss Sakers went to attend a meeting of the Flannel Society. This is a useful institution for the manufacture of flannel garments and their distribution to the deserving poor. While the members are at work, one of them reads aloud. I had at one time thought of offering my services for this purpose. Natural feelings of delicacy with regard to the garments manufactured restrained me.

The afternoon being fine, I went out to watch the cricket on the recreation-ground. Although no charge is made, some of the best people in our neighbourhood are frequently to be found there on a Saturday afternoon.

I do not actually play cricket myself. As a boy I made some attempt in that direction, but did not meet with a sufficient measure of success to justify me in carrying the thing further. If I do a thing I like to do it well, and the wisdom of this principle cannot, I think, be doubted. However, I trust that I am enough of a sportsman to enjoy watching the game.

I cannot tell exactly how it happened, but I am inclined to think that in watching the course of the ball the sun caught my eyes. At any rate, I sneezed suddenly and violently. It was not till it was all over that I was aware that I had produced that large blue duster in mistake for my pocket-handkerchief. I returned it to my pocket as quicky as possible, but I gathered from the expression of two silly girls who were standing near me that it had been observed. I therefore walked away and joined another group. As I approached the other group some boys began to giggle. I was utterly at a loss to understand it. The thing went on. Everybody who saw me began to smile. I was not aware that, as a rule, there is anything absurd in my personal appearance, and the incident annoyed me. I left the cricket-field.

On my way home I met Gladys wheeling the baby in the perambulator. As soon as they saw me the child screamed with terror, and Gladys burst out laughing. I told her sharply to be a little more careful what she was doing, and passed on. Once in my own room, I saw, of course, what had happened. That duster had been used for some grossly improper purpose. I removed the black marks from my face – they were on the nose principally – and went down to speak about it.

Eliza had just returned from the Flannel Society. She began before I could get a word in.

'I thought you said you were going to dust that piano yourself. You made enough fuss about it.'

I gave one short, sarcastic laugh and walked straight out into the garden.

I sometimes think that more things of this kind happen to me than happen to any other man, and I wonder why.

An Independent Opinion

I REALLY had no idea that it was becoming at all noticeable. It is true that the man who cut my hair mentioned it, but I could understand his motive. He simply wanted to sell me a bottle of his own rubbish. I told him pretty sharply to get on with his work and not to pass remarks.

Eliza said, 'I was looking over the stairs when you were standing in the hall this morning. I don't know whether you know it or not, but soon you will not have a hair left on your head.'

'That,' I said, 'is an exaggeration. I am perfectly well aware that my hair is less luxuriant than it once was. But I still have ample. It depends upon the way in which I brush it. Brushed in the right direction, you would hardly detect any sign of baldness.'

'I should go and brush it in the right direction,' said Eliza.

This was an absurd remark, as it was already brushed in the right direction. There is nothing I detest more than interference of this kind. It can do no good, and it is in the worst possible taste.

At the office old Pridgeon, who is my subordinate, said, 'It's lucky you've got a berth, and are not looking for one.'

'Why?' I asked.

'Because if you were looking for one you would not get it.'

'Do you think so?' I said coldly. 'You happen to be wrong. I venture to say that there are plenty of firms in the City who would simply snap at me, and be glad to have the chance. My testimonials —'

'Oh, I wasn't thinking of that,' said Pridgeon. 'They go by appearance nowadays, and they'd spot that circular bald place at the back of your head at once. Seems to add ten years to your age. I wonder you don't do something for it.'

'What is your recommendation?' I asked, sarcastically.

'Ordinary paraffin. Rub it well into the scalp. Marvellous effect that has.'

'Thank you,' I said. 'I am not at present thinking of making any change, but if I were applying for a new berth I think the appearance of dignity and experience would not detract from

216

my chances, and that a strong smell of paraffin possibly might. In future you can keep your advice until it is asked for, Pridgeon.'

Next morning Eliza said that her poor dear mother had a recipe for a hair restorer which had done wonders. She would see if she could find it. There were several things in it. So far as she could remember, it was principally paraffin.

'Understand once and for all, Eliza, that I am not going to use any form of hair restorer, and that I do not wish the subject to be discussed. In the first place, I am not going bald. It is merely that my hair is a little thinner than it formerly was on the top. In the second place, if I were going bald, it would be a positive advantage to me in the City. My appearance of youth has always been against me. You are making far too much fuss about it. Nobody else ever notices it.'

The next day I was working in Mr Bagshawe's room. I was sitting, and he was standing behind me. Presently he said, 'How long have you been with us?'

'Very nearly sixteen years now, sir. And I hope to your satisfaction.'

'More or less,' he said, in his grudging way. 'I have had worse men in the office, and better. What made me ask was that I see you are getting as bald as a coot.'

Naturally, with Mr Bagshawe one adopts a different manner.

'Only too true, sir,' I said. 'Extraordinary thing, too, because in most respects I am supposed to be younger than my years.'

'Yes,' said Mr Bagshawe. 'You haven't learnt as much as you might have done in the time, if that's what you mean.'

It was, of course, not at all what I meant, but I did not think it worth while to argue the point. He had been to the dentist that morning, and was not at his best, and his temper is always a weak point with him.

That evening I overheard Eliza saying to the baby, 'You'll soon have more hair on the top of your head than your daddy's got – won't you, ducky?'

I asked her to be good enough to stop that nonsense, and to let me have no repetition of it.

Although I did not admit it, I was slightly worried. I could understand the hairdresser's assistant, and I attached no importance to him. Pridgeon's remarks I put down to simple jealousy. Mr Bagshawe rarely misses a chance to say something unpleasant, if he can find one. Eliza, in all probability, was simply actuated by a desire to try her mother's recipe for the hair restorer. Women are always fond of concocting things of this kind. What I wanted was an independent opinion, and it seemed to me that I might as well apply for it frankly to young Gillivant.

'Gillivant,' I said, 'I am going to put rather a curious question to you. Has it struck you of late that I am getting at all bald?'

'You want an absolutely candid answer?'

'Absolutely.'

'Well, it has not struck me. It could not have struck me, because, of course, you are not going bald. It was only yesterday, or it may be the day before, that I was saying to somebody or other that you didn't look your years. I am sorry if this annoys you, but it is a fact. I dare say it would be an actual benefit to you if you were going bald.'

I was not annoyed at all.

'What makes you think that?' I asked.

'Well, people may say what they like, but there is no doubt in my mind that a reasonable amount of baldness gives a kind of dignity to a man.'

'I've heard something of the kind,' I admitted.

'You may take it from me that it is a fact. One of my uncles went bald when he was only thirty, and he told me himself that he felt the gain in general respect at once. When people meet a bald man, they say to themselves, "It's no good monkeying with him. He's been about, and he knows the world." '

'Well, Gillivant,' I said, 'you may be right. At any rate, I am much obliged to you for your opinion. Good evening.'

'Half a minute,' said Gillivant. 'I am getting some money in on Saturday. Strictly speaking, it ought to have come on Thursday, but I hear it won't be till Saturday. That will enable me to repay then the eighteenpence that you very kindly advanced.'

'I am pleased to hear it,' I said.

'I thought you would be. I was wondering if you would care to make the debt up to five shillings, as until Saturday I am practically without means. If you wanted any security, I have got a set of studs that —'

I may have been wrong, but I happened to have some loose silver in my pocket at the time. On the understanding that the loan was until Saturday only, I advanced a further three shillings and sixpence.

The curious thing is that I had somehow a kind of feeling in my mind that he had earned it.

The Unexpected Visit

IT was a hot Sunday afternoon in August. Eliza and the baby were out in the garden. I thought myself that it would be cooler in the house. The sofa in the drawing-room is particularly comfortable, and I occasionally rest there on Sunday afternoons, though I rarely close my eyes. I was just drawing down the blinds of the drawing-room window when I saw, to my astonishment, a large private motor-car stop in front of our house. I came to the very natural conclusion that something must have gone wrong with the machinery of the car.

And then, to my great surprise, the door of the car opened, and out stepped Mr Bagshawe. He was wearing a light tweed suit and a straw hat, and I had never seen him in such a costume in my life before. I had never even imagined him in any other clothes than those which he habitually wore in the City. But still it was unmistakably Mr Bagshawe. And, presumably, he had come to call upon us, although he had never given me the slightest hint of any such intention on his part.

I rarely lose my head in an emergency. I decided at once not to let Parker answer the bell, but to go to the door myself. Such, I understand, is the etiquette on the occasion of a royal visit, and this was the same thing, though on a smaller scale.

'Hallo!' said Mr Bagshawe. 'Surprised to see me, ain't you? Well, I didn't come to see you. I can do that any day of the week. I happened to be motoring in this part, and I thought I'd call on my godson. And if your wife offers me a cup of tea I shan't refuse it.'

I took him through into the garden, and really it was most unfortunate. Eliza was lying at full length on the grass, and the baby was climbing over her. We are well provided with garden chairs, and there was no necessity for anything of the kind.

I expected at least that Eliza would apologize for the extremely undignified position in which she had been found. But she did nothing of the kind, and Mr Bagshawe did not seem to expect it. In fact, when I offered to bring a chair for him he said that he would prefer to sit on the grass, too. He began talking to baby, and the poor child, knowing no better, took to him at once.

Presently Mr Bagshawe said to me: 'Look here; you go for a run in my car for half an hour. My man will take you anywhere you like. I want to have a talk to your wife and to this young gentleman here.'

I was a little surprised, and at first not particularly pleased.

However, I humoured him, as I generally do, and said that I should find the drive most enjoyable. The driver seemed a very respectful and nicely-spoken man. He touched his hat to me, and asked me if I would like the car open or shut. Mr Bagshawe had had it shut on account of the dust. I said that I personally should prefer it open. It is not of much use to drive about in a handsome private car unless people can see that you are doing it. In the course of the drive I met several acquaintances, which was satisfactory, although I do not know why they wore that puzzled look. I determined that if the thing was to be done at all it should be done handsomely, and on my return I offered the driver two shillings. He thanked me in a most respectful way, but said that it was more than his place was worth to take it. It was strictly against Mr Bagshawe's orders. This also was very satisfactory.

I found Eliza and Mr Bagshawe having tea in the garden. The baby was still there. He should, of course, have been sent up to the nursery, but it appeared that Mr Bagshawe had asked that he might remain. Eliza was chattering nineteen to the dozen, and anybody might have thought she had known Mr Bagshawe all her life. I could only hope that she had shown a certain amount of care and tact in what she said to him during my absence.

After tea Mr Bagshawe produced a briar pipe from his pocket and lit it. It was not even a good briar pipe, and he said that he had given fourpence for it, and seemed rather proud of the transaction. He told me where I could get one like it, and I replied that I should not hesitate to avail myself of the opportunity. But I must confess that I was surprised. In the City after luncheon Mr Bagshawe always smokes one cigar. He smokes another on his way back from business. I should have supposed it to be an impossibility for him to smoke anything except a cigar, and a very expensive cigar, too.

He remained altogether for one hour and a half. I accompanied him to his car when he left, expecting that he would take that opportunity to confide in me his motive in coming. But he did nothing of the kind. He said that I had got a snug little place, and that if I liked he would give me a shilling for the baby. He was actually being jocose. I may add that on the following morning I heard him talk to a clerk who had put two letters in the wrong envelopes. Nobody on earth could have imagined that this was the same man that I had entertained on Sunday afternoon.

When I rejoined Eliza in the garden I said to her:

'I must give you a word of warning about Mr Bagshawe. I do

not, of course, know what he said to you, but I am familiar with
his habit of deprecation. I have no doubt whatever that I could
easily explain anything he said about me, and even give you his
reason for having said it. He is naturally cantankerous. I
believe, however, that his bark is worse than his bite.'

'What are you talking about?' said Eliza. 'I think he is the very
nicest and kindest old gentleman I ever met in my life. He did
not say very much about you, but what he did say you would
have liked.'

'You do not happen to remember the exact words?'

'Not to swear to them. It was when he was talking about the
business.'

'Mr Bagshawe talked about his business to you!' As a
surprise this really reached the limit.

'Yes. He is not the least bit like what you described. I got on
with him like a house on fire. Lots of interesting things he told
me. He has got no children himself – had two, and they both
died. Lucky that baby took to him, wasn't it? Oh, and he talked
about my business, too.'

'I have yet to learn that you have any business.'

'I mean the money I had from mother. He thinks I could do
better with it. Tell me, is Mr Bagshawe's business perfectly
sound? Would it be safe to put my money into it?'

'There are larger businesses in the City of London, but I will
guarantee to you that there is none sounder. I have access to the
figures, and I know what I am talking about. The Bank of
England is wild-cat compared with Bagshawe and Co. But you
need not make any mistakes, my dear, about your money. You
will never get a chance to put it into Bagshawe's business. He
has got all the capital he wants, and can have as much over
again by putting his head out of the window and whistling for
it.'

'Yes, he said that he did not need capital, but that he could
not see his way to give you even a small partnership unless you
– or I, on your account – had money invested in the concern.'

* * *

It is an extremely difficult thing to describe one's emotions at
the supreme moments of one's life. I was pleased, but still more
I was astounded. On more than one occasion Mr Bagshawe had
gone out of his way to declare that never, under any circumstances, need I expect to be taken into partnership. I pressed
Eliza with questions, and never have I regretted more her
inability to remember the exact words used. It appeared,
however, that Mr Bagshawe told her that he had once had as his

partner a man with plenty of money, considerable knowledge, and no steadiness. I knew, of course, to whom he referred. He was now thinking of trying the experiment of taking a man with less capital and knowledge, but on whose steadiness he could absolutely rely.

It was rather a question to my mind whether I should open the subject to Mr Bagshawe on the following morning when I went to business. Eliza said that I had better do nothing of the kind, and wait until he started upon it. As she seemed to have the management of the affair pretty well in her own hands, I accepted this suggestion. Mr Bagshawe kept me for one hour and a half after ordinary business hours, and it was only during the last half-hour that he spoke of the subject at all. He then said six things about myself, and five of them were distinctly uncomplimentary; in fact, he had quite returned to his normal business manner. But still, it did appear that he seriously contemplated taking me into partnership.

Weeks have elapsed since then, and the final details are not yet arranged. But there is very little doubt that the thing will go through. Ambition no longer has anything to offer me. In future my interests and activities will be concentrated entirely in the firm, and I shall have no time for any further record of those scenes from my domestic life on which I have hitherto been engaged. I can only hope in conclusion that the advice which they contain, and the example which they offer, may be of service to others in their upward career.

ELIZA'S SON

Introducing Ernest

ON my last birthday but one, pa gave me a large notebook, and said that he thought I might find it useful in my studies at school. I thanked him quite properly, and said I hoped he had made the man who sold it take something off, as it was clearly a shop-soiled article. The truth then came out. He had bought the book twelve years before.

'I had intended,' said pa, 'to write in it some illustrations of my methods in the management and education of a son. It would, perhaps, have been a useful guide to young fathers. But when I decided to go into partnership with Mr Bagshawe —'

'When you which?' asked ma.

'My expression is correct, Eliza. The partnership was offered. I decided to accept it. There was no occasion for any interruption. When the business of my firm absorbed me, I was compelled to relinquish authorship. However, I thought the book would come in one of these days, and it has done so.'

Ma said that pa didn't work any more now than he did before he was a partner, and took more holidays. And pa said there was such a thing as mental strain, which was the real reason why he sometimes dozed off after dinner.

I took the notebook to school and tried to sell or swop it. The only offer I got was one small apple, and apples were plentiful that year. So no business was done. I was naturally not going to use it for school exercises. The notebooks I get for them are paid for by pa, and I saw no reason why my birthday present should be used to save him money. It was a measly sort of present, anyhow. A shilling was the most he ever gave for it.

I have now got an idea. Pa had been going to use the book to write about him and me. Very well, then, instead of that, I'm going to use it to write about me and him.

I've got the same name as pa. It was a rotten notion, and it has never worked. After the twentieth time that pa had run upstairs to find that it was me that ma really wanted, he said that it was just as if it was done on purpose, and ma said he had brought it on himself. I was very young then – not more than six – but I have always been old for my years, and I said that, if I were asked, I should like to be called Ernest. Ma agreed, and gradually pa got into the way of it, though he said he shouldn't. It is a suitable name for a boy of a serious disposition. At school the boys generally call me Cockeye. The reason for this, if it can be called a reason, is that I wear glasses to correct a slight strabismus.

Ma said that as a baby I was pretty, but that I now get more like pa every day. I asked her if she thought that was an improvement, and she said one could easily think too much about appearances. I have often noticed a man is not judged by his looks, but by something far higher – namely, by what he can make. All the same, I wish pa did not insist on my wearing an Eton jacket. I am not at Eton, but at a potty grammar school. The Eton jacket does not suit my style of figure, which is rather on the thick side; it does not wear well, and it is the cause of vulgar remarks by other boys. I heard our doctor tell pa that Eton jackets provided no proper protection for the kidneys. But a plucky lot pa cares about my kidneys, so long as a thing is good style.

The reader should not be misled by the above remark. I love, honour and obey my parents. I have been taught to do so, and I do it. But I am not blind to their faults, and, if this book is to be a truthful record, I may sometimes have to allude to them.

We are nearly all day-boys at the school, and almost all classes are included in it. The fact of the case is that the school gives a first-rate education for a very low fee. This is a chance for poor parents, and even the swells find it too good an opportunity to chuck. Sometimes they use it as a preparatory school for their sons until they are old enough to go to the public schools. Pa said that he felt rather nervous about sending me there, and he hoped I would be careful not to mix with boys of inferior social position. Of course, there are a good many boys at the school, such as young Buddilow, who are supposed to be superior to me. I asked, and pa said it would be all right for me to mix with them. Then I asked what their parents would think about it, and pa said: 'Do stop this everlasting questioning.'

As a matter of fact, I don't mix much with any of the boys; they seem to me to have very little sense. They have no proper ideas about money, and spend it in foolish ways, and often on sweets and other food which they do not really need. They think more about games than getting on in the world. I doubt if there is a boy in the school except myself who has made careful and serious plans for his future. Fortunately for me, the fact that I wear spectacles prevents me from taking any part in their games. I am not popular with the boys even now, and they sometimes make fun of me, but I get on better than I did. At first the fun was rather rough, if you could call it fun at all. It does not seem to me amusing to take a new cap from a boy's head and fling it over a wall, so that the owner must commit trespass at great risk to himself to recover his property. Where is the fun in rolling a boy violently down a high and steep bank? A serious accident might happen. However, such incidents rarely befall me nowadays. The boys who were the leaders in such things were, as was to be expected, lazy and unintelligent, and in school they found me very useful. I have written Latin exercises for them, with enough mistakes in them to be possible, but showing improvement. In two or three minutes before prayers I have run over with them the Ovid that they were supposed to have prepared the night before. They in return have not only left me in peace themselves, but have even ragged other boys who were trying to rag me.

It will have been gathered that I am good at work, and I may without vanity say that I am. I am one form higher in the school than any other boy of my age, and I am top of that form. Pa has bought a special bookcase to keep all my prizes in, and always points them out to anybody who comes to the house. He even did it to the man who came for the gas-meter. And he always calls them 'trophies of my son's scholastic prowess'. It's the kind of thing he enjoys saying. I have never yet had a report from school which did not say that I was a hard worker, and had unusual abilities, and that my conduct was excellent. So you would think that at any rate I should be very popular with the masters; but, as a matter of fact, most of them seem to dislike me, and say sarcastic things about me. I believe they try to provoke me to answer back, so that they can punish me for being disrespectful. But I see through them, and never give them a chance. Very poor incomes they have, I believe, though I've not yet been able to get the actual figures.

Ma says that she's afraid I don't act the right way to get myself liked. But if you do act the right way, you may be led into doing things for nothing, which I should object to very strongly. You can do without popularity, but you cannot do without money.

All the same, I was asked to young Buddilow's party,

although it happened in rather a funny kind of way.

Young Buddilow cheeks the masters, neglects work for play, has been publicly caned for laughing in prayer time, and has no common sense. But he is popular, and that shows what popularity is worth. He is good at nothing except games. He can throw stones hard and straight. At one time he never saw me without throwing a stone at me, though I repeatedly asked him to remember that I wore spectacles. He is particularly foolish with respect to money. I suppose he gets more pocket-money than any boy in the school. It is paid him regularly every Saturday morning, and by Saturday evening he never has a penny. It does not all go to the sweet-shop by any means; in fact, when he is in training, as he calls it, he does not eat sweets at all. Almost all shops seem to have temptation for him. He buys just for the fun of buying. There is hardly anything that he will not buy. He buys things that he does not want in the least, and, perhaps, gives away the next minute. He bought a pocket corkscrew last week, and within five minutes exchanged it for silkworms. That sort of thing looks to me like madness.

One Saturday afternoon, as I was going to the free library, I met Buddilow coming from cricket.

He said, 'Hallo, Cockeye. Got any money in your clothes?'

It seemed better to say that I was afraid I had not.

'Pity,' he said. 'If you could have let me have twopence I'd have given you threepence for it next Saturday.'

'Well,' I said, 'how could one be sure of that? Sometimes you spend all your money before you get to school.'

'But I wouldn't if I owed it, you hog! Look here, Cockeye, you can wait outside our gates Saturday morning and get me as I start for school. I must have the money then, for I shan't have had a chance to blue it.'

I said that in that case I would feel in my pockets to see if I had made any mistake. I found twopence and handed it to him, though with some misgivings.

During the whole of the following week he only shied stones at me once, and called out in quite a friendly way that I needn't get in a funk about my blinkers as it was my shins he was going for. This showed a marked improvement on the previous week. At a quarter to nine on Saturday morning I met him outside the gates of his father's grounds, and he paid me the threepence quite cheerfully.

Next week he borrowed fourpence, and returned me sixpence. And so it went on week after week. He always borrowed something, though I would never go beyond fourpence, and he always paid me punctually. I saw to that myself, for I was always at the gates on Saturday to catch him before he could spend his week's allowance. Sometimes, while I was waiting for him, I used to see through the gates a rather shabby old woman wandering about the drive in an aimless sort of way. I thought she might be the lodge-keeper's wife.

These pleasant relations with young Buddilow had lasted nearly a term, when it became known that Buddilow was to have a party on his birthday, and that his parents permitted him to ask anybody he liked to it. A term before I should not have expected to be asked. But now things were different. Money-lending is strictly forbidden at the school. Pa has forbidden it as well, and says I must check my generous impulses. So I was really running a very great risk for Buddilow's sake, and an invitation to his party would have been a way of showing that he appreciated it. But though he asked a lot of boys – some of them boys of what pa calls an inferior social status – he never asked me.

Of course, as I held no security whatever, it was not money-lending in the usual sense of the term. If it had been I should not have done it, for I am always careful to obey the school rules. But the risk was just the same, because it might have been mistaken for money-lending. So it was distinctly mean not to invite me, and meanness is a vice that I hate.

Two or three days before the party took place I happened to be in our stationer's shop buying a box of pens. I always keep a stock of pens at school, and less careful boys who find themselves without a pen come to me for one. I sell them at a fair profit, and thus, helping others, I help myself. As I was buying my pens, a large motor-car stopped in front of the shop, and out stepped the old lady whom I had seen in the drive at Buddilow's place. She did not look at all shabby now. As soon as she got into the shop she stared very hard at me through eye-glasses with a handle to them.

'Bless my soul!' she said. 'I know your face, my boy. Where have I seen you?'

So I told her.

'Of course. So you wait there to walk with Reggie to school. Most touching. David and Jonathan. Then I shall see you at Reggie's party, of course.'

I explained that I had not been invited.

'How like Reggie! He has no mind and forgets everything. However, I invite you myself, and be sure you come.'

I thanked her politely and said I should be glad to come if my parents permitted it.

Pa was pleased about it, though he pretended not to be.

'The Buddilows?' he said. 'Yes, I remember, your mamma and I spent an afternoon there once. Nice little place as far as it goes.'

'When we went,' said ma, 'it was a charity entertainment, and we paid to go in. Had to pay for our tea, too. Had to pay for everything.'

Ma was not so pleased as pa. She said I could go if I wanted to, but she would sooner the boy had asked me himself. Pa became very busy. He went over my clothes and sent them to be cleaned and pressed. And he made a note to buy a white evening waistcoat and gloves for me in the City next day. Then ma said, 'And don't forget the diamond buttons,' and pa said, 'Restrain yourself, Eliza!'

The next morning at school I told Buddilow all about it, and said that his mother was very kind.

'Yes,' he said, 'that's probably the reason. And then, of course, she didn't know.'

'Didn't know what?'

'Didn't know you.'

'I accepted. It's all right, isn't it?'

'Quite. Jolly decent of her to ask you, and you'd be bound to accept. You couldn't tell her why you waited for me at the gate. Well, what will stop you from coming to-morrow night will be a headache.'

'I never have such a thing.'

'You've got to have it, Cockeye. If you can't get it any other way I shall shy bricks at you to-morrow afternoon and make a certainty of it. Now, are you going to give me all that trouble, or are you going to arrange it for yourself?'

I said that I would arrange it for myself, and I did, but it was most unpleasant, and I ought not to have been treated in that way at all. Pa was most annoyed, and said that he had spent eight shillings or more on my account, and it was practically money thrown into the gutter. Ma was more decent. But they both agreed that they would have to be very careful about my diet for the next few days, and they gave me hardly anything for supper except pills. Very well. In a few days' time Buddilow will be trying to borrow twopence again. It pays me much better to get sixpence from pa for a box of pens and to sell them to other boys at a halfpenny each. And I do not know of any rule against this, whereas if I lend Buddilow money there is a risk that I may be falsely accused of money-lending.

If I do let him have that twopence, he will have to return fourpence next Saturday. If he does not choose to act like a friend, he cannot expect to be treated like one.

A Present from Mr Bagshawe

HERE are a few of the things I've noticed.

My godfather is pa's partner. I used to call him Uncle Bags when I was a child, and I still do, though he's not really my uncle. But pa generally says 'Mr Bagshawe'. Sometimes he says 'sir', and then corrects it.

Another thing. Sometimes in the evening I take pa a difficulty in my work. If it's anything in commercial arithmetic, he's all over it, and he's always right. He even criticizes the question sometimes, and says they show lamentable ignorance of ordinary practice in the City. If it's geography, he may chance it or he may not. History he's very shy of. And if it's French, Latin, Algebra or Euclid, he says that the only way I can learn self-reliance is by tackling my difficulties for myself. That kind of talk does not kid me, of course, though from respect I do not tell him so.

Some more things. Pa does up parcels just a bit too well. He must have had a lot of practice at one time. He blows to any extent about the importance of 'my firm', as he calls it, but he tells me precious little about his early days before he was partner. What he does say is sometimes swank, and I always know when it's swank, because ma has her knife in it. 'The last time I was travelling in France', pa began one day, and than ma said he had never been out of England but once in his life, and then it was only a day excursion.

Putting these and other things together, I came to the conclusion that pa never had any proper education, and was at one time in a very lowly position – probably as errand-boy. I asked ma if this were not the case, and she said I was all wrong; but she only hoped I should get on in the world as well as my father had done. She didn't half let me have it – seemed quite angry about it. That's so queer about ma. She gives pa socks to any extent herself; she doesn't go the full length if I'm in the room, but there is not much that happens in the house that I don't get to know about one way or another. But she never lets me say a single word against pa. This seems to me most unfair. Why should I be asked to shut my eyes to the facts?

Whatever ma may say, one thing is perfectly certain – that pa's in a mortal funk of Uncle Bags. If he says a thing 'would annoy Mr Bagshawe extremely', he seems to think that disposes of it. At one time Uncle Bags used to order pa about and make him run around. I'm dead sure of that, whatever ma says. Even now, from the figures which I have been able to pick up from time to time and have subsequently put together, I can see that

Uncle Bags draws at least eight times as much from the business as pa does.

Pa's funk of Uncle Bags was never more surely shown than in the case of that dog. Pa did not want a dog. Ma did not want a dog. I myself did not want a dog. And nobody on earth would have wanted that particular dog. But we had to have it, because Uncle Bags made pa a present of it.

This was the way it came about. Uncle Bags's sister had decided suddenly to spend the summer and winter touring about abroad. She had just bought the dog, and could not take it with her because of the trouble and the quarantine. So she sent the dog to the office with a note for her brother to say that she would be glad if he would take it.

I know what Uncle Bags said to pa about it, because pa told ma about it in the garden and my window happened to be open.

Uncle Bags said: 'Most unreasonable – I can't take the infernal dog home with me; my own dogs would eat it. Have you got a dog?'

Pa said: 'No, sir; but —'

'Then that's all right. I make you a present of it. It'll be a guard for your house. It'll be a companion for your wife when you're away in the City, and I dare say your boy will like it. Every man ought to keep a dog – why, I've got six myself.'

So pa thanked him, and Uncle Bags dictated a letter to his sister to say that he wished she would not do these impulsive and idiotic things. He had found a good home for the dog, where it would be well looked after, but he hoped she would never give him the same bother and trouble again. Why should he be expected to waste the entire day in looking after other people's dogs? And some more of the same kind. Rather hot stuff, Uncle Bags.

So pa brought the dog back with him on a lead, and even on the way home from the station it gave trouble. It walked round a lamp-post and sat down and howled. Pa began to unwind it, and the dog thought it would help, but got the wrong direction. So while pa was unwinding, the dog was winding up again. Pa put out his foot quite gently to get the dog to reverse, and an old lady told him he was a brute and not fit to have the charge of dumb animals. Pa carried the dog the rest of the way to avoid accidents, and was rather heated when he arrived home. He had taken the number of a policeman who had done nothing but grin instead of rendering assistance and keeping the crowd off, and pa said it was just about time some man in that division got a sharp lesson; but he never did anything else about it.

There must really have been quite a number of people where pa and the dog got mixed up about the lamp-post. Everyone seemed to know pa had got a dog. Two men called that evening to know if they could have the job of engraving the address on the collar, and we had three lots of dog biscuits on appro, from different shops, and a photographer wrote that animals were his speciality, and he hoped to be favoured with pa's esteemed order.

When pa had got the dog home he came and told ma and me about it, and he seemed very depressed. It was one more responsibility piled on his shoulders, as if he had not enough to bear already. It would mean endless expense – dog licence, collar, chain, food, vet's bills, and compensation to the people the dog bit. A dog would be absolute ruin to the garden on which he had spent years of labour, and perhaps it would be better to move at once into a smaller and cheaper house where there was no garden at all.

Ma said of course it was annoying, but pa need not talk in that silly, exaggerated sort of way. She didn't want the dog herself, but, still, lots of people did manage to keep a dog without making much fuss. However, if pa felt like that about it, perhaps he had better give it back to Mr Bagshawe.

'I wish, Eliza,' said pa, 'that you would not say what you know to be absurd. Mr Bagshawe gave me the dog as a present. Mr Bagshawe said that I ought to keep a dog. If I had been in a position to return the dog, I should have returned it there and then; but I was not in that position.'

'What's its name?' said ma.

'Don't know,' said pa snappily.

'What's its breed?' I asked.

'None,' said pa, showing his teeth as if he'd been going to bite me.

'Where is it now?' said ma.

'In the coal-cellar. And there it can stop till it dies, for all I care.'

'Has it had anything to eat to-day?'

'Mr Bagshawe said it was not to be fed till the evening, and that Miss Bagshawe had overfed it already. It has had some water, and it ate the back off a letter-book. Now I've got to go out and buy dog biscuits for it. Dancing attendance on a dog – nice work for a gentleman that is.'

After pa had gone I took a candle and went into the cellar to look at the dog. It sat on a large lump of coal, weeping; it was always howling about something or other the whole time we had it. It was really a kind of fox-terrier, but with more than the usual number of spots on it and very long in the ears and tail.

I said 'Hallo!' and the dog suddenly went for me. I don't mean that it tried to bite me – it never tried to bite anybody – but it wanted to get out of the cellar and I was in front of the door. It went through my legs, and I fell over. I bit a piece out of the candle in the fall, and got a lot of coal-dust on me. In fact, I was made to wash my face and hands at once – though it was so near my bedtime that they might very well have been left till next morning.

Pa came back with his lot of dog biscuits, and found the other three lots which had been left in his absence. The dog refused to eat them; they were almost the only thing in the house that he never even tried to eat. Pa's temper was now getting beyond his control, and I voluntarily offered to go to bed, though it was some minutes before my right time. It seemed to be safer.

The dog never disturbed me all night, but I am an unusually sound sleeper. When I looked out in the early morning I saw a pair of pa's boots in the middle of the lawn, and the dog was eating one of them. Then I knew there had been more trouble. I looked out again an hour later. The boots had gone, and pa was walking about the garden with a stick in his hand, saying, 'Come here, sir. Just you come here, sir.' I think he was looking for the dog, but I did not see it anywhere. I doubt if the dog was quite such an absolute fool as pa always said he was, though he was certainly eccentric.

Things were miserable at breakfast-time. There was no milk, because the dog had knocked the can over. Pa came in from the garden and said: 'The Lobelia cardinalis which I planted yesterday morning has been scratched up and destroyed. More money wasted!'

Ma said: 'Jane's given notice because she says kitchens are one thing and dog kennels are another.'

Then pa opened two letters from our neighbours complaining. The dog seemed to have kept everybody awake except myself.

'And after all the trouble we took to make a comfortable bed for him,' said ma. 'It does seem too bad.'

'One more night like the last,' said pa, 'and I speak to Mr Bagshawe, come what may.'

'I don't see why you shouldn't tell him this morning that you find the dog a nuisance and you can't keep him.'

'No good in the least. He'd only say I hadn't given the thing a fair trial.'

They weren't exactly angry. They just looked worn-out and heart-broken. Nothing I said seemed to be right for them, and I left for school earlier than usual.

When I returned at midday ma was quite cheerful again. But she said that Jane had taken the dog out for exercise and had had the misfortune to lose him. I offered to write out notices describing the dog and offering a reward for his return, but ma said she would wait till pa got back and she found what he thought about it.

Pa said it was careless of Jane, but as she was probably not used to dogs it might be as well not to blame her for it. Ma said she had not blamed her.

I asked pa if I should write out a few notices for people to put in their shop window. Pa said that perhaps it would be better to leave it for a few days. If tradespeople obliged you in one way, they always took it out of you in another. 'We must just wait, and hope the dog will return of his own accord.'

'Hope what?' asked ma.

'Precisely what I said. Do not forget that it was a present from Mr Bagshawe. He inquired to-day how the dog was getting on. It's a providential thing, by the way, that I have not yet taken out the licence.'

I wonder why pa wouldn't say he was glad the dog was gone. Of course, anybody could see that he really was glad. At breakfast-time he had called the dog names that he would never have allowed me to use. But now he said: 'Poor little chap! I wonder where he's roaming?'

I said: 'They may have got him at the police-station. Shall I go up and see?'

He told me that I had homework to prepare, and he would thank me to concentrate my attention on that, and not to be for ever interfering in matters which did not concern me.

Just then Jane came in to say that a man had brought the dog back and would like to see pa about it. One of the first things you learn at school is not to smile when you want to. I did not smile at all. Pa did not smile either, but I don't think he wanted to.

As he left the door ajar I could hear a good deal of what pa and the man said in the passage.

'Yes, sir,' said the man; 'I knowed it was your dog because I saw you trying to tie it up to a lamp-post yesterday evening. And I don't suppose there are two of this sort alive. One by himself, he is. Head rather reminds you of a mule, don't it, sir?'

Then the dog began to wail, and I missed the next bit. When it stopped the man was saying:

'Well, sir, I leave that entirely to you. I'd some trouble in catching him, and, of course, it's a three-mile tramp for me.'

Pa said something in a low voice that I could not hear. And

then the man said: 'Afraid I couldn't do that, sir. You see, I've got no room to keep a dog, and then, of course, he ain't everybody's dog. More like a curio, ain't he, sir?'

I did not ask pa at the time how much he had given the man for bringing the dog back, but I found out afterwards that it was ninepence. In his place I should not have paid so much as that, even if I had wanted the dog back. But, of course, pa can be talked over – I've done it.

They took a lot of trouble to make the dog comfortable for the night, and it did sleep for a good part of the time. But it howled at intervals, for about a minute at a time, once every half-hour. After five a.m. there was no more howling. It never woke me once, but the rest were not so fortunate. When pa got down in the morning he found that the dog had eaten most of the rope it was tied up with, had eaten the new Lobelia cardinalis, and had gone. It was Sunday morning, which was more than some of papa's language was; but I wish to be just, and I do not think he intended me to hear it.

And then came a bit of papa's special luck. Uncle Bags drove up in his new car about tea-time unexpectedly.

Pa was in no end of a stew. 'What on earth am I to say to him about that dog?' he said.

'Oh, I'll talk to him about that,' said ma.

Ma and I are not nearly so frightened of Uncle Bags as pa is.

As a matter of fact, nobody had any need to say much, because Uncle Bags had run over the dog and killed it about half a mile from the house. He was not particularly apologetic about it; but, then, that is not Uncle Bags's way. He said it was all the dog's fault, and it was better dead, and what his sister had ever bought such a monstrosity for was more than he could say. He did offer pa another dog, but ma chipped in and said there was so much traffic in our road she hardly liked to take the responsibility. He drank three cups of tea, took down the name of the fertilizer pa uses for the roses, called me a genius in rather a sneering sort of way, but gave me five shillings, and went snorting off again.

Very hot stuff, Uncle Bags!

However, everybody was pleased, and pa let me off church that night.

That is a queer thing about parents. Whenever they really want to give you a treat, they either let you do something they know to be bad for you, or they let you off doing something they know to be good for you. Looks as if there must be a mistake somewhere.

April the Thirty-First

WHAT with the people pa's stopped knowing and the people that he hasn't begun to know, he doesn't seem to have a lot of friends. Ma's got more; but then her friends are all female. On ma's first Thursday I've known as many as six ladies in the drawing-room at one time. Ma never wanted to have any first Thursday, but pa worried at it off and on for about three years, and at last he tired her into it. If it's in the summer and a fine afternoon, they have tea in the garden and play croquet. Ma's good at it, pa's rotten, and I never try it myself. If it's in the winter, they just sit inside and talk. I never go in now. I am sick of being told that I have grown and of handing things for other people to eat. So while they sit in the drawing-room I am in the dining-room, which opens into it. I take tea more seriously than they do, and sometimes I prepare work for the next day, and sometimes I do my accounts. I can hear pretty well everything that is said in the drawing-room, and so occasionally I pick up things I should not otherwise have been told. But mostly it is uninteresting stuff about servants and hats and kids. I would far sooner hear men talk business.

On the first Thursday pa always comes back by an earlier train that gets in at 4.38. If it's punctual he enters the house at a quarter to five. He opens the dining-room door very softly, and comes in on tip-toe. I then hand him a paper on which I have written the names of the ladies who are there – I know the voices of all of them. Neither of us says a word, and pa tip-toes out again. He arranged all this himself, because he says it enables him to be dressed appropriately for the occasion.

For instance, if there is nobody there but Miss Sakers he just washes his hands and sails straight in. If there are three or four, he changes his coat and puts on patent leather boots. And the day that there were six, including one lady who had never been to the house before, he must have changed every rag. It was twenty to six before he came down, and by that time they had all gone except Miss Sakers; and he wasn't half ratty about it, either! He takes a lot more trouble about them than they ever do about him. He is my father and a man of experience, and he may have reasons of which I know nothing. I am not criticizing him, but I must say it looks to me like a mug's game.

Pa always buys two evening papers on the first Thursday. Other days he only buys one, and if he has been able to pinch one that somebody has left in the train he does not buy any. He takes his two papers into the drawing-room with him, and begins speaking about them to ma as he comes in, as if he had not expected to find anybody else there. He says: 'Nothing much in the papers to-night, my love,' or 'The suffragettes are giving more trouble,' or 'Another strike threatened, my dear.' And then he switches round suddenly to the visitors and says: 'Ah! good afternoon, Mrs Poplington. How do you do, Miss Sakers?'

Many a time I have heard pa going through that act, and I have put aside the quadratic equation I was working on, or the savings-bank account I was checking, and wondered what on earth he did it for. I did ask him once. At least, in a respectful sort of way I gave him the chance to explain it. He said it was simply and solely a question of tact. The evening papers provided pleasant and safe topics of conversation, and people were interested to have the latest news. It's all very well as far as it goes, but if you've naturally got nothing to talk about, then why talk? I don't see where you come in on it.

There was just one of ma's first Thursdays when I should have liked to have been in the drawing-room. But I was not there, and did not see what happened. I was not even in the dining-room, and so I did not hear either. But I got to know all about it afterwards, partly from ma, partly from Jane, and partly from pa himself. For two days pa hardly talked about anything else.

We had been having a spring-cleaning, and the drawing-room and two bedrooms were to be repapered. Pa went to a decorator and chose the papers with ma's help, and told the man to send in an estimate. That estimate simply made pa snort. He said he would show that den of thieves with whom they were dealing. Most men would have sent a post card with 'Estimate declined' or something like that on it. Not pa. That's not his way. He sat down and composed a letter with sarcasm in it to send to the decorator. It took him the best part of an hour. He said there appeared to be some misapprehension, that he merely required his rooms to be papered with the papers selected by him at the price per piece as marked on the patterns. He did not require his drawing-room to be papered with Bank of England notes, nor did he wish the walls of his servant's bedroom to be gold-plated. He read it all out to ma and me when he had finished, and seemed as pleased as Punch about it. He was still more pleased when the decorator called round next morning. 'Aha!' said pa, 'I thought that letter would have its effect on Mr Busher.'

So it did, of course. And a post card would have had the same effect and been less trouble.

Pa got the figures cut down as low as he could, and then gave the order. So, as pa had sweated off most of the profit, Busher didn't send his best men. We got two young chaps who were very slow, and didn't make the pattern fit in properly, and the whole thing looked absolutely rotten. Pa used to stand over them while they were at work and say sarcastic things to them, until they lost their tempers and made disrespectful personal remarks. So off went pa to Mr Busher. Pa said his drawing-room had been ruined by the incompetence of Mr Busher's workmen, and, in addition to that, they were foul-mouthed blackguards, who never ought to have been sent to a gentleman's residence. Pa said it was a grave question with him whether he should pay anything at all for the so-called work which had been done, and in any case Mr Busher could consider the order for the two bedrooms cancelled.

Mr Busher said he was sorry there had been any unpleasant-ness, but he couldn't have any cancelling. Pa had accepted the estimate, and it was a contract.

'That estimate,' remarked pa, 'states in the clearest and most definite terms that the work is to be done to my satisfaction. And it is not done to my satisfaction – very far from it.'

By this time Mr Busher himself was beginning to lose his wool. He asked pa how on earth men could be expected to do their work satisfactorily when they were being everlastingly interfered with.

'Who interfered with them?' said pa.

'Why, you did. Mooning about under the ladders, and passing comments, and trying to talk like a comic paper – my men complained to me about it, and no wonder. Enough to put anybody off.'

Pa said that if that was to be the tone, he totally and altogether declined to hear another word. The order was cancelled.

Mr Busher said that goodness knew he was not keen on having the job. There was no credit to be got from decorating these third-class houses and getting good workmen upset by a lot of fat-headed interference. And there was no profit in it, either. Personally, he would be glad to be quit of it. But, as a matter of principle, he was not going to allow himself to be swindled by pa or any other City clerk, and he should put the matter in the hands of his solicitor at once.

Pa replied that Mr Busher could not possibly do anything which would please him better. It was exactly what he wanted. And pa's own solicitor would be instructed to fight the case – right up to the House of Lords if need be.

Then Mr Busher said: 'Meantime, get out of my shop; I am busy.'

And then pa left.

The case never got as far as the House of Lords – in fact, it never started. Mr Busher met pa in the street, and said he was afraid he had been a little heated the day before, and might have dropped some expressions which were not quite the thing. Win or lose, lawyers only meant expense, and he would be glad to come to some arrangement. He was sure a gentleman of pa's standing would not suggest anything unreasonable.

He got round pa all right. Pa says they compromised it. Mr Busher did not insist on painting the bedrooms, because he jolly well knew that he couldn't insist. And pa paid 14s. 6d. too much for the drawing-room. I had figures to prove this, but thought it better not to show them to pa.

When ma heard about it she said it was all very fine, but those two bedrooms really wanted doing, and she would sooner her spring-cleaning got finished some time this side of Christmas.

'You may make your mind perfectly easy, Eliza,' said pa. 'Those two bedrooms will be done, and they will be done properly. And I venture to think that the style of the work and the price paid for it will compare favourably with anything that Mr Busher's men could produce.'

'Who is going to do them?' asked ma.

'Ah,' said pa, 'that is a little surprise which I am reserving for you. You will know all about it in due course, and I am confident that you will not be displeased with it.'

So, of course, I knew that pa meant to paper the rooms himself. He had not been watching Busher's men for nothing. I rather fancy that ma knew it too. But we both pretended to be puzzled, and that pleased pa. As he seemed to be in a suitable frame of mind, I took the opportunity to ask him something.

A boy at school that day had wanted a pen in a hurry, and had no actual money with which to buy pens from me. But he had a free pass for the sixpenny seats at the picture palace on the following day. After a certain amount of discussion, I gave him three pens for it. I believe now I could have got it for two.

So I said: 'If you don't mind, pa, I thought of going to the picture palace after school to-morrow afternoon. One of my schoolfellows has kindly given me a pass for it.'

As it was a sixpenny pass, and the boy had only got three pens for it, he had, of course, practically given it.

Pa raised no objections at all, and said he hoped I should see some amusing and instructive films.

I knew that the next day was Thursday, May 1st, and consequently one of ma's first Thursdays, and I naturally supposed that pa knew it as well. But it seems he did not. He knew that it was Thursday, but he had got it into his head that it was Thursday, April 31st. Of course, he knows as well as I do that April has only thirty days, but he did not happen to think about it. The right date was on the paper he read in the train and on the letters he signed at the office, but it never soaked through, as you might say. Perhaps he was thinking too much about the paperhanging he was going to do, and what a surprise it would be to everybody. Anyhow, he came back by the early train, things being slack at the office, and entered the house with the fixed idea that it was the last Thursday in April, whereas it was really the first Thursday in May.

He said afterwards that this mistake was the most extraordinary thing that had ever occurred in the whole course of his experience. He called it a psychological phenomenon, and several other things. Of course, pa would not say what he knew to be untrue, but I think he must be wrong. Even in my brief experience I have come upon several blunders as to the day of the month, and should say that they were not uncommon. But pa has got rather a habit of finding things very extraordinary.

He had all his paperhanging tools and materials ready – rolls of paper, scissors, paste-pot and brush – everything. He took off his coat, waistcoat, collar and tie, put on an old pair of trousers, a long white apron and carpet slippers, and rolled up his shirt-sleeves. He thought the time had then come to play off his little surprise on ma. So he hung the scissors round his neck, took the paste-pot and brush in one hand, put a roll of paper under his arm, and trotted downstairs. He burst into the drawing-room, announcing loudly: 'Behold the paperhanger!'

There was a lady there who had never seen pa before. She thought it was really the paperhanger, but that he had gone mad. She screamed.

Miss Sakers knew that it was pa, but she thought that pa had gone mad. She turned faint.

For a second or two ma was inclined to think the same as Miss Sakers, and was also rather frightened. Then she saw what had happened, and pa in his agony dropped the paste-pot.

And to think that I should have been spending my time at an ordinary cinematograph show when things like that were happening at home!

Ma says that, the way things worked out, it was the most successful Thursday she ever had, and about the only one that was at all amusing. Pa explained and apologized frantically. He kept on saying that he was extremely sorry it had occurred. He had quite thought that ma was alone, and he was playing off a joke upon her. 'Merely a little of my fun,' he said desperately.

Once they had grasped that it was a joke, they would not leave it. Everybody laughed continuously, except pa, and he never even smiled. He said: 'You will permit me now, I hope, to go and put on some attire more suitable to the occasion.'

But they would not let him go. They said it was too good to alter, and they had never seen anything like it in their life before. Even when two other visitors came in, they still kept him, and the other visitors joined in the laughter. Miss Sakers wanted to fetch her camera and take a snapshot of the paperhanger at tea. And the more serious and dignified pa became, the more they all enjoyed it.

But if ma liked it, pa did not. He said: 'The thing was carried very much too far. The right course would have been to have laughed in moderation at my joke, and then to have permitted me to resume the garb of an ordinary English gentleman. The way that Miss Sakers and the other lady stood in front of the door when I wished to escape was, to be frank, not quite ladylike. I think, Eliza, that a little remonstrance from you would not have been out of place. Let us be merry and wise, that is what I always say. Moderation in all things. Laughter, but not hysteria. A drawing-room should be treated as a drawing-room, but on that occasion it was pandemonium or even worse.'

He said all this at breakfast, and it was just like a man delivering a lecture. I thought he had finished, but he just took a gulp of tea and went on again:

'I must request you, Eliza, to make no mention of the occurrence in speaking to any of your friends who were not actually witnesses of it. And you, Ernest, will be particularly careful to say nothing whatever about it to any of your school-fellows. You understand me? Nothing whatever. Not a word.'

'Yes, pa', I said. 'I had never meant to say anything.'

'Very good. It is not that I fear ridicule. I have, perhaps, less cause than most men to fear that. As a dramatic impersonation the thing was a success. It is that I object to misrepresentation, and that in a case like the present is not improbable.'

One more gulp of tea, and he was off again:

'What, if I may say so, Eliza, you have failed to see, is that this little domestic incident really has a serious scientific interest. Here am I, a man in the prime of life, and in full possession of mental faculties that are not, I believe, below the average, not subject to hallucination of any kind, and yet at 4.50 p.m. on the first day of May I still have the conviction that it is the last day of April.'

And then ma got in just one punch.

'Ah,' she said. 'We thought it was the first day of April that you'd mistaken it for.'

'As a retort, not bad,' said pa; 'otherwise, silly. More tea, please.'

The Presentation

I DO not like gardening. When I am grown up, if I think my means justify it, I shall employ somebody whose time is less valuable than my own to do work of that kind. If not, I shall not have a garden. However, I put my own inclinations aside when my parents ask me to do anything, and this afternoon pa asked me to run the mower over the lawn, and not to wobble it as much as I generally do. I did about two-thirds of the lawn, and then ma came out and finished it while I looked on. Pa had just come back from the City, and he came out of the house as ma was doing the last turn. He began to speak, but the mowing machine made too much noise for us to hear what he said. This annoyed him.

Ma called out, 'What?'

Pa shouted back, 'I decline to shout.'

However, in a minute or two the lawn was finished, and pa got an opportunity to speak.

'I have rather an important piece of news for you, Eliza. I am to take the chair at a public dinner and deliver an address.'

Ma said, 'Oh?'

'Pridgeon is leaving us after eighteen years' faithful service. He has saved money, and an uncle has left him a little more, and he is retiring. The rest of the staff have subscribed for a testimonial to Pridgeon. The presentation is to be made at a dinner which we are giving him. Mr Bagshawe subscribed a couple of guineas, but regretted that he was unable to take the chair at the dinner. The duty therefore devolves upon me. I am determined —'

'How much did you subscribe?'

'I did not see that I could give less than a sovereign.'

'If you had asked me,' said ma, 'I could have told you. If Mr Bagshawe's got money to throw away, you have not. Ten shillings would have been enough for old Pridgeon.'

Judging the question on an arithmetical basis, both my

parents were wrong. If my figures are correct, as I have reason to believe, pa's income from the business is one-eighth of Mr Bagshawe's. Consequently, if Mr Bagshawe subscribes two guineas for a charity connected with the firm, pa should have subscribed precisely five shillings and threepence. However, although a boy may not be able to shut his eyes to the mistakes of his parents, he is not expected to call attention to them, and I said nothing.

'Unfortunately,' said pa, 'the time is short. The dinner takes place a fortnight from to-day.'

'Well,' said ma, 'you ought to be able to change your clothes by then if you stick at it.'

'As usual,' said pa, 'you do not see what is involved. I have already told you that I am to deliver an address. On such an occasion I do not think the address should occupy less than ten minutes. A great deal of care will have to be given to the composition of it – to the selection of suitable phraseology and the introduction of occasional humorous touches. I must make a fair copy of it, and from that two other copies must be typed.'

'Why?' said ma.

'Because I have some reason to think that it would be a graceful act on my part to present Mr Pridgeon with a bound copy of the address delivered on that occasion. The other copy is naturally required for our family archives.'

'I never knew we'd got any,' said ma.

'If everybody thought like that,' said pa, 'there would never have been any family archives at all. Everything must have a beginning. Then, again, there is the question how the money subscribed is to be spent. I have been consulted, and I must have time to decide what I shall advise.'

'It is generally a clock,' said ma.

'Whatever else it is on this occasion, it will certainly not be a clock. Mr Pridgeon's only fault in his office work has been a slight tendency to unpunctuality. The gift of a clock would seem to remind him of this, and would be in the worst of taste.'

They then sent me into the house on the excuse that I had my preparation work to do for school. Of course, what they really wanted was to be able to speak with greater freedom. I took my work to a table by an open window, but I could hardly hear anything that was at all amusing. Ma began. 'How can you be so cantankerous?' But then, unfortunately, she lowered her voice.

I heard no more about the presentation that day.

Next day pa said that after a great deal of consideration he had decided what the present to Pridgeon was to be.

'What is it?' asked ma.

'It is to be a clock. Everybody else seemed to want a clock, and so I withdrew my suggestion of a tea-service. However, the choice of the clock will be entirely in my hands.'

And we had very little peace with pa for the next few days. The trouble seemed to lie in the amount which had been subscribed for the testimonial. All the clocks that pa saw and approved either cost too much or too little. Occasionally he did find one which was just the right price, but it was always one which, so he said, had no artistic merit. All the time that he could spare while he was in the City he spent in clock-shops, and all the time he was at home he talked about clocks. I made a note of the figures, and on his showing pa had been insulted by the assistants in nine clock-shops in the East Central district of London. He found the right clock at last, and had it sent to the office. Pa said he was very sorry that ma and I could not see that clock, for it was really a beautiful piece of work. He described it off and on during the greater part of one evening. As far as I could make out, it was just like any other old clock.

Then the trouble took a new form. A silver plate with an inscription engraved on it was to be attached to the clock. Pa had got an inscription already, covering about a sheet and a half of notepaper. But the expense of it would have been too great. It had to be cut down to twenty-four words. Pa was constantly busy with pencil and odd bits of paper. The first words were always the same:

TO JAMES PRIDGEON, ESQUIRE, AS A SLIGHT TOKEN OF ESTEEM FROM

After that the thing went variously. Sometimes it was 'from the partners and staff', and sometimes 'from a few friends and business associates', and sometimes 'from his fellow-workers in the firm of —' At breakfast-time I used to see pa playing an imaginary piano on the table-cloth. Then I knew he was counting words for the inscription, and I was careful not to interrupt. Ma was not so careful.

Ma said, 'There's one thing that beats me altogether.'

Pa said, 'One moment, please. Twenty-one, twenty-two, twenty-three; I made sure it was twenty-four. However, no matter. You were saying, Eliza?'

'Oh, nothing. I said there was a thing that rather puzzled me.'

'If you will let me hear what it is I may possibly be of some assistance.'

'Well,' said ma, 'if there is to be this almighty fuss every time a clerk leaves his place, how do you manage to find time in the City for any business?'

Pa controlled himself perfectly. His eyes seemed to stick a

little farther out of his head, but he spoke quite calmly. This was an exceptional case. Pridgeon was an old and valued servant. The organization of the whole thing had fallen upon pa. Pa was determined to make it a success. He represented the firm. Time spent on cultivating pleasant relations between the staff and the employers was not time thrown away. The limited company with its hide-bound rules and narrow limitations never obtained the same devoted service from —

Then ma said that pa had got just time, and only just, to catch his train. He spent two minutes in arguing about what the time really was. He missed that train.

But naturally the worst trouble of all was about the address. Pa sets himself a very high standard in everything. He had determined that the address ought to last ten minutes. But he could not find enough things to say about Pridgeon to last even two. He put in all that bit about cultivating pleasant personal relations between employers and staff, but even then there was a considerable shortage. He kept on reading out addresses and asking us to time them. One can have too much of almost anything. There were times when I wished there had never been any Pridgeon or any testimonial.

It is a very curious thing that though pa seems to be able to go on talking any length of time and rather to enjoy it, when he starts writing he finds he has said all he has got to say in about a dozen lines. Try as he would, he could not get that address beyond six minutes. I made one or two suggestions as to things which he might put in, but they were not well received. Last of all, he put in a long quotation from a leader in one of the daily papers, which brought the thing up to seven minutes thirty-five seconds, and at that he left it. He was very particular about the way it was typed. It was done on special paper, and there were wide spaces between the lines to make it cover the largest possible number of pages. One copy of the address, together with a list of the subscribers, was sent off to be bound in vellum. It could not be finished in time for the dinner, but was to be forwarded to Pridgeon afterwards. Ma said it was a needless expense. I thought so, too.

The dinner was fixed for a Saturday evening, and pa spent the whole of the afternoon up till five o'clock in rehearsing his speech and sucking voice lozenges in the drawing-room. I heard it through twice, and said that I thought it went splendidly. Pa said he was afraid that I was a somewhat prejudiced critic, but he told me I could go to the cinematograph, and paid for my entrance. Kind words, I find, are not always thrown away.

Pa went up to dress at five. The dinner was not till eight, but he had to fetch the clock from the office and make the final arrangements at the restaurant. It was about six when he left the house, and the story of his subsequent troubles we heard from him on the following day.

The clock being heavy, pa decided to have a taxi-cab from the office to the restaurant, and on the way there he made a further study of his copy of the address, trying different effects of intonation. I should say his mind was a good deal preoccupied with that address. He reached the restaurant at seven, which gave him an ample margin of time. He wanted it. He inspected the room which had been reserved for the dinner. He arranged about tipping the waiters. He telephoned to the man who was to take the flash-light photograph. With these things he managed to fill in twenty minutes, and then he made the rather shocking discovery that he had left the clock behind him in the cab.

'Not for an instant,' he said, 'did I lose my head. There was still time to save the situation. I got another cab and drove to Scotland Yard, telling the driver to go as quickly as was compatible with safety. As I expected, the clock had been brought there, and after the usual formalities it was handed over to me.'

'How much did you have to pay?' asked ma.

'There is a regular tariff for these things. I was back again at the restaurant at a quarter to eight, resuming the study of my speech on the return journey, and being specially careful this time to keep the clock in my mind.'

Pa said that the dinner was quite satisfactory. Even in France he had seldom seen anything of the kind better done. The waiters were efficient and attentive. Everybody, including Pridgeon, thanked pa very much for coming and for all the trouble he had taken. And then came the awful moment. Just one minute before he had to deliver the address pa found that he had left his copy of it in the cab in which he had brought back the clock from Scotland Yard.

When he was telling us about it, he said again that not for one moment did he lose his head. It seemed to have been about the only thing he did not lose that night. The long quotation from the newspaper had to go. It was impossible to remember it. He found, too, by a very curious coincidence, that the things he remembered most easily were the things which at mature consideration he had decided to leave out. He says that he also trusted to a considerable extent to the inspiration of the moment. He must have spoken for at least two minutes. He did not appear to think much of Pridgeon's reply. It was far too long, and although it caused much laughter, it was not in the best of taste. It seems to have included several stories about pa in his early days. I wish I had been there.

At the end somebody proposed a vote of thanks to pa, and pa made another speech. This had not been prepared at all, and lasted for fourteen minutes, which, pa said, showed the irony of fate. Ma said it showed something or other, anyhow.

Pa got the last train home all right, and was rather proud of the fact that he woke up nobody in the house on his return. The only strange thing about it was that he left his latchkey in the door. The milkman saw it there next morning and called attention to it. Pa said it was nothing to make a fuss about. It might have happened to anybody.

The bound copy of the address was not wasted after all. It was true that it had never been delivered, but pa said it was something like the address which he actually delivered, and he had good reason to believe that Pridgeon would not remember any discrepancies. Pridgeon sent pa quite a nice letter of thanks for it, and said it would be one of his proudest possessions.

I do not want any more of these presentations. One way and another they cost a good deal of money, and afterwards we get the reaction, and that affects me personally. When I pointed out to pa that the new programme at the picture palace was of exceptional interest and contained many things which would have a real educational value for any boy, he said that if I liked to fool away my own pocket-money on things of that kind I could, but he shouldn't encourage it. I tried ma, and she seemed to think the same.

And what has pa got for the money? He has got a flash-light photograph in a frame, which cost six shillings, and has been a bitter disappointment to him. The really important people, he says, by which he means Pridgeon and himself, seem to be sitting about a mile away and have come out very small. On the other hand, two junior clerks (one of whom has since been dismissed for intemperance), as they happened to be sitting next to the camera, occupy far more space in the picture than their position could have justified. The price of the clock with the inscription was £6 15s. 6d., and so pa must have paid ten shillings at Scotland Yard. This is not a mistake in arithmetic, because I know perfectly well pa would not have put the price of the clock a farthing higher than £5 to the policeman.

The only people who benefited were the cabman and the restaurant people and Pridgeon, and I do not see any reason to oblige any of them. I hate unnecessary expense with nothing to show for it. If pa had just handed over that money to me, I should have done much better with it.

Of one thing I am quite certain. When I am at the head of that firm, as must in the nature of things happen some time – Uncle Bags being my godfather, and not, I should think, a good life – there will be no more presentations.

The Unsuccessful Sinner

IT has very seldom happened that I have received any punishment at school or have deserved any. On one occasion I was punished when I was in the right and had rather deserved to be commended. We were sitting at our desk, writing answers to a Scripture paper. I was at one end of the form and Balgood was next to me. He knew nothing whatever about the subject, and had never tried to know anything. Consequently, he attempted to copy from me the account which I was writing, correct in every detail, of St. Paul's first missionary journey.

Balgood at this time had a habit, if he ever saw me in the playground, of giving what he called 'An Exhibition of the Intelligent Jumping Cockeye'. He hurled things at my feet which might have hurt me considerably if they had struck me, and naturally I jumped to get out of the way of them. It would have been foolish of me if I had not done so. While doing this he would shout out 'Hoop-la!' and other expressions used by the trainers and exhibitors of performing animals. Other boys, as idiotic as himself, would gather round and laugh. So I was not disposed to oblige Balgood, unless I received some assurance he would cease these silly 'exhibitions', as he called them, in future. Besides, a boy who copies is cheating.

So I sat somewhat sideways at the desk with my back turned towards Balgood, and arranged my paper so that he could see nothing. I quite expected he would whisper, 'Let's have a squint, and I'll let you off jumping.' I should then have changed my position, so that, if he cared to take the responsibility, he could see what he wanted.

But he did not do what I expected. He completely lost his temper, charged into me violently, and sent me off the end of the form on to the floor. So great was his impetus that he came down on the top of me, and, having lost his presence of mind, he clutched at an inkpot and brought it down with him. It was the merest chance that my spectacles were not broken. I got some of the ink on my face and hair, there was a good deal on

Balgood's collar and neck, and the rest went across the floor.

Of course the disturbance, the ink, and the laughter of the other boys irritated Mr Mellish, the master who was taking the class, but he might have kept some sense of justice. As soon as I could get up I said, 'It was not my fault, sir'; but he never even inquired into the facts of the case. He punished us both. We each had to write out a hundred times: 'I should try to act like a gentleman and not like a gorilla.'

We were kept in after school in the afternoon to do this imposition. I wrote it as quickly as was compatible with neatness, and was then allowed to go. Balgood, however, made up twenty-five different ways of spelling 'gorilla', and used each one in turn. I have not the least idea why he did this, and I doubt if he knew himself. But when he showed up the imposition, it was detected, and he was made to do it all over again twice. This made him all the more angry with me, though quite without reason. I had never asked him to play the fool with the imposition in that way.

He caught me in the playground next day. Regular cricket is played on the cricket field, of course, but there are generally a few old stumps in the playground. Balgood had collected these, and as soon as he saw me he called out: 'Ladies and gentlemen, I will now present to your notice the highly trained jumping pig, Cockeye. One, two, three, and up! Observe his action.' When he had finished throwing the stumps at me, he picked up a few small stones and said he would now feed the beast. It was most unpleasant, and more than once I had a great mind to hit him. However, I am glad to say that next day he got the measles, and that finished with him for the rest of the term.

But I must say I was surprised at the way ma took it when I told her I had been punished by Mr Mellish. She was pleased. Of course, she pretended that she was not, but grown-up people do not take me in quite so easily as they suppose. Anyhow, I felt so certain of it that I never even told her that it had not been my fault. I said I had been punished for ragging with another boy during school. She said it was silly of me, but she supposed all boys had to have a lark sometimes. I had not had a lark – very far from it – but I said nothing.

I got some further light on the subject later, when I happened to overhear a conversation between pa and ma. She was telling pa about it.

'I say,' she said, 'I do believe Ernest's going to turn into an ordinary human being at last. He has actually managed to get himself punished at school.'

'For nothing disgraceful, I trust?' said pa, a bit anxiously.

'Of course not. Ernie's all right. Just high spirits. He was rotting with another boy when he ought to have been at work.'

'Ah, well!' said pa. 'I dare say I was rather a young devil when I was at school myself.'

'Not you!' said ma. 'Tell that to somebody who don't know you.'

'I may as well point out, Eliza, that at that time you didn't know me. If I cared to tax my memory, I believe I could recall several instances in which I behaved most improperly. Did you give Ernest a good talking to?'

'Of course not, and don't you do it, either. He's had his punishment already. As a matter of fact, I was rather glad – seemed more natural.'

'Well, it's a curious thing,' said pa, 'but I do believe Mr Bagshawe would take the same view. In fact – well, yes – I shall mention this to him if I get a chance. It has become quite useless to speak of the prizes which Ernest has taken. The last time I did so he said he'd far sooner hear that the boy had knocked up a good score at cricket, or had been licked for cheeking a master. A funny thing to say, I thought.'

'Oh, old Bagshawe knows what he's talking about. You bet he's right.'

Now, here was a very extraordinary state of things. It really bothered me. All my life I had been taught to be good. My parents, and even Uncle Bags himself, had always been rubbing it into me. It was the same thing over again at school. I believe I was the best boy that ever went to a school. I tried to be, and I never did anything wrong. It was because I was good that I got prizes. Boys who were bad got punishments. In fact, Mr Mellish had punished me just because he thought I had done wrong, though I do not see how he can have thought it. When a boy hurts himself by falling violently on the floor with a heavy boy on the top of him, and has ink spilled on his face, which must sooner or later involve extra washing, you may be sure that he is not acting intentionally.

If people had meant me to be generally good, but occasionally to have high spirits, they ought to have said so. How was I to know that they wanted me to rot about with other boys instead of doing my work? They had always told me the exact opposite. It did not seem to me to be reasonable, but I know it is not for me to criticize those who are older and wiser than myself, and I quite saw that I should have to make some alteration in my conduct.

In this decision I was thinking of Uncle Bags especially. I had seen for some time past that he was not satisfied. When I took my first lot of prizes he was very smiling, and gave me a sovereign. When I got my last lot, he called me a genius in a sneering sort of way, and never gave me anything. You can't help noticing things like that. He had also called me a plaster saint and a young nincompoop.

I now saw what was the matter. My spectacles do not permit me to play at cricket, a game which wastes much valuable time; but I could, though it was distasteful to me, get into some mischief, if that was what he wanted. There was no immediate hurry about it. He calls about three times a year, and a visit from him would not be due for at least a month.

For a month I kept, as I prefer to do, to the paths of virtue, and made good progress with my work. I was also enabled to make a considerable addition to my bank account at the post office. I had been trying to explain the arithmetic of chance and the folly of betting on horse races to some boys, and had only been laughed at for my pains. I had, therefore, to convince them in some practical way, and the simplest seemed to be to allow them to bet with me on the Derby. I made twenty-five and twopence after clearing expenses.

And then papa announced that Uncle Bags would be motoring on the following Sunday, and had said that he might look in for a cup of tea on his way back. It was time, therefore, that I did something wrong. Some people might think I had done wrong by keeping a 'book' on the Derby, but this was not really so. My only object – or almost my only object – had been to show other boys the folly of betting, and it cannot be wrong to do that. But apart from that, I thought Uncle Bags would prefer something with a little more fun and high spirits in it.

It was on the Friday night that I heard, and Saturday is a half-holiday. So I really only had half a day to get myself punished.

I started quite early by telling the French master that he was a cuckoo. I was afraid at the time that I was overdoing it, and that it might lead to a caning, which I did not want, instead of an imposition, which I did. However, the French master knows little English, and he must have misunderstood. All he said was: 'I was not desiring that you flattair me.'

The next hour I was with Mr Mellish, and with him I had every hope. What he hates most is for a boy to eat sweets in class. He is quite smart at detecting it, and it makes his eyes bulge out of his head. I had not got any sweets because I never buy anything of that kind. I like them, but it amounts to eating money. The boy next to me had got quite a lot, but selfishly refused to lend me one. The only thing I could do was to suck a small marble which I had picked up in the playground. When I was put on to construe, I removed it from my mouth under cover of blowing my nose. This trick hardly ever succeeds with him, but it did this time. Whenever he seemed to be looking at me, I sucked violently or pouched the marble so that it made my cheek project. It was difficult to believe that he could miss it, but he did. If that marble had been a real sweet, and I had wanted to eat it undetected, he would have caught me in the first two minutes. As it was, at the end of an hour I was still unpunished.

I finished the morning with the headmaster, and it was not safe to risk much with him. As a rule, if he punishes at all, it's a much larger-sized punishment than I was looking for. But he generally gives a small imposition for writing untidily and making blots on your paper. I showed him up a Latin prose that was written on a slant, and I had also dropped the paper on the floor and put my foot on it to make quite certain. All he said was: 'Don't let this occur again. Your work is generally satisfactory, or you would have had an imposition this time.'

So there it was. At the end of the morning I was still without a punishment. I had done my best – or perhaps I should say that I had done my worst – and I had got nothing to show for it. It was not much good to say that I had done a lot of these dare-devil things unless I had got a punishment to prove it. If I had done so, Uncle Bags would only have said I was bragging.

It was most disheartening. It looked as if I could only get punished for things that I had not done. The only thing left, so far as I could see, was for me to play off some little practical joke on Uncle Bags himself when he came. This would amuse him, and show him that if his godson did not play cricket, he was still a bright, high-spirited boy. This, in its turn, would lead him to give me a tip, and I rather wanted half a crown to make my bank account up to even money.

I may as well say at once that I never got the half-crown. I did the practical joke, but it did not work right.

While Uncle Bags was having tea in the garden, I went out to the chauffeur and said: 'Mr Bagshawe says you are to take the car home, as he will be returning later by train.'

I could not help smiling to myself as I imagined what Uncle Bags's look of consternation would be when he came out and found the car gone. But it worked out differently. Uncle Bags heard the man start the engine, and came out to see what he was up to. Pa and ma came with him. And every one of them was angry with me.

Pa said it passed his comprehension how any son of his could be such an idiot. Uncle Bags said that a boy who played the fool and thought it was funny was mostly the better for a good hiding. Ma said I was a perfect nuisance. The chauffeur scowled at me as if he would have liked to kill me. I was sent up to my room for the rest of the day, and was not given a proper amount and variety of food. And in the temper in which they all were – Uncle Bags seemed to have lost all control of himself – it was hopeless to attempt to explain.

This is my last experiment of the kind. They seemed to want me to be a mischievous, high-spirited boy, and I did my best to oblige them. Then when they had got it they did not like it. It is much easier for me to go on in my ordinary course, always behaving properly and speaking respectfully, and never playing jokes on anybody, and on the whole I find it more remunerative. I have made a resolution never to do anything high-spirited again. And I shall keep it.

But I see now where I was wrong. It is generally accepted that all boys must be a nuisance, and that there must be something wrong with them if they are always good. But the adult likes the boy to be a nuisance to some third party, and not to himself or his friends. That is where the catch is.

Mr Graham Campbell

WHEN pa first took up with photography ma was quite pleased about it. She said she liked a man to have some occupation outside his business. But at that time pa had a five-shilling camera, and got the films developed and printed by the chemist, and it did not satisfy him for very long. I dare say the chemist was partly to blame. He talked to pa and told him about the different things he might buy, and made him ambitious. The next camera cost £3 10s., and pa bought it from the chemist. He also took lessons in photography from him. Ma was slightly sniffy about the second camera, but by this time pa had become rather learned about lenses, and said he must either do the thing properly or leave it alone. He took a series of photographs of the garden, which made it look as if it were about four miles square, and much finer than it really is. He took two photographs of me, but even ma says that I do not photograph well, and then pa fitted up a dark room in a corner of the big attic, and took to calling the attic the studio. Hardly anybody could enter the house now without being photographed by pa. He even photographed Uncle Bags. He filled some big scrap-books with his photographs, and asked people if they would like to look at them. He would stand over them to see that they did not go through the books too quickly and paid proper attention to everything. He took one of the photographic papers regularly now, and ma told him that she liked moderation in everything.

And then one day he came back from the City with yet a third camera. It did not look much bigger than the second. I asked pa how much it cost, because I always like to know the price of everything, and he told me to mind my own business. Later, when ma asked him how much it cost, he said it was impossible to get a camera which would do such good work any cheaper. But when I was not there she got the actual figures out of him, and she was very much annoyed. She said that if she had known that photography led men to fool away money like that, she would never have encouraged him to begin. He might almost as well have started a motor-car or racing stable. They then shut the door, and I could not hear the rest. Next morning at breakfast pa said he should now be able to get some very interesting views of interiors, and ma said he had better photograph the interior of the bankruptcy court. Later on from other allusions I gathered that the price of the camera was not under £20.

After that for quite a long time pa did not buy anything photographic, so far as I actually knew, but sometimes he came from the City with his pockets rather bulgy and went straight up to the attic. When he came down again the pockets no longer bulged, and he looked as if he had committed a burglary.

Late one afternoon I was preparing my work for next day and pa was mounting some photographs in one of the albums, when a man called to see pa. His card said that he was Mr Graham Campbell, author and journalist.

'I've not the slightest idea what he wants,' said pa, 'but I suppose I may as well see him. Show him in.'

As pa did not tell me to go away I remained where I was. Mr Graham Campbell was a well-dressed man of about forty. His eyes were all over the place. He must have seen everything in the room as soon as he got inside it. He was very polite, and began by thanking pa very much for seeing him.

'The fact of the case is,' he said, 'that I have been engaged by an important firm of publishers to prepare a large illustrated work entitled "Workers at Play". It deals with workers of all kinds, professional men, City men, statesmen, artists, and their hobbies. It will be most sumptuously produced, and the price of it will be three guineas net.'

'I'm afraid I could not think of it,' said pa.

'But, my dear sir, you misunderstand me. I was not proposing that you should buy a copy. Your name was given to me as a representative City man, and all I wanted was to ask you if you would oblige me with some information as to your own hobby, if you have one. If you are so kind as to do this, of course a complimentary copy of the book would be sent you.'

'Oh,' said pa, 'that certainly puts rather a different complexion on the matter.'

'I think you will have no reason to be ashamed of the company in which you will find yourself in that book. The Prime Minister and the leader of the Opposition will both be there. The Archbishop of Canterbury has also promised. Lord Kitchener is practically a certainty. Now if I get to work at once on that understanding, perhaps you will be good enough to tell me what your hobby is.'

'For some time past I have been taking a great interest in photography. I think I may say that for an amateur I have been moderately successful with it.'

'I wish I were you,' said Mr Graham Campbell regretfully. 'I have done a little photography with a snapshot camera, but, of course, that kind of thing is no use for a book like "Workers at Play". I did show some of the publishers my attempts, but they told me frankly that they were not up to the mark. That is a pity, too. If I were at all expert, I could have made a hundred pounds or more by taking the photographs for that book. As it is, they will have to employ somebody else.'

'Well,' said pa, 'perhaps you would like to see some of my latest productions.' He brought out two of the scrap-books. 'One of these,' he said, 'contains what I call my garden series. The other consists of studies of child-life.'

Mr Campbell went through the books very carefully. He seemed greatly interested, and praised everything he saw. He said he never would have believed it possible that an amateur would turn out such work. He put a pencil mark against two or three photographs which he said he should like to reproduce in the book.

'Do you think they would be up to the publishers' standard?' asked pa.

'I can say without hesitation that they will. It is extremely improbable that there will be anything better in the book. Of course, a fee will be paid you for any of these that are reproduced.'

'Well,' said pa, 'it is a work which fascinates me very much. I like doing it. I believe I have some aptitude for it. Do you think it would be possible for me to undertake the other photographs for the volume?'

'I really cannot say,' said Mr Campbell. 'They may have already engaged a photographer. But it is extremely unlikely, for I have only just left them. If you will permit me I will submit specimens of your work to them to-morrow morning, and let you know. At what time are your services available?'

'Any day after four in the afternoon, and after midday on Saturdays. I might even be able occasionally to get away for a morning. I am obliged to you, Mr Campbell. Perhaps you would now like to come up to see the studio.'

They were upstairs for nearly half an hour, and when they came down Mr Campbell left, and pa looked extremely pleased with himself. He said that Mr Campbell was one of the most intelligent men he had ever met, that it was a pleasure to show work to anybody so appreciative.

'Are you going to get the job, pa?' I asked.

'I should prefer, Ernest, that you did not use those vulgar phrases. I am in all probability going to accept a commission from the publishers of this important book. It is not certain, and I will say no more about it at present. I shall know to-morrow afternoon when Mr Campbell will be here again.'

But as a matter of fact pa did say a lot more about it. He talked about hardly anything else that evening. He said that thoroughness in all things had always been a motto of his. It was true he had paid a large sum for a camera, but if he received this commission the expense would be fully justified.

Ma said that there must be a catch in it somewhere. She did not see any reason why pa should be put into a book of that kind. Pa's firm was not a particularly big firm, and pa was not the senior partner by a long way.

'I think, Eliza,' said pa, 'that you tend to over-suspiciousness. I am not asked to subscribe to the book. I am not asked for any money at all. On the contrary, money is to be paid me. Mr Campbell will submit my photographs to the publishers to-morrow morning, and will let me know their decision in the afternoon. It is just possible that the publishers will have already engaged a photographer, or that they will not show the same appreciation of my work that Mr Campbell did. In that case I may make nothing, but under no circumstances can I lose anything. Be reasonable, Eliza.'

Mr Campbell arrived on the following afternoon in a taxi-cab. He seemed a little excited. He said it was all right – that the publishers appreciated the photographs even more than he had done, and that they would be glad to give pa the commission. But there was one condition.

I guessed at once what the condition was: that pa was to pay a sum of money down as security, or something of that kind; and I may admit that my guess was entirely wrong. Mr Campbell never asked for money.

'The fact is,' said Mr Campbell, 'that the publishers are in a bit of a hurry. Several of the distinguished people who are to be included in the book have already fixed dates for the interviews and photographs, and we cannot very well ask them to alter these dates. One of these people has fixed on this afternoon, and I am just off to see him. If you can come with me, bringing your photographic apparatus with you, you can have the commission for the whole of the photographs. If not, I am instructed to arrange with a professional photographer. Well now, there is the taxi-cab outside – the publishers pay for that, of course, and if you are free we can start at once.'

Pa accepted the offer eagerly, and hurried upstairs to get his apparatus. He decided to take both his cameras with him. He would not let me help him to carry the things down for fear of an accident. He packed both the cameras carefully in the cab, and then an idea seemed to strike Mr Campbell.

'I say,' he said, 'I wonder if you would do me a kindness. You've got a small snapshot camera upstairs. If you would bring that down I could take one or two photographs with it on my own account – not for the book, of course, but just for my own pleasure. You would be able to show me how it worked, and what were the best bits to select, and so on.'

Pa seemed very grateful to Mr Campbell for all he had done for him, and said he would be only too happy to fetch the little camera, and would explain the working of it to him as he went along. So he ran upstairs to the attic for it. When he came down again the taxi-cab had gone, with Mr Campbell and both cameras and a lot of other apparatus inside it.

Pa gave him plenty of time. I do not know why, but the idea came into his head that Mr Campbell had gone to buy a notebook and would return. In about ten minutes pa found ma, and said to her that he thought it was very ungentlemanly of Mr Campbell to keep him waiting in this way. Ma heard the story, and told him to go to the police-station at once. I do not think he would have gone, but ma said that if he did not she would.

Next day a man came down from Scotland Yard to see pa. He was a detective, and he had got a photograph of Mr Campbell in his pocket which pa recognized.

'Yes,' said the detective thoughtfully, 'we've been wanting him for some time. His real name is Smith, and he has any amount of aliases. He has had seven years for this kind of thing. Sometimes it is a clock, sometimes it is a motor-car. He is specially fond of following up expensive cameras. He understands all about them, and is a very good mechanic. He can alter a camera so that no one could recognize it. A description of your two has been circulated, of course, to all the pawnbrokers, but I do not think there is much hope that they will be recovered.'

'How did he get to know that I had a camera?' asked pa. 'I suppose he bribed the assistant who served me to give him my name and address.'

'Unlikely,' said the detective. 'He could manage to see the label when the thing was sent out without much trouble.'

'And does he tell everybody the same story that he told me – about giving them a commission to take photographs for "Workers at Play"?'

'Oh, no. He tells many stories, and chooses one which he thinks will suit the case. Very often he represents himself as a man from the shop, and says that an inferior quality of camera has accidentally been delivered, and that the firm wish to change it. He shows the firm's trade card as proof of his bona fides. Of course, it is no proof at all. Anybody can get a trade card by asking for it. We know of five different cameras that he has had this week.'

'Well,' said pa, 'it is a most amazing thing. How did he know what story to tell me? He'd never seen me in his life before.'

'He knows the type of man he is dealing with in two minutes. Once he gets inside the house, the clock, or the camera, or whatever it is, is as good as gone.'

'And you don't think you will be able to get my cameras back again for me?'

'We might. We shall get Smith all right in the end. We are setting one or two little traps for him. If he has not disposed of your property by then, you will get it back. But I don't hold out any hopes of it.'

For some time pa was rather depressed, and told us every day that the loss must be made good by the strictest economies. It was not of the slightest use to talk about picture palaces to him, and if I had not made a little money by a private speculation at school I should have been deprived of these educational forms of entertainment.

And then pa became rather proud of the whole thing, though I don't know why. He liked to tell the story to people, and when he did so, if ma was not there and he thought I was not listening, he always overstated the price of the camera. He also always said that Campbell was recognized by the police to be the cleverest thief at large in Europe at present. Now the detective had not said that. If I myself were a thief, I should look a little higher than twenty-pound cameras, but I am glad to say I have no inclinations towards dishonesty or vice of any kind. My last school report again states that my conduct has been uniformly excellent.

Pa has not recovered his camera, and so far Mr Campbell has not stepped into the police trap. One of the bad results of the incident is that pa has become very distrustful, and will allow nothing to be taken out of the house without written permission and fuss of that sort. The boy left the wrong newspaper at our house the other morning, and came back for it, but pa would not allow it to go. Of course, it is not for me to criticize him, but I can't shut my eyes to the fact that he is inclined to carry things too far. Ma said so too. That was the day she had told the shop to send for the knife-machine that needed repairing, and pa refused to let it go when the man called for it. In fact, pa was just sending out for a policeman when luckily ma returned.

By the Silver Sea

MA says that there never was a boy like me since the beginning of the world, and she doesn't seem altogether pleased about it. Yet the only time I ever tried to act like other boys and to do something spirited and mischievous, she objected as much as anybody. Personally I see a good many boys at my school, and I have no wish to resemble them. I think that, with my abilities and industry, and my sense of the value of money, I ought to do better than any of them. They are a lazy lot. They all love holidays, whereas I myself hate them.

It is supposed that during the holidays boys can do as they like. If they wish they can play rough games, such as cricket and football. They can collect butterflies or birds' eggs. But my spectacles make rough games unsuitable for me, and I never indulge in them. I have made inquiries, and I find that the very best professional players do not make an income which would satisfy me, and they soon get too old to make anything at all. That being so, why should I try to play games? As for birds' nesting and butterfly collecting, they are messy occupations and may be actually dangerous. And when you come to sell your collection, you get little or nothing for it. What I should like to do would be to sit in the house and busy myself with my own occupations, and occasionally to visit a cinematograph. But I find that in the holidays I can very seldom do what I like.

Yet all my occupations are quite innocent and helpful to

myself and others. In the morning I like to study the advertisements in the papers, and learn what the prices of things are. At
present I can tell what almost every motor-car I meet on the road
cost when it was new. I find out how much people make in
different professions and trades. Schoolmasters seem to get
very little, although they give themselves such airs. When I
think it worth while, I write for free samples. I was forming a
complete medicine chest in this way, and had already got
several different kinds of hair-restorer and three cures for
obesity. I also obtained a good deal of cocoa by this method. But
a post card costs a half-penny, and the sample sent is so small
that it would be almost cheaper to buy it at the shop. Ma
stopped this occupation, because she said it did not seem to her
honest, and she thought it was dangerous to play about with
medicines. After all, there is really not very much profit in it.
Very often the advertiser will only send you one thing free if
you buy something else from him. I am fond, too, of studying
anything connected with the business. I am teaching myself
book-keeping, shorthand and commercial letter-writing. But
frequently I am taken away from my work and made to go for a
walk. I am also compelled at times to play croquet. This constant
interference with serious occupations is very annoying.

But it is the summer holidays that I dislike most, for then we
spend a fortnight at Selton-on-Sea. I dislike swimming, which
turns me blue, and I dislike rowing, which makes me sick, and I
am compelled to do both. I dislike our lodgings. I dislike the
smell of the sea. I dislike everything about it. But pa and ma
have got into a groove now. They will go to Selton-on-Sea every
summer for the rest of their lives. Ma really enjoys it, pa thinks
he does, and I have to pretend I do.

It was the usual thing this year. Pa always has three seats in
the train reserved for us, but he also insists on being at the
station half an hour before the train starts. He spreads things
over all the seats, to make them look as if they were all taken. He
gives a porter sixpence to lock the door. He stands at the
window and talks loudly about scarlet fever. He does everything
he knows (short of paying for the extra seats) to get us the entire
compartment to ourselves. And he has never once succeeded,
and he never will succeed. About two minutes before the train
starts, the guard comes along, unlocks the door, and puts
another family in on the top of us. Trains to the seaside are
always full in the holiday season. I think pa must have great
patience and perseverance. If I tried a trick every year for three
years, and it never came off, and there were good reasons why it
never could, I should give up trying it. Perhaps pa may have

some special reason for it, and for the sandwiches too.

We start just after luncheon, and we reach Selton just before tea-time, but pa always takes sandwiches with him. He seems to have got the idea that it's not legal to travel without sandwiches. He eats one or two himself, and we have to finish the others later in the day, when they have curled up at the edges and are perfectly beastly. I wish somebody would tell him.

Our landlady was all smiles when she received us, which was to be expected. If I had a £30 house and were letting half of it for £3 a week I should smile myself. Of course, we have nothing like the same comfort that we have at home. There is only one sitting-room, and I can never get on with my work. If I am not interrupted in one way I am in another. Pa says: 'Come along, Ernest, and get some ozone into your lungs.' If ozone is what the beach smells of at low tide, I would sooner have plain air.

Of course, it is not for me to criticize, but to me the whole thing seems too silly. At home ma always shows a sense of the value of money, and if pa spends too much on anything he always makes up for it by spending too little on something else. But at the seaside they spend money just anyhow. It goes on all day. They pay to walk on the pier, and they pay to sit in deck-chairs, though you can walk in the street and sit on the sand for nothing. This year they paid for the brake to Skilby Castle, and they paid for admission. They did the same last year and the year before. Why? There was precious little of the castle left the first time we went, and it has not got any bigger since. Pa always photographs it, and it always come on to rain. I am fed up by Skilby Castle, and I don't care how historical it is; I would cheerfully pay money to be left at home and practise my shorthand. But I always have to go, and I am always expected to regard it as a treat. I need hardly say that we take far too many sandwiches with us, and get the sandwiches for breakfast next morning.

But, as a source of expenditure, the musicians annoy me most. This year there are two gangs of them – 'The Masked Minstrels' and 'The Screamers'. I dislike any kind of music myself. Pa and ma really like 'The Screamers' best, because they are comic, but they also patronize 'The Masked Minstrels' because they are high class. But why give them money? They have no legal claim. If they choose to provide an entertainment on a public beach, that is their affair, and anybody has a right to listen to them for nothing. But pa always subscribes.

Pa and ma had rather a disagreement about 'The Masked Minstrels'. Pa asked ma what she supposed they were.

'Ordinary street performers like the others. Those masks are just a bit of kid.'

'On the contrary,' said pa, 'they are black satin.'

'What I meant was that they only put them on just to humbug you into thinking they're somebody special.'

'I think, Eliza, that I have as much power of observation as most people. Perhaps more. I have been complimented on it before now. I go by the intonation of the voice, the choice of repertoire, and the general manner. And I say without hesitation that "The Masked Minstrels" are not ordinary street performers.'

'Oh? What are they, then?'

'Talented amateurs who wear masks to conceal their identity, and are really doing it for the love of the thing.'

'Well, they're pretty handy with the collecting-box considering. However, have it your own way.'

'It is not a question of my own way, Eliza.'

'Then have it the other way. I don't care, anyhow. Your blessed "Minstrels" are out for what they can make, just the same as the "Screamers" are.'

Pa was out all next morning, and when he came in to lunch he was excited and important.

'I've solved the mystery, Eliza.'

'Solved which?'

'I know who the "Masked Minstrels" are. At any rate, I know who their leader is.'

'Oh, did you ask him?'

'I did not. Neither have I been told. Neither have I seen him without the mask. But I have recognized him, and it turns out to be one of the most extraordinary coincidences that have ever occurred. Believe me or not, the fact remains – that man is one of my own clerks, Williams by name.'

'Well, how did you come to know?'

'Because I observe and remember details which would escape most people. He was singing "The Lost Chord" – a good song and one which ought to be more widely known – and in the position in which he was standing the sun lit up his open mouth. I saw that he had three gold stoppings in his back teeth. Williams also has three – in just exactly the same position.'

'Oh? And when did you see inside of the clerk's mouth?'

'That was due perhaps to the one indiscretion in his career. He was speaking to a bookmaker over the office telephone. Mr Bagshawe and I had entered unobserved. When he looked up and realized that Mr Bagshawe had heard him put a dollar each way on Antelope for the Cesarewitch his jaw dropped. That was how I came to see. The gold stoppings were most noticeable. Mr

Bagshawe gave him a most serious warning, and fined him ten shillings for improper use of the office telephone.'

'That makes four gold stoppings altogether.'

'Do not trifle, Eliza. You must see that this is most remarkable.'

'I don't see that it proves anything. Lots of men have got gold stoppings in their teeth.'

'That, taken by itself, might not have been conclusive, but everything else fits in. I happen to know that Williams has his holiday now. Williams is the same height and build as this man, and has hair of the same colour – though done differently, which is what one would expect. His speaking voice is not quite the same, but naturally a man who masked his face would also alter his voice. Taking one thing with another, there can be no doubt of it. The leader of "The Masked Minstrels" is no other than Williams, my clerk.'

'Did he recognize you, pa?' I asked.

'He must have done, of course, though naturally he was not going to give himself away. The interesting thing is that he will not have the slightest idea that I have recognized him. Later, at the office, I shall tell him that I know how he spent his holidays – saying something about it in a light and chaffing way. But I shall never tell him how I found out – that will be a mystery to him as long as he lives.'

This incident seemed to give pa a taste for detective work. He bought two detective stories that same afternoon, and was very pleased to be able to say he had spotted the guilty man long before the detective in the story did. But for the cares and responsibilities of his business he says that he would write a detective story himself, which at any rate would be totally different from anything the world has seen yet.

Otherwise the holiday this year has been very much as usual. The weather has unfortunately been uniformly good, and I have in consequence been made to swim in the sea every day. The man whom pa paid last year to teach me to swim was a brute, who ought to have six months' hard labour. He frequently allowed me to come within an ace of drowning, and when I complained that I had got a mouthful of sea water he simply laughed. I have read somewhere that, when shipwrecked sailors on a raft are compelled by thirst to drink sea water it always drives them mad, and they then eat one another and jump overboard. I complained several times about my instructor to both pa and ma, but I never could get them to take a right view about it. In fact, ma is always wanting me to do things. This year I was as nearly as possible taught to ride. Fortunately the charge for the hire of ponies at Selton-on-Sea is so much in excess of the usual rates that I managed to get this post-poned.

This bathing business is the more shameful because pa himself never does it. Pa can't swim. He never will say that he can't, and I never can get ma to admit that he can't, but I am not easily deceived. They only tell me that sea-bathing is unsuitable at his time of life. This, of course, is skittles, because my instructor was at least five years older. But the whole thing is most unjust. I cannot see that a knowledge of swimming is any use to a boy who intends to embrace a commercial career. Pa never had any knowledge of swimming, and there can be no doubt that he has got on quite a good deal. If I had spent the time that I have been made to waste in this way on acquiring a knowledge, say, of the law as affecting limited liability companies, I should have been acting much more sensibly. Pa has the advantage of me that he at any rate spends his holiday just as he likes.

He goes on the pier every day, and sometimes twice a day. He sits on a deck-chair (price twopence), and reads novels (price sixpence), and buys bananas (price two for three-half-pence) totally in excess of his real requirements. But if I try to do what I like, which would be to sit at home and study shorthand, pa immediately begins to talk about ozone.

The holiday came to an end at last, as even the worst things will, and we had the same old farce at the railway station going back. Pa tipped the porter and spread out the luggage just as before, and the guard put in another family two minutes before the train started, just as before. By a coincidence it was just the same family with just the same baby, and the baby was just as sick as it had been on the journey down. It is a relief to me to feel that it is all over until next year.

Next morning pa went up to the City in quite a cheerful frame of mind. He was looking forward to chaffing Williams about his leadership of 'The Masked Minstrels'.

When he got back in the afternoon, he came straight into the room where ma and I were sitting, and said: 'Eliza, a most extraordinary thing has happened.'

'What – again?' said ma.

'You will remember that I was able to identify beyond any possibility of doubt the leader of "The Masked Minstrels" as being our clerk, Williams.'

'Is that all?' said ma.

'You would perhaps like to know the nature of the evidence. It appears that Williams obtained permission from Mr Bagshawe to change holidays with another clerk. Williams preferred to

take his in September, because his aunt, who happens to live in
Dulwich —'

'Oh, never mind about his aunt.'

'It is not uninteresting, but if you do not wish to hear it you
need not. All that I need say is that Williams was at work at the
office every day while we were at Selton.'

'I see,' said ma. 'Well, that rather dishes the extraordinary
coincidence you made such a fuss about.'

'Nothing of the kind, Eliza. You should really reflect a
moment before you give these hasty judgments. If you did, you
would see that it makes the coincidence still more extraordinary.
Here we have two men, probably strangers to each other, acting
without any mutual arrangement or collusion, going about the
world with their back teeth stopped in exactly the same
manner.'

'At least two men, I should think,' said ma.

'And in addition to that, both those men happen to come
across me under circumstances which enable me to examine
their back teeth: in one case from the exigencies of music, and
in the other from fear and surprise. It would make an
interesting subject for a letter to one of the newspapers.'

But ma managed to persuade him out of it.

An Account and a Prospect

I HAVE just paid the penalty of an act of carelessness.

I am by nature more careful and methodical than most boys.
In fact, ma says that in this respect I am more like some old
woman than a boy; but the incident which has just occurred
shows how even the best of us may be guilty of an occasional
lapse. It is a little strange too, because the lapse in this case had
its origin in an effort which I make annually to realize my exact
financial position. I refer to my Christmas Present Account.

Every year when the Christmas season comes round I give
and receive presents. At one time I used to give two presents –
one to pa and one to ma. But I have now found it more
economical and quite as satisfactory to them to give them one
present between them. It is generally some trifle of household
use. Last year it was an inkstand, I personally having been
inconvenienced often by the shortage of inkstands in the house.
The money which I expend in this way I enter on the debit side.

On the other hand, I receive presents regularly from pa, ma,
Uncle Bags and Miss Sakers. I sometimes receive one from

Uncle Frank, but he is not to be depended upon. I make a list of these with a fair estimate of their cash value and enter them on the credit side. I then balance and see how much I am to the good on that Christmas. This seems to me to be a very wise precaution. It prevents one's generous impulses from running one into undue extravagance. It shows you exactly how you stand. If I found that in any year I had expended more than I received, I should, of course, correct it in the following year. It is, I am convinced, sound business. But at the same time I am tactful enough to keep these accounts locked away in the desk, which I reserve for my business papers. They concern nobody but myself, and I know how easily things of the kind can be misunderstood.

I also practise an economy which may seem to be trifling, but it is those who take care of trifles who ultimately become rich. When pa and ma receive letters at breakfast-time, which are written only on the one sheet, I always get them to give me the half-sheets. I keep these in a little case, formed of the covers of an exercise book. The waste of paper which goes on, even in well-conducted households, is much to be regretted.

Last year I made out the Christmas Present Account as usual, and then came the act of carelessness. I cannot remember exactly how it happened. Probably I was putting away my things hurriedly, or somebody spoke to me and distracted my attention. At any rate, instead of locking away that account in my desk, I put it in the case where I keep those half-sheets, and now, several months later, this act of carelessness has been visited upon me. I have been much misunderstood. For instance, the thing that I am blamed for is not carelessness at all. But I make no complaint about that, feeling that, after all, I have brought it on myself, and hoping it will teach me to be more careful in future.

It happened in this way. Miss Sakers had been playing croquet with ma. They are just about equal and very keen on the game. They never play for money, and it can lead to nothing, and I do not see what there is to be keen about. There is, perhaps, some reason for it which a boy cannot understand. Anyhow, they nearly always lose their tempers over the game, and are especially polite after it to show that nothing serious was intended. This afternoon they had just got to the polite stage. Miss Sakers said that ma's game had improved enormously. Ma said that she had only been lucky, and that on a really good lawn, such as the vicarage lawn – which is where Miss Sakers lives – Miss Sakers would always beat her. Then it was Miss Sakers's turn, and she said she had always been meaning to ask ma where she bought her tea. It was so difficult to get good China tea at a reasonable price, and ma's was so much better than the tea they had at the vicarage.

Ma said that she always got it from the same place in the City, and that Ernie should write down the address for her.

Miss Sakers said it was too sweet of her.

Ma added: 'Not at all.'

I took a half-sheet from my case and wrote down the address. Miss Sakers thanked me and put the paper in the bag she was carrying. I did not know it till next day, but I had written that address on the back of my last Christmas Present Account.

Some people if they found that, by accident, an address had been written for them on the back of a private memorandum, would be too honourable to read the memorandum. And nobody with nice feelings could make use of information obtained in that way. At least, I should have thought so, but no doubt I was wrong, for Miss Sakers did read that memorandum, and did make use of it in a spiteful way.

I think I know what made her so spiteful. That Christmas she had given me a stylographic pen, and I had entered the value of it in the account as one shilling and sixpence. It was a fair estimate. I know of two shops in our neighbourhood where precisely similar stylographic pens can be bought at that price. Apparently, she paid three shillings and sixpence. At any rate, she says she did. And I suppose it made her angry to find that her present had not been appreciated at its full value. I am not a vindictive boy, and have been taught to make allowances for others, and so I try to find what excuse I can for her. Perhaps she did not even know that she would be getting me into trouble when she brought that account back and showed it to ma. But I think she might have guessed.

I was not in the drawing-room when she called, and had not the faintest idea that there was anything wrong. Out in the garden I could hear ma and Miss Sakers laughing. In fact, they laughed so much that I almost thought of going in to see if they had got anything amusing. But I did not go. I have been so often disappointed before.

And after Miss Sakers had gone there was no more laughing. Ma called me in, and she didn't half pitch into me. Then she told pa, and he took a turn at it. He said he trembled to think what Mr Bagshawe would say if he ever got to hear of it. There was no reason why he ever should hear of it, and if he did I could not see that it mattered what he said. But I did not point this out. I took it all quite meekly. At one time I got rather nervous, because they talked about abolishing Christmas presents for me altogether. That would not suit me at all. My Christmas Present Account has so far always shown a balance on the right side, and for a boy in my position a rather considerable balance. Not seeing exactly what to say, I just kept on expressing regret until I could get time to think something out for them. At first I was a good deal taken aback, because the charge they were bringing against me was so totally unexpected. It was so incredible as to be ridiculous. But I have only to set it down to show how absurd it was. They actually accused me of meanness. What my own conscience accused me of was carelessness. I like order. There should be a place for everything, and everything in its place, as it says in the Bible. Business papers should be kept locked up, and should not be allowed to fall into the hands of people who may take advantage of the accident. That was where I reproached myself.

However, I soon got to understand their point of view, mistaken though it was. I went to bed early; as I was being treated as a kind of leper there was no particular encouragement to sit up. In my own room I at once saw the line to take and worked out the details.

Next morning I came down to breakfast with everything ready, and appeared depressed. I said that, of course, I was not defending myself, but I should like to explain how it had happened. I had known that I was to go into business, and had tried to fit myself for it. I had made accounts out of all manner of things, simply for the sake of practice, and not because I really cared whether there was any profit or loss. I had even made out an account for the garden for one month, although it was not my garden, showing an expenditure of sixteen and three and an income of one penny in respect of a lettuce. It was just a sort of game, and I was very sorry it had been misunderstood. I did not know there was anything wrong in it, and, of course, I thought just the same about Christmas as they did themselves. However, I would promise, if they wished it, never to do any accounts again.

And it all went very well indeed. In fact, before breakfast was over I could see that they were begining to ask themselves if they had not been too hard on me. But I noticed one thing that I have often noticed before – it is much easier to convince pa than it is to convince ma.

My Christmas Present Account will always be kept locked away in future. And to prevent the possibility of an accident it will be written in shorthand. Nobody in the house can read shorthand. Nor can Miss Sakers. And though, as I said, I am not vindictive, if I ever do get a chance of being even with Miss

Sakers, there is a strong probability that I shall take it.

That night while I was in my room I heard some quite interesting scraps of conversation from the garden. Pa and ma were talking about me and trying to settle which one of them I was more like. I could not hear all of it, because they kept walking about. Pa said that he could not make out how the boy got that love of money, amounting almost to avarice. He himself had always been a singularly open-handed man.

'Yes,' said ma, 'and a pretty fool you'd have made of yourself with your open-handedness if you had not had me to look after you. Do you mean to say that the boy gets his meanness from me?'

'You are always and perpetually,' pa began – and then they moved on.

When they came round again ma was saying: 'Well, he's got your figure, at any rate. I was always on the slim side myself. And he's got your way of talking. In fact, he doesn't talk like a boy at all, and I don't suppose you ever did.'

'But I fancy he'll get on in the world,' said pa.

'Oh, yes,' said ma. 'He'll get on in the world, if that's the only thing to think about.'

It was not altogether flattering, but very much the kind of thing that I had expected. No allusion whatever was made to the numerous prizes that I had taken at school, or to my uniformly good reports, or to my exceptional abilities, and there seemed to be an anxiety to look for faults.

* * *

Some months have elapsed since I wrote the above. I see there are still two or three pages left in the book pa gave me, and I propose to occupy them by recording a very probable change in my future career.

About a fortnight ago, the headmaster of the grammar school called on pa and ma. This was a thing that he had never done before. I knew that he had not called to make any complaint about me, because I never do anything about which a complaint can be made. But it struck me that it might be interesting to discover the reason for the call, and I strolled casually into the drawing-room. I was almost immediately sent out again. The door was shut and I was not given any opportunity to hear what was being said. After the headmaster had gone, pa and ma had a long discussion together in private. Next afternoon Uncle Bags came down, and there was another conference of the three of them, while I was sent out in Uncle Bags's motor-car.

However, I was not kept long in suspense. The next day I was told that the headmaster had suggested that it might possibly be worth while to send me to Oxford or Cambridge. The matter had been discussed with Uncle Bags, and it had been decided that I should go if I could get a scholarship. I understood that the headmaster had said that in his opinion there was very little doubt that I should get a scholarship if I continued to work as well for the next few years as I had done in the past. Uncle Bags had offered, of his own accord, to defray part of the expenses, which, of course, was very decent of him.

I cannot say that just at first the prospect appealed to me. The sooner one goes into business, the sooner one becomes experienced in it. The assistant masters at the grammar school had all been to a university and had all taken degrees, and whatever else it had done for them it had not helped them to make money. Probably though, they had not a good business to step into as I had – nobody becomes a schoolmaster if he can possibly be anything else. I agreed with the headmaster about that scholarship. I have always been good at work, particularly mathematics. But what would it come to? Perhaps sixty or seventy pounds a year for three years, and during those three years my expenses would be very much increased. If the decision had been left to me I should have carried out what had always been my plan – to leave school at sixteen and go straight into the business.

But then, of course, the decision was not left to me, and everybody seemed so certain that it was a splendid chance for me, that I have gradually got resigned to it. Pa is very pleased about it, and has now told everybody in the place that he has decided to send his son to Oxford. He would prefer Oxford, if possible, because he has found on inquiry that there is a better social tone there. It was an old Oxford man who told him.

The headmaster seemed pleased, too, though in a more solemn way. I shall get some special coaching, as all the boys do who are in for anything competitive. He said that he hoped that at the last I should come to love learning for its own sake, quite apart from any emoluments that it may bring. (I think this improbable, but I said politely that I hoped so too.) For this reason he says it would be better on the whole if I went to Cambridge, where the scholarship is perhaps a little sounder. He happens to be a Cambridge man himself.

Uncle Bags seemed almost savage about it, but this may be merely his manner. I mentioned what my own ideas had been. 'Stuff and nonsense!' he said. 'When you're eighteen you'll be a greenhorn and a nincompoop, just as you are now. Three years at a university may knock it out of you. I've got no use for your sort in this office in the green state. You've got to mix with men to know them. If business were only a matter of sums, which is what you seem to think, any fool could be a successful man of business.'

Well, there are some years yet before I shall be leaving school, and when the time comes the decision will, as a matter of fact, rest with me. I am to be sent to a university only if I can get a scholarship. If I choose I can always fail to get a scholarship. So the thing does not worry me.

But I expect I shall go. There are plenty of university men in the City, and the only way they are handicapped by it is that they seem unable to resist a taxi to Lord's on fine summer days. The temptation to watch cricket during business hours would not, however, affect me. The other day I came across this sentence in an obituary notice in a newspaper: 'He was not only a successful man of business, he was also a man of considerable academic distinction.' I should be quite willing, when the time comes, for my obituary notice to begin in the same way. It sounds well. I would always sacrifice swank to money, but why not try to have both? It is just as well to aim high. Every boy ought to start from the point where his pa has stopped. It took pa twenty years or so (and a bit of luck) to get into a partnership. With my superior abilities, in twenty years I might be almost anything.

As for the choice of a university, I shall leave that till the very last. I shall go in for scholarships at both universities, and select the one which is willing to pay me most. That is the sound way to look at it. A scholarship is really a cash discount offered by a college to its best customer, as far as I can see.

Pa and ma will be proud of me one of these days. At present I do think they might be a bit prouder than they are. They ought not to discuss what they (wrongly) suppose to be my faults in the way they do. One day they will be sorry for it.